BODY COUNT

Julie Mae Cohen is the darker side of Julie Cohen, an award-winning author whose novels have sold over a million copies worldwide. Her thriller debut, *Bad Men*, was a BBC Radio 2 Book Club pick in 2023 and was shortlisted for the RNA Jackie Collins Award for Romantic Suspense. Julie grew up in Maine and now lives in the UK with her family and a terrier of dubious origin.

Also by Julie Mae Cohen

Bad Men
Eat Slay Love

BODY COUNT

JULIE MAE COHEN

ZAFFRE

First published in the UK in 2025 by
ZAFFRE
An imprint of Bonnier Books UK
5th Floor, HYLO, 105 Bunhill Row,
London, EC1Y 8LZ

Copyright © Julie Mae Cohen, 2025

All rights reserved.
No part of this publication may be reproduced,
stored or transmitted in any form by any means, electronic,
mechanical, photocopying or otherwise, without the
prior written permission of the publisher.

The right of Julie Mae Cohen to be identified as Author of this
work has been asserted by her in accordance with the
Copyright, Designs and Patents Act, 1988.

This is a work of fiction. References to real people, events,
establishments, organisations, or locales are intended only to
provide a sense of authenticity and are used fictitiously. All other
characters, and all incidents and dialogue, are drawn from the
author's imagination and are not to be construed as real.

A CIP catalogue record for this book is
available from the British Library.

Hardback ISBN: 9-781-80418-933-7
Trade paperback ISBN: 9-781-80418-934-4

Also available as an ebook and an audiobook

1 3 5 7 9 10 8 6 4 2

Typeset by IDSUK (Data Connection) Ltd
Printed and bound in Great Britain by Clays Ltd, Elcograf S.p.A

The authorised representative in the EEA is Bonnier Books
UK (Ireland) Limited.
Registered office address: Floor 3, Block 3, Miesian Plaza,
Dublin 2, D02 Y754, Ireland
compliance@bonnierbooks.ie
www.bonnierbooks.co.uk

À Gisèle Pelicot. Merci, Madame.

BODY COUNT (noun)

1. The number of people that someone has had sex with. Popular especially in misogynist internet circles, to shame women for being sexually active. *'I'm a high-value man and I want a virgin, not a slut with tattoos and a high body count.'*
2. The number of people that someone has killed.

Chapter One

It's a quarter past three on a Friday afternoon and I'm sitting in a chain coffee shop, wearing a wig and terrible shoes, pretending to be having an online meeting and watching a man who could be my father.

I say 'coffee' shop. What I mean is 'brownish burned-tasting water loaded with artificially flavoured sugar syrup and topped with fake dairy foam' shop. There is something in the plastic cup in front of me that supposedly contains caffeine. It's purely a prop. I wouldn't taste this stuff.

The guy I'm stalking loves it. He's halfway through his second crappuccino. The baristas here know him; as soon as he walked in the door, they started preparing his drink. He didn't even have to order or queue up. He went straight to the counter, past all the waiting customers, and they handed him a tray with two foam-topped cups, a bottle of sparkling water and a chocolate-chip cookie. No money changed hands.

They made me wait fifteen minutes for my drink and wouldn't take my order until I gave them a fake first name.

I mime taking a sip and peer over my fake glasses at Sir Thomas West. He's a remarkably easy man to stalk – not just because he's famous, or because he goes everywhere shadowed by a muscular six-foot-five bodyguard with the longest mullet I've ever seen. Mostly it's because he's a creature of habit. He frequents this particular branch of an international coffee shop, a five-minute walk from his house, at least four times a week. This is the third time I've sat across the room from him in this very café, though admittedly it's been quite a gap since the last time. I've had to make a few sacrifices in my pursuit of a new relationship.

Anyway, now that I have a proper boyfriend, it's good to be back in the saddle. Even though this wig itches like hell.

Sir Thomas is wearing a frankly terrible pair of faded Boomer jeans, a light blue polo shirt, rimless glasses and, I kid you not, sandals with white socks. He has shopping bags piled up at his feet. His hair is snow white and fluffy. His hands are oddly delicate, like those of a pianist or brain surgeon.

I glance around the café. Everyone else is watching him, too. Most people are pretending not to. Sir Thomas is feigning obliviousness, scrolling on his phone as he drinks his sugary beverage. It's quite the charade all round, and exactly the reason why I have restricted my activities thus far to surveillance.

The only person who's not pretending at all is the bodyguard. Mullethead is sitting at a booth, his beefy arms resting on the puny table, his stony gaze never once leaving his boss. He stares as a woman approaches Sir Thomas.

She's in her mid-thirties and she's holding a little girl of about four or five by the hand. When they get to his table, West looks up and smiles. 'Hi there,' he says.

'Tommy— I mean, Sir Thomas,' she says. Her face has gone bright pink and her voice is breathy and high-pitched.

'Yes, that's me. What's your name?'

'I'm Rebecca.'

'It's lovely to meet you, Rebecca.'

People have stopped pretending not to watch, now, and are staring openly at Sir Thomas and the woman. Mullethead has relaxed a little. Clearly he hasn't been hired to protect against small children.

'I'm sorry for approaching you in public, but I just have to say that I absolutely loved you when I was a little girl.'

'Did you? I'm delighted.'

And he looks delighted, too – as if this is the first time this has ever happened to him.

'I used to watch *Tommy's Treat* every day. My mum says I wouldn't even eat my dinner unless you were on the telly.'

'That means so much to me. Thank you.'

'I know you must have people telling you this all the time. I mean, everyone watched *Tommy's Treat*.'

'It's always special to hear it.'

'I didn't have a father, you see. He left us, and I was an only child. So you were almost a father figure to me. I'd watch the telly and it made me less lonely, I guess?'

'That's exactly why we made the programme, for little girls like you, Becky.'

She giggles, and in that moment, she sounds like the little girl she used to be. 'Actually, I haven't been called Becky since I was a child.'

'It's important, isn't it?' he asks kindly. 'Those feelings we had as children. The names we had, too.'

'Would you ... would you mind signing something for me?' She holds out a paper napkin. 'This is all I have. If I'd known I was going to meet you ... I still have all my *Tommy's Treat* annuals.'

'You hang onto them. They might be worth something someday.' He grins and winks at her, and she giggles again as he signs the napkin. I can't see what he writes, though I'm familiar with his signature: big, looping and bold and practised. Rebecca reads it and gasps a little.

'Oh,' she says. 'Thank you so much.'

'You're very welcome.' His voice is sweet, like all the sugar he drinks in such quantities and which doesn't seem to rot his teeth or make him gain weight. 'And who is this? Is this your daughter?'

My hand tightens on the flimsy plastic cup.

'Yes, this is Ferne.'

'Ferne.' His voice, that voice broadcast all over the world for so many years, not every day now but still on talk shows and charity appeals, grows warmer and sweeter. His mouth seems to savour her name. 'How old are you, Ferne?'

'I'm five.'

'She just started school,' says Rebecca. She pushes her daughter forward slightly, as if in offering.

'School, eh? You're getting to be quite a grown-up girl. I'm Tommy. It's very nice to meet you.'

He holds out his hand, and Ferne looks at it, uncertain. Like all little girls – like me, when my mother paid attention to me – she has been told never to talk to strangers.

'Go ahead and shake Sir Thomas's hand, Ferne,' says Rebecca.

Ferne raises her little hand, slowly, towards Thomas West's delicate, brain-surgeon's grip.

I stand up and quickly gather my things. It's too public here. Mullethead is lurking. I'm not learning anything I don't already know. I can't do anything useful. I'm wasting my time.

I can't bear to see him touch her.

I turn away before I can see it, and rush for the door, fake hair falling into my face.

And run straight into a man.

I knock into him full-force, and knock the mug out of his hand. Hot coffee splashes down the front of my outfit and soaks into my canvas trainers, burning my toes.

'Ow!' I shout, jumping back, taken totally and uncoolly by surprise.

'What the fuck!' shouts the man.

I see him for the first time: he's wearing the sort of cheap grey suit beloved by mediocre middle managers everywhere. His face is flushed red with anger.

'I'm so sorry,' I say. 'It was an accident, I didn't see you there.'

'What's the fucking hurry?' he shouts.

'I'm really sorry,' I say. My toes throb. I look down at myself; my outfit/disguise is totally ruined by coffee stains, which is actually a bit of relief because it is seriously ugly. The man's suit seems unscathed, worse luck. He's a jowly, balding guy with a paunch and small bloodshot eyes and the red, broken-capillaried face of someone with high blood pressure.

Everyone in the café is now looking at us. So much for keeping under the radar.

'You silly fucking bitch. Why don't you look where you're going?'

'Are you OK? You didn't get burned, did you?' I stoop to pick up the empty mug from the floor.

'Do you even have a brain in there, or is it all in your boobs?'

The pain in my toes goes away. I stand up straight, all my muscles at ease, all surprise gone, my head entirely clear.

Despite this, my voice is meek. 'I really do apologise, sir. You're right, I was being silly. Let me get you another cup of coffee. What were you having?'

'Macchiato, double shot, extra-hot. Do you think you can manage that?'

'Of course, no problem, coming right up. Can I get you anything else?'

He grunts and turns away, muttering. I go to the counter, wait in the queue while the attention in the café returns to laptops, phones, private conversations. No one seems to be taking my photo, though I can't rule out someone having videoed the collision for TikTok.

I glance over at Sir Thomas; Rebecca and Ferne have gone back to their own table, and he is reading a newspaper and licking his fingers in an absent-minded way. The same hand that touched Ferne's. I focus my attention on the croissant display.

The barista who eventually serves me grimaces in sympathy. She points to my cheap, coffee-stained floral top. 'Are you OK? You didn't get burned, did you?'

'I'm fine,' I say with fake cheer. 'It was all totally my fault, I wasn't looking where I was going.'

She lowers her voice. 'Every time that guy comes in, he has a go at someone. Last week, he screamed at me because I made his extra-hot coffee too hot. Then the next day, he screamed at my colleague because she didn't make it hot enough. He complained to head office and we both got written warnings.'

'Oh no. I'm sorry.'

She shrugs. 'It's nothing compared to the way I've heard him talk to his wife and kids. That guy has a temper on him. It's going to bite him in the arse one day.'

'Karma's a bitch.' I give her a smile, and she smiles back.

'Here,' she says. 'Have a biscotti on me, in sisterly solidarity.' As she passes over the coffee and the biscuit, I fumble in my unchic handbag and come up with a five-pound note for the tip jar. It's not enough, but I don't want to be too memorable.

Nobody's watching me at all as I walk to Mr Anger Issues' table, slipping an emptied plastic ziplock bag into my coat pocket.

'Took your sweet time,' he grumbles.

'Sorry.' I hold out the tray.

He gulps the coffee immediately, extra-hot notwithstanding. The guy must have an asbestos throat. He needs it, to tolerate all the abuse coming out of it. 'Huh. Look at that, you actually got the order right.'

'I hope you enjoy it and that you have a great rest of your day!'

'Just watch where you're going from now on, stupid cow.' He takes another gulp and turns to his phone, resuming his urgent game of Candy Crush.

I do watch where I'm going. I return the tray to the stack of used ones and walk slowly and carefully back to my original table in the corner, bumping into exactly zero patrons and upsetting no one at all. I return to my abandoned hardly touched beverage, open my laptop, put on my headphones, log into a fake Teams meeting, and wait.

It doesn't take long. I've only taken a couple of nibbles on my free feminist biscotti (almond and chocolate chip – better than you'd think) when I hear a faint choking sound. I start typing urgently, as if my boss has just asked me an important question. The choking gets louder. I register Sir Thomas West, OBE, leaving the café, giving a cheery wave to his fans. His bodyguard trails in his wake, mullet fanning magnificently in the breeze.

I'll deal with him later. That's a promise. But first …

A chair scrapes back. For the second time in twenty minutes, a mug falls to the floor.

'Mate, are you OK?'

I pretend not to hear a thing because of my headphones. At his table, Mr Anger Issues is clutching at his chest. His face has gone purple.

I'm not generally a poison sort of girl. It's too risky: it doesn't always work and it might be detected in an autopsy. But on a person with known cardiac issues, like Sir Thomas and, incidentally, this guy, why not try to help things along?

The crash of a body on the floor is loud enough that I can't pretend to be oblivious any more. Several people have gathered around the choking, gasping man. A fellow customer kneels by his side and starts thumping on his chest. I don't think that's how you're meant to do CPR, but I'm no expert.

'Someone call 999!'

Everyone's instantly got their phones out. Some are calling. Some are filming. What is wrong with people? I mean, sure, I caused this heart attack, but I wouldn't dream of *filming* it. Some things are private.

The feminist barista rushes out from behind the counter and starts taking control. 'Can everyone please clear the area?' she calls. 'Give the man room, clear space for the paramedics to do their job.'

There's no evidence of paramedics arriving any time soon, but people put away their phones and start leaving, and I take the opportunity to do the same. I give the man on the floor a wide berth, but even from here I can see that his face has gone grey. His limbs jerk every time the do-gooder pushes on his chest, but otherwise, he's motionless.

He's no longer a heart attack waiting to happen.

I guess I'll have to replenish my poison supply for the next time I see Sir Thomas.

Chapter Two

So, for those of you who are new here and need to catch up: my name is Saffy Huntley-Oliver, and I'm a serial killer. But I'm not one of those inadequate, pathetic, fragile-masculinity murderers that you binge-watch documentaries on Netflix about.

I don't kill for a sexual kick like BTK or Fred and Rosemary West. Ew, how gross is that? I definitely don't kill for necrophilia like Ed Kemper. Ew ew ew ew ew ew ew ew. No.

I don't kill because my mummy and daddy didn't love me enough like David Berkowitz, or because I hear homicidal voices in my head like Peter Sutcliffe, or because I'm a grandiose loser in my real life like Ted Bundy, or because I find it impossible to talk to real-live human beings like Dennis Nilsen.

No.

One, all of those were men.

Two, I am beautiful, wealthy, intelligent and charming. I'm a treble-heiress, a former model, a fashion muse, and I've raised tons of money for charity. I might be a narcissist, but I have a good excuse because, whatever way you look at it, I am fabulous.

Three, I'm completely in control of my own life, not at the mercy of impulses and neuroses or my own psychopathy.

I kill people for a *reason*.

I kill bad men. Specifically, men who hurt women and girls. I've been doing it since I was twelve (with breaks, of course, for school, work, charity fundraising, travel, amassing a killer wardrobe and, lately, getting a boyfriend).

Did you know that almost every woman and girl who is murdered, worldwide, is murdered by a man? And the vast majority of those men are known to the victim. Fathers, husbands, boyfriends, brothers, rejected would-be lovers. As a female human being, you have an almost infinitely larger chance of being killed by someone you love than getting to meet Keanu Reeves.

How messed up is that? Everyone should meet Keanu Reeves. I met him once, in a vegan restaurant in San Francisco. He was adorable.

Murder is just the tip of the iceberg when it comes to how dangerous life is for women. We're not even talking about rape statistics, here. Or domestic assault. (Although, did you know that domestic violence increases by thirty-eight per cent every time England loses a football game?)

Or every single little misogynistic, catcalling, threatening, butt-pinching, mansplaining, wage-gapping, slut-shaming, baby-trapping, victim-blaming action that we see over and over and over in everyday life.

In fact, there are so many bad men out there that even when you're stalking one, it's difficult not to get distracted by another. They just seem to pop up everywhere you look. Which only proves that I'm doing the right thing.

I don't kill men for pleasure. I kill them to redress the world balance. To make it a safer place for people who are not bad men.

Although ... it can also be pretty fun.

* * *

This part of London is well-equipped with CCTV cameras, so after I leave the café I stroll unhurriedly to a nearby park where there is a friendly sheltered bench. There, I sit down to use a little cleaning cloth to remove smears from my glasses, and also any fingerprints from the plastic ziplock bag. I fold it up into a tissue and linger for a few minutes to enjoy the late-afternoon urban sunshine.

It takes longer than I'd expected to hear the approaching ambulance siren. The NHS is so stretched, isn't it? It's a national shame. I know it's a cliché that wealthy people hate to pay taxes, and I've met plenty of them who complain, but personally, I don't begrudge a single penny. I didn't earn my own money, after all, unlike the people working in healthcare.

Fortunately, I myself am blessed with excellent health, but that's all down to genes and an active lifestyle – luck, not superiority. Despite my hobby, I'm not devoid of compassion for others. For example, I would hate to be a person, even a misogynistic jerk, suffering a very public heart attack in an international chain café, having to wait for an ambulance until it is too late. It shouldn't happen in a major city.

However, I can't deny that it is quite handy for me.

I tuck my fake hair underneath a baseball cap, shrug on a light cardigan and blithely make my way to the nearest Tube station. I take the Elizabeth line east to Abbey Wood, where

I dispose of the ziplock bag in a bin outside a chip shop and the wig and glasses in a domestic refuse bin near a block of flats. Another few changes of Tube and a black cab later, I reach my gym (expensive, private, discreet), where they have excellent showers and where I store several changes of clothes and a full complement of makeup in case of spontaneous workouts and/or murders.

By the time I reach my own front door of my bijou mews house in Kensington, I'm glowing with health and good cheer.

When I open the door, there's a scrabble of little paws on my hardwood floor as the world's ugliest dog, Girl, sprints to get as far away from me as she possibly can. I glimpse her stubby tail rounding the corner into the kitchen. There's an inviting scent of something baking, fresh flowers on the console table, Radio 4 burbling comfortably in the background, a man's jacket hanging on the peg next to mine.

'Hi, honey,' I call. 'I'm home!'

* * *

Wherever Girl goes, there's a high chance that Jonathan is there, so I follow the dog's retreating backside into the kitchen.

And there he is, my beautiful, adorable, angelic, messy-haired, sexy-voiced, murder-obsessed new boyfriend (boyfriend!!) Jonathan Desrosiers, at my kitchen island with his hands in a bowl of flour.

'Hey,' I say, delighted to see him. I am always delighted to see him (even when he is walking in on me killing a bastard Tory, but more on that later). 'How's your day been?'

'Hmm. Could be better. I can't seem to get the hydration balance right with this spelt flour. How about you?'

'Oh, you know, the usual grind of being an unemployed wastrel.' I kiss him on the cheek, and then he turns his head so he can kiss me on the mouth.

I melt.

It has been nearly three weeks since our first kiss – that glorious first kiss, in that weird little man Simon Simons' basement, both of us drenched in blood and surrounded by badly stuffed cats – and difficult as it is to believe, kissing Jonathan Desrosiers has only got better and better. He's a good kisser: just the right balance of lip and tongue and teeth, sweetness and lust.

Girl grumbles in the corner. She still hasn't forgiven me for adopting her from a smelly dog shelter and then promptly trapping her in a well. I keep reminding her that the whole dog-in-well thing was only a ploy to get Jonathan to notice me. I knew all along that he would rescue her. She wasn't in any actual danger.

Well. Not much.

In any case, it all worked out perfectly, Jonathan adopted her, and since then, she's been living in the lap of luxury. So she should thank me, really. But apparently even ugly dogs are good at holding a grudge.

I ignore her and keep kissing Jonathan. My hands push up under his T-shirt to touch the warm skin at his waist.

When I come up for air, I murmur, 'Why aren't you touching me?'

'My hands are covered in flour. I'm afraid you'll kill me.'

'I would never do that,' I say. And in that moment, I mean it.

Chapter Three

WHAT JON DID NOT MENTION was that he had spent most of the afternoon looking at photographs of severed heads.

It was a mistake to go online so soon. It had been less than a month since his very public unmasking of Simon Simons – Jon's mild-mannered ultra-fan, who was a secret serial killer of an untold number of cats, multiple elderly neighbours and a single decapitated former nightclub owner. Simon Simons had, incidentally, also kidnapped Jon and severed his little toe.

Fortunately, that toe had been found and reconnected, though Jon was never going to wear sandals again. Since he'd never worn sandals in the first place, he considered himself incredibly lucky to have escaped.

There was trauma, of course, from having been abducted, kept hostage in a basement, threatened and tortured, and then from Jon having to shoot and kill Simon to keep him from harming Saffy. But Jon coped with all that trauma in the same way he coped with everything: by ignoring it and hoping it would go away.

It hadn't gone away.

The news hadn't died down at all. It didn't help that, for his now-discontinued podcast, he had a Google alert for news of UK homicides. As soon as he logged on, the headlines popped up.

TRUE CRIME PODCASTER AT CENTRE OF ANOTHER SERIAL KILLER CASE

GRANNY KILLER'S CONFESSION: *I POISONED OLD PEOPLE BECAUSE THEY SMELLED FUNNY*

SIMONS COPYCATTED 'BIN BAG KILLER' TO GET IDOL'S ATTENTION

A REAL-LIFE DEXTER? PORTRAIT OF SERIAL-KILLER KILLER, JONATHAN DESROSIERS

Ugh.

His agent, Edie, refused to tell the media where he was staying; thus far, none of them had tracked him down to Saffy's mews house in Kensington. He was hiding here as if he were in an expensively furnished bunker in one of London's most exclusive neighbourhoods. He only ventured outside to walk Girl, and made sure he wore a baseball cap and sunglasses.

Things were, at least, slightly better than the last time he'd been the focus of national media attention. When he'd found a headless dismembered body on his doorstep eight months ago – the morning after his wife left him – he had fled to a remote cottage in Scotland in order to drink his body weight in whisky. Now, he was more likely to share a bottle of vintage champagne . . . and he wasn't alone.

He glanced up from his laptop screen to survey his surroundings. He felt distinctly scruffy next to the furnishings of Saffy's guest bedroom, with its fluffy white rugs on polished hardwood floors, pristine white high-thread-count bed linen, and raw silk cushions (also in white). The walls were painted what he'd call white, but he was sure that the paint was a very precise shade of white, probably called Elephant Breath or Virgin Bride. There were two oil paintings, one on the wall behind the bed and one across from it. He was no expert, but he suspected that one of them was an actual Georgia O'Keefe.

Girl the dog lay on the bed at his feet, her snubby profile silhouetted against the Georgia O'Keefe. When he'd first come to this house, back when Saffy was a near-stranger and before he'd even dreamed of killing Simon Simons, he'd tried to make Girl sleep on the floor. But every morning he'd wake up with Girl curled up next to him on the pillow, shedding wiry hair on the Egyptian sheets, leaving small circular patches of drool and a distinct scent of mutt.

How would he know how to train a dog? He'd never had one before a few weeks ago. He hadn't even planned on having this one. He settled for buying a cheap blanket and putting it on the bottom of the bed. Girl seemed to get the hint, though sometimes he still woke up with her arse in his face.

Some days – most days – Jon had literally no idea how he had ended up here. Sometimes it felt as if someone was looking down at him, pulling strings, watching him dance.

His email pinged and by instinct, not even paying attention or remembering that it was a really bad idea, he opened the message on the top of his inbox.

What do you think? read the subject line.

Dear Jonathan,
I'd like your opinion on these photos.

The return email address was a bunch of numbers followed by @gmail.com. He should be wary of anonymous online accounts. There was an attachment which he should delete immediately.

According to DI Atherton of Scotland Yard, Jonathan Desrosiers was a blighted hack who profited off the misery of others and encouraged the worst in human nature. But despite that, Jon was still a journalist. And this email had been sent to his personal address, the one he didn't give out to anyone except for people he knew.

So he clicked on it.

It was a zip file of several photographs. When he opened the first one, he recoiled violently enough that his laptop almost went flying.

He caught it. Then he uttered a heartfelt 'Fuck.'

Girl, who had jumped to her feet at his reaction, woofed at him and nosed his leg.

'I'm all right,' he told her. But he wasn't so sure. Someone who was all right wouldn't look at the photograph again.

But he did. It was a picture of a man's severed head lying on a pitted linoleum floor, and although he had not seen this photograph before, he had seen the head. He'd *touched* the head. Eight months ago, he had found it in a freezer in his mate Cyril Walker's house, and then when Cyril had tried to kill him, Jon had grabbed the head and thrown it at him.

He could still feel the sensation now in his hand: the weight of the head, the cold and terribly hard texture of the skin on the face and neck, ice crystals on the surface, like a frozen leg of lamb.

Meat. It felt like meat, and sometimes in the middle of the night when, yet again, he couldn't sleep, he tried to rewrite history and make himself believe that it had been meat – a package of mince, a joint of gammon – because it was less monstrous to use those things as a weapon to save yourself. Roald Dahl had written a story about a leg of lamb as a murder weapon and it was funny.

But then there was the hair, and that was horrifyingly, indisputably human. Hair that had been combed and cut, and shampooed and styled, and that Jon, in his desperation and fear, had grabbed hold of and pulled.

In this photograph, the man's eyes were half-open. Jon knew, now, that this man had been named Milo Berryman. He was a part-time Deliveroo cyclist. He had grown up in foster care in Liverpool and spent a bit of time in prison for drug offences. Three weeks after moving to London, he'd stopped replying to his mates' texts. Nobody raised the alarm because even though Milo was trying to get clean, he'd gone missing before and always turned up sooner or later, sometimes with a hangover and blacked out memories, more often with his cheeky grin and his trademark outrageous stories, stories that couldn't possibly be true, of pranks and parties and incredible coincidences. He loved being up high and spent a lot of time on fire escapes and roofs. One time Milo swore up and down that he had fallen asleep in Stanley Park and when he woke up, there was a giant boa constrictor curled up on top of him, also asleep.

He'd had to lie absolutely still until the sun came up and the snake warmed enough to slither off him, away and into the bushes. None of his mates believed this story, but it was pure Milo, they agreed. Sometimes they called him 'Snake Charmer' and it always made him laugh.

No one had reported him missing.

He'd moved to London to try to connect with his birth mother. When the police found her and spoke to her, after Milo's head was identified and linked with his body, which had been found months earlier, cut up in a bin bag and dumped in a patch of waste ground in Walthamstow, his birth mother said that Milo had never got in touch. She didn't even know he was in London, until he was dead.

Milo's favourite song was 'There She Goes' by The La's. His favourite food was chips and curry sauce. His foster mum had all his certificates for perfect school attendance still hanging up on his bedroom wall. He rode a third-hand bike that he'd bought online and had its serial number scratched off, so it had probably been stolen. Although his body, and then his head, had been found, no one had ever found his bike, or if they did, they didn't know it was his.

Jon knew all of this about Milo Berryman because he owed it to him, and also because he had to. It was important to recognise Milo as a person, a whole person, with troubles and joys. Not something grisly he had discovered by mistake and used in self-defence. Not nightmare fuel ... but the indescribably sad ending of a life.

Over the years, he'd investigated several murders and covered many of them in his true crime books and his podcast, *Stone Cold Killers*. He had made his living out of other people's deaths.

The only way he could square this with his conscience was to tell himself that he was writing for the victims' sake. That he was humanising them for the reader. Memorialising them in his words. Making people understand that murder wasn't entertainment; it was a real-life human tragedy, and the people touched by it would never, ever be the same.

He had first-hand experience of that.

Now, Jon gazed at the photograph of Milo's head. It had been taken not long after he'd removed it from the freezer. It could be a police photograph, though he didn't see any evidence markers on it. The head appeared to have been thawed out a little (how long would it take a head to thaw?); the muscles of the cheeks were slack and the mouth was drooping slightly to one side, as if Milo had fallen asleep on the floor minus his body. There was no blood or other fluid leaking from it, and although Jon remembered ice crystals on Milo's eyelashes and beard stubble, he couldn't see any in this photo.

Who took it? Who sent it to him?

What opinion was he supposed to have about it?

He clicked on the second photo. He was pretty sure he knew what this one would be, and he was right: it was Cyril Walker's freezer. The freezer was an old one – a compartment above the refrigerator – and the shelves had been removed to accommodate four severed heads. When Jon had seen them in real life, he'd been too terrified to take in the details, but since then he'd learned who the victims were, so he could identify them: Stephen Wójcik, Diego Little, Les Galloway, and Jack Banks. Three were white men with longish dark hair (Cyril had a type – Jon had thought more than once that he himself belonged to that type). Another white man had a shaved head. The fifth man was Black with close-cut hair and an earring visible in his left ear. All of them had slack mouths, frozen eyes. All of them had been washed clean of blood from the clean, neat cut between the C4 and C5 vertebrae. They were upright.

There was a package of potato waffles crammed between Wójcik and Little. Jon hadn't noticed that before. He wished he hadn't noticed it now.

Aside from that, there was nothing for Jon to have an opinion about. He'd given a full statement to the police, the most sensational details of which had already been covered in the press. Cyril Walker had confessed to all of his crimes in detail and indeed was eager for Jon to make them the subject of his next book.

These photos, however, hadn't been shared with the press, as far as he knew. So where did they come from?

There were two more in the zip drive. Girl, who had been nudging his ankle in hopes of a scratch, huffed and jumped off the bed.

The third photograph was also something he had seen before. The freezer this time belonged to Simon Simons, and it was a more up-to-date model, with drawers underneath the fridge. The top drawer was open, exposing three carefully sealed ziplock freezer bags. Again, Jon hadn't appreciated this at the time, because he was busy being afraid for his and Saffy's lives, but the freezer bags were each labelled with a printed date and a name. *Mittens. Fluffy. Sir Augustine.*

Another severed human head lay beside the frozen cats. This one was face-up and the victim had black hair and an impeccably groomed goatee. His name was Francesco Fanducci and he was a nightclub owner and cricket player, a father of four who occasionally mixed things up by setting fires and assaulting women.

Jon had found the rest of his body, minus the hands, in a bin bag on his front doorstep eight months ago, and had briefly been a suspect himself for the murder. His and Saffy's investigation of the crime, to clear his name, had led almost nowhere until the head was found in Simon's freezer. Then they, and the police, were able to piece back Simon's crime as an attempt to get Jon's attention.

'These cases are solved,' he muttered to himself.

But that had been his speciality as an investigative journalist and podcaster, hadn't it? To examine cold cases, but also cases that were supposedly solved, but were really a miscarriage of justice. He still got Christmas cards every year from the man he'd cleared of Lianne Murray's murder.

His journalist days were long over, though. He had no more desire to go picking around in other people's tragedies – or their freezers. Especially as he'd come so close to being a victim himself.

Still. He clicked on the fourth photograph.

It was yet another severed human head. One he'd never seen before.

Girl jumped back up onto the bed and plopped down on the blanket at his feet. She had a pink shoe in her mouth, which she chewed enthusiastically.

'Girl!' Jon cried, shoving the laptop aside and lunging for the shoe. Girl clamped down on it. It took several minutes of tugging and prising Girl's jaws apart before he extricated the shoe: a delicate kitten-heeled sandal that Jon was pretty sure he'd seen Saffy wearing a couple of days ago. It was covered in dog slobber and teeth marks. One strap hung unattached from the sole.

'Bad dog,' Jon told Girl. 'You can't chew Saffy's shoes. You can't.'

Girl eyed him and started licking her genitals.

'She pretended not to care about what you did to her lemon tree on the patio, but I think you are on thin ice, my friend. She literally saved your life! Leave her shoes alone.'

Girl's back leg was up in the air and she was paying special attention to her anus.

Jon sighed and stashed the shoe under his pillow. All he had to do was keep it a secret until he could ask Saffy's sister Susie what the shoes were, and get her to help him source a replacement. Most likely it would max out his final remaining non-maxed credit card.

'Here,' he said. He scooped one of his battered running shoes from the floor and put it in front of the dog, who ignored it. 'Chew on this instead. All you like. Have a feast.'

Then he retrieved his laptop, closed up the grisly photos, shut down the laptop and put it in a drawer. Despite her choice of chew toy, Girl had done him a favour. He'd had enough of death and danger and bloody severed heads for several lifetimes. He had the nightmares to prove it.

He'd track down the source of this email, and those photos, later.

It was time for him to concentrate on something healing and wholesome and productive. Like making bread.

* * *

'Hi, honey, I'm home!'

Saffy came in from her workout a few hours later, freshly showered, smelling gorgeous, smiling beautifully, and still so out of his league that if he wasn't wrist-deep in dough, Jon would have pinched himself. She kissed him on the cheek and he was tempted to mention the photos. She might have some ideas about who had sent them, and what the last photo was about. She loved playing amateur sleuth.

But then he thought about her mangled shoe. And the bloodbath they had witnessed in the basement of Simon Simons' home. And the fact that his previous relationship had fallen apart because he couldn't stop being obsessed with murder.

So he kept quiet.

Chapter Four

We are on our second double date with my sister Susie and her terrible boyfriend, Finlay. The first date was in a crowded but infinitely Instagrammable restaurant in Chelsea, where it was impossible to hear anyone over the squeals of Generation Z. In other words: perfect. I spent the entire night holding Jonathan's hand under the table and nodding without comprehension or interest to anything that Finlay said.

Tonight, Susie has decided that the four of us should have an actual conversation. Finlay has invited us for dinner at his place. Obviously neither my sister nor her boyfriend are aware of how many times I have murdered Finlay in my head. Susie, bless her, is a sweet innocent person who believes the best in everyone. And Finlay – well, Finlay is just stupid.

Finlay's place is exactly what you would get if you fed an AI image generator with the prompt *'douchebag tech bro's industrial-modern Shoreditch loft'*. All the windows are tall, all the walls are naked brick and stone, all the furniture is black. The downstairs is entirely open-plan, which means that half of the living area is taken up by exercise and computer equipment, with a metal spiral staircase going up to the mezzanine level.

The television is the size of a cinema screen and the lights, the heating, the fridge, the window shades, and probably the toilet are all operated by Finlay's smartphone.

Finlay greets us and ferries Jon away to inspect his selection of hyper-local craft ales, while Susie waylays me beside the large sliding steel door.

'I'm so glad we could make this happen,' she says. 'Finlay has been cooking for days.'

'Finlay is cooking?' I say in alarm.

'Yes, isn't that adorable?'

'It's . . . interesting.' I sniff the air, which has no detectible cooking scents.

'He's very concerned about the level of additives in pre-prepared food,' says Susie, as if she has not been living off Deliveroo and vodka for her entire adult life. 'Anyway, how are you? You look good.'

'Alaïa. Ready to wear.'

'No, dummy, I mean *you* look good. Your skin is glowing. All that sex suits you.'

My sister is the most important person in my life. We have been inseparable since she was born. For obvious reasons, I'm often obliged to tell her untruths, but I try to be as honest as I can about other important things such as clothes and boys.

'Well,' I say.

'What?'

'We . . . are taking it slow.'

Her forehead wrinkles – as much as it can. Susie is a devotee of preventing ageing before it starts.

'You mean you haven't done it yet?' she asks.

I glance at the open-plan kitchen, where Finlay is explaining beer. As usual, he's wearing no shoes, shorts, and a shirt unbuttoned to his navel and rolled up to expose his tribal tattoos, like a wannabe Jason Momoa. Jonathan is wearing jeans, trainers, and a button-down white cotton shirt, the ultimate in geek chic. The two of them seem not to be paying attention to us.

'There's no hurry,' I say in a lowered tone. 'He's recently divorced. We've both been through some things.'

'You're living together.'

'Yes, but we're not *living* living together. He doesn't have anywhere else to stay in London. He stays in the guest bedroom.'

'You mean he's your lodger?'

'No, he's my boyfriend. But we value our personal space. Also he's recovering from surgery.'

'That was on his *toe*. I don't know what sex positions you like but most of them don't involve the little toe.'

'I'm enjoying being old-fashioned. It's very romantic.'

Susie is shaking her head. 'You spent weeks moping around my flat, moaning about how bad you wanted to screw his brains out.'

'Maybe I've learned patience.'

'At your age?'

'Hey! Less with the age.' I am six years older than Susie, though impeccable genes and skincare belie the fact. 'So, have you found any more messages from Finlay's Russian side piece on his phone?'

'I told you, Finlay explained everything and the whole thing was a misunderstanding.'

'Hmm.'

'Besides, I've forgiven him.'

'Why would you need to forgive him if he's done nothing wrong?'

'Anyway, I'm more interested in you and Jon. Why haven't you shagged yet? Can't he get it up?'

'Oh, he can get it up.' I smile at the memory of our earlier makeout session in the kitchen.

'So what's the problem?'

'There is no problem,' I say. 'Everything is total bliss. Please open a bottle of champagne immediately.'

'I'm making mojitos,' she says, and leads me to the built-in bar, which is conveniently situated next to Finlay's surfboard and saxophone.

'Can I have a martini?'

'You are so boring,' she says, but she proceeds to make me a martini: dry and dirty with three olives, just the way I like it. I take an appreciative sip.

'I've trained you well.'

'Please. You can't take the credit. They taught me to make martinis in finishing school.' She begins to pound mint in the bottom of a glass, and shoots me a sly look. 'So, why do you have cold feet?'

I feel a warm hand rest on my hip, an arm around my waist, and because I have lightning-fast reflexes, for a split second I stiffen before I realise it's Jonathan. My delectable boyfriend. I smile up at him.

'Who has cold feet?' he asks.

'Nobody,' I say, and to prove it I give Jonathan a deep, lingering kiss that completely ruins my lipstick.

'Whoa,' says Finlay from behind us in his fake-Australian accent. 'I didn't realise this was that kind of party.'

'It really isn't,' I say.

The urge to shove my martini glass straight into Finlay's throat, severing his jugular and making him spray dark sticky blood all over his man-toys, is a fraction of what it was a few weeks ago. This is not because Finlay himself is any less of a dictionary definition of the word 'cockwomble'. It is purely down to the fact that he gave me some small technical assistance in tracking down Jonathan after he was kidnapped by Simon Simons, therefore most likely saving Jon's life and, with it, our relationship.

Since then, there has been a truce, at least on my side. I have not made any plans to kill Finlay. And Finlay, to give him credit, has been nothing but friendly to Jonathan.

Finlay seems to be thinking of the same incident and his part in it, because he drapes an arm around Susie's shoulders, raises his can of craft beer and says, 'Cheers, guys. Here's to you not being dead.'

'I'll drink to that,' says Jonathan.

Susie raises her eyebrows at me. I ignore her.

* * *

Our starter consists of a strand of asparagus on a very large plate, but this is at least palatable so I have raised my expectations of Finlay's culinary skills to above floor level. The conversation, however, is less promising. As I predicted, Finlay is doing most of the talking, and most of that talking is about either super-optimised exercise routines or crypto.

Susie, who I assume has heard all of this ad nauseam and yet still fancies this toerag, keeps on shooting me looks. She's sitting at the end of the table to my right, and Jonathan is across from me, so I'm answering her unspoken questions by gazing at him lovingly. Since my sister and I are so busy with this charade of meaningful glances, Jonathan, the poor beautiful sod, is having to feign interest in our host's monologue, every now and then interjecting with 'I see' and 'Oh, how fascinating.'

This is heroic good manners. How unlike the boor who I poisoned earlier. I have chosen my boyfriend *so well*. I am a literal genius.

I slip off my peekaboo-toe heel and reach my bare foot under the table until I encounter Jonathan's ankle. I'm rewarded by a slight widening of his eyes as I make contact. I slide my foot upward, into his trouser leg to the top of his sock so my toes touch warm, bare skin. I lightly caress his shin with my toes.

Is Jonathan a foot man? A boob man? A bum man? Or is he, as I hope, the kind of man who appreciates every part of a woman equally? I have so many things to discover about him. We have so many things to discover together.

There's really no hurry. Meanwhile, I am showing my sister that Jonathan and I can't resist each other.

'So, dude,' Finlay is saying, 'I hear you write books?'

Jonathan sits up a little straighter at this suggestion that he might actually join in the conversation. 'I've written a few,' he begins.

'Like, how do you do that? Do you just sit down, or . . .?'

'My books are journalism, so I spend quite a bit of time doing research and getting it all in order. The writing itself is—'

'Don't they say that everyone's got a book in them?'

'I wrote true crime focusing on murder victims,' says Jonathan dryly, 'so most people would probably prefer not to have that sort of book in them.'

I reward him for this wit (and for unconsciously emphasising how special I am) by wiggling my toes a little further up his leg. He sends me half a naughty smile.

Finlay's watch buzzes. 'Oh, the main course is ready.' He hops up, man-bun bobbing, chest hair wafting in the breeze, and goes to the kitchen area, where he fusses with some sort of appliance. It's only when the top of it opens and he begins plating up that I finally detect the scent of cooking, and the unmistakable aroma of ...

'Is that beef?' I ask.

'Sous vide,' Finlay says, sprinkling micro herbs. 'Wagyu.'

'I'm a vegetarian,' I say.

'Everyone needs protein and this is super-plus optimal?' He puts down a plate in front of me. It contains a piece of meat, oozing blood.

'When I say I'm vegetarian, it means that I don't eat flesh.'

'Babes, I told you,' says Susie, pouting. 'Remember?'

'Did you? I don't remember.'

Oh, he remembers all right. I can see the smirk on his face. I might be holding up to my side of the truce, but Finlay has just trampled all over it. He thinks I owe him one for helping save Jonathan's life, and therefore must eat crow.

Or cow.

'Just have a little bit, Saff. It won't hurt you. I promise you, this is so tender, you'll think you're eating silk.'

What happens to a man's severed penis if you cook it sous vide, I wonder?

'Babes, Saffy hasn't eaten meat since she was a kid.'

'There are no animal welfare issues with this beef,' Finlay tells me. 'If that's your problem? These cows are treated like royalty, right up to the minute that they quickly and painlessly die. They're happier than we are?'

Oh, how I would love to make Finlay beg for such a quick and painless death right now, on this black dining table. But I can't. I can't. My sister would never forgive me. My boyfriend doesn't know I'm a murderer. Nobody knows I'm a murderer. And that's the way I intend to keep it, forever and ever.

But. All the knives in the kitchen. All those lovely, sharp knives, arrayed on a magnetic holder on the wall ...

I close my eyes and breathe deeply, realise this is introducing molecules of cooked meat into my body through my nostrils, and hold my breath and count to ten instead.

'I'll Deliveroo some noodles,' says Susie.

'We could order a pizza,' says Jonathan.

'I've got some whey powder,' says Finlay. 'Do you want a glass of that instead?'

'It's fine,' I say. I open my eyes and smile dazzlingly at Finlay, the moronic man-bunned meatmonger. 'I'm not actually that hungry. That starter filled me right up. Susie, would you mind making me another martini?'

'I'm sorry, I honestly didn't know,' says Finlay, forking the meat from my plate onto his and cutting off a bite.

'It's an easy mistake to make,' I lie. 'Pardon me, I'm just going to use the loo and refresh my lipstick. Please, don't wait for me.'

My re-donned stilettos make clicking sounds as I climb the spiral staircase to the mezzanine, where lurk Finlay's bedroom and ensuite. Against all of my expectations, he seems to have changed his bed linen recently – although it's black, so it's hard to tell without getting close, and I am *not* doing that. I wonder why he leaves his stinky workout gear all over Susie's flat, but somehow manages to pick it up in his own space.

(Why am I kidding myself? Finlay pays a woman to do all of his housework. She must have to shower in bleach afterwards.)

I can hear the conversation going on downstairs without me. Susie is saying, 'Yes, babes, I told you several times' and Finlay is answering with 'OK, OK, I'll find something else if it's that important.'

Up here, I am invisible. I put on a pair of latex gloves before removing a plastic ziplock bag from my clutch. Then I open the wardrobe door. His cleaner doesn't touch anything in here – it's a jumble of clothes and flip-flops and unused hangers and it emits a strong scent of Invictus. Gingerly, I move some of the clothes to one side, clearing a space near the very bottom. I extract, from the ziplock bag, a black and pale blue striped Eton tie.

Handling it only with two gloved fingers, I plant it in Finlay's wardrobe and then replace clothes on top of it, as if the tie is a fossil trapped in layers of sedimentary rock.

I touch up my lipstick in the black polished concrete bathroom and go back downstairs, considerably more cheerful.

Finlay has replaced my bloodstained plate with a bowl of salad. Susie has made me a martini with seven olives. I settle back into my chair. Jonathan asks, 'Are you OK?' and I merely smile at him, slip off my shoe again, and put my bare foot directly on his inner thigh.

'Everything is great.' I wiggle my toes. His cheeks go pink. Slowly, and with great relish, I pop an olive between my red lips.

'So, back to the book stuff,' says Finlay, chewing. 'You know, I've always thought that I should write a book?'

'Is that so?' Jonathan asks politely.

'Yeah, I've got some real stories. You wouldn't believe the shit that has happened to me.' He swigs from his can of craft beer. 'How long does it take to write a book, anyway?'

'It depends on a lot of factors. Anywhere from a year to several years, on average. I had to write my second book, *In the Dark of the Night*, quite quickly because it was a well-known case and the family of the victim wanted to set the record straight.'

'How quickly was that?' asks Susie. 'Like, weeks?'

'About eight months.' He glances at me, where I am sipping my martini with Zen-like calm and not betraying that I am feeling him up under the table. 'There was a lot of material to get around, and some of it was pretty sensitive. It was a lot of seven-day weeks, and twelve-hour days. It didn't do my marriage any favours.'

'I thought you were divorced?' Susie pounces.

'Yes, I'm divorced. We've both moved on. She's engaged to a man she met at work, and I've found someone much, much hotter than me, who inexplicably seems to like me.'

His hand settles on my ankle and strokes up my calf.

'And are you usually a workaholic?' Susie is vetting my boyfriend.

'I was. But I'm trying to be better. I've given up doing the true crime books and podcasts, anyway. The topic is too harrowing.'

'Oh? What are you doing?'

'I'm trying to find my new niche. Something more positive, I hope.'

'He's baking sourdough,' I volunteer, making my way further up his thigh. 'Working on the perfect rise.' My toes encounter something gratifyingly and perfectly risen.

His cheeks are now flaming.

'What about sex?' suggests Susie. 'That's a fun way to pass the time. You could start a new podcast about shagging.'

Jonathan chokes on his beer. He swallows hard and drinks some more.

'Seriously?' I say to Susie, but it's her turn to ignore me.

'I mean, if there's a choice between sex and death, I know which one I'd rather hear about.'

'Eight months,' says Finlay, disappointed. 'It really takes that long just to write one book? Like, you could make a whole human baby in that time.'

'That's nine months, sweetie.' Susie turns to Jonathan again. 'See? You could make it, like, educational.'

'I'm not sure I've got the expertise,' Jonathan says modestly, but laughing now.

'But wouldn't it be fun getting the expertise? Doing the mileage?'

'Anybody can do sex,' I say, loyally. 'It takes someone very special to do murder.'

'I could maybe do a month to write a book,' says Finlay. 'Go someplace isolated and spiritual, do a few ayahuasca journeys, and just get it all down, you know? I just feel like I've got a lot to say that would, like, resonate with people.'

'You could certainly try,' says Jonathan.

Finlay snaps his fingers. 'I've got an idea! You're looking for something new to do? Why don't I tell you my stories, I can dictate and send you the recordings or something, and you could write them? I bet it would sell like crazy. We could split the money, like sixty-forty because it's my life and all you'd have to do is basically type it.'

'You've got some interesting suggestions,' Jonathan says. 'I'll give them some thought.'

'Jonathan is bullshitting you,' I tell Finlay. 'Nobody wants to buy a memoir unless it's under the name of a football player or a member of the royal family.'

Susie asks cheerfully, 'Who wants another drink?'

'I think I need one,' admits Jonathan, as my foot trails up and down his crotch. 'Could I have a whisky? Neat?'

'Beer, me,' says Finlay.

'I'll take another dirty martini. Only one olive this time, though.'

'It's funny that you drink those,' says Susie, taking my glass.

'Why is it funny?'

'They always seemed more like a man's drink to me. Didn't Harold drink those?'

Cold sweeps through me. Under the table, my foot stills.

'I don't remember,' I lie.

Chapter Five

'God, that was excruciating,' I say as soon as the door of the black cab shuts behind us.

'*Some* of it was excruciating,' Jonathan agrees. 'Some things were nice.'

'Name one thing.'

'The steak was good ...'

I roll my eyes.

'So was the whisky.'

'I bought that whisky for last year's Secret Santa.'

'I cannot picture you doing Secret Santa.'

'It was my sister's idea.'

'That makes sense.'

'Don't tell me you like Finlay.'

'He's fine,' says Jonathan, with heroic fairness. 'He's got some ... ideas. But he's fundamentally sound, I think.'

'I don't understand why my sister loves him.'

'But she does, so ...'

'I can't interfere,' I sigh. 'Please don't ghost-write his memoir, though.'

'I don't know. It does sound fascinating. Bitcoin, blockchain, and ice baths.'

'You're a horrible human being. I love it.' I lean back in the seat and groan. I feel hungry, drunk, frustrated, and also quite horny. 'So the steak and the whisky were the only good things?' I lift my foot and wiggle it suggestively.

'You're right. There was one other good thing.' He rests his warm hand on my bare knee, his little finger just under the hem of my dress.

'Mmm, and what was that?'

'You are beautiful,' he murmurs, and leans over to give me a deep, passionate kiss. I twine my arms around his neck and return it, with enthusiasm.

Now this evening is getting good.

* * *

By the time the cab pulls up outside my Kensington mews house, I'm sitting on Jonathan's lap, snogging him like a teenager. My dress is wrinkled, my lipstick is all kissed off, my hair is totally ruined from his hands running through it, and the cabbie has probably had quite a show, but I don't care about any of that.

I'm the complete opposite of a simpering young damsel and I don't, in general terms, agree with the chauvinistic system of a man paying for everything on a date because, let's face it, they usually want something in return. Despite these feminist ideals, when Jonathan, currently unemployed, pays the driver and adds a substantial tip, my knickers just about melt.

I pull him inside the house by his shirt collar and as soon as the door has closed behind us we're pressed up against the wall, ripping at each other's clothes. My hands are up underneath his shirt and his are up underneath my dress and he's kissing me with a hunger that he hasn't kissed me with before, almost desperation, and although desperation is not generally a turn-on, this desperation is wonderful – like he's suffocating and his only air supply is my mouth, my neck, my skin.

I unbutton his shirt and lick his collarbone. He tastes of salt and deliciousness. When my tongue touches his skin he groans and lifts me up, closer, rucking my dress up around my hips. With my back against the wall, I wrap my legs around his waist and can feel his erection through his trousers and my knickers. My hands buried in his curls, tugging them, I kiss him harder. I bite his lips. I suck at his tongue.

I was right when I told Susie that anticipation made everything better, because I fancied this man before, but right in this moment, with only a couple of scraps of fabric separating us, I want him so much that I think if I don't get him, soon, right now, I might die.

I hear a snort.

It's a strange noise to make when you're in the middle of an extremely heavy petting sesh but in every other way Jonathan is pretty much ideal and he feels amazing, so much unexpected strength in his wiry frame and what feels like a very lovely impressive package under his jeans, so I am prepared to ignore any strange sounds. I press myself up harder against him, tilt my hips to get better friction. He groans again in pure, sexy need.

Another snort.

Jonathan raises his head from my chest. His eyes are unfocused, his lips wet, his cheeks flushed.

'What's that?' he says.

'It's my left breast. My right one is a tiny bit more perfect, so you've made a wise choice starting with the left, so you won't be disappointed later.'

'No, I mean ...'

Snort.

Our heated gazes leave each other and converge on a spot in the middle of my living room, where Girl is standing watching us, her eyes narrowed.

'It's just the dog,' I gasp, tugging at Jonathan's hair, turning his head back to mine so I can kiss his lips. His scrumptious, sexy mouth.

I can feel the dog's eyes watching us. I concentrate on the texture of Jonathan's tongue, the way he tastes faintly of expensive whisky and my own more expensive perfume. I think about him picking me up and carrying me upstairs to my bedroom, throwing me on my bed, pushing my thighs apart and ...

Girl whines.

I pull my head back. 'Girl, go into the kitchen, sweetie. Good dog!'

She does not go into the kitchen. I free one of my hands and point to the kitchen door. Girl merely stares at me.

'Girl, go to your bed,' Jonathan says, to no avail.

'Let's just ignore her.' I nibble on his ear.

'I fed her before we left. Maybe she needs to go out.'

'I also have needs,' I remind him.

'Believe me, I have the same needs. I'll just ...' He lowers me to my feet and disentangles himself, pushing his hair into greater messiness. His shirt is askew and there is a visible outline of his needs in the crotch of his jeans. He looks down at himself, and then quirks a smile at me: half-sheepish, half-aroused, wholly adorable.

'I'll be right back. C'mon, Girl, let's go out.'

He walks past Girl towards the kitchen at the back door to the courtyard garden. The dog doesn't go with him. In fact, her gaze remains on me and, as soon as he is out of sight, she pulls back her top lip and growls at me.

'Oh, stop it,' I tell her. 'Just because you've been spayed doesn't mean that no one else can have any fun.'

'Girl!' calls Jonathan, out of sight.

Deliberately, the dog squats and pisses on my parquet floor.

I crouch, look her in the eyes, and hiss, 'I'm the alpha predator in this house. Back off.' She snorts again and turns around, giving me a close-up view of her rectum.

At this moment, Jonathan returns and sees the spreading puddle.

'Oh no! Girl! Bad dog! I am so, so sorry, Saffy. Girl, go outside right now!'

The dog trots off happily to the garden, stubby tail waving. Jonathan retrieves paper towels from the kitchen and begins wiping up the mess. 'I don't believe she did that! She must have been really desperate to go. I'm sorry, Saffy, it's my fault. I should have let her out right away, as soon as we got in.'

'You had other things on your mind,' I say, straightening up. I pull the hem of my dress back down. He should still have other things on his mind, not dog piss.

'Agh, it's everywhere. I need more paper towels. Where do you keep the disinfectant spray?'

Five seconds ago, he needed a condom. Seething, I fetch the cleaner's supply of Purdy & Figg from the cupboard under the stairs.

'I don't know what got into her.' He starts spraying, filling the room with the scent of vetiver. 'I'll make it up to you, Saffy.'

'I think it's the dog who owes me an apology.' I'm beginning to think I should have left that mutt in the well in Scotland, where I put her in the first place.

'She's just a dog. I wonder if she's sick?'

'Well,' I say, 'she's killed the mood, anyway.'

'She has rather. We could have a nightcap, try to rekindle it?'

I sigh. It's not the puddle of pee, or the sight of a dog's anus that's ruined it; it's more that I, a creature of normally superior brains, beauty, and righteous rage, have been cockblocked by a dog in my own home. I feel deflated, as if some vital part of myself has also been pissed on.

'I'm tired,' I say. 'Let's take a rain check, shall we?'

I kiss him on the cheek and go up to my chaste bed, alone.

Chapter Six

In the small, battered notebook that he usually carried in his back pocket, Jon had the beginning paragraph of an abandoned manuscript draft. He'd written it six months ago in a small cabin in Scotland. His handwriting was sloppy and lots of it was crossed out, as if he were drunk when he wrote it, because he was indeed drunk when he wrote it:

When I first met Cyril Walker, four years ago, I liked him. He helped me solve a case, and then he stuck around. He came to my house. He met my wife. We played darts together in the pub sometimes. I thought he was a good bloke. A little quirky, maybe, and he wore too much body spray deodorant, but I thought he was fundamentally sound. He was laid-back and funny. His brother had been jailed for a crime for which he was later exonerated, an incident that gave Cyril a strong sense of justice. I could relate to that. I trusted him.

But the whole time that Cyril and I were friends, he was luring young men to his house and killing them. Which goes to show that ~~anyone can be a murderer~~
  ~~I am a really fucking terrible judge of character~~
  ~~if I'd caught him sooner, I could have saved Milo's life.~~

Jon was thinking about those crossings-outs now, as he stowed the notebook and pen, plus his wallet and phone, in a locker in the prison visitor centre. It was only the second time he had been to this particular building, but the routine was already familiar. Show his ID, lock up his stuff, walk through a metal detector, and submit to a search. Then wait to be escorted to the visiting room. This time, though, he had the presence of mind to take in the details: the concrete walls, the scent of bleach, the echoing footsteps. No comfort anywhere; no style. Prison was the polar opposite of Saffy's house.

The guard unlocked the gate into the high-security visiting room and Jon passed through. There was only one person sitting in there, his wrists attached to the table in chains. Last time Jon had seen Cyril Walker, he'd still been on remand and was wearing his own clothes. Since then, Cyril had had his court date, where he had pleaded guilty and been sentenced to life in prison for murdering five men, dismembering them, and putting most of their remains in black bin bags. Now he wore a grey prison tracksuit. His hair was neatly combed, his face clean-shaven. As Jon approached, he stood, his expression serious.

'Cyril,' said Jon, wary.

Aside from the time that he'd tried to kill Jon, Cyril had always acted like a nice guy when they were together. But jail could change a man, make him desperate. Deprivation and solitude could make him want to take revenge against the person who'd put him there.

And that person was Jon.

Jon held back, leaving a safe distance between him and his former friend. There was a guard at the door, and chains attaching the killer to the table. But Jon had seen far too many imaginative methods of murder in his life. They haunted his dreams. And some of them began with exactly this moment: two men, old friends and new enemies, facing each other across an empty room.

Cyril did a slow visual survey of Jon, from head to toe and back again. His face never altered from its deadly serious expression. His nostrils flared, and Jon had the distinct sensation that Cyril was trying to smell him. Actually, he probably was – Cyril had a weakness for cologne. But to Jon, it felt as if the other man was trying to smell his fear. And right now, he was sure it was coming off him in waves.

He forced his hands not to clench and resisted stepping backwards. His shoulder throbbed in memory of pain. Even in chains, Cyril had the skill and cunning to kill in a split second. A loose handcuff, a blade concealed in his mouth, hands wrapped around Jon's throat …

Cyril opened his mouth. Despite his best intentions, Jon took a step back.

Cyril said, 'Hello, Clarice.'

Jon relaxed and Cyril broke into a smile.

'It's good to see you, mate! I wasn't sure you'd use the visiting order.'

'I wasn't sure I'd use it either,' confessed Jon. 'But I found myself unexpectedly free.'

Because this morning, when he'd made a tray of coffee, strawberries and freshly baked buttered bread and brought it up to Saffy's room and knocked on her door, hoping to apologise and make up for their ruined evening … she hadn't answered. And when he'd pushed open the door – tentatively, in case she was in the shower or changing – her bed was made, her room spotless and empty. She'd left no message.

So instead of brooding about how he'd fucked up his chances with the most beautiful woman he'd ever met, he'd figured he might as well spend some time with a murderer.

'How the hell are you?' the murderer was asking.

'I'm OK, thanks.'

'Shoulder all healed up?'

'Where you stabbed me? Good as new.'

'How about that toe?'

Jon lifted his foot to show Cyril that he was wearing a normal pair of trainers.

'Glad to hear it.' Cyril sat, and gestured with his chin for Jon to do the same on the chair opposite.

'How are you keeping?' Jon asked.

'Pretty good. Not too bad. The food's terrible, mind.'

'Well, that's what you get for cutting people up. No more caviar and champagne for you.'

'Fair. Though frankly, I'd settle for a decent pie and chips. Listen, I've been thinking more about this. When you write the book about me, I don't want you to call me the Bin Bag Killer. Like I said, it's disrespectful to the victims. I cared about those men.'

'I'm not writing about you, Cyril.' Jon thought about the abandoned draft in his notebook and shuddered.

'You're gonna write about the guy who took your toe first, eh? It's your decision, but granny killers are not as exciting as sex killers. You want the big money, you should write about me.'

'I'm not writing about anybody.'

Cyril sucked his teeth and shook his head. 'Mate, you know as well as I do that you can change your clothes or your hairstyle, but you can't change your essential personality. Take me, for example. I look like your typical red-blooded heterosexual builder. Just like my dad, who was a player and cheated on my mum every chance he got. Now me, I tried dating women when I was a youth. Even got married, if you can imagine that. No matter what I did, it was never any good. I couldn't get it up, you know? But I kept trying. I thought being gay would be the worst thing that could happen to me.'

'Most would say that it's significantly worse that you're a murderer.'

'Oh sure, yeah, that too. I'm a killer, dyed in the wool. Have been since I was a little kid and used to torture kittens. It would have been a lot easier for me if I wasn't, but there it is. But tell you the truth, I was more scared of being gay than being a murderer. Internalised homophobia is terrible. The minute I started to accept my gayness, I was much happier.'

'... And you could start killing people.'

Cyril waved that aside. 'It's the same with you, mate. You're a writer. And you write about murder. It's in your blood. You need to accept it.'

As twisted as Cyril's words were, there was a grain of truth in them. Jon had sworn to leave murder behind. True crime podcasts glamorised violence in a way that was bound to increase the prevalence of real-world violence. And he was just as guilty as anyone else of finding thrills in the horrific.

But murder kept on finding him. And it was also true that his happiest moments had been when he was tangled up in a case, sifting through facts and evidence, wrist-deep in the blood of innocent victims.

'My dad loved his job. The only time he was a decent human being was when he was at work,' Jon said, surprising himself.

Cyril nodded.

'Yeah, I get it. My old man was a beautiful plasterer. When he got done with a wall, it was a bona-fide piece of art. He was famous all over South London for his work. And he was a pleasure to watch. He took real pride in it, you know? And yet he made our mum's life a misery.'

'My dad was a detective. People called him a hero. At home, it was a different story.'

'All cops are bastards.'

Jon felt that Cyril was probably prejudiced on this issue, but he took the comment in the sympathetic spirit in which it seemed to be meant.

'Sometimes I think I'm the opposite of my dad,' Jon said. 'I've tried to be a good man in my private life, and then in my work life, I'm perpetuating harm. I feel that I need to be a decent person all the time, or it doesn't count.'

'Nah, don't give me that. No one is all good, or all bad. Your work exonerated some innocent people, didn't it? Including me. I never killed that Fanducci fella that you found on your doorstep.'

'Speaking of, I wanted to ask you—' Jon said, and then winced as he realised what he'd been about to do. 'Never mind.'

'Oh, you can't do that to me, mate. I'm stuck in here with nothing to do except play chess in my head. If you have something interesting to ask, then ask away. I'm an open book, now. I promise not to lie.'

'Did you ... have the police found all of your victims?'

'Ah,' Cyril said, and his cheerful face shifted a little, became crafty. 'Well, that would be telling.'

'That means they haven't. You've killed more people than you've confessed to.'

'Listen, I said I'll be honest with you, and I will. The truth is, I'm a prisoner. I've got a certain amount of celebrity here, but it doesn't translate into any privileges. I'm still quite a young man. I have to think about my future. If leading the filth to another body or two or whatever would help me at some point, I have to keep that up my sleeve, don't I?'

Another body. Or two. Or *whatever*.

The idea sent a chill down Jon's spine.

'Plus,' Cyril continued, 'some things are just personal. I deserve a private love life, just like anyone else. A gentleman doesn't kiss and tell.'

'Cyril, your definitions of words can be concerning.'

'But you're a friend of mine, and I'd like you to be my biographer. So you're a special case. If you, say, had a crime that you were investigating, and you wanted a little hint or two ... I could help you out. With what I remember, or what I hear in here, or whatever.'

'You're volunteering to be my murder consultant. Like Hannibal Lecter and Clarice Starling.'

Cyril's nostrils flared. '*Sometimes you wear L'Air du Temps, but not today. God, I love that movie.*'

Jon took a deep breath. He looked behind him, at the guard, who was staring off into the middle distance, seemingly oblivious.

'I got an email,' he said in a low voice. 'An anonymous one, with a tip.'

'Aww,' said Cyril. 'That's how you and I met. The beginning of a beautiful friendship.'

'This particular email had a picture of a severed head attached to it.'

Cyril smiled. A strange and sinister light came into his eyes. 'What did he look like?'

This was a very, very bad idea. Still, the mystery tugged at the back of Jon's brain, begging to be solved. And maybe it was in his blood after all.

He thought back to that grisly photo. Tried to imagine the person who that head had belonged to: a person who thought, and worked, and talked, and loved.

He'd only seen the photo once. When he'd tried to look at it again, this morning, the email had disappeared from his computer. He'd checked the deleted messages file, his spam file, his entire inbox . . . nothing. Gone.

He knew he hadn't deleted the email. Which meant that whoever had sent it had made it vanish. They wanted him to get a message, but not know who they were.

This was nothing new. He got lots of anonymous tips. All you could do was to follow them.

'The victim was white,' Jon said, 'somewhere in his forties, I think? He had a beard. Salt and pepper.'

'Hmm. More salt, or more pepper?'

'About even. The photo was taken in a freezer, so there may have been some frost. It was a full beard, not a long hipster beard. He had a high forehead and curly hair, a little more grey than the beard. Brown eyes. Pierced right ear.'

Cyril was rapt. 'What's his nose like? Eyebrows?'

'Fairly prominent nose. His eyebrows . . . I didn't notice anything specific about them. Just eyebrows.'

'Is he attractive?'

'Cyril, he was a severed head.'

'OK, OK, don't kink-shame me. Let me think.'

He lapsed into silence, and Jon thought, queasily, that it was difficult to tell whether Cyril was trying to remember, or whether he was enjoying his mental image of a corpse. Maybe both. His expression was dreamy.

'Was he one of yours?' Jon prompted.

'I'm sorry to say that he isn't. But I can try to find out more. There's a guy here who's a bit of a connoisseur of stuff like this. A little bit like you.'

'Maybe you should get him to write your biography.'

'No, I want you. You're the best. We would make a great team.'

'It's not going to happen.' Jon stood, and Cyril grinned up at him.

'Come back next week and I'll let you know if I've found anything out. Off the record, as a favour to you.'

Jon nodded and headed for the exit.

'And Jonny,' called Cyril after him. 'I've thought up a new name for myself. No more "Bin Bag Killer". From now on I'm "Cyril the Serial". Got a ring to it, innit?'

Chapter Seven

THE REASON WHY WOMEN ARE so good at multitasking is that, historically and in the present day, the work done by them is simultaneously restricted and devalued by the patriarchy. So instead of being allowed to do one big important thing, like writing world-famous Elizabethan drama or conquering Asia or walking on the moon or making *The Godfather* trilogy, women have been expected to do all of the small and multitudinous yet vital things that men can't be bothered with, like raising babies or making sure that the toilet paper doesn't run out.

While all of this stuff is in fact very important (and essential, if anyone is to do anything Big), it is also quite frequently boring and only scrapes the surface of one's intellect.

So we need to do several things at once, basically to preserve our sanity.

Which is one reason why the day after my aborted date with Jonathan Desrosiers, which is the day after I didn't get a chance to kill Sir Thomas and killed Mr Anger Issues instead, I'm sitting in a restaurant, having lunch with a different man.

I met Kurt on Hinge, where I had set up a profile specifically to match with him. Kurt is six foot two, thirty-one years old, BDE, a self-proclaimed entrepreneur whose hobbies include travel, driving fast cars, and the great outdoors. On his dating profile, he has six photographs, three of which consist of him holding a dead fish.

(Oh, by the way, if you're not up on Hinge-ese, 'BDE' means 'Big Dick Energy'. Make of that what you will.)

Kurt is quite specific in his requirements in a partner. According to his Hinge profile, he requires a petite and feminine woman, aged nineteen to twenty-three and submissive, with no tattoos. He does not want single mothers, gold diggers, or women with a high body count. He says he is open to all races but prefers Asians and/or blondes.

Fortunately I am blonde and have no tattoos or children, and I have no need for any man's money. The rest ... well, let's say I'm good at fiction writing.

'Thanks for meeting me at such short notice,' I said to him when we met for the first time outside the restaurant. 'I wouldn't normally say this, but thank goodness my hairdresser had to cancel!'

(I had my hair done yesterday before my double date with Jonathan. I have standards.)

'Yeah, I had a last-minute opening,' he said, glancing at his phone. 'Great to meet you, Sarah.'

On Hinge, my pseudonym is Serena.

On our way into the restaurant, he rested his hand on the small of my back. To give him credit, he did pull out my chair for me at the table.

'What a gentleman!' I enthused.

'It's one of my most important values,' he said. 'I think a lady deserves to be taken care of.'

'Oh, definitely. And it's so rare these days.'

'I know.' He raised his hand and snapped his fingers at the waiter. 'Bottle of prosecco here,' he called, and then flashed his teeth at me. 'A little treat for you. I know you ladies like your champagne.'

Then why didn't you order it?, I thought, and smiled.

While the waiter poured our drinks, Kurt told me about a great deal he was just on the verge of closing, and how lucky I was that he had a spare couple of hours for lunch, because usually he didn't do lunch dates. 'Lunches are for business,' he said, 'and dinners are for *business*.'

He winked in the manner of the creepy uncle that you try to avoid at Christmas parties.

You might be wondering why, when I keep going on about how much I am in love with Jonathan, I am currently on a date with Kurt. And really, I hadn't planned to be here. My actual plan was to spend all night making passionate love with Jonathan Desrosiers, and to then spend the hours between 8 a.m. and noon having lazy morning sex, which, after a pause for a double espresso and maybe a smoothie, would merge seamlessly into a good chunk of time indulging in afternoon delight.

But then Girl deliberately cockblocked me. And yes, yoga and chamomile tea help with the feelings of sexual frustration and rage, but they can only go so far.

'To first meetings,' Kurt says, holding up his glass. I toast with him, and take the most demure of sips.

I'm not cheating on Jonathan, you understand. I am merely multitasking.

Kurt orders for us without consulting me: he has a steak, well done, with chips, and I am allotted a Greek salad. (I fancied the veggie burger with extra avocado; my life for the past twenty-four hours has been rather dominated by salad leaves. But Kurt got in there before I had a chance, and who am I to challenge his manliness?) By the time our lunch has arrived, I have learned all about his dating philosophy, which is essentially that he is a high-value man who has worked on himself and deserves a woman who will reflect his essential greatness and never challenge his autonomy. Women these days are handed everything on a plate, feminism has made them believe they are invulnerable and entitled, nothing is ever good enough, and if females today are ever crossed in whatever trivial way, they will immediately cry rape or fake a pregnancy and a poor lad's life will be utterly ruined through no fault of his own.

Of course, I agree. What a torrent of good sense this Kurt possesses.

'You're not dating anyone at the moment, are you?' he demands, pointing his fork at me as he chews.

'No, I'm a one-man woman.'

He nods, and shoots his gaze to the waitress and her short skirt. She is not the person serving us, better luck to her.

'I'm not ready to settle down and limit my options,' he says.

'Wise,' I say.

On his way to the men's room, he snaps his fingers at the waiter again. 'I'll take the cheque right away,' he says. 'Time is money. Chop-chop.'

I pour the rest of what's left of the bottle of prosecco into his glass and also slip in a roofie.

The feta in my salad has a yellow cast to it, and the tomatoes look as if they were grown in 1986. I don't complain. I push my food around my plate, smile sweetly at Kurt when he returns to the table, and continue agreeing with everything he says as he finishes up his meal.

Despite the evidence to the contrary, I'm not much of a poisoner. I prefer my victims to be more or less aware of what's happening to them in their final moments: that's the point of justice, after all. However, you can't ignore maths. I am slender and delicate, I favour tiny clutch bags, and though I move much more quickly than your average female while wearing three-inch-heeled ankle boots, I am a mere mortal.

Kurt is the type of guy who chugs, rather than sips, his drinks. By the time the waiter returns with the bill and a card reader, his eyes are becoming unfocused. 'You should be paying me,' he slurs, fumbling his card out of his wallet and missing the reader when he tries to tap it.

I take his card smoothly from him. 'Let me help you.' I add a hundred per cent tip and tap the card. 'Low blood pressure,' I mouth to the waiter, who looks the happiest he's been since we arrived.

On the way out the door, Kurt leans heavily on me. His hand rests on the top of my breast, which might be deliberate, but then again he is pretty wasted, so I let him keep it attached to his body for now.

'Whaddya say?' he mumbles. 'You wanna piece of this?'

'Who wouldn't?' I croon. 'Let's find someplace more private.'

I lead him down a side street and into an alley unsullied by passing traffic or CCTV cameras. London is so convenient for rats and murderers. This particular alley is narrow, framed by tall buildings made of dark bricks, redolent of rotting food and drains. There's a shallow gulley down the centre of it, damp with stagnant water, and a tide mark of rubbish strewn along the sides.

'Does this place ring a bell, Kurt?'

He's stumbling now, pawing at me clumsily, and doesn't seem to have heard me.

'I think it's a sexy spot, don't you? Just the place where most women would want to have a *piece* of you.'

Something about what I've said catches his attention. He stops walking suddenly and looks around him.

'Gonna be sick,' he says, and lurches forward. He leans against one of the damp walls and retches up his steak and chips onto the filthy ground. It spatters onto his shoes.

I sigh. Seriously? This place is gross enough. Still, at least his back is turned to me now, which will make my job easier. I slip on my latex gloves.

'Kurt Rider,' I say. 'Don't you remember this place? This stinking, ugly alleyway? I suppose there's no reason why you would. After all, what happened here hardly changed your life at all.'

I take out the flexicuffs from my Chanel clutch and before Kurt has finished puking, I've got his hands bound behind his back.

'What the—' he sputters, trying to turn around. I hook my foot around his ankle, push hard, and he thuds to the ground. I jump onto him, straddle his back, and slip a prepared slender noose over his head, pulling the slipknot tight.

It's the work of another moment to jump off again, loop the end of the noose around his feet and pull that snug, too, so his legs are bent back towards his head. It's a form of hog-tying called incaprettamento, elegant in its own way. Simple as it is in concept, it's quite difficult to pull off in execution without a lot of practice. I don't recommend you try it at home.

However, one of the advantages of this method is that all of your hard work is now done. You can step back at your leisure and relax while the victim strangles himself.

I go to Kurt's head, and squat down in front of him, careful not to step in his regurgitated lunch. He seems to have sobered up a bit now that his life is in danger.

'What are you—' he chokes.

'Shh,' I say to him. 'Save your breath. You haven't got much left. You remember this alley now, don't you? I'm not surprised it took a minute; you haven't been here for over a dozen years. Of course, I'm pretty sure that Becky Kita, who you raped in this alley when she was nineteen, still sees every brick of this place in her dreams.'

Kurt's eyes roll. He struggles against the ties that hold him. This serves to make the slipknot around his neck tighten further. His face is very red.

'In court, you said both of you were drunk. For you, this was supposed to mean that you couldn't control yourself. In Becky's case, from your point of view, being drunk meant she was asking for it. It's funny, isn't it, how alcohol removes a man's responsibility for his own actions, but it makes a woman even more responsible for the actions of everyone else? Even men who are nearly twice her size?'

Kurt can't answer this. His face is starting to go purple and he's making guttural noises in his throat.

'What's that, Kurt? You were found not guilty? Yes, that's true. Becky had to go through a physical examination. Her clothes were taken from her. Her phone was taken from her. Police officers went through her laptop. She had to give multiple statements. Her name was leaked on social media, so she had to endure continued harassment from your friends, your fellow students, and complete strangers. She had to leave university and quit her job. Despite all of this, she gave evidence against you at trial, where you were found not guilty. All the evidence wasn't enough to convince the jury that the act was non-consensual. No witnesses, just like now. It's a he-said/she-said situation. After the verdict, you bragged about it. You couldn't be tried again for the same crime, and you'd got away scot-free. You said, and I quote, that "she brought it on herself".'

I stand. I take off my gloves, put them back in my handbag, clean my hands with an antibacterial wipe. My dress is a mess of wrinkles, though, and I'm going to have to bin these shoes.

I look down at Kurt. Despite the falling oxygen levels in his brain, he's still intelligent enough to realise that all of the struggling is only making things worse for him. He's trying desperately not to move. His bulging eyes are pleading. He has started to drool.

Now *that's* Big Dick Energy.

'Anyway,' I say cheerfully, 'when you pass out, which will be any minute now, your legs will relax and that will tighten the noose enough to finish you off. But there is one piece of good news, Kurt! You can take comfort in knowing that you've brought all of this on yourself.'

Chapter Eight

Jon was on the way to the park with Girl, enjoying the fresh air after the prison, when he saw Saffy strolling up the street in the distance. She wore a white sleeveless dress and big sunglasses, her loose hair a golden mane around her head. She walked, as she always did, with careless grace, as if she knew that wherever she went, she would be welcome. She looked like a model, with all of Kensington her catwalk. There was an extra spring in her step this afternoon – he saw the people near her smiling, as if her good cheer was contagious. More than one man in her vicinity did a double-take as she passed.

He had to do a double-take himself. How was it that this stunning woman, rich, beautiful, clever and funny, good-natured and fascinating, was interested in *him*? Scarred, unemployed, heartsore, uncertain, raised in a totally different social class and milieu ... a person who spent all of his time with the dregs of humanity?

She spotted him and her face lit up. 'Hello, hello,' she sang, and danced up to him and the dog. She paused to kiss him on the lips (her lipstick tasted of roses and vanilla), and to give Girl a little pat on the head.

'You're in a good mood,' Jon said. 'What have you been up to?'

'Lunch with a friend, and then a little shoe shopping.' She held up her bags. 'How about you?'

'Also visiting a friend.' He wasn't about to confess that he'd been in prison, seeing Cyril. Even though the corpse he'd found on his doorstep had brought him and Saffy closer together, he'd told her he was finished with all of this darkness. It wouldn't go down well if he mentioned that he'd been casually hanging out with a man who'd murdered and dismembered at least five men.

At least.

'Sounds as if we've both had brilliant days!' She linked her arm through his and fell into step beside him towards the park. 'I think it's so important that couples have separate interests, don't you?'

'Is that what we are? A couple?'

'Well ... we're not *not* a couple.'

'We're making our way towards coupledom,' he suggested.

'We're seeing how it goes,' she agreed. 'But I do think we can definitively state that we are more than housemates.'

'Roommates who want to tear each other's clothes off?'

'So much,' said Saffy, flashing him a perfect smile, and Jon was once again baffled at what she saw in him.

But how could he ask that? It might make her reconsider whether she wanted him after all. He wasn't that stupid.

'Thank you for letting me stay with you,' he said as they entered Kensington Gardens, strolling along the wide flower-edged path. 'I know we said it was for while I recovered from my surgery—'

'Don't be ridiculous. You can stay as long as you like. I enjoy having you around.'

'And I'm sorry about last night,' he said. 'I don't know quite what happened.'

'I know what *didn't* happen.'

'Next time I'll put Girl outside.'

'There's going to be a next time?'

'I hope so.'

'Me too.'

The dog sniffed the base of a tree. Jon took Saffy's bags from her, and kissed her on the cheek. 'But to tell you the truth,' he said, 'I'm scared shitless.'

'Why? I have all the same parts as any other woman. Are you worried you won't know what to do?' She sparkled at him.

'I'm pretty sure I know what to do. But you can tell me if I get it wrong.'

'And maybe punish you.'

He licked his lips, his mouth suddenly dry. 'We have a lot to learn about each other, don't we?'

'We certainly do.'

'So . . . it's OK if we take it slow, isn't it?'

'Of course! Or fast is also good. I'm pretty flexible.'

'It's just that . . . it seems like your sister has some opinions, so I wondered if you had said anything to her.'

Saffy lost a bit of her chirpiness, and sighed. 'Susie always has opinions. I love that about her, but also it frequently is annoying. I didn't tell her anything, though. In fact, I told her we were taking it slow on purpose.'

'Are we?'

Girl picked up the pace again, and Saffy didn't answer for a few moments, until the dog had paused to greet a Miniature

Schnauzer, the two animals wagging their tails and sniffing each other's arses before, by mutual consent, they moved on.

Why couldn't it be so easy for humans?

'Susie thinks that I deliberately choose men I don't care about very much because I'm frightened of commitment,' said Saffy at last. 'She thinks that as soon as I get a boyfriend, I'm looking for excuses to drop him. And while she's not right about everything, she might be a teensy bit right about that. All I know is, I like you more than I've liked anyone for a very long time. Maybe ever.'

He shouldn't ask; he had a modicum at least of emotional intelligence, and he knew asking this sort of thing so early in a relationship made him seem insecure and needy, but he did anyway: 'But why *do* you like me?'

She shrugged narrow, elegant bare shoulders. 'I've had a crush on you since the first time I heard your podcast. And even more after reading your books.'

'You like me for my work?'

'For what your work shows about you. It's like what I said the first time I met you, Jonathan Desrosiers: you're a good man.'

'Am I?'

'You are. Yes. Also, you have that whole geek-chic thing going on. All skinny and dishevelled. I think on TikTok they call it the "hot rodent look".'

He grimaced. 'OK, if that does it for you, who am I to judge?'

'Aren't you going to tell me why you like me?'

Who wouldn't?, he thought, but from everything he knew about women, he knew that would be a totally inadequate answer. And he also knew that she was very aware of her own beauty and intelligence, her social cachet, and her wit. Saffy had many fine qualities, but, he'd learned, modesty was not one of them. So instead, he went for the first quality he'd noticed about her just now, when he'd spotted her walking down a Kensington street towards him.

'Sunshine,' he said, and when she looked surprised, he explained, 'When we met, I was in a very dark place. I'd thrown away my marriage and my career. I'd nearly been killed, and I was reeling from trauma as much as the physical injury.'

'It was also raining quite a lot,' she agreed. 'And you were living in a literal shithole in the arse end of nowhere.'

'With excellent scenery and whisky,' he pointed out. 'But yes, that cabin in Scotland was terrible. It was only suitable for newts. But more than that, Saffy – when I met you, I didn't know who I was any more. I felt useless and lost. And when you appeared, even though I didn't know it then … everything became lighter. I could see better – not only the world, but myself.'

She gazed at him, her eyes wide. 'Oh my God. That is so beautiful. I don't believe I called you a hot rodent, and then you came out with that.'

'I'm not as good with animal metaphors, clearly.'

'Yes, weather metaphors are much deeper.'

He laughed, then became serious. 'I do notice, though, that a lot of what you say you like about me is stuff that I've been trying hard to distance myself from. My work in true crime, for one.'

'Whatever you do for a living, you'll still be one of the good guys.' She squeezed his arm against her. 'I'll admit, I do think the true crime stuff is cool. But it's who you are that's important, not what you do.'

'I wish I had that faith.'

'Don't worry,' she said. 'If I ever think you're being a bad man, you'll be the first to know.'

'So . . . are we taking it slow?'

She shrugged. 'Maybe. Maybe not. I guess we can see what happens. I don't know if there are any right or wrong answers when it comes to relationships. Like I said, I haven't been in many real ones before.'

'I really am sorry about last night.'

'So am I.'

They stopped and kissed. Girl tugged at the lead and whined.

When they broke apart and resumed walking, Saffy said, 'I was thinking, though, maybe we're going about this backwards. We started seeing each other when we were solving a mystery, instead of dating like normal people. And now you're staying in my house, and we're doing things like double dating with my sister and her boyfriend. Maybe we need a bit more mystery. A bit more sense of occasion.'

'You think that might dissolve some of the awkwardness?'

'It might be fun to try.'

'What do you suggest?'

'I've got a gala this weekend. A charity thing, black tie, for something I'm on the board of. I wasn't planning to go. It's the least favourite of my charities – it finds homes for aged donkeys. Not that the donkeys aren't deserving of love like anyone else, but they do quite often have fleas. However, it's very popular and the charity does put on a good gala, and the donkeys aren't actually there so you don't have to worry about getting fleabitten. Would you like to be my date?'

'Black tie?' he said doubtfully.

'We'll go shopping for you. Don't worry, you'll be the best-dressed hot rodent there.'

He thought about champagne and dazzle, an exclusive London location, surrounded by the wealthy and the earnest. He thought about himself in an uncomfortable formal suit, the son of a policeman and a housewife. His world had been shadows, prison cells, dark rooms with reams and reams of information – just him and his laptop, with the most horrific human stories beyond imagining.

Then he thought about Saffy in a slinky sequinned dress.

'Let's do it,' he said.

Chapter Nine

POLICE APPEAL FOR INFO ON MISSING MP

Metropolitan Police have issued an appeal for any information on the whereabouts of Rupert Huntington-Hogg, Member of Parliament for Swinley. Huntington-Hogg, 59, was reported missing by his fourth wife, Fenella Huntington-Hogg (née Farquhar-Wickham), on 12 May after he failed to attend their five-year-old daughter's birthday party at Pizza Express in Wokingham.

'He promised me he would be there,' said Mrs Huntington-Hogg, 32. 'Edwina adores her father and it broke her heart when he didn't show up with her gifts as planned. That was when I knew that something was definitely wrong.'

The last authenticated sighting of Huntington-Hogg was at a Tarts and Vicars party at his private members' club, Dulpeepers in Mayfair, on 1 May. His last known appearance in Parliament was two weeks before. At the time of his disappearance, he was residing in his Marylebone home while his family stayed in their house in Berkshire. He has not been seen in his Swinley constituency office since February.

This is not the first time that Huntington-Hogg has vanished; in 2001, when newly elected to his first constituency in Boarly North, he failed to attend a Parliamentary select committee. In that instance, the alarm was raised by Ines Schvarkovski, who was at the time the MP's personal assistant and eventually became his second wife. Six days later he was photographed in Phuket, Thailand. He returned to the UK soon after, explaining he was conducting negotiations on behalf of party donors to raise investment.

Huntington-Hogg is no stranger to controversy. He briefly served as Health Secretary but resigned to the backbenches after an outcry over a past *Spectator* column saying care home patients should be 'culled off' by refusing to provide them with seasonal flu vaccines. After an acrimonious break-up in 2018 his former mistress, Becky Winston, brought a charge of sexual assault and harassment against him, which was settled out of court. When contacted by ITV News about the MP's disappearance, Winston, 38, said, 'I hope he stays gone.'

Downing Street released a statement this morning, reading in part: 'Our thoughts are with the family of our colleague, The Right Honourable Rupert Huntington-Hogg, who has served this country for many years, and we hope he will very soon be restored to his loved ones and constituents.'

Police have canvassed the neighbourhoods in London, Berkshire, Swinley, and Penzance, where the MP maintains residences, but have not managed to record any confirmed sightings of Huntington-Hogg. CCTV footage taken at Reading Station on the evening of 20 May could contain images of the MP, but this, too, is not confirmed.

Detective Barking of the Metropolitan Police stated, 'We are keen to hear from members of the public who may have some information about the whereabouts of The Right Honourable Rupert Huntington-Hogg. If you or someone you know have relevant information, please contact Crimestoppers or the Metropolitan Police.'

Chapter Ten

SUSIE AND I ARE LYING side by side on wooden benches in a sauna while sweaty muscular young men in shorts wave scented leafy branches over us.

'I'm just saying,' says Susie, although she has in fact *not* said anything for the past thirty minutes, 'that people in glass houses shouldn't throw stones.'

I turn my head to look at her. Like me, she is wearing a white bikini, and like mine, her skin is dripping with perspiration.

'What brought that particular cliché to mind?'

'Look, I know you don't like Finlay.'

'I haven't said that.'

She raises her sweaty sculpted eyebrows.

'I haven't said that *lately*,' I amend. 'What's this about? Did you have an argument after the world's worst dinner party?'

'No. Well ... sort of.'

'About the dead animal on our plates?'

'I know you didn't like it, and I was a bit annoyed that he didn't listen to me about you being vegetarian, but he tried, at least, and that's the important part, isn't it?'

'It's amazing,' I comment to the wooden ceiling, 'how even when men fail, somehow they get the credit.'

'Well, I think it was the important part. I couldn't have cooked any of that. If it had been up to me, we'd have been eating bags of Doritos. So I was quite impressed.'

'He was trying,' I concede.

'Oh, there you go with another one of your word games.'

'What do you mean, word games?'

'When you say one thing and totally mean another, but you're not technically lying because it's not your fault if the person you're talking to didn't understand you.'

'Do I do that?' I ask innocently.

'Or, instead of answering something directly, you ask a question that implies the opposite of the truth.'

'I forget sometimes that you have a degree in English and American Literature.'

'I don't forget it,' says Susie. 'I am still permanently scarred from reading Henry James. So do you mean "trying" as in making an effort, or "trying" as in trying your patience?'

'I meant both,' I say. 'But, I will admit that it was nice of him to invite us round.'

'I saw you feeling up your boyfriend under the table, by the way. It was sort of gross.'

'I thought you wanted me to have an active sex life!'

'Not in front of me, where I can see it. You, like, practically raised me. It's like watching your mom and dad have sex. Ew!'

'I'm not your mother, and Jonathan is not your dad.'

'I know, it was just an analogy. Anyway, I don't want to see it, but I'm fine with hearing about it. Did you have hot monkey sex when you got home?'

My silence tells her everything she needs to know.

'I thought so as soon as I saw you,' says Susie. 'You've got a line between your eyebrows.'

Instantly, I feel my forehead, searching for a furrow. 'No. No, I don't. Wait, do I?'

'It's only very faint. Call my Botox lady when we're finished here. I'll give you her number.'

Oh God. Is this it? Have I hit the slippery slope? Has lack of sex made me old before my time?

'This is why I said glass houses,' Susie says. 'Nobody's relationship is perfect.'

'Of course nobody's relationship is perfect. Not at first, anyway.'

'So you don't have to criticise Finlay.'

'I'm not. Currently. Although you are being very defensive.'

'No I'm not!'

I don't reply. I turn over onto my front and let the young man fan steam onto my back with the branches.

'You're weaponising silence,' Susie says.

I still don't reply.

'OK,' she says. 'I'm sorry that I picked on your little verbal quirks.'

'Thank you. And I'm sorry I called you defensive.'

'Thank you.'

'But if there is something wrong with your relationship with Finlay, I love you and I will listen without criticising.'

I cross the fingers on the hand that she can't see, because although I don't intend to criticise him aloud, I won't promise not to mentally push him into a wood chipper and then dance naked in the resulting cloud of blood.

'He doesn't answer his phone,' Susie admits.

'Ever?' I wouldn't put it past Finlay to suddenly decide that mobile phones give you ear cancer.

'No, only sometimes. Usually at night, when he's told me he's chilling at home alone. Or when he's supposed to be at the gym, or working. He says that's because he's got it on silent, but ...'

'He never has his phone on silent.'

'Right. And then about ten days ago, when he'd told me he was tired because he'd been on a fast and he was going to go to bed early, he rang me about midnight and when I picked up, it was obviously a pocket dial because he didn't say anything. But I could hear what was going on in the background, and it sounded like he was at a party.'

'He's cheating on you,' I say instantly.

'You said you wouldn't criticise!'

'I'm not criticising. I'm reaching the logical conclusion. He did have that whole thing with that Ulyana.'

'But he's not acting like he's cheating. He's, like, really affectionate. When we're together, he keeps telling me he loves me and our sex life is great. He checks in on me all the time by text, which is why it's so weird that he doesn't answer when I call. And he doesn't call me by another woman's name, or get any mysterious messages when we're together, and also—'

She stops. I wait, and eventually say, 'What?'

'I'm embarrassed to say this.' She glances up at the half-naked Russians who are fanning us, who remain stoic. 'I went through his phone.'

'Susie!'

My little sister. I'm so proud.

'I know it's wrong! But I didn't find anything. Nothing suspicious at all.'

'Finlay is good with tech. He might have hidden the evidence.'

'I just don't think he's cheating. But what if something else is wrong? What if … like … he has cancer and he doesn't want to tell me? What if he's been secretly having chemo and he's going to die?'

Susie sounds like she is going to cry.

This is only one of the reasons why I love her so much, and also why I need to protect her. She is so innocent and good that she thinks it's more plausible that her perfectly healthy boyfriend is having secret chemotherapy than that he's followed his dick into yet another OnlyFans star.

I reach over the gap between our benches and take her hand, squeezing it tight. She squeezes back.

'It'll be OK,' I tell her. 'I'm sure there's a perfectly reasonable explanation.'

'Yeah,' she sniffs. 'Yeah, I'm sure it's something totally innocent.'

'Maybe work has been difficult and he doesn't want to worry you.'

'Maybe he's planning some wonderful surprise for me.'

'Maybe he really does put his phone on silent.'

'Yeah. Yeah, you're right. I'll try not to worry.'

I don't believe any of this for a second so I add, 'But if he is cheating on you, do I have your permission to cut off his dick and feed it to him, bite by bite, on toast?'

Susie smiles. Before she can answer, one of the Russian spa men says, 'Hot part done now. Time for cold.'

* * *

We plunge into a freezing-cold pool, have our skin scrubbed with ice, and then lie, cleansed, detoxed, glowing, and faintly traumatised, side by side on lounge chairs by the pool, wearing robes and sipping sea buckthorn tea. I'm wondering whether Susie would have given me permission to castrate Finlay so I could do it guilt-free. I think she probably wouldn't, but a girl can dream.

'Oh, I forgot,' Susie says lazily. 'Finlay wrote down some of the stuff from his childhood that he wants Jonathan to write about. I've got it in my bag in my locker. Remind me to give it to you later.'

'I don't think that Jonathan is interested in ghost-writing Finlay's memoir.'

'Well, just in case. Finlay says it's fascinating.'

'Have you read it?'

'No, it's in an envelope, and that would be snooping.'

'You went through his phone.'

'That was different, duh.'

'I'll pass it on.'

'You're the best sister ever.'

'I know.' I blow steam from my tea. 'Anyway, Jonathan and I have decided we need a proper romantic evening together, so I'm taking him to a black-tie event. Champagne, dancing—'

'—And a low-cut dress!' She claps her hands. 'Let's go shopping after this!'

There are the magic words. We are going shopping, and my sister is no longer fretting. I relax into my lounge chair and sigh happily, picturing an afternoon of perfect complexions, retail therapy, and perhaps a cheeky glass of champagne in Harvey Nicks, everything right with the world. I can feel the non-existent furrow in my brow melting away.

And then my sister goes and ruins it all.

'I just worry sometimes,' she says dreamily, her fingers trailing along the tiled and glossy floor. 'Maybe I am sabotaging myself.'

'What do you mean?'

'I wonder whether because you and I never had any good parental role models, we're incapable of normal relationships.'

I tense. I have thought this sometimes too, but I've never discussed it with Susie. I only ever wanted her to be normal and happy.

She continues, 'I don't even remember our birth father, he died so soon after I was born. And I barely remember our mother. The only parent I ever really knew was Harold.'

'He wasn't our parent. He was our mother's husband. And barely that.'

'I used to call him "Daddy".'

'I try to forget about that fact.'

'Why won't you ever talk about him?'

'Because there's no point. He's dead.' Bleeding out in a swimming pool in Rhode Island, like a chunk of ginger-haired chum. Good riddance.

'I remember that he used to give me horsey rides on his back, didn't he?'

'He did.' The thought makes me sick.

'And he smoked cigars. And he liked *The Three Stooges*. Remember, he used to have all those DVDs in the library? He let me watch them sometimes. It was about people hitting each other. He thought it was so funny, he would laugh and laugh, so that made me laugh too, although I didn't quite understand it because you're not supposed to hit people? I was too young, I guess.'

'Why all of a sudden are you interested in Harold?'

'I just wonder about him sometimes. I wonder if he'd lived, what it would have been like. Whether our lives would have been more normal.'

I take a moment before I answer, while light reflects off the pool in ripples on the ceiling.

It happens that I have a good idea what our lives would have been like if Harold had lived.

He molested me from the age of six, when my mother died, until the age of twelve, when he decided I was too old and it was time to move on to my baby sister. Fortunately, before he could lay a single finger on Susie, I killed him in his own swimming pool.

But what if I hadn't?

I wouldn't have been able to stop him with words. Every single person in that big Newport mansion, every person in his Manhattan town house – the staff, our tutors, the nanny, his personal assistants, the people who wrote flattering news articles about him – all of them were in his employ. He had power over their lives. If I had said anything about what he'd been doing, no one would have listened to me. At that time, Susie and I didn't go to school like normal children. We didn't have any outside friends.

If I'd gone to the police, they would have visited Harold. Money would have changed hands, or he'd have had a word with their superiors, and my accusations would have disappeared.

Things could have got worse. I've learned enough about what wealthy and powerful men can do with women and children under their control. What monsters paedophiles are. How sometimes, they share.

I'm a strong person, and also I happen to be a psychopath. I've read up on this, and apparently psychopathy is something you're born with. My very lifeblood is pretending to be normal and manipulating every situation to my advantage. If I hadn't become a serial killer, I could have learned how to play Harold, blackmail him, end up with everything I wanted. And I might have become a serial killer anyway, in the end. I like to hope I would, because I enjoy my hobby very much and my life would be very boring without it.

So if I hadn't killed Harold, my life would be much the same. But Susie's wouldn't.

Susie is not a psychopath. Susie is a well-adjusted, empathetic, compassionate, easily wounded human being. Susie is an optimist, a person who believes in the best of human nature. She is the person I pretend to be.

Harold's abuse would have killed the little sister I loved.

Physically, she would have survived – I would have made sure of that – but she would have been a shell of the person lounging next to me right now. No money or privilege would have been enough to save the girl she used to be. Maybe she would have turned to drugs, like our mother did. Maybe she would have hurt herself, wreaking the wounds that Harold caused onto her own body. Maybe she would party to exhaustion, join a cult, cut herself off from everyone, believe she was worthless, find herself in a psychiatric unit, believe she was damned.

Men do these things to women and children.

I murdered Harold, and I saved Susie from all that.

But of course I can't tell her any of this.

'I don't think our lives would have been that different,' I lie. 'Harold wasn't that interested in being a parent. He was always going to pack us off to boarding school. Now if he'd lost all his money instead of dying, our lives might have been different.'

Susie waves her hand. 'Oh, we had Mummy's money, so we would have been fine. He couldn't touch that. Anyway, it wouldn't have been such a bad thing to get jobs and live like normal people.'

So says Susie, who has never held down a paying job for more than three months, lying in a £1,000-a-day spa, planning our shopping trip later.

Bless her. I wouldn't change her for the world.

Chapter Eleven

'Jonathan,' said Edie as soon as he answered her call. 'Brace yourself.'

Jonathan's agent had never been one to mince words. He reached for his coffee and replied, 'Edie! How are you? How is Marj? Are you still in France? Any news on the house?'

Jonathan's crazed stalker had burned down Edie and Marj's house. Yet another thing for Jon to feel guilty about.

'I'm fine, she's fine, the cats are fine, yes, we're still in Arcachon and we're waiting for the insurance money, which should come through any day now that the criminal case has been resolved. Marj wants to get a new kitchen. I'm more worried about restocking my library. But that's not why I called. Are you sitting down?'

'No.'

'Sit down, instantly.'

'OK,' he said, still standing.

'I have had a pre-empt offer for a book about Cyril Walker.'

'I don't want it.'

'I haven't finished. You're not sitting down, are you?'

'No.'

'Well, it's on your own head.' She then proceeded to tell him the amount that had been offered.

He sat down on the floor with a whump.

'I warned you,' said Edie.

When he could breathe again, he said, '*How* much?'

She repeated the figure.

'If you wanted to throw in a follow-up book about the granny killer who destroyed my home, I'm confident I could negotiate the fee upwards of three times that much.'

'But ...'

'I know what you're going to say, darling, and can I just say right now that I respect your scruples, hugely. I understand that you have been through significant trauma at the hands of both of these men and that you're not in a hurry to revisit that. May I suggest, however, that if you accept this offer, you are going to be in a position to afford all the therapy that one could possibly desire.'

'It's not the trauma. It's my conscience. These people shouldn't have their lives glamorised. Their victims were real people, with families and loved ones. They're the ones who shouldn't be traumatised. They've had enough already.'

'I cannot begin to tell you how much I admire you for your principles, Jonathan.'

'But you don't agree with them.'

'Of course I do. But also, Netflix has been in touch. Repeatedly.'

'That's even more exploitative.'

'And I have a call scheduled with an American publisher this afternoon. If I tell them about the pre-empt, we'll have a bidding war. And then there are the media appearances. You could be a very rich man, Jonathan Desrosiers.'

'I'm not going to abandon everything I believe in for money, Edie.'

'I knew you'd say that, and again, I admire you hugely for everything you believe in. If more people in this world were like you, we could negotiate world peace and solve the climate crisis in a matter of weeks. But ...'

'Edie—'

'Hear me out. True crime is huge business. If you don't write this book, and the next one too, somebody else is going to write it. And that somebody else may not have your sense of empathy, compassion, and justice. They might sensationalise the stories. Or portray the killers as some sort of celebrity. This is happening already with these cases, by the way, all over the internet and in the mainstream media. These people really *are* exploiting the victims' families.'

'But at least it won't be me who's done it.'

'But it will be you who allowed it to happen.'

'How am I supposed to be responsible for other people's actions?'

'Jonathan, you have always felt responsible for other people's actions. That's one of the things that makes you special.'

'It's one of the things that gave me a mental breakdown!'

He could hear her take a drag of her cigarette on the other end of the line. He tried to relax his hold on the phone a little bit, and breathe. Girl came over and sat on his foot.

'You can donate the profits to the families,' Edie said. 'Or to victim support charities.'

'Minus your ten per cent.'

'Minus my ten per cent. I'm a craven capitalist who doesn't have your scruples, much as I admire them. And also I think

I deserve it, for being in the line of fire and having my house burned down by a serial killer. But you – think of the good you could do.'

'Edie,' he said, 'you are trying to manipulate me.'

'Well, yes. I'm good at it. That is why you pay me a commission. But also, Jonathan, I am right. You can keep control of the narrative, do it the way you think is ethical and fair, and get paid a whopping amount of cash to do with as you like. Or, you can absolve yourself of all responsibility like any normal Joe. I, personally, do not think you are a normal Joe.'

'Sometimes I wish I were.'

'No you don't. You are far too talented, and, may I say, weird. So, darling, please don't answer now. Think about it all. We have a few hours to decide.'

'A few hours!'

'A couple of days. I can stall them. It might make them more keen, actually.' She was using her calculating voice.

'Edie, I lost flesh and blood to these two men. And now you're asking me to lose my soul.'

'Don't be so dramatic, Jonathan. There are lots of ways to have a soul. Think it through. OK, speak soon, ciao!'

He sat on Saffy's kitchen floor, holding his phone. Girl nudged his hand and he absently scratched behind her ears.

No. He wasn't going to do it. He couldn't spend the rest of his life wrestling with his conscience and encountering disembodied heads.

The doorbell rang and Girl leapt up, barking and scampering for the door. Jon followed more slowly, slipping his phone in his pocket, glad of the opportunity for distraction.

'She's friendly, just likes to say hello loudly,' he told the person in the motorcycle helmet who was waiting outside.

'Delivery for Jonathan Desrosiers,' said the person, holding out a garment bag and a shoebox and ignoring Girl's frantically wagging stump of a tail.

He brought the bag to his bedroom, hung it from the bathroom door, and opened it. Inside was a tuxedo, with a crisp white shirt, black silk bow tie, red pocket handkerchief. The box contained a pair of shiny black shoes.

Jonathan was not a person who appreciated clothes for their own sake, but he did appreciate what they meant. He had learned when he arrived at university to study journalism against the wishes of his father that what you wore betrayed your origins. His new clothes from Marks & Spencer made him stand out as someone who was trying too hard, who was uncomfortable in his skin, who was the first of his family to attend tertiary education. Within weeks he had given those clothes to a charity shop and instead bought second-hand jeans with holes in them, T-shirts with the necks stretched out, button-down shirts that were too long in the sleeves and had to be rolled up. He saved up from his weekend job and bought a pair of Doc Martens. These clothes made him invisible among the rich students who liked to look poor.

When he came home in those clothes, his mother clucked and tsked and his father told him he looked like a perp. His mother, who wore dresses from Debenhams. His father, who wore a shiny permanent press suit to work as a detective. He knew then that he was getting it right. That he could define himself against his parents.

His uniform as a journalist and a podcaster was jeans, a white shirt, occasionally a soft jumper, running shoes. Comfortable clothes that would fit in anywhere, that would not intimidate anyone, that were easy to wash and replace. The less he had to think about them, the better. And he knew that being able to not think about clothes was a privilege afforded to him now that he was comfortably educated and a member of the chattering classes, and also of course because he was white and male and straight.

But this. This tuxedo, and tie, and pocket handkerchief, and shoes. This was a uniform of a different kind; the uniform of a class that he had never belonged to. He looked at the label in the jacket. It was a name he had never heard of, but which was definitely not Primark or Next.

His phone buzzed in his back pocket. It was a text from Saffy:

Have you had a delivery?

You bought me a suit?

I couldn't resist! Out shopping with Susie. I think this will look so sexy on you. Have you tried it on?

Do you even know my size???

Size, schmize. I showed Gustav a picture of you. He is a genius. We have time to get it altered though. Try it, send me a selfie!!

'Gustav,' he said aloud. 'Who the hell is Gustav?'

But he banished Girl from the bedroom (she moulted white hair, whatever the season apparently), stripped off his jeans and white shirt, put on the suit, and looked at himself in the full-length mirror on the back of the bathroom door.

It was a revelation.

The tux was made of some lightweight material that nonetheless had substance and structure. It fitted him effortlessly: not tight, not restricting, not too loose. The cut of the jacket made him look broad-shouldered, masculine; the trousers somehow made him look taller. The whole look was let down by his messy hair and unshaven chin, but even so, it was as if some tailoring fairy had waved a magic wand over him and said, 'You will transform from a scruffy unemployed journo to a charming sophisticated British spy!'

Was this what clothes could do?

Selfie!!!!!!!! demanded Saffy by text.

He put on the shoes. They fitted him too. Apparently Gustav *was* a genius. It took several minutes for Jon to work out how to take a full-length photo of himself in the mirror, but when he looked back over the shots, he looked good in all of them, albeit missing a martini.

He sent one to Saffy. A barrage of messages followed:

OMG ☺ ☺

Send another!

He did.

I cannot wait for Friday night!!!!!

I AM SWOONING YOU LOOK SO GOOOOOOOOOO OOOOOOOD

I want to BITE you

(only in a good way, I do not eat human flesh)

Do you like it?

Did he?
I don't look like myself, he texted. *Maybe that's a good thing.*

You look like yourself in a really hot suit, she replied, followed with many fire emojis.

Thank you for buying it. I'll pay you back.

No need. You are my guest.

He turned and tried to see himself from a rear view in the mirror. He looked better from this angle, too. Maybe he had been making a mistake all these years by not wearing better clothes?
Isn't this the plot of Pretty Woman? he texted.

God, that movie is problematic. On the other hand, I love a gender flip! See you soon, I am just trying on lingerie. ☺

Girl scratched at the door. Jon took off the suit and carefully hung it back up on the door, high enough to be out of reach of the shedding zone. Then he read the labels on the clothing and let Girl back in to lie on the rug while he sat beside her in his underwear and googled the cost of each item. The numbers were so large that he had to use the calculator app to reach a total.

It was eye-watering. He would have to max out several credit cards that he hadn't applied for yet. And this was just for one night.

Yet Saffy could shrug it off with a few emojis.

He owed Saffy so much already. She had given him a place to stay, rent-free, while he was in London, and had paid for more than her share of food, coffee, and expensive liquor. He'd been trying to pay for things, but in Kensington, most things seemed to arrive at the doorstep without any money obviously changing hands. He bought dog food, but everything else was magically supplied. And then this extravagant gift. There was no way he could ever pay Saffy back financially – even if she would allow him to, which he doubted she would.

Obviously this was going to be a consideration if he was going to date someone so far above him when it came to wealth ... but it made him uneasy. What was his role in all of this? Arm candy?

For the second time in an hour, he was reminded of his dad. Who kept control of the chequebook and balanced it every Thursday night, making Jon's mother explain every single withdrawal, down to the last penny. Who never bought anything he could not afford to lay out cash for, including holidays and cars, who overpaid his mortgage, who put away money for Jon's university education so that he would not have to get any loans.

'A man pays his debts,' he would tell Jon, when Jon wanted a new pair of trainers that were too expensive, when he asked why they had never been abroad like his schoolmates. When Jon had seen him scream at his wife, Jon's mother, for buying something frivolous. That time when he had got a promotion and Mum had bought a new television to surprise Dad, as a gift, to replace the one that still worked, when Jon had stood between them, tears streaming down his face, holding out his arms so that his father could not reach his mother to beat her.

'A real man pays his debts,' he would tell Jon, in his smoker's voice. 'You buy what you can afford, and no more. Anything else is stealing.'

Chapter Twelve

THE GALA IS IN THE ballroom of a Park Lane hotel. You know the hotel ... the one formerly owned by that friend of Jeffrey Epstein. The one where that rock star was found after her overdose. The one where that oligarch strangled his mistress. The one where the crown prince of that small European country lived for years after being exiled. The one where that gangster opened fire on the lunching clientele. The one where that actress fell from the window to her death.

Anyway, it's beautiful.

In the taxi over, I shimmy closer to Jonathan and I whisper in his ear, 'Let's make a pact.'

'What about?' he whispers back.

'If either of us gets cornered by someone boring, or if we can't stand making small talk for another minute, or if we have a wardrobe malfunction, we'll have a code word so the other one knows we need to escape.'

'Good idea. What's the code word?'

'Something unobtrusive, that we could slip into normal conversation without people noticing.'

'With this crowd? Hmm. Like "tax loophole"?'

I elbow him. 'Like "cup of tea".'

'But what if one of us wants a cup of tea? That's too common. How about "Myra Hindley"?'

'We are not going to be having any sort of conversation where that name is unobtrusive. Worse luck.'

'Why are we doing this, again?'

'To cultivate mystery.' I plant a soft kiss on his cheek, and wipe off the lipstick mark I've left. I let him inhale my perfume. 'To seduce each other.'

'And to raise money for donkeys.'

'Right. So our code word can't be any sort of hoofed animal.'

'How about "Henley Regatta"?'

I think about it. 'That could work. OK.'

He takes my hand and squeezes it. 'I like that you have an escape plan.'

'Oh, I usually have two or three, at least.'

The taxi stops, and I reach for my clutch bag, which contains my stepfather's folding hunting knife.

'I'll pay for the taxi,' says Jonathan quickly. 'And for the drinks tonight, by the way. And dinner, if it's not included.'

'It's all included. But thank you for getting the taxi.'

He pays, and when the doorman opens the taxi door, he gets out first and offers me his arm. I graciously take it. As we walk along the red carpet to the entrance, he glances down at me and I see him bite his lip.

I want to take a short detour here to talk about cleavage. For one thing, the word itself, whose the origins and connotations are frankly dodgy. 'To cleave' is to cling tightly to something, or alternatively, to chop it off. And as a feminist, I'm disturbed by the fact that men, in particular, either want to grab my boobs or tear them off of me. 'Cleavage' itself means 'split', which is also sort of gross, because that implies that women have one big boob, which is split into two mini-boobs with a space between. The whole terminology is steeped in violence or dependence, neither of which are particularly sexy.

However. Like most women, I have come to understand the power of cleavage itself, the real thing, the controlled, corralled, elevated, augmented, and exposed flesh of my chest and the artificially created gravity-defying illusion of a narrow valley between my breasts. These few inches of fat and skin have toppled empires. Or rather, not the fat and skin themselves, but the heterosexual men who have become irrationally obsessed by them.

There is no better symbol than cleavage for the way that women have been systematically objectified by the patriarchy and as a result have been forced to use that objectification to claw back any semblance of control and autonomy. We hide our boobs if we want to avoid being harassed or assaulted (it often doesn't work). We play peekaboo with our boobs when we want to get something (risky, but it sometimes works).

There is a whole boob code, which changes constantly. Too much boob is slutty. Too little boob is prudish. We must never show our entire boob, because then we have lost control altogether and we are asking for it. But the very subtle distinctions of how much boob we can show in any given situation, without showing the entire thing, down to the millimetre, in order to create the precise effect that we want from all angles – it's an art form. Even more so when your clothes are also a mask, when you're trying to distract from the knife in your handbag, or the bear spray hidden in your bra.

This dress I'm wearing is calculated both to expose and conceal. The bodice is high, but projects slightly outward. So from a distance and most angles, I am elegant, demure, neck and shoulders rising from a froth of metallic silk, light as a cloud. But from above and to the side, the dress presses upward and flares, presenting the tops of my breasts like pale cupcakes on a silver platter.

Which is the exact view that Jonathan has now, as he escorts me into the hotel.

I sparkle up at him. 'My goal,' I whisper, 'is for you to be so turned on by the end of the evening that you can't even remember your name. How am I doing?'

'Who am I?' he murmurs.

And then we're in the ballroom, under glittering chandeliers and murals of half-naked goddesses, surrounded by balloons and streamers and black-suited waiters carrying trays of champagne and canapés, the high earners and the trust fund children, the famous and the would-be famous, the It girls and the Eton boys, the sports stars and the minor royalty, all dressed in designer clothing and regarding each other like vultures.

Above the stage hangs a giant banner, gold stitching on scarlet cloth. It says the name of the charity: SAVE OUR ASSES.

Jonathan stops dead.

'You have got to be kidding me,' he says, and bends over in silent laughter.

'I told you, it's a donkey charity.'

'Save our—'

'—Poor neglected beasts of burden that require good homes to live out their retirement,' I finish for him.

'Why are we at this charity thing, in particular?'

'I'm on the board.'

'The ass board.'

'The donkey board.'

'Wow. How did you come to be on this board?'

'Blackmail, mostly. Champagne, please.'

He takes two flutes from a passing waiter. We toast, looking deep into each other's eyes.

'Remember your name yet?'

'I think it starts with J.'

I link my arm with his and speak quietly. 'How many of these gala things have you been to?'

'None. My publisher had a party one time and I left after half a beer.'

'Right, so the technique is as follows. One, circulate the room, but never spend more than five minutes talking to anyone. Ten minutes, at an absolute stretch. Two, do not eat the canapés.'

'Why not?' asks Jonathan, watching a waiter glide by with a tray of mini blinis.

'Because three, there is always a photographer lurking somewhere close by and you do not want to feature in *Tatler* while stuffing food into your gob. Which leads to four, try to ensure you are in at least three photos, but not too many because you don't want to look desperate for attention.'

'Why be in any photos at all?'

'In case you need an alibi,' I say, and wink.

'Good thinking.'

'I know. Five, don't get drunk until the party is over and you're in private. Six, if anyone gropes you, just extricate yourself and laugh, but keep names and receipts.'

'This is getting grim.'

'Men *are* grim.'

'God, I'm sorry.'

'Me too.' And I'm about to say more, but at that moment Anya Ayers-Atkinson, the chair of the board, swoops down upon us, her smile glinting like the teeth of a victorious hyena.

'Seraphina!' she hoots, 'isn't this *marvellous*! I'm so *glad* you could make it! Is this the man in the newspaper who catches *serial killers*? You must tell me *all about it*!'

Jonathan's eyes widen in panic. He mouths, *Henley?*

He is such an amateur, bless him. *Not yet*, I mouth back, and turn to Anya with a charming smile.

'How are you, darling?' I ask, double-air-kissing and not wincing at her overpowering perfume. 'And how is your sweet little PawPaw? Still being carried in her Birkin?'

'Oh, *PawPaw*,' screeches Anya, and the next five minutes are taken up with her talking about her Sphynx cat who suffers with a mysterious skin condition between her toes that makes walking impossible. Then she spots someone across the room. 'Oh darling, there's Rafe, I must say hello! Talk later, sweetie? Ciao!' She air-kisses us both again and disappears in the crowd.

'That was masterful,' says Jonathan.

'This is not my first rodeo. Now, follow my lead. I know the conversational Achilles heel of at least two-thirds of the people in this room, and with the other ones, you can usually deflect with school fees or the impossibility of getting good help.'

* * *

It's while the first course is being served that I spot him properly. I caught a glimpse earlier – snow-white hair at the far side of the ballroom – but here in the dining room I have a straight-line view of him two tables away. If I listen, I can hear the unmistakable timbre of his voice, exactly as it used to sound on telly. As I watch, he delicately cuts into a seared scallop and raises it to his lips.

Wouldn't it be glorious if Sir Thomas had a seafood allergy, if he started clutching his swelling throat and going purple? As a witness, I would have all of the pleasure and none of the risk. I could even run up and pretend to be doing CPR so I could make sure to see the dying light in his pale blue eyes. It's not as fun as stabbing or even poisoning, but the result is the same.

Though for preference, I'd kill him myself and make sure it was done properly.

'Are you all right?' Jonathan whispers to me. 'You look like you've seen a ghost.'

'Just thought I might have a bit of spinach between my teeth. The horror! Do I?'

'No, you're fine.'

'What a relief.' I lick my lips and give him a coy look. 'Also,' I say, dropping my voice, 'I've got a secret.'

'What is it?'

I glance around the table. The seating plan put us with three older couples, all of whom know each other and none of whom are interested in serial killers or, apparently, donkeys. Since we've sat down, the men have been talking to each other about investment portfolios and the women have been talking about a mutual acquaintance of theirs who has left her husband for the tennis coach. This isn't the fun table or the famous table, and some people might resent being placed here. But for me, it's a fortunate state of affairs, because it means that no one is paying attention to me, and I can give all of my attention to Jonathan.

Except when I'm giving my attention to the man across the room.

'You'll have to find out,' I say, fluttering my eyelashes and resolving to be less obvious about watching Sir Thomas West.

I knew he would be here. And while my main reason for coming to this gala is to see Jonathan Desrosiers in (and, hopefully, out of) a finely tailored suit, why not do little bit of light stalking while I'm at it?

I'm just watching Sir Thomas tonight. He's a marked man, but I don't have specific plans right now. I've armed myself, sure – but that is merely a wise precaution. At present, I'm information gathering. I feel better if I know where Sir Thomas is, and what he's doing.

I don't see his bodyguard anywhere, though that doesn't mean anything; for such a large man with so much hair, Mullethead is very good at melting into shadows. Sir Thomas doesn't appear to have a date, either. He's seated between Anya and a napping viscount in his nineties. Sir Thomas is famously a bachelor. 'Never met the right woman,' he's said in every interview.

This is *not* the reason why he's never been married.

He's also famously good at raising funds for charity, which is why Anya's drinking in every word he says, nodding and smiling and touching his arm flirtatiously. That must be the reason, mustn't it? She must want something out of him badly enough to compromise her ideals?

Because surely, *surely*, she has heard the same rumours that I have? Surely everyone has, even though no one is acting on them.

No one except me.

Chapter Thirteen

WE'RE DANCING, JONATHAN DESROSIERS AND I, in a ballroom full of spinning stars. We've danced before, once – at a seedy nightclub called Majicks, when we were on the trail of a killer – but a few things are different tonight. For one, we're already a couple. For two, the floor is a lot less sticky.

Other than that, it's just as full of magical sexual tension. He's not an accomplished dancer, especially as he still can't put all his weight on his left foot, but who needs an accomplished dancer when all you really want to do is press your body up against someone who you lust after with all of your heart and soul? He's warm and solid in his beautiful Givenchy suit; one hand holds mine and the other one rests just right on my waist; I can feel his breath on my cheek. Our bodies sway gently to the music, in perfect time.

We're talking about our favourite topic: a dead guy.

'I didn't know that Rupert Huntington-Hogg was the patron of this charity,' Jonathan is saying. He's referring to Anya's after-dinner speech, where she asked for donations, and also prayers for our missing patron. 'He's been missing for how long? A month?'

'Something like that,' I say, as if I didn't know the exact date that I killed him.

'Do you know him?'

'I've met him a couple of times at these events. Each time, he had a different wife.'

'I met him once.'

'Did you?' I ask, interested.

'He gave my father a medal for bravery when I was about ten years old. I was at the ceremony.'

I don't mention the fact that Jonathan almost met him another time, in my house, when Rupert H-H was tied up and bleeding in my bath and Jonathan came by to pick up his stuff.

'What did your father do to be awarded a medal?'

'He stopped a man with an axe from attacking a bus driver.'

'Wow!'

'He wasn't even on duty at the time. He was just taking the bus to the football.'

'Did the man with the axe have beef with the bus driver?'

'I think the man with the axe was generally homicidal. They said my dad was a hero. He was, I guess.'

Jonathan sounds sad, so I press myself a little closer against him. In these heels, I'm only about an inch shorter than he is – the perfect height, because it makes everything easy to reach. I whisper in his ear, 'Enough about him. Let's talk about me. Aren't I gorgeous in this dress?'

'You're always gorgeous, Saffy. But you're especially gorgeous in this dress.'

'Wouldn't I be even more gorgeous out of it?'

'Yes, you would.' His grip on my waist tightens. 'You're the most beautiful woman here, and by far the most interesting. I can't believe my luck.'

'Now you're talking.' I nibble lightly on his earlobe, and he shivers. 'Do you like being bitten?'

'I never thought about it.' I bite him again, a little harder, and he groans. 'It seems I do.'

'By the right person.'

'By the right person, yes. Specifically, you.' His hand slides from my waist upward, to the bare skin at the small of my back. Now it's my turn to shiver.

'I could eat you up,' I murmur, and I kiss down from his ear along his jawline. My lipstick leaves blood-red marks on his skin. The colour is satisfying. He tastes delicious.

'When we get home,' he says, 'you can have anything you want.'

'Absolutely any part of you? I have permission?'

'As long as you don't use bolt cutters.'

'Consent is so sexy,' I breathe, and lean in for a long, deep kiss.

We stop dancing and let the world turn around us, let the couples whirl by. None of that matters. Only the two of us in the universe, dancing under a banner that says SAVE OUR ASSES.

When we break apart my head is spinning and I'm ravenously hungry for his naked skin next to mine. I want to know what he tastes like all over. I want to see his orgasm face, and most men have absolutely ridiculous orgasm faces, so you can tell I've got it bad.

'Wanna know my secret?' I ask.

'Badly.'

'I reserved a room upstairs.'

'For us?'

'For us and this massive sexual tension we're carrying around.' He pulls back a little. 'Saffy, that's expensive.'

'It's a donation. Almost all of the money is going to the charity. They threw in the room as a sweetener. I decided to use it tonight.' I give him a smouldering look. 'That is, if you'll use it with me.'

'And by "use" the hotel room, you mean . . .'

'Use the bed. And the sofa. And the shower. And the walls. And the desk chair.' I can sense he's not quite convinced, so I kiss him again, sucking his tongue into my mouth, giving him a flavour of exactly what I want to do with him in all of these places. By the time I'm done, he's panting.

'Unless you don't want to . . . ?' I pout my wet red lips at him.

'I want to. I really want to. But—'

'But?' Slowly, I grind my hips against him. This is really disgraceful behaviour on a dance floor, especially for someone like me, who has cultivated a reputation in these circles for ice-queen elegance, but everyone has had a lot of champagne.

'No buts,' he gasps. 'Yes.'

'"Yes please, Saffy"?'

'Oh God. Yes. Yes please, Saffy.'

'Let's go down to reception and get the keys.'

Jonathan bites his lip. 'I don't think I'm in any state to walk across a fully lit hotel lobby right now.'

I glance down and am glad to see he's right.

'Why don't you have a seat and . . . compose yourself? I'll go get the keys, and I'll text you the room number when I'm in it.'

'Good idea.'

'Don't forget to wipe off the lipstick.'

He touches his mouth self-consciously. I wink at him, and sashay away, feeling his gaze following me.

The lobby is one floor down. I have a quick safety stop in the ladies' on the way, to refresh my makeup and fix my hair.

In the mirror, my cheeks are flushed and eyes are bright, the pupils dilated. I look like I'm on some amazing drugs. And this does actually prove I'm not a pervert or a sex criminal, because after I've killed someone, I look cool, calm, and collected. The two drives, sex and murder, are entirely different.

Except when Jonathan talks about murder. But that's more like a soul mate thing.

Titivated, I check into our room at the reservations desk and request a bottle of champagne to be brought up. Then I make my lone and distracted way to the bank of Art Deco lifts and step through the embossed bronze doors.

As I press the floor button I'm already thinking about what to do when I get to the room. Should I take off my dress and be waiting for Jonathan in my lingerie? Or should I wait for him to come and unwrap me like a priceless gift? Should I lie enticingly on the bed, or be waiting to pounce on him at the door? Should I send him, along with the room number, a selfie of a mystery bit of my body and make him identify it before he's allowed to touch me? Or should we just get naked immediately and pour champagne all over each other like horny teenagers?

The lift doors slide shut but at the last moment, someone's hand appears between them and they spring open again. 'Room for another small one?' says a voice and, without waiting for an answer, a white-haired man slips into the lift and reaches over my arm to press the button for the top floor.

The doors shut.

I am alone in a very small enclosed space with Sir Thomas West.

Chapter Fourteen

MAYBE IT'S A PREDATOR THING, but at moments like these, time seems to slow down. My senses become sharper. Every molecule of my being focuses on a single person: the one person whose destiny has become fatally intertwined with mine.

I imagine it's how prey feels, too.

No sooner has Sir Thomas West stepped into my lift than I am aware of all of him at once. His cologne: Tobacco Vanille by Tom Ford. His shoes, glossy and polished to a mirror shine. His bow tie that has a tiny print of bow ties on it. A whiff of seafood from his dinner, a hint of red wine, an iota of talcum powder and Elnett. His hands, so tidy and well-manicured with a dusting of silver hair on each finger; the heavy Rolex on his wrist. He is forty years older than me, ten stone heavier, five inches taller. A flood of information, some of it important, some of it not.

The massive bodyguard is nowhere to be seen.

I smile at the old man in a friendly manner. Out of the corner of my eye, I look for CCTV cameras. I don't spot any, but there could be some hidden behind the mirror.

'Enjoying your evening?' Sir Thomas asks me in his genial way, the way that charms everyone at first.

I can hear his heart beating. The breath in his throat.

I didn't intend to kill him tonight, but I've been stalking him for ages, and I've never seen him alone before.

'Very much,' I say. 'You?'

'It's an important cause. Are you heading back to the dance floor?'

In the time that it takes West to ask his question about dancing, I have rehearsed the entire scenario in my mind, how I can do it.

A laugh, a flirtation. I'm not his type, but he has an image to maintain. A question about the cigar poking its Cuban head out of his breast pocket. He has pressed the button for the penthouse suite. We leave the lift together, we walk to the suite and there I slip a powder into his nightcap, the same powder I gave to Mr Anger Issues in the café. The powder that was meant for West.

'I haven't decided yet,' I say.

Or maybe there isn't any CCTV in the lifts. Maybe we are truly alone.

My knife is in my handbag. Well-oiled, whisper-sharp. I can open it with one hand. And he's turned slightly towards me, a white-toothed smile on his face, his body relaxed.

A quick, efficient swing of my arm, point outward, into the place where his leg meets his body. The knife cuts into his flesh like butter, so sharp he doesn't even feel it, so sudden that to his unaccustomed brain, the sensation of bright arterial blood flowing from his femoral artery feels as though he has wet himself. Like an old man. The old man he is. An old man who cannot control himself.

But I can control him, here in this lift. And he bleeds and bleeds and bleeds, while I watch. Enough blood to flood the bottom of the carriage, enough blood to drip through the doors and down the shaft to spatter on the floor below, where people are still dancing.

Enough blood to avenge every single one of his victims.

In my mind, it's happened already. In real life, I will not get away with it, unless I am both quick and lucky. Unless I am justice.

But I *am* justice.

My hand creeps into my handbag and opens the knife.

Chapter Fifteen

Jon sat in a quiet corner of the ballroom for a few minutes, drinking ice water and trying to compose himself. With Saffy gone, the strangeness of this entire scenario was all too clear to him. He didn't fit among these people. These clothes weren't really his. And while he thought donkeys were fine and deserved good lives, he couldn't understand a mind-set that believed that spending thousands of pounds on champagne and pleasure was actually going to help reduce inequality or suffering.

Think of all the good you could do with this money, he heard Edie's imagined voice saying.

He assumed that these people had considerably more than his book deal would bring in, and they belonged to a class where that was normal. But if he did have all this wealth, he wouldn't spend it on tailored suits or hotel rooms when he had a perfectly comfortable home less than a mile away.

Or would he? Did having money change you? When you could afford things like this, did you just not think about them? Was he judging the way that Saffy chose to spend her wealth because he felt inferior? Did he have any right to judge anyway? It was her money, and she did spend a good chunk of it on charities, and she was always ready to help other people. She'd saved his life. She was a good person.

And Jon wasn't exactly a raving Marxist. When he'd been living in a cheap shack in the Highlands, to punish himself, he still made sure to drink single-malt whisky. He'd tried to refuse Edie's pre-empt offer, but to be honest, he enjoyed the ego boost that came with it. And yes, when he had been a full-time crime author and podcaster, he'd donated some of his royalties and revenue to the victims of the killers he discussed – but he'd made a profit from them, too.

Which led to the question: were his scruples because he was principled or because he was joyless?

He downed his water. The fact was, all moral and economic arguments aside, he really wanted to go upstairs to a very expensive hotel room with Saffy and have sex with her all night on the high-thread-count sheets. Maybe he was being led by his dick and not his ethics. It would not be the first time a man had made that choice.

On the other hand, there was nothing like a moral dilemma to kill a hard-on. At least now he was OK to walk across a crowded room without having to grab a tray from a waiter and hold it in front of his crotch. Jonathan looked at his phone; there was no message from Saffy yet, so she was probably in the process of checking in. He got up and threaded his way out of the ballroom to the corridor where the lifts were.

The doors slid open almost immediately to reveal Saffy, flawless and beautiful, with her hand in her clutch bag. Incredible how the sight of her removed all of his doubts. 'Hello,' he said, smiling widely, and stepped into the lift along with her.

She looked startled to see him. 'Oh,' she said. 'Hi.'

This was not the greeting he'd expected. 'Are you OK?'

'Yes. Yes! Fine.' The doors shut and the lift started upwards. She took her hand out of her clutch bag and pushed back her hair, although it was already perfect. She looked almost dazed, as if she'd been pulled out of a daydream. 'I was just about to text you, that's all.'

'I couldn't wait,' he said, and wound his arm around her waist to pull her closer and kiss her, because whenever he kissed her, he had zero second thoughts whatsoever. Then he noticed for the first time that they weren't alone. An elderly white-haired man shared the lift with them. From his outfit, he was also a gala guest.

He caught Jon's eye and smiled, and Jon recognised him. 'Oh, wow! Are you Thomas West?'

'Guilty as charged.'

'Wow!' Jon said again. 'I'm – I'm not usually star struck, but I watched you all the time when I was a kid.'

'Thank you. It's such a pleasure to meet viewers.'

'Seriously. I wanted you to be my dad.'

'Oh.' Sir Thomas chuckled self-deprecatingly. 'Well, that's very kind of you.'

'Not as kind as it may sound. My real dad was a shit.'

'I'm sorry to hear that.'

'But you – I loved *Tommy's Treat*. It was a huge part of my childhood. The skit about the detective bear, who solved crimes about stolen honey to help the bees?' Jon remembered sitting on the floor in his parents' front room, rapt, in the hours between school ending and his father coming home. Sometimes his mother would sit on the sofa behind him and they would laugh at the same jokes. 'It was genius. Thank you.'

Sir Thomas smiled. 'What is your name?'

'I'm Jonathan. And this is Saffy. Did you watch *Tommy's Treat*, Saffy?'

Her expression was distant, and he thought suddenly that he was making a fool of himself.

'No,' she said. 'Alas, I didn't grow up in this country. British children's TV is as mystifying to me as the Henley Regatta.'

He stared at her. What was she saying?

'Well, it's fabulous to meet you, Jonathan and Saffy,' said Sir Thomas, holding out his hand. Jonathan was reaching out to shake it, when the lift pinged and the doors opened.

'This is our floor,' said Saffy. 'So lovely to meet you, Sir Thomas.'

'Tommy, please. Hope to meet you again.'

Saffy moved away quickly, so that his arm was no longer around her waist. She really could walk fast in heels. He shook Sir Thomas's hand briefly and followed after her down the hotel corridor.

'I know,' he said. 'I should have played it cool.'

'It's fine.'

'Well, I can see that it's not.'

'What makes you think that?'

The corridor was long. He practically had to run to keep up.

'I know that in your world, you see celebrities all the time. And if it were Samuel L. Jackson or Taylor Swift I wouldn't have said anything. But back in the day, Tommy West was a proper hero to a lot of kids. So I lost my head a little bit. I didn't mean to embarrass you.'

'Nothing embarrasses me.'

'He didn't seem to mind.'

'No, he loved every minute.' They reached a door and Saffy produced a key card from her handbag. Without a glance at Jon, she opened the door and went in.

The hotel room had floor-to-ceiling gold-coloured drapes on the windows and a king-sized bed with gold brocade cushions. It was bigger than the living room in the house he'd shared with his ex-wife. The carpet was so thick that his feet sank into it. It smelled of something exotic and expensive, probably frankincense and myrrh.

Saffy dropped her handbag on an armchair and turned to Jon, smile back on her face.

'Sorry about that,' she said. 'I'd had a whole scenario planned out in my head, and it didn't include running into you in the lift. It took me a minute to adjust.'

'What was your scenario?'

'It involved the very small pieces of silk and lace that I am wearing underneath this dress.' She tossed her hair, exposing the length of her creamy neck.

'I'm not sure that my underwear game is up to yours.'

'Even more reason to get rid of yours as quickly as possible.' She crossed to him and tugged on his belt.

He was probably going to regret this later, but he put his hand on her wrist to stop her.

'Are you sure you're OK?' he asked her.

'Other than sexual frustration?'

'No, I mean ... this place. This whole thing.'

'What about it?'

'There are so many unwritten social codes that you understand and I don't. I feel like I keep on screwing things up. And making you angry.'

'I'm not angry.'

'You sound like you are.'

She sighed, and dropped her hand from his belt. 'If you don't want to sleep with me, you can just say so.'

'I do! But there seems to be a lot we're not saying to each other.'

'What am I not saying to you?'

'I don't know. You haven't said it.'

'You are literally making no sense right now.'

'Saffy – my marriage broke down because we couldn't communicate. I don't want to make that mistake again.'

'Ah,' she said. She crossed her arms over her chest. 'Your ex-wife is back in the room.'

'No! No. I'm not thinking about her. I'm thinking about you. About us.'

'Half an hour ago, on the dance floor, there was an us. Now, there's you and your ex-wife *Amy* arguing with me for no reason.'

'I'm not trying to argue.'

'You're doing a good impression of it.'

'I just want to know why you used our escape word in the elevator, when I was having a harmless conversation that was going to end in a second anyway. I didn't talk to him to annoy you. He used to be one of my heroes, that's all. It was the only conversation I actually enjoyed all night, except for when I was talking with you.'

'I wanted to get out of the lift and into this bedroom with you.'

'And you got annoyed when I didn't jump to do what you wanted?'

'I wanted everything to be perfect, that's all.'

'Because you paid for it?'

She threw her hands up. 'I have no idea what you want me to say, Jonathan. Yes, I paid for everything because I wanted to and I can afford to. Yes, I would prefer to fuck you instead of talking to an old man. No, I wasn't angry with you, until you decided to ruin the mood by analysing every word that comes out of my mouth.'

'I'm trying to figure out where I fit in here. This is really not my world, at all.'

'It's not anybody's world. It's a charity gala.'

'It's your world. You fit in perfectly.'

'And confidence is sexy, Jonathan. It's sexier than a tailored suit or the right accent. If you don't think you're good enough for me, then maybe you shouldn't be here.'

That. That was it. She had said it: the very thing that he had been thinking.

It was worse coming from her.

'You're right,' he said. 'I'll go.'

Chapter Sixteen

THE HOTEL ROOM DOOR CLOSES behind him. I kick the dresser much harder than these shoes are designed to do, and hurt my foot.

'Bloody hell!'

I hop around on one foot, aware that I have not only ruined my plan for an entire night of mind-blowing sex, but have tipped off Jonathan that I'm hiding something beneath my cool and polished exterior.

I should have just stabbed Sir Thomas like I was going to. Right there in front of Jonathan in the lift. At least it would have given my boyfriend something to do besides pick a fight with me for no reason at all.

'Stinking wanking bollocks!'

I give up hopping, kick off my shoes, and fall back onto the bed. Alone.

I want to rip the world apart.

'Why is this so difficult?' I moan to the ceiling. Why do I have to be heterosexual? Why am I attracted to the same gender that I prey on? Why can't I be satisfied with a high-quality vibrator and a photograph of Idris Elba?

Why are men???

There's a knock on the door. He's come back! He's changed his mind. He's decided he can't live without me, and will fling me onto the bed and we will fuck like cocaine-fuelled rabbits all night long.

I spring from the bed and run to the door. It's only as I'm about to wrench it open that I realise exactly how desperate I am behaving, like a pathetic lovesick wretch, and while I've got it bad, I do not and will never have it *that* bad, so I pause, take a deep breath, compose myself, pull my bodice up, on second thoughts pull it back down a smidge, and open the door.

'Room service,' says the uniformed woman next to a cloth-covered trolley on which sits a silver ice bucket of champagne and two glasses.

Way to kick a girl when she's down.

I tip her, and when she's gone I sit back down on the bed and glumly survey my options.

I can lie here in my misery, drink this entire bottle of champagne and watch terrible films on television alone, like a wealthier and better-dressed Bridget Jones. This is such a cliché of helpless womanhood that the mere thought makes me shudder.

I can do the same as above, except I can ring Susie and get her to come over and do it with me. This is much more appealing and feminist, women supporting women and all that, but it has the major downside that I have to reveal my failure to my sister, who naturally looks up to me.

I can go try to find Jonathan. This is beneath my dignity. I do not chase after men, unless I am planning to slit their throats.

Well, to be fair, I sort of did chase after Jonathan before we met. But that was just to get his attention in the first place. Now that I've got his attention, chasing after him would be pathetic.

No. None of these options are any good. But I am full of pent-up desire and rage, far too much of both, and I have to let them out.

So there's only one option, really.

I get up and take the bottle of champagne to the bathroom. The cork popping makes a loud sound against the marble tiles. I take a big swig right from the bottle, swill it around my mouth, and spit it out into the sink. I limited myself to two glasses at the gala, but now I want to reek of booze. To gild the lily, I dab some champagne under my ears and in my décolletage, like perfume.

Then I tuck my hunting knife into the bodice of my dress, my key card into my knickers, and leave the room.

There are three suites on the top floor of this hotel, but I know which one Sir Thomas is in because he is a creature of habit and he did a photoshoot and interview with *The Sunday Times* in the Mazarin Suite three years ago. I also happen to know that to get to the top-floor suites, you need to have a specific key card, which I don't have. I've come woefully unprepared for this sort of operation. I don't have any lock-picking tools and no roofies, no plastic wrap or gaffer tape. It's just me and my trusty knife.

But I do have my wits about me. And I really, really want to cut Sir Thomas West.

Chapter Seventeen

*B*UT WHY? YOU ASK. WHY would a principled and disciplined avenger such as myself want to murder a famous, beloved, and respected star of children's television? One who has produced, directed, and starred in thousands of hours of quality programming, and devoted countless hours to raising funds for charities? Who has brightened the lives of millions of kiddies and never met with anything but adulation in the media?

Surely Sir Thomas West is one of the so-called Good Guys?

To explain, I have to take you to an afternoon about a year ago when I heard three words that would change the trajectory of my life.

I was sitting in my hair salon, sipping a double espresso and undergoing a deep-conditioning treatment. I had a glossy magazine open on my lap, but I wasn't reading it. A new stylist had joined the salon and I was half-listening to her gossiping with the receptionist, talking about her earlier career working in film and television, which she'd left because 'it just isn't worth it, girl'. She was being totally, delightfully indiscreet, listing the celebs she had styled, who'd had work done, who wore a hairpiece, who tried to feel her up, who spoke to her like shit, who was shagging everyone on set. In short, it was a perfect Wednesday afternoon and I was enjoying myself immensely.

Then she said the words. She whispered them, actually.

'He likes kids.'

At that moment, the rest of the world disappeared for me. I held my breath and I listened with every fibre of my being.

And that is how I learned about Sir Thomas West. Beloved children's television figure, national treasure, and paedophile.

As soon as I left the hairdresser, I began working on finding out more about Sir Thomas, without seeming to do so. With a man that powerful, I knew there was no point in speaking with television executives or media bigwigs – no one who had a stake in the game. A quick internet search told me that Sir Thomas was still active in producing television, which meant that millions of pounds and lots of jobs depended on his good name.

And we all know what happens when a rich and powerful man commits crimes against people with no power. Everyone turns a blind eye. They might whisper about it, sure. But they don't *talk* about it. Even post-#MeToo and Weinstein and Cosby and Savile and Epstein and so many other men who got away with endless harm. There's too much to lose. For the victims, the burden of proof is too high.

So I had to investigate how I usually do: discreetly. I spoke to the women who nobody listens to.

I mentioned Sir Thomas to Punam, the woman who does my lashes (she's a genius with LED lashes – they withstand water, makeup remover, and arterial blood spray). She'd seen some things, and gave me some names. I had casual conversations with camera operators and assistant producers. I chatted with former interns who no longer worked in the industry. I bought drinks for indiscreet journalists and publicists and I bought cocaine for the woman who used to edit Sir Thomas's bestselling series of books for children.

All of this was hearsay, though, and while that's generally good enough for the Homicidal Court of Saffy Huntley-Oliver, a high-profile target is higher risk. Especially when he has a bodyguard.

That is why I told everyone I was spending two weeks in Bali and instead checked myself into an exclusive rehab centre under a fake name and an even faker painkiller addiction, where I met a certain actress with a fondness for fentanyl.

And that's where I heard more than three words. A *lot* more.

I won't say her name, because you'd know it. And even though I'm not really an addict, I still consider myself bound by the 'anonymous' part of the twelve-step programme. But in group meetings and in quiet, late-night one-to-ones, the actress revealed her story to me.

She started out in beauty pageants aged four. She had a talent agent by age six. At age seven, she made her debut on *Tommy's Treat*. Thomas West (he hadn't been knighted yet) was quite taken with her. He called her a 'rare talent'. He said she had 'a great future'. He promised to help. He ingratiated himself with her parents and before long, they were all being hosted in his country house outside Chipping Norton, with the swimming pool and the tennis courts and the go-kart track and the home cinema and the make-your-own-sundae bar.

Uncle Tommy, as she called him, got her parents to sack her talent agent and sign her on with a different one, who Tommy knew personally, who owed Tommy some favours. And the work did start rolling in, it was true. Ads, small parts on telly, pantos, larger parts on telly. Wasn't she lucky to have met Tommy, who had such good connections? Weren't her parents proud of her?

So lucky. So proud.

So full of secrets.

Tommy didn't abuse her right away. He waited until she signed with the new agent and the offers started. She was eight. By then, her parents trusted Tommy enough to let her travel alone with him in his car. And that's where the abuse started, but it was in his house, too. And the studio. And his dressing room. And her dressing room.

'I love you,' he said to her. 'This is a game we're playing. You're my special girl. Haven't I been good to you?'

And he had.

For five years, he played his secret games with her. Not every time he saw her; sometimes he just brought her gifts – toys and clothes and books and DVDs. Sometimes he was the benevolent, loving uncle that he pretended to be. And sometimes he wasn't. But she couldn't say anything to her parents, or to anyone.

Because she owed everything to him. Everyone said so.

It stopped one day when she was thirteen and had landed a role in a West End play. Uncle Tommy stopped by to see a matinee and when he turned up in her dressing room (when he was *let into* her dressing room, when he was *led there* like royalty), the actress was drinking from a bottle of vodka. She didn't have time to hide it before he walked in. He saw her, he frowned, and he walked right back out again.

'And you know what haunts me?' the actress said to me, lighting another cigarette with yellow-stained fingers. 'I felt ashamed. Not because of what he'd done to me, but because of what I'd done to him by drinking. I'd let him down. But he never touched me again after that. He was disgusted.'

I have my own opinions about that moment in the dressing room, and why Sir Thomas never touched her again. It wasn't because she'd let him down: it was because she'd grown up.

I know a thing or two about predators moving on to younger prey.

But I didn't say anything. I nodded and listened hard.

She breathed in deep, and her next words came out in puffs of smoke. 'I never said a goddamn thing, because no one would believe me of course, and even if they did believe me, how could I prove it? But also, I'd got to where I was because of him. Everyone was always reminding me of it. My own talent wasn't enough. I needed *him*. And I needed the booze and the drugs, because that was what saved me from him.' She laughed, a rough laugh that sounded strange coming from her petite frame. 'He took my childhood, and he took my parents, and he took my self-belief, too. But hey, at least I had the dope, huh?'

Chapter Eighteen

Downstairs at the gala, the band is playing 'Mac the Knife' and Anya Ayers-Atkinson is on the dance floor with the corpulent scion of an oil family. Her evening bag is hanging on the back of her chair. I wouldn't trust half the people in this room with my pension plan, but at least white-collar criminals very rarely stoop to petty theft.

I have no such scruples. I dip into her bag, find her key card, and on my way out I help myself to the teensiest miniature lemon tart from a passing waiter's tray. I told Jonathan no canapés, but murder uses up quite a few calories. I enjoy it while riding the lift to the top floor of the hotel and considering whether I'll remove Sir Thomas's scrotum first, or his hands.

How many children did he touch, over the years? I've heard of several others, beyond the actress. My guess is that it was more than several. Sir Thomas would have had access to an almost unlimited number of children. Good old Uncle Tommy.

Oh, I'm going to enjoy killing him.

As soon as I step out of the lift my mood plummets. Because standing in the plush corridor, wearing black as always, is Mullethead. His hair is truly spectacular, by the way. Short on the sides, puffed up on top, and cascading down his back. I have rarely seen someone so committed to a hairstyle.

'Evening,' he says to me. 'Nice night for it.'

This is the first time I've heard him speak and his accent is pure Somerset. I wonder if he knows what Sir Thomas likes to do to children. I wonder how many secrets he is keeping. Closer up, I can see that he's wearing a diamond stud in one ear and an Omega on his wrist. Bodyguarding clearly pays quite well these days.

I take a chance and tap my purloined key card at the second suite door, and to my relief it opens. I'm greeted by a rusty meow and the sight of Anya's bald cat PawPaw lying curled up on a discarded Yves Saint Laurent evening gown. PawPaw is wearing a pink cashmere jumper and as always, she looks like a giant aborted rat who has undergone some very unfortunate plastic surgery.

'Good kitty,' I croon, and reassess my situation.

Much as I would love to, I can't kill Sir Thomas here. It's far too risky, even without Mullethead outside.

However. I am still furious at being cockblocked.

Fortunately, there's always a Plan B.

* * *

At night, this part of the park is always in shadows. The streetlamp died months ago, and the Corporation of London has not yet got around to replacing it. Fortunately, my dress is sparkly enough to light up the place like a beacon. I'm limping, not because my foot hurts any more – I rarely feel any pain when I'm on the hunt, which is really something that scientists should look into because it could alleviate a lot of human suffering – but because I want to look weak. A lame prey animal separated from the pack.

And sure enough, sooner or later, a hyena will turn up.

'Hey little girly, what's up?'

'You hurt yourself, sweetheart?'

There are two of them. They're wearing tracksuits and trainers. One has a baseball cap and one has a pot belly. They're each holding a can of Stella. One of them has his mobile pointed at me.

I don't answer, just keep limping, and they get closer.

'You OK, love?'

'You're getting this, aren't you?'

'Fuck, yeah. Look at that fucking dress. We got a posh one here, man.'

'C'mere, sweetie, lemme help you.'

'We got what you need, girly.'

'Why you out here all alone and by yourself? C'mon, gizzus a smile.'

'Leave me alone,' I whimper.

'Hey, we're nice guys.'

'We just wanna have a drink with you.'

'We just wanna talk a little.'

Baseball Cap makes a grab for me. Pot Belly is still filming.

I stumble, deliberately, and Baseball Cap catches me. 'Whoa, girly, watch it!' he says, as I twist my arm around and stab him right in that special place, the place I've already picked out for Sir Thomas, the place where the leg meets the groin. The knife is sharp and his tracksuit is flimsy. It's really just a flick of the wrist. He doesn't even feel it.

He does feel it when I kick him in the balls.

He squeals and falls backwards, clutching his crotch. As he writhes on the ground, his hands quickly fill with blood. It's literally spurting out of him. I guess he's got healthy blood pressure, at least. Now his squeal has turned into a full-lunged scream.

'What's the matter?' I ask him, stepping out of the trajectory of the spray. 'Can't you take it like a man?'

Pot Belly screams too. 'What the fuck what the fuck what the fuck what the fuck?' Apparently Pot Belly's vocabulary is quite limited.

I'm completely ignored as he drops to his knees beside his bleeding buddy. I notice he's still filming on his phone. Blood spatters onto his face and tracksuit.

'What the fuck?' he yells. Baseball Cap is still screaming, but more weakly.

'This is getting way too noisy,' I say. Blithely, I skip over to behind Pot Belly, reach around him, and slit his throat.

He stops swearing immediately and gurgles instead. It's an improvement.

I pluck his phone from his hand as he starts clawing at his neck. Flicking blood from my gloved fingertips, I stop the video recording and delete it. It's a shame to erase my handiwork, but at least I have fond memories to look back on.

Pot Belly collapses forward onto his friend. Baseball Cap tries to scuttle backwards but he's mostly beyond movement. His hands haven't slowed the bleeding at all.

'It typically takes about three minutes for someone to bleed out after the kind of injury you've got,' I tell him. 'That doesn't sound like long, but it can feel long when you're waiting for death. With any luck, you'll remain conscious for all of it.'

'Help,' he slurs. 'Help me.'

'You mean, like the kind of help you wanted to give me? Ew, no thank you. I'd rather you kept it in your pants.'

While he moans on the ground beneath his buddy, I put Pot Belly's phone on the ground and smash it with the heel of my shoe and the handle of my knife. I fish out the SIM card and the memory card, and kick the rest into a nice handy gutter grating. I hear the splash. Thank goodness for London's Victorian sewer system.

'Well,' I say to Baseball Cap, 'that was fun. Thanks for letting me work out some tension. Enjoy the rest of your night!'

* * *

Back in the hotel room, enjoying a well-earned cup of peppermint tea, I notice that the hem of my dress has a few spots of blood on it. And I thought I'd been so careful. It's a beautiful couture dress, and I'm going to have to burn it.

Plus, I missed a text from Jonathan, and it's too late to reply.

On the other hand, I do feel much better now.

Chapter Nineteen

Back at Saffy's, Jon changed out of his suit and back into his normal jeans and shirt. In the mirror, he was a normal schlub. A normal schlub, whose masculinity was so threatened by a woman who was richer and more powerful than he was, he'd rather pick an argument and storm out than face the fear that he wouldn't be able to perform.

'I'm the problem,' he told himself.

Girl, who'd been delighted to see him, nudged his leg with her snub nose.

'I know,' he said to her. 'I neglected you to go to a party. And I've kept Edie waiting about my final decision about the book. I don't seem to be living up to the requirements of any of the females in my life.'

But the dog, at least, he could make it up to. He clipped on her lead and took her out for a walk.

Girl was so used to the neighbourhood by now that he didn't have to think about where to take her; she chose the path with her favourite lampposts and the quickest way to the park. Just as well, because his self-recrimination took up most of his attention. But what was he supposed to do? Ignore the fact that Saffy was upset about something that she wouldn't reveal to him?

Pretend that her demeanour towards him hadn't undergone a total hundred and-eighty-degree between the dance floor and the lift, and another one as soon as they got into the hotel room?

He was trying to be sensitive, when what was required was caveman sexual aggression. How could he even win in that situation?

At this time of night, Kensington Park was nearly empty: a few revellers on their way home, a homeless person huddled in a sleeping bag under a tree. He spotted a woman walking on her own and he steered Girl in the other direction so she wouldn't think he was following her. He remembered the time that his ex-wife Amy had sat him down and told him about what everyday life was like as a woman: how women had to check their surroundings, how they held their keys between their fingers as makeshift weapons, how even the most innocuous-seeming man could be a potential threat.

By then he had spent thousands of hours investigating the murders of women, so he should have got it. But he didn't, not really. Not until he'd been a victim himself and learned that violence could come from the most unexpected places, from people who you dismissed or those you trusted.

Still, here he was out alone after midnight with no protection other than a scruffy dog who was more interested in sniffing pigeon shit than looking out for danger. That was a privilege, he supposed.

Girl wandered aimlessly from scent to scent, trailing him behind her. At night and with few people around, it was difficult to tell how much time was passing. He didn't even notice that they had crossed from one park to another until he looked up and saw the hotel he had left earlier in the evening. From the outside and a distance, it was all white and gold, like a lit-up wedding cake.

He stopped and gazed up at it. One of those windows might be Saffy's. Had she gone to bed? Or was she still up, disappointed and fuming?

He thought about crossing the road to the hotel, going up to the room and apologising. But he had Girl with him, and he didn't know if the hotel allowed dogs. He thought about ringing Saffy and checking that she was all right. But she might be asleep. He took out his phone anyway and poised his thumb over the 'call' button for a moment, before deciding that it was best to leave it for tonight. He'd let her cool down. He'd try to figure out what was wrong with him.

He texted her instead. `Sorry for ruining the evening. This is why I can't have nice things.` He waited a little while, but it remained unread.

She was asleep. Just as well. She'd wake up and see his text, and with any luck, tomorrow they could work it out. They could joke about how solving murders was so much easier than having a relationship.

Girl pulled at the lead and he followed her, feeling a bit better now that he'd taken the first move to make up with Saffy. Not like his own father, who would never back down in an argument, never admit he had made a mistake.

More like his mother, who always apologised for everything, who always took the blame even though none of it was her fault.

He shook his head. That was a false equivalence. This situation was nothing like his parents' marriage. Neither he nor Saffy were violent, for one thing. (Despite the fact that Jon had killed a man. He had *killed a man*. Something that his father had never done.)

And for another, being wrong or right didn't divide itself down strict gender lines. Men and women were both human, and they both made mistakes. A healthy relationship acknowledged that. But someone had to make the first move, someone had to soften. It was his turn this time, that was all.

Girl had her stubby nose to the ground and was sniffing loudly and straining at the lead. 'Smell a fox?' he asked her, amused by her earnestness. Girl, the mighty hunter. Maybe she had a bit of bloodhound in her.

He let her pull him down a side path, along a clump of bushes, away from the lights of the road. He'd let her hunt the fox or rat or whatever for a few minutes and then make his way back to Saffy's house.

It was unlit in this section of the park and at first he took the dark shapes in front of him for bushes or shadows. Then he and Girl got closer and suddenly he could smell it, too.

You never forgot a smell like that. And not the sounds and sights and feelings attached to that smell, either. It was red and screaming and full of pain.

He fumbled for his phone again and turned on the torch.

One of the bodies was sprawled on its back, eyes and mouth open, skin bleached in death. The other slumped on top of him. Jon couldn't see any wounds from here, but the two men had been wounded, all right. Some of what he had taken for a shadow was actually a large pool of blood spreading over the path. The light from his torch gleamed in it.

Girl sniffed at the blood. He looked down, and one of his feet was standing in the pool. He moved it away quickly, and when he put his foot back down, the bottom of his trainer was sticky. He was probably imagining it, but it felt as if his foot were clammy, as if the blood had soaked through his shoe, as if the last bit of residual warmth from those men's lives was coating itself on his skin.

He shone his torch over the men. The one on the bottom was clearly dead, but he couldn't see the face of the man on the top. He didn't appear to be breathing. Jon crouched and angled his phone and saw that the top man's throat had been slit from ear to ear. The man beneath him wore a green tracksuit which had been soaked nearly black. They had not done this to each other. They had not been dead for long.

There was a killer somewhere nearby in the darkness.

He called 999.

'I've just found two bodies,' he said. His voice was surprisingly steady. 'I think they're dead.'

He knew they were dead, but it seemed rude somehow to say it within their hearing.

The sirens started up almost right away, getting closer. Quickly, furtively, Jon took several photographs of the scene, walking around the dead men to get as many angles as possible. Old habits. The urge to understand. That was all.

There were no bloody footprints except for his, no weapons that he could see. Two cans of Stella lay on the grass nearby. Splinters of something shiny littered on the path. The men were young; whoever killed them must have been strong, or it could have been more than one person. From the amount of blood, he'd guess they'd severed an artery of the person lying on his back. He couldn't see much more without moving the bodies, and of course he wasn't going to do that.

By the time the first officers arrived, his phone was back in his pocket. Girl greeted the policemen as if they were old friends.

Chapter Twenty

I ALMOST NEVER DRINK ENOUGH TO get an alcohol hangover, but I've found that there is such a thing as a murder hangover. Killing a person creates such a potent cocktail of excitement, hyper-arousal, elation, and satisfaction that sometimes the next day you can feel a bit flat. There's the muscle strain too, if you've had to get physical and slash at slightly odd angles, like I did with the hoodlums in the park, or if you've got to move a heavy body, but that's not the main part. It's the emotions that cause the hangover.

For a few moments while you're planning and executing the murder, you are immortal. You are all-powerful. You are an avenging angel. You are Death.

It's difficult to go back to being a human being who is merely fabulous.

I take a long soak in the hotel room bath, drinking room service coffee and mineral water and eating a fruit salad. Post-homicide hydration is so important.

Jonathan sent an apology text last night, and I haven't replied to it. If I'm honest, I want him to suffer a little bit. But also, reconciliations are much better in person.

When I'm drying my hair, a courier arrives with a fresh outfit. Lightweight trousers, silk blouse, low-heeled shoes, all in demure neutrals: casual and breezy to say 'I rise above rejection' but soft enough to say 'I am ready for you to appeal to the better side of my nature'.

In the cab going to Kensington the driver nods at the police cars clustered around the entrance to the park and says, 'Something happened there last night. Two young lads killed in a fight, I heard.'

'What a waste,' I murmur.

'They're all doing drugs and carrying knives these days,' the cabbie informs me, and spends the rest of the journey telling me how he would sort out the youth of today by reinstating National Service and requiring everyone under eighteen to undergo weekly drug testing. As with many men, he doesn't require any input from me to bolster his conviction that he is fascinating, so I zone out and plan the nuances of the expression I will wear when I enter my home.

I wonder if Jonathan's had a sleepless night. I wonder if he's been pacing the floors and googling 'How to make it up to your girlfriend when you've been an idiot'.

'Hello,' I call as I step into my house.

There is no answer.

I sniff the air. There is no scent of apology flowers.

'Hello?'

I don't hear the tell-tale sound of canine toenails scuttling away from me. Perhaps Jonathan has taken Girl for a walk, preferably past a florist that sells massive apology bouquets. But the house has a vaguely neglected feeling to it, as if no one has been breathing in it for a while.

Has he moved out? Did I ruin everything by not replying to his text?

To my relief, there's still a pair of his running shoes inside the door of his bedroom. The bed is made. I touch the pillow and it's cold. In the bathroom, his toothbrush is dry.

He didn't sleep here last night.

I stare at my reflection in the guest bathroom mirror. He wouldn't, would he?

No, he wouldn't. Jonathan's a good man.

But ... he is a man.

I care about Jonathan, but there are limits. If that man left my five-star hotel room and took his dog to another woman's shag den, he is going to die. I will do it with sadness and regret, but I will do it. I will tie him to a chair in a plastic-lined room and make him tell me every single detail of what he did and why he regrets it, and then I am going to slice off his body parts, one by one, starting with his testicles. I am going to put the body parts into big glass jars of preservative and I am going to use them in an art exhibition entitled FUCK AROUND AND FIND OUT.

Joke. I'm going to bury them in scattered unmarked graves where they won't be discovered. I'm angry but I'm not an idiot.

The door opens, I hear the jingle of Girl's collar, and momentarily, I panic. Planning the disposal of a potentially cheating boyfriend is one thing, but what am I going to do with his dog? I don't kill animal-animals, only human animals. Am I going to lose a boyfriend and gain a pet?

Get it together, Saffy. Your murder hangover is making you slow. Susie will take the dog.

'Saffy?' calls Jonathan. It's only one word, but he sounds odd. Weary, and yet ...

I poke my head out from his bedroom and he's there. Unshaven, hair uncombed, looking as if he's been up all night, with his cheeks strangely flushed and his eyes bright.

He has sex face. He has *sex face*.

I calculate the distance from his bedroom door to the knife block in my kitchen.

'Oh,' he says, 'you're home.'

'I just got back. I was looking for you.'

'I haven't been to bed yet.'

'Why?' I ask, with preternatural calm. Maybe I won't reach the knife block in time, and I'll have to strangle him with my bare hands. That would be satisfying, too. I'd be able to see the reaction on his face.

His beautiful face. The face I have become infatuated with. This is so conflicting. How do people even have relationships?

'I've been down the nick,' he says.

This, I did not expect.

'Why? Did you commit a crime?'

'I found a murder scene.'

'*Again?*'

'They do seem to follow me, don't they?' He laughs hollowly and goes past me into his bedroom, where he falls face-first on the bed. 'It was two lads who'd been stabbed in the park,' he says, slightly muffled by the duvet. 'I was out walking Girl and she sniffed them out.'

He found my dead hoodlums.

We both have a murder hangover. For the *same murder*.

Instantly, all is forgiven. I sit beside him on the bed and stroke his tangled hair.

'You poor thing!' I lie. 'You must have been terrified.'

'Strangely, not. Mmm, that feels good.'

I keep running my fingers through his hair, smoothing out the curls. 'Why weren't you scared?'

Could you see me in the wounds? Did my crimes call to you?

'I don't know,' he says. 'Maybe I'm used to it by now.'

'How did you feel?'

'More fascinated than anything.'

I want to purr. He's fascinated by me! This is a girl's dream come true.

'I've been answering questions all night. Morning. Whatever this is.'

'What did they want to know?'

'The same thing over and over again. Whether I saw or heard anyone in the area, if I'd moved anything, what direction I was walking in, why I was out that time of night ...'

'Did you see or hear anything?'

'I didn't hear any screams. I did see some people as I was walking, but no one unusual. No one hurrying or spattered with blood or anything. And there was a lot of blood.'

I think, with a pang, of my wasted dress.

'Any of the people I passed could have done it,' Jonathan says. 'The two of them couldn't have been dead much more than half an hour.'

'Why did they need to ask you so many questions, if you didn't see anything?'

'They just wanted to get every detail, I guess. I was glad to do it, in case I'd forgotten anything.'

'You're not a suspect this time, are you?'

He sighs. 'I definitely have a reputation with the homicide detectives. But no, I don't think so.' He turns on his side, pulls me down to lie next to him, and then spoons into my back, his arm around my waist. 'This is so nice,' he says into my hair, his warm breath on my neck.

'Yes, it is.' I pull his arm tighter around me.

'I'm sorry about last night and my fragile masculinity.'

'I'm sorry for losing my temper and being entitled.'

'It seems like a silly argument, when people are getting killed.'

'It does put things into perspective, for sure.'

'Can we start again?'

'Of course.'

He kisses the back of my neck. I melt with lust. This is going to be even better than what I'd planned for last night, and much *much* better than killing him. We've shared something profound and beautiful. Life and death. What's more intimate than that?

I tilt my head to the side and wait for him to keep kissing me.

And wait.

His arm around my waist grows heavy. His breathing behind me slows.

He's asleep. I wiggle a little bit, but he's out for the count. Poor man's all tuckered out. I sigh and cuddle in closer, and he makes a contented sound in his sleep.

I close my eyes. I can't remember the last time I lay like this in the arms of someone, like a little spoon. I'm not sure that I ever have. My life doesn't allow for a great deal of non-lethal personal contact. I've tended to select my boyfriends for their temporary basis and lack of clinginess; I've never allowed any of them to stay overnight in my bed. Until now, I've seen that as a sign of my strength.

I hug my sister, of course. I have long-ago memories of being held by my mother. But this is different, being held by a man and feeling safe there.

As a cure for a murder hangover, this isn't what I wanted. But it's not half bad.

Chapter Twenty-One

Jon was back in prison, back in the same chair at the same table, across from Cyril again.

'Thanks for coming in, mate,' said Cyril. 'I keep on thinking you're going to get pissed off with me for stabbing you that time and decide not to see me again.'

'I wish you hadn't stabbed me,' said Jon. 'It aches when it rains.'

'Didn't have much choice, buddy.'

'That's one of the many topics on which our opinions differ.'

'Didn't want to end up here, did I?' Cyril gestured at the uncomfortable windowless room, the chains on his wrists, the omnipresent walls.

'What's the worst part about prison?'

'The clothes,' said Cyril immediately. 'Cheap leisurewear does not suit me. And the hygiene. Contrary to rumour, the showers aren't actually that bad, but we're not allowed to do it enough. I've picked up a foot fungus.'

'Too much information.'

'Yeah. Sorry. Also the food is terrible, as I was saying last time. It's worse than my mum's cooking, and that's saying a lot. We need to get Jamie Oliver in here. Nearly cracked my tooth on something that was supposed to be a Yorkshire pudding.'

'Are you bored?'

'So bored, mate. My lawyer's stopped coming, my brother won't talk with me, I've done all the psychiatric tests until they were coming out of my wazoo and they all find me sane.'

'In what universe are you sane, Cyril?'

'I'm a psychopath, obviously, but that's not in question and it's not treatable. I'm not deluded; I've got a firm grip on reality. I understand the consequences of my actions, and I understand that they were wrong.'

'But you did them anyway.'

'Yeah. I made a rational choice to kill those men, dismember them, and dispose of their bodies, because I wanted to and it was fun. And I acted normal enough not to get caught for a very long time. In my book, that makes me sane.'

'You're a good conversationalist,' said Jon. 'I would not call you sane or normal.'

'Anyway, those tests are a joke. Blunt instruments. You'll do better at explaining my psyche than those shrinks. You really get me.'

Jon couldn't help asking, 'Has anyone else been in touch, asking to interview you?'

Cyril waved his hand, which made the chains clink. 'Oh, I've had tons of those. I say no to all of them. I've already chosen my biographer.'

Edie had been ringing non-stop. This morning, she'd left a message saying that Jon's silence had paid off – the publisher's offer had been increased by twenty per cent.

'I'm not writing.'

'You will,' said Cyril. 'Anyway, I've got some news. I might have a name to go with that head you were talking about.'

Jon leaned forward. 'Who is it?'

'First, though, I have a question for you. Have you told the police about it yet?'

He had spent nearly eight hours in the police station on Saturday morning answering questions about other murders. The last thing that his old frenemy, DI Atherton, had said to him before he left was, 'Desrosiers, tell me the truth: do you know anything you're not telling us?'

'No,' he'd said then.

'No,' he said now. 'I haven't mentioned it.'

'Why not?'

'I don't have the photo any more. I don't have any other evidence. For all I know, it's a special effect. AI, or a dummy head.'

'Seems like most people would still ask the police about it though.'

'How exactly are you placed to know what most people would do?'

Cyril chuckled. 'That's where you and I are similar. Neither one of us is like most people. Why haven't you told the cops? Do you like having a secret, all to yourself?'

'I was waiting to see if you could give me a name. What is it?'

'I think it's because you want to solve the case yourself.'

'Why would I want to do that? I'm through with true crime.'

'Because it's what your entire identity relies on. And it's hard to hide your identity. I've been in the closet, mate. It's a terrible place to be. Even harder than prison, in some ways.'

'I'm not in the closet about being a true crime investigator.'

'No – you're not trying to hide. You're trying to convert yourself into something that society believes is "normal". And that's also terrible.'

Jon huffed in exasperation.

'We're friends,' said Cyril. 'We go way back. You can tell me. Don't you feel a little lost? Like you don't fit in? Like you're not sure who you are any more? All your confidence is gone. All your *spunk*. Your instincts tell you to do things, but you're always second-guessing them. Always censoring yourself. It's no way for a man to live. Are you thinking about your dad a lot these days?'

'Yeah,' answered Jon, before he could stop himself. 'A lot.'

'Me too. My dad. What was your dad like?'

'He was a violent son of a bitch.'

Cyril nodded. 'I hear you. But you loved him, right?'

'He was my dad.'

'So the association of violence with love runs deep in you, too?'

'I'm not violent to the people I love.'

'But violence comes to them, doesn't it?'

That made Jon pause.

Cyril continued, 'I think it's a real tragedy of modern life that boys don't have good role models for masculinity. Our dads, that whole generation of British men, and all the generations before, they never talked about their emotions. I never once saw my dad cry, you know?'

'Me neither. It would be unthinkable.'

'Right. And then us, you and me, we want to be different types of men than our dads were, but we have no idea how. The women have the feminist movement, but what have we got, your everyday blokes? Incels spouting toxic masculinity on every social media platform. If we want to be a different type of man than our dads were, we have to make it up as we go along, with no guidance. So we define ourselves against our old men, instead of defining ourselves by who we actually are.'

'You defined yourself by killing people.'

'Which proves my point. My dad was a philanderer and a cheat. I knew I could never do that to anyone I loved. But you can't cheat on a dead man, can you?'

'Cyril,' said Jon, 'that is fucked up.'

'Like I said, mate. We haven't got any proper role models or guidelines so we can't help but fuck it up.'

'Ten minutes,' said the bored guard at the door.

'What do you think?' asked Cyril. 'Am I right or am I right? I hit a nerve, didn't I?'

'I think you should write your own book.'

He shrugged. 'It's more fun if I can psychoanalyse you at the same time. Like I said, it gets boring in here. I like to have a project.'

'Well, now that you're done poking around in my brain, can you tell me the name that I came here for?'

'Ah. Yeah. So I found that out in about six seconds, but I don't get many visits, so I had to hang onto it.'

'Who is he?'

'I asked around the gen pop for a head of his description. Turns out he's quite well known. His name's Tony Jones.'

'His murderer talked about him?'

'No – he's a former inmate. Incarcerated for stalking. I sort of feel sorry for the guy. At least me, I'm a serial killer and also I'm a man's man, you know what I mean? I'm respected around here, nobody gives me any shit. But this guy, Tony, he was in for stalking. That's not as bad as being a paedo, obviously – everyone hates the paedos. But stalking is low. Stalkers don't even have the balls to approach someone or kill them like a normal person—'

'Once again: that's not normal, Cyril.'

'Right, right, but you know what I mean. Stalkers lurk around in the shadows. They're creeps. All mouth and no trousers. And even after he'd been put away, Tony Jones was still obsessed with this woman he was stalking. She was just a normal woman, not rich or famous or anything, but she had the guts to turn him in and testify against him. He told everyone in prison that she was really his girlfriend and she loved him, and that when he got out they were going to get married and have babies. He was delusional, like a guy who lives in his mum's basement and tells everyone he's dating a supermodel from another country. Everyone laughed at him to his face. I wasn't here yet, but some of the lifers told me. When Jones got released, they were all waiting for him to bounce right back in, because there was no way he was going to stop harassing that woman. But he never came back.'

'Because if the head is his, someone killed him first.'

'Bingo.' Cyril tilted his head. 'That's made you happy, hasn't it? You've got a real light in your eyes.'

'Do you know what that light is? It's the knowledge that I'm about to walk out of here into the fresh air.'

An exaggerated wince. 'Meow.'

Jon stood up. 'Thanks for the information, Cyril. That, I appreciate.'

'Any time. Do you have any more mysteries for me to solve?'

'Not for the moment. I'm going to take this one to the police now.'

'Uh-huh. I'll believe that when I see it. How's that blonde girlfriend of yours, by the way?'

Jon froze, fear striking his heart in a way it hadn't when he'd been face to face with two freshly killed people.

Had he mentioned Saffy to Cyril? That would be a major error. Especially with the sharp insight that Cyril had pointed at him, that violence tended to find the people that Jon cared about. Violence had already found Saffy, and he didn't want it to happen again.

'Relax, mate. You didn't say anything. Even in here we get the odd copy of the *Sun*. She looks like a stunner. Not my type, obviously, but you've done well for yourself.'

'Nice of you to say. Goodbye, Cyril.'

He walked quickly to the door.

'Jonny,' Cyril called to him, before Jon could escape, 'next time, can you bring me a cream or something for my foot fungus?'

Chapter Twenty-Two

Susie and I are side by side on treadmills, smashing our workouts. She's all in pink. I'm all in black.

'Has Jonathan had the chance to look at Finlay's notes yet?' she asks me.

'I don't know. He hasn't mentioned it.'

'Any luck with the old . . .' She makes an obscene gesture with her tongue in her cheek.

'Still working on it,' I admit.

'You know, there's this amazing woman on TikTok called Liza Chessington. She's, like, a sex and intimacy coach? I watch her all the time and she is so good.'

'How does a person become a sex and intimacy coach? Do they hang around people's bedrooms blowing a whistle every time someone can't find the clitoris?'

'She's worked with loads of couples,' Susie continues. 'And she has a lot of incredible videos. Here, I'll send you one.' She taps on her phone, which is resting next to her pink water bottle. 'You should check her out. She's really inspirational.'

My own phone buzzes. I wipe my hands on my leggings and open the link she's sent me. I have the volume off while I'm in public, because we live in a society and I am not rude, so all I see is a video of a dark-haired woman in a low-cut blouse speaking to the camera with animated all-caps auto-generated captions.

IT'S NOT THE BODY COUNT . . . IT'S THE BODIES THAT COUNT.

'Wise,' I say, though I am not entirely sure of what this means and how it refers to sex and intimacy and not, say, serial murder.

'So wise,' agrees Susie. 'So insightful. I've got an idea – you should go see her!'

'I don't want to talk to a stranger about my sex life.'

'You've got to visualise it to achieve it, and sometimes everyone needs a little help.'

A gym bro appears in front of us, between our treadmills. 'Did one of you ladies say you needed help?'

'No, thank you, we're fine,' I say.

'You know, it's all about muscle mass these days.'

'We've already lifted. We're on the cardio portion of our workout.'

He peers over at our displays. 'Actually, if you're looking for maximum cardio effectiveness, you should do intervals.'

'We're good, thanks.'

'It's easy, you can reprogram mid-workout. Here.' He presses a button on Susie's treadmill and it starts speeding up. Susie runs harder.

I plant my feet on either side of my treadmill and stare at the man, hands on my hips.

'Are you sisters?' the man asks, oblivious.

'Yes,' pants Susie.

'You're hot.'

'We've got boyfriends,' pants Susie.

'Can I have both your numbers, for me and my friend?'

'No,' I say. 'Go away.'

He returns my stare for a split second and then looks down. 'Not that hot anyway,' he mutters, moving away.

'Yes, we are!' I call after him, and resume my workout. Susie slows her treadmill back down and mops her forehead.

'I think we should move gyms,' she says. 'There's a female-only one in Fulham.'

And give up a good proportion of my killing pool? Not likely.

'You said when we were on the chest press that you had some news,' I say. 'What is it?'

'Oh.' She bites her lip. 'Actually this is oldish news, but I didn't want to tell you until I knew it was going to work out. I've got a job!'

I do a little skip on my treadmill. 'That is great news! What is it?'

'Well, it's not really a job-job. It's a volunteer job. But it's a proper one, with a title and everything, it's not just rocking up between parties and putting a few hours in. It's three nights a week and I've had to do training and everything.'

'It sounds amazing. I'm so proud of you.'

'In the past I've found it hard to stick with things, you know?'

'You haven't found the right fit,' I say loyally.

'I think it's more that I get bored easily. It used to make me feel bad about myself. Like I'm not serious enough or smart enough to do anything real, and I'm only suited to be a socialite or marry well or whatever.'

Like our mother, who had two degrees in music and played the harp like a literal angel but gave it up when she married our father. I never heard her play, not once. I only saw her in old photos that she kept hidden and I found years later, after she had been dead for most of my life.

'You're smart and serious enough to do anything that you like,' I tell Susie. 'You always have been.'

'I think that's part of the problem too? Like, as long as I never try anything too difficult then I don't have to worry about failing? Anyway, I'm older now, and I can't spend all my time partying and having fun and shopping and whatever. I need to make a difference to the world, somehow. Make it a better place, if I can.'

'I can understand that.'

'Right? You're always working so hard for those charities. You're a real inspiration. We've been given so much, so it's important that we can give back.'

'With great power comes great responsibility,' I say.

'Oh, Saffy, that's *Spider-Man. So* cringe.'

'It's true though.'

'Yes,' she says, and stops the treadmill. I do the same. We wipe ourselves with towels, and reach for our water bottles.

'So what's the job?'

Her cheeks are flushed, but she blushes more. 'It's volunteering at a suicide prevention hotline.'

'Susie-sue!' I exclaim in delight. 'That's amazing!'

'Yeah, it sort of is. And, I sort of love it.'

'What do you love about it?'

'Helping people. Really listening to them. It's unbelievable but an hour, a few minutes even, can be life or death to someone. Obviously it's all confidential or whatever and it's hard, the hardest thing I've ever done, but I feel like I can do it, like it's worth it. I've never really felt that way, you know?'

I hug her hard. 'I am so proud of you.'

'Thanks. I'm proud of me too, I think.'

'Have you saved anyone's life?'

'It's impossible to say. It's all anonymous and you don't know what happens when they hang up. You have to let people go after talking to them, or you'll spiral, just wondering. That's part of the training. Anyway, I do feel like I've helped sometimes. Often it's very sad, but sometimes it's unexpectedly joyful.'

'What made you decide to do it?'

'You know, it's partly the talking you and I have been doing about our parents? Like you and I dealt with so much loss when we were growing up. I think it means that I can connect with other people who are dealing with loss. And I do feel like Mummy's death could maybe have been prevented, if someone had been there to listen to her. I don't know, maybe not.'

'Maybe,' I say. 'I've thought about that. That maybe I should have done something.'

'You were too young, Saffy. It was not your fault. And also, you've done what she would have wanted. You're making the world better for women. All those women's charities that you help with? It's inspiring. It's inspired me.'

'Thank you,' I say, and we hug again, ignoring the sweat.

'We don't really talk enough about the deep stuff,' says Susie. 'I like it when we can do that. Even if it hurts.'

We head for the showers to wash everything away.

Chapter Twenty-Three

THE PUB WAS SURPRISINGLY BUSY for mid-afternoon on a Wednesday. Jon bought a pint and had just managed to find an unoccupied table in the corner when DI Atherton entered the pub, spotted him, and came over.

DI Atherton and Jon had known each other for some time, and most of that time had been marked by mutual distrust. Atherton had never concealed his opinion that Jon, like all true crime journalists, was a vulture who profited from other people's pain. In addition, he had tried to arrest him for a crime he didn't commit. Jon, for his part, thought Atherton was a grumpy son of a bitch who was too much like his own dad for comfort.

But he was Jon's closest contact in the Metropolitan Police.

'That dog is still ugly as hell,' Atherton said by way of greeting.

Girl, undeterred by the insult, wagged her tail and panted at the police detective.

'Pint of Best and a packet of salt and vinegar,' said Atherton. Jon left Girl tethered to a chair and went to the bar. When he got back, Atherton was begrudgingly scratching her behind an ear and Girl looked as if she were in heaven.

'I've seen prettier faces on dead rats,' said Atherton, accepting his pint and crisps.

'Thanks for agreeing to meet with me,' Jon said.

'I just saw you a few days ago.' They'd met in the hallway of New Scotland Yard, as Jon was leaving from being questioned about discovering the bodies in the park, and Atherton was beginning his day at work.

'Yes, but unofficially. Off the record. I appreciate it.'

'I'm hoping it's because you have some further information for me.' Atherton took a slurp of his pint.

'I don't know anything about the park murders, other than what I said in my statement.'

'If you're looking for information from *me*, you can look somewhere else. The park murders aren't my case.'

'It's about a different case. And this is weird, so bear with me.'

As Atherton steadily made his way through his pint, Jon told him about the disappearing severed head photos on his phone.

'So let me get this right,' Atherton said. 'The photos are gone, and you're not sure if they're genuine?'

'The other photos, of Cyril's victims and Fanducci, are genuine. I could have taken them myself.'

'Did you?'

If he'd had the presence of mind, he might have. But he told the truth: 'No. I was too busy being scared shitless.'

'So you're suggesting there's a leak somewhere within the Met. Or that someone in the Met sent them to you?'

'I don't know. And I don't know if I could tell you, even if I did. Even though I'm not podcasting, they're still anonymous information to a journalist from a source.' Not for the first time,

Jonathan wished that his previous contact at the Met, DCI Harrison, hadn't retired and moved to Melbourne. 'What I really wanted to do was tip you off that there's another severed head out there.'

'Maybe. In a photograph that no longer exists, taken in a place we can't verify, at a time we can't verify. That severed head, if it's real, could be in Kazakhstan. Which is way out of my remit.'

Jon pushed over a piece of paper. 'I've written down a description of the man.'

Atherton glanced at it and accepted it. 'Missing persons appeals turn up anything?'

'I didn't look.'

'You didn't do even a basic search?'

'No. You warned me off doing investigations, remember?'

Atherton grunted. 'You mean that instead of getting off your own arse, you'd rather that the Met wasted the time and manpower to substantiate a very shadowy rumour.'

'I'm not involved in true crime any more.'

He half-snorted a laugh. 'Oh that's right. These days you leave your crime scenes up to Ugly the Wonder Dog.'

Jon opened his mouth to defend Girl, but she didn't seem to be offended and besides, for Atherton, this was practically bonhomie. He was usually much more rude.

'I did speak to Cyril Walker.'

Now Atherton looked interested. 'Was it one of his?'

'He insists it wasn't, and I believe him.'

'What did he say?'

Now was the time for Jonathan to pass on the name that Cyril had given him. Tony Jones, the stalker. That was why he'd asked Atherton to meet. So he could pass on information to the police, like a normal person, and then go blithely on his way and leave it behind.

Instead, he replied, 'Cyril said he wasn't his type.'

'That man is a sick son of a bitch.'

Jonathan couldn't disagree with that. What he didn't know was why he'd just failed to tell Atherton about Cyril's ID. Or why he had a strong compulsion to change the subject.

'Actually,' said Jon, 'when I received the email, for a split second, I wondered if you'd sent it.'

'Why would it be me? Oh, wait, I know – because I needed some help, because the Met can't solve murders without you.'

'Because you knew Cyril would talk to me.'

'Interesting theory.'

'By the way, Cyril also hinted that he had more victims out there.'

'Oh, I'm sure he does. Did he hint at who, or where we'd find them?'

'No. He's planning to use them as leverage.'

'What an arsehole.' Atherton drained his pint and held out his hand. 'Give over your phone, I've got some bods who can try to find the photograph.'

By instinct, Jon reached for his pocket. Then he remembered the photos he'd taken in the park while he was waiting for the police to arrive.

'I left it at home,' he lied.

'We're not interested in your sexting or whatever. We're not allowed to dig around in your private life. We'll only look for this deleted photograph, with permission of course.'

'I understand, but I honestly don't have my phone with me.' Inwardly he prayed that no one would choose this moment to ring him. 'I can drop it in the next few days.'

'I can get a warrant if that makes the decision easier for you.'

'I'll drop it,' Jon repeated.

'Great.' Atherton stood and shoved the last handful of crisps into his mouth. 'Try not to find any corpses for a while, eh?'

'I'll do my best,' said Jon.

'Do better than that.' Atherton brushed dog hair off his trouser leg and strode out of the pub.

Chapter Twenty-Four

I pause outside Liza Chessington's office, which is in a magnificent brick building on Harley Street. According to the brass plaque outside, she shares the building with a plethora of other people. She's the only one without a 'Dr' in front of her name. However, there are several sets of letters after her name on the plaque, none of which have a meaning that is obvious to me.

Inside, the lobby is floored in marble and everything is painted in Bone by Farrow & Ball. I check in with the receptionist, who is nearly invisible behind several pots of magnificent orchids, and take a lift up to the top storey, where I check in with a second receptionist and take a seat. Liza Chessington's waiting room is empty except for me. This room is painted in Cabbage White by Farrow & Ball, and furnished with austerely modern wooden chairs and a series of large framed posters on the walls. Each of these contains a quote or an aphorism, printed in bright block letters. While I wait I read them, though they aren't exactly *War and Peace* so it doesn't take me long.

JULIE MAE COHEN

ACCEPT WHO YOU ARE.

DON'T WAIT. THE TIME WILL NEVER BE JUST RIGHT.

THE ONLY LIMITS WE HAVE ARE THE LIMITS WE BELIEVE.

YOUR FANTASIES ARE REALITIES WAITING TO HAPPEN.

None of the quotes have citations, so I assume this implies that Liza Chessington is the author of all of them.

How did I get here? More importantly, *why* did I come here, to the office of my sister's favourite TikTok obsession?

The practical answer is that Liza Chessington, whose schedule is full until midway through the twenty-first century, mentioned a last-minute cancellation in one of her stories and I happened to be online at the time and I messaged her to book it, on a whim.

The real answer is that I was online at the time because I was in my bed, alone. And I was in bed, alone, because Jonathan and I spent last night sitting on the sofa together, eating his latest batch of sourdough cinnamon buns, cuddling and watching television. And not even true crime documentaries, for the pointers. No, we watched a show where real human beings competed to turn a lump of clay into a pot that is so satisfying that it will make one of the celebrity judges cry. And then we kissed sweetly goodnight and went to our separate beds.

I know. What's next? Will I take up needlepoint and start making sandwiches? Will Jonathan buy a pair of comfy slippers?

The most worrying part of all of this was that I quite enjoyed it.

'Ms Huntley-Oliver?' says the receptionist, and she nods to a plain ash door.

When I open it, I'm greeted by a rush of glossy hair and essential oils and cleavage. 'Saffy,' gushes the person I assume is Liza Chessington, as she kisses me on both cheeks and takes me by both hands and beams into my face. 'It is so good to meet you. I'm so excited for the journey we are going to take together. Come in, come in. Please make yourself comfortable. Choose a sofa.'

She gestures to three love seats arranged in a loose triangle. One is upholstered in an aubergine leather, one is covered in soft grey tweed, and the other is dusky rose velvet. I choose the velvet, placing my handbag beside me, and Liza claps her hands twice in something like ecstasy.

'Good choice, good choice,' she says.

'I didn't know it was a test,' I say.

'Everything's a test.'

'Did I pass?'

'With flying colours. This is what I call my vulva sofa. It's designed to be attuned to your yonic energy. The divine feminine, which exists independent of physical being. It's particularly powerful in you.'

'Thank you!' I say, matching her energy, while wondering how much of this I can take before I have to go kill someone. 'I suppose I do feel extra feminist today.'

Liza surprises me by bursting into laughter.

'You think this is total bullshit,' she says.

'Well. I didn't want to be rude, but yes. And the idea of a vulva sofa is quite off-putting. It's like the upholstery should be moist.'

'Good. I love a woman who knows her own mind. Well, Saffy, this is a great start. With any therapeutic journey, it's important that you feel free to take what you need, and leave the rest. We can only change what we're ready to change.'

'Actually,' I say, 'I'm not crazy keen to change myself. I like myself a lot already just as I am. I made an appointment with you because I'd like some relationship pointers.'

Liza sits in what I assume is her divine therapist chair, which is a black leather Philippe Starck. She crosses her legs and clasps her hands on her lap. She looks exactly the same as she does on TikTok, which is surprising because I thought nobody looked exactly the same as they do on TikTok. I'm wondering if she uses fillers, and if so, which, when she asks, 'What do you feel are the sticky points in your relationship?'

Now, I have a confession to make: I have never been in any sort of therapy before.

Arguably, I should have been in full-time therapy from about the age of six, but my stepfather never considered it for obvious reasons, because he was the cause of all of my problems. After he died, my guardians just didn't take that much of an interest. I went off to boarding school and channelled all my emotions into team sports, looking out for my sister, and nurturing my homicidal tendencies.

One time when I was twelve, not long after Harold died, the well-meaning matron of my boarding house asked me to her study for tea and tried to have a heart-to-heart with me about how I felt about being an orphan.

Even at that age I was a very good liar. I felt fine about being an orphan, seeing as I had been the one to bump Harold off, but I knew better than to say that. No one who had lost three parents was supposed to be fine with it, even if it did mean that their parents' deaths had provided them with a personal fortune that would sustain several nations.

I cried and I said I missed my mother. And how horrible it had been to discover Harold's body. And how I worried about what would become of us, and how I had resolved to protect my sister so that she would never have to worry about anything. (The last point was true – if you have to tell bald-faced lies, it's always good to throw in a soupçon of truth to make it more convincing.)

Anyway, I must have been very convincing, because one night not long after I broke into Matron's study and read her notes about me. *Seraphina is coping well*, she had written. *Although she is understandably sad, she is emotionally mature and optimistic for the future. With appropriate nurturing to support her grieving, I believe she will adjust to her new normal.*

(The 'appropriate nurturing' remark was how I knew that I could get away with absolutely anything, including permission to skip lessons, extra days of holiday to visit my sister, and repeated uniform violations. All of these were necessary, especially the latter, because the uniform for that school was a horrific shade of puke green, which did not flatter my complexion at *all*.)

This conversation with Matron was my one foray into anything like therapy because, frankly, I am the sanest person that I have ever met.

Liza Chessington is gazing at me with a face full of what I assume is compassion and interest. 'Let me assure you,' she says, 'that everything that you say here will be kept in the strictest confidence. There is no feeling that is wrong, or secret that is too dark. This is a judgement-free zone.'

Somehow, I don't believe that Liza would be judgement-free if I admitted how many corpses I have created. However, I do want relationship help so I stick with the truth on this limited topic.

'I've got this really hot boyfriend, but we don't seem to be able to have sex with each other.'

'And you want to have sex with him?'

'In the worst way. I keep on ruining pairs of silk underwear.'

'So what's stopping you?'

'When we first started seeing each other, he was recovering from a bad break-up and he couldn't even kiss me without thinking about his ex.'

'Rough.'

'Right? Especially, and I don't mean to brag or compare, because the heart wants what the heart wants, but she was a very basic brunette. But he's over that now, I think. Well ... mostly.'

'OK, he's got baggage. Everyone does. What else?'

'Then he had an injury that he had to recover from, so that took a little while. Then, once he healed sufficiently, one night we were about to go for it, literally one inch away from the deed, and his dog pissed on the floor.'

'I see.'

'And then we tried again last weekend, but he was feeling insecure, I think.'

'How did that manifest?'

'He picked a fight with me.'

'Hmm.'

'We made up, but since then ... we've only been cuddling. Which is nice, but I would very much like to see him naked.'

Liza is looking thoughtful. She has produced a pen from somewhere, perhaps her bra, and is tapping her lips with it.

'What I'm hearing is – and correct me if I've got this wrong – that something external keeps on getting in the way of the two of you being intimate?'

'Yes.'

'And that something external is always his fault?'

I sit back on the vulva couch and consider. 'I hadn't looked at it that way, but ... yeah.'

Wow! This is worth the substantial consultation fee already!

'So you're saying that our lack of a sex life is because of him, not me?' I say eagerly.

'Let's explore that idea a little. What do you think that would mean?'

'Maybe ... maybe I've chosen wrong.'

'Why did you choose him?'

'Because he's hot, and he's clever, and we have a lot in common. And he's also a really good person.'

'These sound like good reasons for choosing someone.'

'Yes, but maybe that's not what I actually need. Maybe what I should have been looking for all along was a man who is both pretty and stupid, who will ravish me senseless and not have to think so deeply about everything.'

'Does that appeal to you?'

I screw up my face. 'I've tried it. There's something missing.'

'Why?'

'Because ... I want a boyfriend. Someone I can connect with on the same level. Not a fuck machine. Though a little bit of fuck machining would be very welcome.'

Liza nods. I was wrong: on TikTok she looks like a complete flake but in person there's something about her, something expansive and wise. I don't know that I've ever had anyone listen to me so deeply. Then again, I am honest with very few people.

'What I'm hearing,' she says, 'is that you often find relationships disappointing. Is this correct?'

'Absolutely!' I say with feeling. 'I'd stopped dating altogether before I became interested in Jonathan. It just didn't seem worth it.'

'Have you ever had a romantic relationship that you felt entirely happy with, while it lasted?'

'No, I can't say that I have.'

She leans forward, her elbows on her knees, hands clasped in front of her. 'And what do you think is the common denominator in all of these relationships?'

That's easy.

'*Men*,' I say. 'The common denominator is that I am a heterosexual woman and therefore I have no choice but to date my own worst enemy. If I were a lesbian, life would be easier.'

'I hear that fairly often from straight women,' says Liza gently. 'But it's not easier for lesbians.'

'Yes, fair enough, I was being glib. I take that back. At least as a heterosexual woman I'm not subject to homophobia as well, or the added strain of being a woman who by nature opposes patriarchal norms. I have a huge amount of privilege, in so many ways, and being straight is just one of those privileges. Plus, I'm sure lesbians have their own relationship issues. But being attracted to men is objectively terrible. I would choose the bear, but I don't want to have sex with bears. I want to have sex with men.'

'So you're saying that the thing that all of your failed relationships have in common, is that you had them with men?'

'Yes.'

'Even though you have no desire to have relationships with women?'

'Right.'

'Do you think there's something else in common?'

The other obvious common factor is that none of the people I've had romantic relationships with are murderers. Only a murderer could really share my interests in a wholehearted – or should I say, full-blooded – way.

But the problem is that male murderers are, by any definition, bad men, and I kill bad men, so dating a murderer would be a crackling conflict of interest layered on top of a whole lot of juicy ethical dilemmas and it seems healthier to steer clear of that whole pastry.

'What do you think?' prompts Liza.

I can't tell her what I've been thinking, so I say, 'What do you think? You're the love guru.'

She clicks her tongue and rearranges herself on her chair so she is sitting cross-legged, back straight, arms open. Like a guru, in fact.

'I think,' she says, 'that the common denominator in all of your relationships is you.'

'Well. Yes.'

I was a little worried that she could read my mind, so I'm relieved that it's something so obvious and non-violent.

'Do you accept that?' she asks.

'Of course.'

'So what are the implications?'

'That I keep on choosing the wrong man?'

'Maybe. And we can definitely spend some time exploring why you choose the partners you do and how you can make better, more aware choices. But you came here to work out how to make your intimate relationship with Jonathan better, right? I don't think you're ready to jettison your relationship with him and choose someone else, at least not right now. You want to focus on this one.'

'I do really like Jonathan. More than I've liked anyone, maybe ever.'

'That's great. So let's pause for a moment and think about you.'

'You think something's wrong with me?'

'I don't like to use value judgements like that. And feelings are never wrong. They just *are*. They exist. We can't choose how we feel, but we can feel our choices, you know?'

'Hmm,' I say.

Usually I am ten steps ahead of everyone in the room, and right now I am not. I don't like it.

'I'm going to suggest, very gently here,' Liza says, 'that if you're not finding the intimacy you want, that you consider that you might be blocking *yourself*.'

'How?'

'I think it's interesting that you mentioned the meme of choosing the bear. I hear a lot of that discourse all over social media and it's a way for women to talk about male toxicity, but there's a deeper truth beneath the surface, which is that this metaphor is actually about fear.'

'I'm not afraid of men. I'm a strong woman. I can take them.'

'That's good. But the thing is, Saffy, that to be intimate with someone – truly intimate with someone – you have to be vulnerable to them. And being vulnerable is scary.'

Liza reaches over and takes my hand in both of hers. She looks into my eyes.

'What are you afraid of, Saffy? Not the bear, not men. What are you *really* afraid of?'

I pull my hand away and stand up from the vulva couch. 'I'm not afraid of anything. This is ridiculous!'

Liza just watches me. For the first time I notice how irritating and smug her face is.

'I'm not scared of having sex with Jonathan. I came here because I *want* to have sex with him!'

'The bear tells us that we're attracted to what we fear.'

I am speechless, and that takes a lot. I'm tempted to brain her with a paperweight or something, but that goes against everything I believe in.

I'm not afraid of Jonathan. If anything, Jonathan should be afraid of *me*.

'I think we'll leave it there for now,' says Liza, serene. 'I'll see you next week, same time.'

Chapter Twenty-Five

I'M WATCHING SIR THOMAS AGAIN, and this time I'm furious.

His town house is in Hackney, a three-storey Victorian terrace that he bought in the 1970s when his TV career was taking off and which has since grown astronomically in value. The media uses this as evidence of his down-to-earthness, conveniently forgetting that he has several other properties and that since Sir Thomas bought this house, the area has become gentrified and this particular house has become rather grand. It's been gutted and completely renovated, including adding a state-of-the-art home security system and a basement swimming pool.

The house is also almost equidistant from two primary schools, one at each end of the street.

The house backing onto Sir Thomas's has been on the market for months. It's overpriced, if you ask me, but then again I would not pay to live in Hackney among all the hipsters. Anyway, it is vacant and has a poorly lit side entrance. It's also unfurnished, so I make sure to pack a folding camping chair along with my binoculars.

The best view is from the roof. It's easily accessible through the skylight and there's a flat area that's big enough to set up the camping chair. From here, you can see the whole of Sir Thomas's garden and the back of his house. He rarely draws the blinds on this side, so there's a great view of his kitchen, living room, study, and bedroom.

What a trusting soul he is. You would think he had nothing to hide.

Except, of course, for the multiple alarms on his doors and windows, and the bodyguard who shadows him in public. All of this is indication that he has a *lot* to hide.

The only way I could kill Sir Thomas from here would be with a rifle with a long-distance scope and the aiming skill of a sniper. I currently possess neither of these things. So this is more of a surveillance mission than a murder mission.

But it makes me feel better to know what he's doing. That there are no children in his house with him.

I set up my lightweight chair. On rainy nights, I sometimes bring a golf umbrella. But tonight is clear. I train my binoculars on Sir Thomas's bedroom – I always look in the bedroom first – but it's unlit and the bed looks empty, so I scan down to the study and living room, which have lights on but are also empty. What a profligate waster of electricity he is, this national treasure.

He's in his kitchen, wearing an apron. It looks like he's alone. I settle in to watch him. He's mixing something in a bowl. Boring. It's no distraction at all from thinking about my session with Liza Chessington this afternoon.

That woman is so full of bullshit. First off, who would trust someone whose office was papered with meaningless social media slogans and equipped with furniture symbolising genitalia?

Second, what did she mean that the common denominator in my failed relationships was me? I am a psychopath, sure. I have no fear of danger, don't believe that rules apply to me, and have trouble curbing my blood lust.

But my love for Susie – and the fact, by the way, that I haven't killed her boyfriend out of love for her – prove that I have feelings like normal people, and therefore I can have a functional adult relationship.

So the problem can't be me. I am *not* the problem.

Sir Thomas starts measuring flour and sugar. He's baking a cake. What a wholesome chap. God, I hate him so much. I hope he chokes on his batter. I hope he mixes in some botulism. I hope he slips on a bit of butter and cracks his skull open.

No, I don't hope any of that. I want to kill him with my own hands, not watch as he dies of an accident. I *deserve* to kill him. And I want him to see me and know why I'm doing what I'm doing.

'What are you *really* afraid of?' Liza asked me.

I'm not afraid.

I'm never afraid.

Why should I be afraid?

In the kitchen, Sir Thomas looks like he's singing as he pours batter into pans. He's an old man. He's got wrinkles, grey hair, age-spotted hands, sinewy arms, eyes that are starting to be clouded by cataracts. He isn't physically strong. He has heart disease. In the natural course of things, he probably has ten years left at most.

I'm not afraid of him.

But yes, I am afraid of something.

Chapter Twenty-Six

I LIED A LITTLE BIT EARLIER, when I said that I never allowed my lovers to stay overnight in my bed.

I did, once. It was about eight years ago. He was called Manuel and he was heir to a Spanish weedkiller empire. He was also an ultra-marathon runner. He had a lanky, sinewy body without a spare bit of flesh, the kind of body where you could see delicious hints of his skeleton underneath. He had a big cock that looked even bigger because the rest of his body was so spare. He wasn't very clever and he wasn't really interested in anything except for ultra-marathons, which made him incredibly boring and also easy to date because he had no interest in settling down and making babies or controlling my life whatsoever. Going out with him made me look normal.

Manuel was very good at energetic, athletic sex. Being in bed with him was a full-body workout. My core and my pelvic floor have never been stronger. However, it was exhausting even for someone like me, who's used to extremes of physical exertion from lugging around dead bodies, etc., so one Saturday night after a particularly strenuous bout of sex, swimming in oxytocin from several orgasms, I fell asleep.

I was awakened sometime later by a hand closing around my breast and an erection poking at my buttock. It was Manuel, of course – he also had a phenomenal recovery time. But half-asleep in the darkness, still in the middle of whatever dream I was having, I did not recognise him. I reacted without thinking.

I pushed him over onto his back, ripped the cord of my bedside lamp from its socket, whipped it around his neck, and pulled it tight.

He was stronger than I was. He could have fought me off. But I'd taken him by surprise, as much as he'd taken me by surprise, and he lost the valuable seconds between my starting to strangle him and the oxygen being cut off from his brain. He thrashed around, eyes bulging, mouth choking for air, and before I could realise how monumentally stupid it was to kill a man in my own bed, he was dead.

No. That's not true. I'm glossing over it, again.

It takes longer than you might think to strangle a man, and time moves more slowly in these situations anyway. I realised my mistake long before Manuel lost consciousness.

I knew that he wasn't a rapist or a murderer or a wife-beater. The worst thing he had done was not explicitly ask for the consent that I would have gladly given him.

But I kept strangling him anyway, until he stopped choking and thrashing, until his limbs went limp and his erection fell dead, until he soiled my sheets, until his heart stopped, until his eyes glazed, until his brain was a lump of useless tissue, until his skin was starting to cool.

Because he had frightened me and that meant he deserved to die.

Chapter Twenty-Seven

Is that what I'm afraid of? Do I think if I get intimate with Jonathan, I will kill him by mistake?

He doesn't deserve to die. He's a good man. He cares about humans and animals. He's funny and cute and smart and modest. He's helped a lot of victims and he's also stopped killers before they hurt any more women.

But let's be real here. I don't want to kill Jonathan, because I like him. But if I have to, I will.

That's always been the deal, in my head anyway. I have a somewhat relativistic view of life and death, compared to most people, and innocent people sometimes are collateral damage.

I don't think that the fear of killing Jonathan has stopped me from being intimate with him. If that were the case, I never would have had sex with a man ever in my life and I would be resigned to the life of a homicidal nun with only my vibrator for company.

It might be deeper than that: by which I mean more selfish.

I care about Jonathan. And if I have to kill someone I care about, I'll have to suffer the pain that my victims' families go through.

I'm not a fool. I know that almost everyone is loved by someone. I know that even though they are terrible human beings, the men I kill have women who love them. Mothers, sisters, daughters, girlfriends, wives. Even if it's only the senile old lady they've been stealing pension money from in order to spend on drugs.

I think about Mandy Brett, the abused wife who didn't want to leave her husband, Chad, who I pushed off a roof in New York, years ago. Women stick with the men who abuse them, because they love them. And although they're better off without them, it still hurts if they're gone.

Bad men cause pain. But death causes pain too. In some ways, the men who I kill are the lucky ones.

I cause pain. And not the fun kind. The mourning, grief-crazy, howling-in-agony kind.

I don't want to go through that any more than I want to repeatedly slam my fingers in a car door.

So killing Jonathan would be a lose/lose proposition. Maybe that's why I'm scared of getting too close. I don't want to hurt him, and I don't want to hurt me.

* * *

Sir Thomas has finished baking. He's removed the cakes from the layer pans and left them to cool on the counter, presumably to ice tomorrow. He's washed his hands and turned off the lights in the kitchen. I watch as the lights go out in the living room, and then in the study as he climbs the stairs. The bedroom light snaps on. He disappears into his ensuite bathroom, which I can't see into as it's got frosted windows, but I can see his silhouette moving around in there, vaguely, like a ghost. After an interval that light goes off too and he emerges, in burgundy pyjamas. He climbs into his bed and turns off the light.

It's all dark. He's all alone. There's nothing to see tonight. I came here for nothing.

Sighing, I stand up, stretch, and begin folding up my camping chair. It's then that I spot something that I haven't noticed before, because I've been so focused on watching Sir Thomas and searching my own soul.

In the corner where the flat roof section meets the main slope of the roof, there is something that gleams white in the darkness. Closer, I can see that it is a white Pot Noodle container. It's empty, it smells of curry, and it has a metal spoon in it.

This was not here the last time I was here.

I do not eat Pot Noodle.

* * *

Sir Thomas isn't going anywhere and I'm not ready to go home just yet, so on a whim I catch a bus headed towards Limehouse. I love driving in London – it is so deliciously homicidal – but on occasion I enjoy public transport, especially the top deck of a bus. I find a seat near the back, comfortably apart from the only other passenger up here, and I settle down to think.

Someone else is using my Sir Thomas-stalking spot on the roof. They could be birdwatchers, but birdwatchers don't generally break into empty houses. Perhaps they are the sort of person who enjoys a quiet evening of burglary, stargazing, and junk food. Maybe they're the jealous ex-partner of one of Sir Thomas's neighbours.

But Occam's razor suggests that the simplest answer is the true one: someone else is watching Sir Thomas. Who is it? Is it paparazzi? A crazed fan? Someone with a crush (ew)?

Or is it another vigilante?

The thought gives me simultaneous feelings of pleasure and of irritation. It's nice to think there's someone out there who shares my values. On the other hand, Sir Thomas is mine. I've got plans for him. OK, I haven't been able to put any of them into practice yet, but I will. I'm biding my time. And it will be annoying if someone else gets there first. After all this effort, I want to see the dying light in Sir Thomas's eyes, and for him to know exactly why he's under my knife.

I'm after justice, not a cheap thrill.

I resolve to arm myself before I go up to my hiding place next time, and to be extra vigilant. If this person, whoever they are, is leaving empty Pot Noodle pots in their super-secret observation spot, they're not worried about being caught, which means they don't know that I've been using this spot too. The last thing I want is to be taken by surprise.

Anyway, this introduces a new complication to my hunt.

I sigh, resting my head on the bus window, and think about the days when killing used to be so easy and fun, and I was merely a carefree slip of a monster, blithely dispensing of bad men in between one social event and the next, leaving a trail of bodies in my wake with nary a care in the world.

And I'm getting that wrinkle in my forehead. Against my better judgement, I feel it with my finger. Right there between my brows. Is this what getting older is all about?

A group of young girls come onto the bus and climb noisily up to the top deck, where they populate the first two seats, laughing and passing their phones back and forth. I watch them as they loudly play videos to each other and pose for selfies. They're about fifteen or sixteen, all wearing short skirts, heels and crop tops, straightened hair and lip gloss, pouting at the camera with their perfect skin and abundance of collagen and filtering the photos anyway.

The patriarchy would have you believe that women are always seething with jealousy of each other: that we're bitches, we're crones, we're avaricious balls of envy. Poor women hate rich women, white women hate Black women, gay women hate straight women, cis women hate trans women, old women hate young women. But that's not the natural way of things at all. It's a ploy. Men in power would like women to compete with each other and see each other as rivals for a tiny slice of advantage, because it stops us from working together to gain our own power.

Feminists know that the only way to lift up one woman is to lift up *all* women, even if they're different from you. So even though I've been sitting here thinking about getting older, and even though these teenage girls are objectively a bit of a noise nuisance, I watch them with fondness. Because this is what being a young girl should be about: fooling around with your friends, making noise, squealing and shouting and being your vibrant, beautiful young self.

I smile, watching them. It gives me a little glow of happiness on their behalf. *This* is what I'm fighting for.

I wasn't like that, by the way. I had so-called girlfriends and I hung out with them and squealed and giggled and traded gossip, but in my case, it was all pretend. It was an elaborate act to fit in. I never shared any of my real secrets. Still, it was nice to be part of something, even if only on the surface. Maybe I should go back to one of those school reunions I've started getting emails about.

The girls are all gathered around one seat, watching something on one girl's phone and exclaiming. The man who was seated in the middle of the bus quietly gets up. I expect him to go downstairs to get away from the chatter, but instead he changes seats, so he's only across the aisle and a few rows back. As I watch, he extends his phone into the aisle and tilts it so it's facing upwards towards the girls, who are bending over their friend's phone.

That slimy collection of tadpoles in an anorak is taking pictures up the girls' skirts.

He's quick with it, too. A real pro. When the girls finish watching their videos and go back to their own seats, he whips his phone back into his pocket and stares out the window as if he never had a filthy thought in his life. He hasn't noticed me, though. Noticing him.

The girls all trundle off the bus in a whirl of joyous hysteria and pound-shop perfume, oblivious to all the nastiness in the world, not a metre away from them. That's how it should be. I'm ready to follow the pervert as he follows the girls, but he stays put in his seat, so I do too. He doesn't press the stop button until we're in Mile End.

I descend after him and follow at a safe distance.

He's scrolling his phone as he walks. Just like people tell women not to do. Women should be aware at all times, especially at night. We should keep our phones in our pockets and constantly survey our surroundings so we can prevent ourselves being attacked and raped. Men, on the other hand, can look at their phones whenever they want. Flitting through photos of teenage girls' underwear. Thinking about getting home and wanking to images of their smooth thighs.

He turns along the side of a church, under the shadow of a crumbling brick wall. It's a bit of a safety hazard, here in London where anyone could trip on a brick. I pick one up.

'Excuse me,' I call. 'Sir? I think you dropped something.'

He turns around. I keep the brick in my left hand behind my back. My gloved right hand holds an object out towards him. It glints in the darkness.

'Huh?' he says. He takes a few steps closer, within arm's reach. He smells strongly of sweat and onions. 'What's that?'

'Don't worry, it's just a spoon,' I say, and swiftly stab the sharp handle end into his eye.

Liquid splashes my hand – it's dark so I can't tell whether it's blood or aqueous humour from inside his eye. I've really never killed anyone this way before so it's all a bit of a unknown journey, what fun! – but I keep pushing. The pervert chokes on his scream, staggers backwards, hands flying to his face.

Apparently a Pot Noodle spoon in the eye hurts quite a bit but it is something less than lethal, so I'm grateful for my brick. I push upskirt pervert man with all my strength and he falls backwards and lands heavily on his back on the ground. Then I'm on top of him, using the brick to pound the spoon deeper into his brain.

Will he die, or will he merely be lobotomised? Like I said, it's an unknown journey, but what a delightful one! It just goes to prove that you're never too old to learn new things.

He starts spasming, arms and legs jerking and his hands and feet drumming the ground. His phone's fallen out of his hand and out of the corner of my eye I can see I was right – he was surveying his stolen booty as he walked. Ugh. Gross.

I give the spoon another pound. By now the bowl's almost to the place where his eye used to be. That's pretty far into his brain.

As an aside, I've read a few articles on the subject, and it appears more medical lobotomies have been performed on women than on men. Isn't that interesting, how our society likes to control women by literally removing part of their minds?

Eventually he stops jerking around, his mouth starts leaking blood, and he stops breathing.

I climb off and pick up his phone to chuck into the canal.

What a lark! It's been a day of intense emotions. It turns out that unknown person who left me the spoon was doing me a favour.

I feel much better now. Youth and optimism restored.

Chapter Twenty-Eight

STOP THINKING ABOUT BODY PARTS AND
START THINKING ABOUT THE PERSON
WHO OWNS THEM.

Because it turned out that Liza was right about my being afraid, my faith in her has been bolstered. I've been watching the videos that Susie sends me again. This week, Liza's lessons are all about intimacy.

'We all use the word "intimacy" when we're talking about sex, but real intimacy doesn't have to be about bodies at all,' she says to the camera, as she walks along a golden beach lined with palm trees. Either she films these videos in advance, or she literally jetted off to the Caribbean right after I left her office. 'Real intimacy, *true* intimacy, is about opening up your mind to another person. It's about sharing emotions and interests and time together. When you're truly intimate with someone, you can find their mind as much of a turn-on as their body. Maybe even more.'

The lesson I take from this is that Jonathan and I need to get to know each other better.

It's true; you can live with someone and be a stranger to them. The two of us have been sharing the same space for weeks now. I know what he likes for breakfast (black coffee and toast with peanut butter); I know when he likes to shower (first thing in the morning, so he appears for breakfast all clean and smelling yummy); I know whether he snores (I listened at his door – he doesn't); I know what tune he hums under his breath when he thinks no one is listening (Mozart's Symphony No. 40 in G Minor – the man is a continual delight).

However. There's so much I don't really know about him.

He doesn't talk about his childhood, though to be fair, neither do I. I know more than I want to about his marriage, but not much about his other relationships. I haven't met any of his friends, unless you count the time that I stalked his ex-wife or the time that DI Atherton came to my house looking to arrest him. We haven't had any late-night philosophical debates about religion or philosophy. If you were going to make a montage of our time together – like the ones they have in romcoms, where the couple is holding hands and laughing while they go around a fairground or whatever – ours would involve more blood than balloons and more corpses than carousels.

Because that's the tricky bit, isn't it? I'd love to know everything about Jonathan, but I can only tell him so much about myself. I mean, out loud. In words.

However, I've done a bit of research and discovered the whole concept of 'love languages'. It's refreshing to be able to do an internet search that wouldn't be flagged by the police, and I learned quite a bit. Some people show love with physical touch; some show love with words of affirmation; some with gifts. I did a few online quizzes and found that my love language is acts of service. I like doing things for the people I care about.

So, to that end, and in the interests of trying to get to know each other better, I knock on Jonathan's bedroom door bright and early in the morning.

Girl barks and I hear some quiet conversation behind the door. When he opens it, he's wearing pyjama bottoms, no top, and he's just putting on his glasses.

I take a moment to soak in the sight. And then, when I drag my gaze to his face, I realise that he is looking a little bit guilty, like I've caught him doing something.

'Did I interrupt you?' I ask.

'No, no, not at all.' Though I notice that he is standing in the doorway with the door pulled behind him, blocking my view of what used to be my guest room. What's he hiding? I hope it's bed sheets rumpled from a morning wank as he thinks about everything he'd like to do to me. 'You look nice,' he says.

I'm wearing a light and flowing frock, and I look better than nice, but I peck him on the cheek, inhaling the scent of sleepy man, and say, 'Do you have plans today?'

'Not at the moment.'

'Good. Then get dressed, because Susie's coming over in an hour to take the dog for the day and I'm going to take you out.' He is still looking a little shifty and worried, so I add, 'No fancy galas or anything. I fancy a nice drive in the countryside, and I've got us a picnic.'

'Oh! That sounds good. OK, I'll ... give me a minute.'

He closes the door again and I hear him speaking to Girl. I can't make out what he's saying, though, and I definitely can't make out her response, so I give up and go to ring the garage to bring my car round.

A Mercedes sedan is all well and good in the city, where you want to ride in comfort and transport bodies with little fanfare or suspicion, but when you're hitting the back roads, you want something light and stylish that handles like a dream. I'm loading the picnic into the tiny boot of my BMW convertible Z4 when Jonathan emerges from the house.

'I like this car,' he says, laying a hand on its gleaming flank. 'Is it fast?'

'Fast, beautiful, and thrilling. Just like me. Get in.' I wink.

As soon as we hit the motorway and I'm able to put my foot down a little, he cheers up even more. By the time we're zooming along B-roads, fresh air streaming by us, he's positively beaming. My hair is tied back in a silk scarf, my eyes shielded by large sunglasses; he's got the top buttons of his shirt open and his hair is adorably ruffled. You'd think we were on our way to Monaco, not buzzing around Berkshire.

'This is fun,' Jonathan says as we take a corner at speed, and then have to slow down to follow a tractor. 'The fastest car I've ever owned was a Mini.'

'What kind of Mini?'

'A Rover Mini Mayfair. 1.5cc engine. It drove like a very tiny rocket out of hell, but I think it felt faster than it actually was. And if you had more than one passenger, it struggled to get up a hill.'

'Did you ever snog someone in the back seat?'

'I did more than snog someone in that back seat. Fortunately I was young and I didn't do myself any lasting damage.'

'I like hearing about your life,' I tell him. 'I feel like we should get to know each other better.'

'I agree.' He smiles over at me. 'I want to know everything about you.'

'Well, you can ask me any question you want, if I can ask you anything I want.'

'Deal,' he says.

'Who should start?'

'You can.'

'What are you worried about?' I ask him, steering around the tractor and speeding up again on the narrow hedgerow-lined lane.

'Hitting a pheasant?'

'No, I mean . . . what were you worried about when I knocked on your bedroom door this morning?'

'Oh! Just Girl being noisy. I don't want to annoy your neighbours.'

This is obviously not the truth. I fling the car around another blind curve and while he's distracted I say, 'Ever since you had a beer with that Scotland Yard detective, you've seemed preoccupied.'

'I—'

At that exact moment, a fox steps out into the road in front of us.

I brake, hard. Precision German engineering stops the car a bare metre from the animal, who is standing still in the road. Her fur is red and lustrous, her paws and muzzle white. Her yellow eyes blink once. She was seconds from death but now she merely gazes at us.

For a moment, Jonathan and I and the whole world hold our breath.

Then the fox makes her leisurely way across the road and disappears through a gap in the hedge.

'That was close,' Jonathan says.

I start the car again, and begin more slowly down the road. I may have callous disregard for human life, but I like wild animals.

'You haven't answered my question,' I say.

'What was the question?' he says, feigning innocence. It takes more than that to deceive a deceiver.

'Why have you been on another planet since meeting with the detective?'

'Atherton gave me a lot to think about.'

'Like what?'

He doesn't say anything.

'He doesn't suspect you of being involved in the murders in the park, does he?' Just my luck to have a man take the credit for all my hard work, *again*.

'No, nothing like that.'

'Then why are you being so vague?'

Once again he doesn't answer right away, and for the first time it occurs to me: does Atherton suspect me of something? Is that why Jonathan is avoiding discussing his conversation with the detective – because he was being pumped for information?

'He came to my house once,' I say lightly. 'When he was looking for you. He didn't find anything. He didn't strike me as the sharpest tool in the box.'

'Something happened during our conversation,' says Jonathan. 'And it's something I haven't figured out yet. When I work out what I think about it, you'll be the first to know.'

'Can I help you work it out?'

'I think it's something I have to do myself.' He reaches over and squeezes my hand. 'But I will tell you, I promise.'

It is difficult for me, a narcissist, to accept that I can't control everything. But I smile and nod, because a relationship is all about compromises, isn't it?

'My turn for a question,' he says.

'Shoot.'

'Why do you think you're so cagey about your personal life?'

I shoot him a glance as I drive.

'You think I'm cagey?' I ask. 'I thought I was an open book. I go to the gym, I shop, I brunch, I do charity work, I shop some more.'

'It's not a criticism,' he says quickly. 'I respect your need for privacy, especially since we're practically living in each other's laps.'

'I would like to *literally* live in each other's laps, by the way.'

'Noted. But ... and don't take this wrong, Saffy, because I think you're terrific. But I've noticed that you know a lot of people and have an enormous social circle, but you don't seem to be close to any of them.'

'You've seen the people in my social circle.' I shift up to fifth gear. 'Do they seem like warm and fuzzy individuals to you? Or do they seem like piranhas in designer clothing? Always jockeying for position, who's got the most money, the most power, the best clothes, the trophy partner? It's like a Jilly Cooper novel without any of the sex or the plot.'

'I'll admit that it's not a milieu I'm familiar with. But they can't all be terrible. You're one of them, you grew up in that world, and you're not terrible.'

'You haven't seen all of me yet.'

'I know you're not terrible, Saffy. In fact, I know you're pretty wonderful. You're funny and astute, you're generous and kind, you've got a strong moral compass, and you're doing what you can to make the world better.'

'Thank you,' I say humbly, though he is in fact totally correct. Except for the 'kind' part.

'But you don't seem to let anyone in.'

'I let my sister in. In fact sometimes I think I let her too far in. She has opinions about everything from my manicure to my menstrual cycle.'

'Susie aside,' says Jonathan. 'And I know I'm not really one to talk. I'm not much of a warm and fuzzy person, either. I've been too obsessed with my career to get close to people. I have a chip on my shoulder, trying to prove to my dead father that I'm a better person than he was.'

'That's the sort of morbid and impossible goal that I can support.'

'So what's your reason?'

'Aside from my tragic backstory? Father dead, mother dead, stepfather dead, no living relatives, a childhood spent skipping from one boarding school to another at the whim of distant trustees, learning that I can't count on anyone except for myself and my sister?'

He's silent for a moment. 'You know, I googled you, back when we first met.'

'If I recall correctly, I told you to, so you could be sure I wasn't an axe murderer.'

I hardly ever lie, but this is especially not a lie. I have never used an axe.

Yet.

'I dug a bit deeper, not long ago,' he says. 'I found some *New York Times* archives. I read that it was you who discovered your stepfather Harold's body in the family swimming pool.'

'Oh. Well. Yes.'

'I hope you don't mind that I looked.'

'It's a matter of public record. Why should I mind?'

'Well, you never told me. I suspect you haven't told many people.'

'It's not something I like to talk about.'

'If there's anyone who understands what it's like,' he says gently, 'it's me.'

'You've certainly discovered your share of corpses.'

'And that means that any time you want to talk about it, I'm here. About that, about anything.'

I glance over at him. He's watching me with soft eyes, with compassion and care. Somehow, that is the sexiest thing I've ever seen.

'I'm glad we're talking like this,' I say. 'Letting each other in.'

'Me too.'

And I drive on, through the wilds of Berkshire.

Chapter Twenty-Nine

Although Saffy drove like a demon, she was as accurate as an angel. Fresh air ruffled his hair and the sun shone between the trees. Every now and then a leaf fluttered down like a butterfly. None of it was as bright as Saffy's hair.

All of the tension that Jon had been carrying between his shoulder blades seemed to have melted away. On a day like this, in a fast car with a beautiful woman beside him, it was easy to forget his problems.

Well. Except for the latest pair of Saffy's shoes that he had discovered in Girl's mouth this morning. He'd had to wrestle them away from her and hide them, once again under his pillow.

How did the dog even find them? Saffy kept all of her shoes in special shoe racks in the massive walk-in closet in her bedroom, with each pair in a transparent Perspex box. They were arranged alphabetically by designer. Or at least, that was what Saffy had told him; Jon wouldn't know a Prada from a Primark.

Every time Edie rang him, the pre-empt offer had gone up. If he took it, he'd be able to replace all of her shoes and she might never know.

He glanced over at Saffy and smiled. They'd spent a good deal of the drive trading secrets, but they hadn't even touched the sides. Wouldn't it be nice if the only secret between them was about shoes?

Saffy slowed the car and pulled into a drive between two tall sandstone gatehouses. The gate itself was open and festooned with red, white, and blue bunting.

'Where are we?' Jonathan asked.

'It's called Hatherstone House. I wasn't sure whether we'd be able to get in today. But if it was open, I thought it would be a perfect spot for a picnic.'

'National Trust?'

'No, private property. Open to the public once a month or so. It's incredible what my fellow rich people will do for a tax break. Form shell companies, open their homes, suffocate their grandmothers.' She nodded at the lines of Union Jacks, which danced along the long, winding drive. 'Not sure what the patriotism is about, though. Well ... not what it's about today specifically.'

The house came into view: a golden sandstone neoclassical confection of a thing, with Ionic pillars and a wide sweeping lawn, decorated with not one but three fountains shaped like various naked gods. Saffy found a parking spot in a roped-off area and Jon got the picnic hamper, an old-fashioned basket, out of the boot.

'This weighs a ton,' he said.

'It's the solid gold caviar.' Saffy retrieved a blanket, draping it over her arm. 'I hope you like fish eggs.'

'I can't say that I'm a fan.'

'That's good, because I'm lying. We've got hummus sandwiches, grilled artichokes, artisan cheeses, fruit, and sparkling apple juice.' They joined hands and wandered across the lawn towards the house.

'It's quite a place,' said Jon.

'Built in the late eighteenth century, designed by John Carr. The Palladian portico was called "the finest in the south of England". There's a hothouse in the back that's full of rare orchids. All of it built from the proceeds of sugar cane plantations in Barbados.'

'It sounds as if you've been here before.'

'I have. I spent an Easter holiday here once, because I went to boarding school with the daughter of the owner. Who you've met, by the way. Hatherstone House was built by Ranulf Hogg, who was the great-great-grandfather of Sir Rupert Huntington-Hogg. How about under this tree for our picnic?'

It was a spreading beech tree, with a canopy of waving leaves and last year's crunchy beechnut shells underneath. They laid out their blanket and Saffy flung herself down on it, pulling the scarf off her head and shaking loose her hair.

'Huntington-Hogg, the missing MP? This is his house?'

'His ancestral home. He's sure to have another in his constituency clear across the country.'

'You didn't say that you knew him well.' Jon sat down next to her.

'I don't. I went to school with his daughter, Letty. Who hated him. She was the youngest daughter of his first or second wife, I can't keep track, but anyway she had to spend half the holidays with him, or at least inhabiting one of his properties. We spent the entire Easter holidays avoiding him as much as possible, which was easy enough because he was never home. We played croquet, watched movies, and got through a big chunk of his vintage port collection.'

'What's she like?'

'Letty? She was a hoot. She was a communist. She had great plans of inheriting this place and then burning it to the ground. She said it had been built because of the labour of enslaved people on the plantations, and the only way she could expiate the family sin was to wipe the proceeds of it from the earth.' Saffy opened the hamper and took out a bunch of grapes. She broke off a stem and handed it to Jon.

'Are those still her plans?'

'No. She died in a car accident when she was nineteen.' Saffy popped a grape in her mouth. 'If I recall correctly, her father used the tragedy to gain sympathy votes in the general election.'

'Wow.'

'Yeah. Still . . . he's done great things for private equity firms.' Saffy spat a grape seed an impressive distance.

'It sounds as if some of Letty's political ideas rubbed off on you.'

'Meh, I don't care much about politics. It's morals that get me going.'

'Were you close to her?'

'I liked her. I couldn't say we were close.' She nudged him with her foot. 'Like we were saying in the car earlier. It's difficult for me to get close to someone. That's one of the reasons why I brought you here, because you said you'd met Huntington-Hogg. It's something we have in common.'

'I hope it's not all we have in common.' Jon leaned in to kiss her, but before he could, a loud round of applause broke out nearby, and 'Rule Britannia' started playing through a speaker.

They both looked in the direction of the noise. There was a marquee set up on one side of the house. Bunting and Union Jacks fluttered around it, and people were congregating nearby.

'Sounds like something is happening,' said Jon.

'Do you want to go see what it is?'

'Might as well, before we get too distracted.' He helped her up and they followed the crowd.

Chairs had been placed in rows on the lawn under the marquee. Some of the gathered people took seats, but Jon and Saffy stood to one side. 'Do you think we're crashing a wedding?' Jon whispered.

'Not unless that's the cake.' Saffy pointed to the front of the marquee, where a large shape stood, covered by a sheet and surrounded by flowers in red, white, and blue. As they watched, a woman in a blue dress and a hat with a veil approached a lectern next to the shape. A bottle of champagne stood on the lectern next to a microphone. The music came to a triumphant end as the woman took her place.

'Hello,' said the woman tentatively into the mic. She cleared her throat and said, a little more confidently, 'Good afternoon. Thank you for coming. As you – as you know, my husband, Rupert, was meant to be making this speech today. But he – well, I – my children and I hope that he will come home soon.'

She bowed her head. This was evidently the poor abandoned current Mrs Huntington-Hogg. Jon searched the crowd for children, but he didn't see any. At boarding school, most likely, or with their nanny. Some of the audience were dressed up for a reception, but most were wearing casual clothing, as if they'd dropped by like Saffy and himself. There were a few obvious journalists in the front row, flanked by photographers and looking mildly bored.

'She's devastated,' whispered Saffy to him, 'but she's looking well on it.'

Jon noted the woman's perfect makeup, rosy cheeks, and coiffed hair.

'Because of circumstances,' said Mrs Huntington-Hogg, 'we had considered delaying this unveiling ceremony until Rupert could be here in person. But I insisted we go ahead. Rupert would have wanted us to celebrate this tribute to his ancestor Ranulf Hogg, and to remember all of the great work he did in the service of this mighty nation. It's a tradition that my husband is proud to have carried on.'

'It's sounding like an epitaph,' whispered Jon. 'I wonder if she knows something we don't.'

'Has anyone ever told you that you're obsessed with death?'

Jon smiled and put his arm around Saffy's waist. She edged in closer to him and leaned her head on his shoulder.

It was that moment that someone screamed.

Chapter Thirty

Jon broke away from Saffy and instinctively ran towards the source of the scream, to help whoever was in trouble.

He stopped short when he realised there wasn't just one person screaming and wailing; it was a group of them, about a dozen people at the back of the marquee, all of them covered in blood.

It soaked their shirts and trousers, spattered their bare feet. As he watched, the newcomers spread to make a circle around the crowd. He saw that they were wearing chains on their wrists and ankles. But they weren't limping.

'This house was built with human blood!' cried one, a young woman.

'This house was built with blood money!' cried a young man.

'No honour in slavery!' yelled another.

'No glory in blood!'

'No statues to slavers!'

'Pull it down!'

'Pull it down!'

'Pull it down!'

The protestors converged on the shrouded figure in the front of the marquee. Some of them produced signs, written in fake blood.

The crowd gaped and murmured.

Mrs Huntington-Hogg yelled, 'Get off my lawn, you—'

The mic screeched with feedback, cutting off whatever she was going to say. One of the protestors threw a water balloon at the shroud. It exploded with a burst of fake blood, dripping down the white material.

'This is better than a zombie movie,' Saffy murmured, appearing at Jon's side.

'You have to admit, they have a point.'

'Oh, they've got a hell of a point. Letty would have been delighted.'

Saffy herself appeared to be delighted. She pulled Jon off to the side to get a better view of the melee that was starting near the lectern.

Just as she did, a phalanx of police officers in fluorescent vests arrived and began driving the protestors back, away from the statue. For a moment, all was confusion and shouts of anger, but it took hardly any time before the stage was cleared and Mrs Huntington-Hogg was back at her lectern.

'That's the most efficient police operation I've ever seen,' said Saffy. 'No offence to your dad.'

'Don't worry.' He watched as a police officer collected one of the protestor's placards and bundled it away, out of sight. 'They must have been tipped off that something was going to happen.'

'It's reassuring to know that playing dressing-up in front of a lump of stone is the most pressing crime going on in Berkshire right now.'

Mrs Huntington-Hogg cleared her throat and the mic squealed another bout of feedback. She adjusted it slightly, straightened her hat, and said, 'Well. Thank you for bearing with us. And thank you to the dedicated and patriotic public servants who are defending free speech today.'

She glanced nervously at the blood-spattered and veiled statue, and then faced resolutely forward. 'Ladies and gentlemen, I give you a great man, the scion of an honourable family who have done so much for this wonderful country: Sir Ranulf Hogg!'

She nodded at a man who was standing nearby. He pulled aside the bloodstained shroud that was masking the statue. Mrs Huntington-Hogg got ready to pop the cork from the champagne.

And that was when the screaming really began.

Chapter Thirty-One

THE CURTAIN IS SWEPT ASIDE, and I relax and enjoy the Big Reveal.

As statues go, Sir Ranulf Hogg is standard. He's made out of bright white marble, but unlike the various classical gods scattered around the property, he's fully dressed. I've seen the family jewels of his direct descendant, and sculpting him in clothing was a wise artistic choice. He's wearing stone breeches and a stone topcoat, with stone ruffles at his neck, quite nicely done in my opinion.

As well as the clothing, there's been some small attempt at historical accuracy. The most flattering sculptor in the world couldn't avoid depicting Ranulf's signature Hogg jowling and the signature Hogg nose; the jowling and the nose that have graced oil portraits and newspaper photos for generations. Even poor Red Letty didn't fully escape that curse, bless her, though I don't recall her having those bristling eyebrows. Maybe she was good at plucking: attacking her face in the boarding school bathroom mirror with a pair of tweezers after all the other girls had gone to sleep.

All the pain that women have to go through to avoid a bit of extra hair. Just to try to fit in with everyone else.

Sir Ranulf stands upright, one of his hands holding a book (meant to make him look smart) and the other holding a piece of some kind of vegetation that I think is meant to be a sugar cane. I'm surprised to see this: most modern sculptors try to sidestep the whole issue of the dodgy ways that rich people gained their wealth through massive exploitation, torture, and murder. Also, I doubt that Sir Ranulf actually ever touched a sugar cane with his own fair white hands. His role was purely to own the land and the people on it, and allow the unstoppable flow of money to him and to his descendants.

To this end, he's been placed fittingly on a large white pedestal so that he is above everyone else. His haughty face is turned towards his domain: the house, the rolling lands, the rose garden, the rare orchids, the orangery, the fountains, all the beautiful and civilised things that he paid for through horror, tragedy, heartache, and death.

Sir Ranulf looks proud. The great white master.

Unlike his scion, the errant Sir Rupert Huntington-Hogg. Member of Parliament, philanderer, rapist, terrible father, misogynist, luster after latex, devotee of water sports of the non-polo type, and rabid consumer of the most expensive whisky in the Strangers' Bar, who has been missing for weeks now and is missing no more.

Rupert H-H has seen better days. And he's not dressed, either.

There are different shades of white, though. There's the cold, pure, hard white of marble: something that's never been alive, no matter how it's carved to resemble something that breathes.

And then there's the cold, mottled, flabby grey-white of a body that once moved and touched and breathed, ate and drank, laughed and lusted, fornicated and sinned, but has now been drained of every drop of blood.

Literally, drained, as in it flowed down the drain of my bathtub and into the great sewer of the beyond, where it belongs.

It turns out that blue blood is just as red as normal blood, and a famous politician begs and squirms just as much as a regular old misogynistic Joe, when you've put a knife to them. Rupert's not bleeding or begging any more, though. He's slumped up against the pedestal with his head resting on his ancestor's foot. His man-boobs and man-belly flop out free, for all to see. So does his penis, which is a little shrivelled worm in the thatch of his untamed pubes. His eyes are open, his mouth open too, jowls slack, teeth yellow, and you can see the precise outline of every single slice I made to the front of his body in order to drain out all of that blood.

A tiny bit of intestine peeps out of a slice in his stomach.

Rupert's home at last.

Chapter Thirty-Two

We've escaped the chaos and are ensconced next to a roaring fire in a sixteenth-century pub about five miles from Hatherstone House and its latest corpse. The pub is, appropriately and gruesomely enough, called the King's Head. We have a double whisky each and a bottle of red wine to split.

'Maybe we should have stayed for the police,' Jonathan is saying. He gulps his whisky. His hands are a little unsteady, but his eyes are bright, his cheeks flushed. Just like they were when he found the murdered miscreants in the park. My man has a little thing, a little frisson, for death.

Do I know how to plan a day out, or do I know how to plan a day out?

I sip demurely. I love it when my hard work is properly appreciated.

'There were plenty of witnesses,' I say. 'I'm pretty sure the police will have all the evidence they need, without us.'

'They were certainly out in force already. For about a split second, I thought the reveal was part of the protest. But then ...' He drinks again.

He's talking about five seconds after the shroud lifted, when he grabbed my arm and rasped in my ear, 'That's a real body. That's really Rupert Huntington-Hogg.'

We'd stuck around just long enough to get a good look. I would have happily basked in the fruits of my labours, but once Mrs H-H started screaming, everyone else pitched in, and it got a little screechy. You'd think it was Armageddon, and not just a deceased and perverted MP who deserved everything he got.

Anyway, we collected our picnic and hotfooted it to the car, pulling into the first decent drinking spot we could find to settle our nerves.

Though no amount of alcohol is going to settle the happy tingle going through me right now.

'Most people thought it was a stunt at first,' I say. 'I think you recognised him before his own wife did.'

'By now, I know the difference between a real dead body and a fake one. I've seen enough of them.'

'His poor wife,' I say, with real pity. Mrs H-H had been a mess. You'd think that woman would be glad to be rid of a flabby philanderer – especially since now that there was a body, she could collect both the life insurance and her inheritance. But I've learned that there is no accounting for the taste of heterosexual women.

'At least his children weren't there,' says Jonathan.

'That's a blessing.' As if I'd be that sloppy. I don't wilfully traumatise children.

Jonathan has finished his whisky and is pouring out a glass of red wine. 'Do you want some of this?' he asks, the bottle hovering above the second glass. 'We've got your car.'

'We can get a taxi to the station. Or back to London, if we want. I'll leave the car here and get someone to collect it in the morning.'

He pours me a large glass. 'Are you OK? That was ... quite a sight.'

'It was very shocking,' I reply, though to be honest I'm talking about having to look at Rupe's teeny-tiny willy again. It's astonishing to me that something that looks like a misshapen and discoloured peanut could cause so much suffering in the world.

Jonathan takes my hand and caresses it.

'I've seen worse though,' I say bravely.

'I know. I'm sorry. I am so, so sorry, Saffy.'

'Why are you apologising? It's not your fault.'

He's quiet, one hand on mine, the other around the stem of his wine glass.

'It is my fault,' he says eventually.

'What? How? You didn't kill Huntington-Hogg, did you?'

'Of course not. But I did kill Simon. Right in front of you, too.'

'That was self-defence. And also, you saved my life.'

(My life was never at risk, but sometimes you have to stroke a man's ego.)

He's shaking his head and looking at the table, which is much less fascinating than my face.

'What's wrong?' I ask.

'I'm remembering what we were talking about in the car this morning. How you found your stepfather's body when you were a young girl.'

'Oh, Jonathan, I'm over that. It was a very long time ago.'

'I understand why you're putting on a brave face, but Saffy – I saw what happened at that dinner party, when Susie mentioned your stepfather's name. You covered it up well, but for a moment, you went white as a sheet.'

'Did I?' I don't know whether to be impressed that Jonathan watches me so carefully, or to be annoyed at myself for being so pathetic. 'I guess I was taken by surprise. Generally, I'm fine.'

'People don't just get over that type of trauma. I know – I've spoken to my share of victims over the years. It lives inside you, somewhere in your body. You had this terrible experience as a child, and you've worked to get over it. And then you met me, and since then, within a couple of months, you've been a witness to two more killings. It's too much.'

'That's not your fault, though, Jonathan.'

'It is.' He abandons his wine glass and takes my hand with both of his. 'It is my fault. I've joked about attracting murders and murderers, but it's true. I keep on getting involved in death, whether I want to or not. It cost me my marriage. I don't want you to get dragged into it.'

'I'm not getting dragged into anything. I've got my eyes open. I knew who you were when I met you, remember?'

'But you're such a sunny person. A good person. You've got an innocence to you, Saffy, which is wonderful, considering what you've been through. I don't want to be responsible for destroying that.'

I grip his hands too. I could not love this conversation more.

'Jonathan,' I say, 'this is total nonsense. I love your work. I admired it before I met you. I like that you care so much about getting justice for victims, and finding out the truth so their families can have peace of mind. You're a good man. I've been saying that since I first met you. And I loved investigating Fanducci's death with you. It was so much fun!'

'But—'

'Like I said, I have my eyes wide open. I understand what it means, to be your girlfriend. The things I might have to witness. And I'm OK with that. More than OK. I think it's important work.'

He meets my gaze. I meet his right back. At first, he's looking like he might keep arguing with me, but I stare lovingly into his eyes until he softens.

'I like that we can talk about these difficult and vulnerable things,' I say.

He nods. 'It's new to me,' he admits.

'Me too. But I think we're doing pretty well.'

He releases my hands, and for a while we drink our wine in silence. I can tell that he is thinking hard, and I know that he won't tell me what he's thinking about until he's parsed it through in his head.

So I take a few moments to bask in my own cleverness. It took some tricky timing and some good old-fashioned physical hard work to set up that whole cadaver reveal, and to get us there for the denouement, but it went like clockwork. The large police presence because of the protestors made it even more fun. I'm pleased with myself for keeping Rupert's body in the deep freeze for a while until I could get everything lined up perfectly.

And then, more than merely being a spectacle, the incident prompts this sort of beautiful heart-to-heart with Jonathan, growing our intimacy even more.

It just goes to prove that right-wing politicians are useful for something after all.

'I have something to ask you,' says Jonathan, when we're ready for a second glass of wine. 'And you can say no. In fact you should say no, if you're in any way uncomfortable with it.'

'What?' I lean forward in my chair.

'I'm not entirely convinced it's a good idea myself, but I can't see any other way forward, not if I want to know the truth.'

'What is it?'

'Will you promise me that you'll say no, if you have even the smallest doubt or scruple?'

'Yes, yes, tell me what it is before I faint from the suspense!'

He pours us each another glass of wine. I'm squirming in my chair with impatience. What is it? Does he have a kink he wants to tell me about? Like bondage? I have quite a bit of experience with that. Or maybe he likes pegging? That could be fun.

Or maybe it's not a kink. Maybe he has murder fantasies! What a dream that would be!

Or maybe he wants another dog. I am less keen on that. Maybe he wants children? Do I want children? Why have I never thought about whether I want children or not?

Maybe he wants to get married.

!!

He isn't going to propose, is he? Before we've even slept together?

I sit on my hands and wait for him to kneel.

But he doesn't. Instead he sips his wine while I rapidly go crazy.

Eventually he says, 'I need to interview a victim of a crime. And because of the nature of that crime, I'm not confident that the victim will be comfortable with being interviewed by a man, especially not a man by himself. It could make a real difference in helping to gain her trust, if you were there with me.'

'You want me to help you with another case?' I cry in delight.

'I don't know if it's a case, so much as a ... suspicion. A lead.'

'Does this mean you're going to get back into solving crimes? Holmes and Watson, when it's the lady Watson played by Lucy Liu? She's hot. Or Mulder and Scully? I could do Gillian Anderson. Hannibal and Clarice? I love Jodie Foster.'

'It's ... well, let's say that for right now, it's just a lead. Something I'm interested in. I'm not committing to following it anywhere. The thing is, there could be some traumatic details involved. And if you'd rather not be tangled up in it, I will totally underst—'

'Are you kidding? I love doing the amateur detective stuff!'

'It's about another severed head. I think it belongs to a man called Tony Jones.'

'Severed heads are the jackpot! We had great luck with them last time.'

He's smiling, but cautiously. 'So, that's a yes?'

'That is such a yes!' I jump up and run to his side of the table and give him an enormous hug and a kiss. 'I'm in! Let's get this investigation started!'

I am *so good* at this intimacy thing!

Chapter Thirty-Three

BLOSSOM YAN LIVES WITH HER mother in a bungalow in Tring. The grass is overgrown and weeds poke through the cracks of the path leading to the front door. All of the blinds are drawn.

'Park down at the end of the street,' Jonathan says. 'We can walk up to the house.'

'She's expecting us?' I ask.

'We're a few minutes early. But we shouldn't arrive before the time we've arranged, and we shouldn't sit in the car outside her house. It's important to be as predictable as we can be.'

'You've learned this from speaking with victims before?'

'You have to do whatever you can to make them comfortable. They've been through enough, through no fault of their own. It's important not to re-traumatise. So if Blossom wants to stop talking, we'll leave, even if we've only been there for a few minutes. We want the truth, but her wellbeing comes first.'

'See, this is what makes you a good guy.'

'To Blossom, there might not be any good guys any more.' He checks his watch, and opens his car door. 'OK, let's go.'

Curtains twitch at the window of a neighbouring bungalow, but at the Yans', all is quiet. There's a cat preening itself on the pavement outside. It gives us a contemptuous look as we approach and walks off, tail held high.

Jonathan presses the doorbell. I notice that it's a Ring, with an integrated camera. The door itself has a peephole and three external locks. This is a quiet middle-class neighbourhood populated with pensioners and normally I would consider this level of security a bit OTT to protect a flat-screen telly and a three-piece suite from DFS.

But Jonathan has told me some of what Blossom and her mother have been through, and frankly, I'm surprised the Yans don't have a pack of Rottweilers, each trained to bite off an intruder's nose.

We've arrived bang on time, but despite this it takes a little while for anyone to come to the door, and even longer for all of the locks to be negotiated and for the door to open. When it does, I don't recognise the woman who stands there, even though I've seen photographs of what she looked like before the trial. She's much thinner, with hollowed cheeks and silver threads in her dark hair.

'Hi, I'm Jonathan Desrosiers,' says Jonathan gently. 'Are you Blossom?'

She flinches slightly and then nods. 'Are you Saffy Huntley-Oliver?' she asks me.

'I am. It's so lovely to meet you. Thank you for agreeing to see us.'

The warmth in my voice makes her visibly relax a tiny bit. I'm used to manipulating people to give me what I want, but in fact I am very glad to be meeting Blossom Yan, so there's no need to feign friendliness and approachability.

Blossom lets us inside. She locks the door behind us. There's a sliding bolt and a chain lock on the inside, as well as the ones I saw before. Inside, all the lights are on so the house is quite bright even though the blinds are drawn. The hallway is papered in florals and there's a pink carpet underfoot.

'I've got a pot of tea,' Blossom says, leading us to the room that is most definitely called a 'lounge' in this household. More floral wallpaper, more pink carpeting, and, as expected, a floral three-piece suite and a flat-screen telly, which is turned onto some sort of gardening programme, but muted. Overhead lights blaze, along with two lamps. Several vases hold artificial flowers. A tray with a flowered teapot and flowered mugs sits on a coffee table in front of the sofa. There are shortbread biscuits on a flowered plate. Everything is pristine, impeccably neat – much more well-kept than you would have expected from the straggly hedges outside.

I take all this in a moment, before Blossom has finished asking if we'd prefer coffee instead.

'Tea is perfect,' says Jonathan.

'It's really kind of you,' I say.

The two of us perch on the sofa and Blossom begins pouring the tea. 'I've got Mum settled, but I might need to check on her.' She points to a baby monitor on a side table. 'We use that to communicate when I'm in another room. It's easier to use than a walkie-talkie because she doesn't have to press a button. She used to just yell, but her voice isn't great.' She adds milk and one sugar to each mug before seemingly realising what she's doing and looking at us, aghast, her thin cheeks flushing. 'Oh no, I didn't even ask if you took sugar! That's how Mum and I take it, and it's been so long …'

'That's how I take it,' I say. 'Milk and one sugar! I was wondering how you read my mind.'

Jonathan and I take appreciative sips. I don't think I've had milky sweet tea since I had that English nanny. At Blossom's insistence, I also take a biscuit. It crumbles in my mouth in another memory of childhood.

'Thank you for agreeing to see us,' Jonathan says.

'I wasn't sure,' says Blossom. 'I really wasn't sure.'

'I understand.'

'But then when I read about your charity,' she says to me. 'That made me feel safer. Like you might know what it's like.'

'I do,' I say, even though I'm not sure which charity she's talking about. I didn't even know that Jonathan's introductory email was going to mention anything to her about who I was or my charity work; I thought I was just along for a female presence. But it seems that he's not above leveraging a bit of information to secure the trust of a witness, either.

'I've never been battered,' she adds quickly, giving me that vital extra piece of information: she's talking about the women's domestic abuse refuge where I serve as a patron. 'At least that's a blessing. But it's feeling unsafe, you know? And maybe if he had hit me it would have been taken more seriously, quicker. Do you think? From what you've seen from the women you've worked with?'

'It's not my charity,' I say gently. 'I do volunteer there, though. I've spoken with quite a few women who are victims of intimate partner violence. I think, sadly, that having bruises as evidence can help with getting the police involved and court cases brought.'

'There's no bruises. No evidence at all that he was trying to frighten me. And he was never my intimate partner either, of course. It was all a crush. I should be flattered. That's what they said the first time I reported him. The desk sergeant even said he was quite a good-looking chap. Like I should think I was lucky that he'd chosen me.'

'Because all we ever want is a man to approve of us, right?'

She turns to Jonathan. 'You said you might have some news about him? About where he is?'

'I'm not sure. I'm following a lead. But I did want to as if you've heard from him at all?'

'No.' She picks at non-existent lint on her trousers. 'Since they told me he was getting out on parole I've been expecting him any moment. I had some peace while he was inside, but now that's gone. I was just beginning to feel more normal. It took four years. Now I don't answer the door. I can't bear to check the post. Mum has to screen everything. She was the one to find your email. She can still use an iPad. The police have been no use, they say they can't park outside my house twenty-four hours a day. They say that he's got a protection order against him. But he never paid attention to that before, did he? That's why he ended up in jail.'

'He was released eight months ago,' says Jonathan. 'He showed up for his first meeting with his parole officer, but disappeared some time before his second. The theory is that he's left the country.'

'The police told me this, but they won't tell me any more. So I'm stuck still thinking that he's going to turn up at any moment. Do you know any more?'

Good news! I want to shout. *All that's left of this man is the memory of a photograph of his severed head!*

I don't say it. I do wonder how Blossom would react to that, though. With horror, or with jubilation?

'It's just a lead at the moment,' says Jonathan. 'I don't want to get your hopes up.'

'Can you tell me about what happened?' I ask. 'Or is it too awful to talk about?'

Jonathan shoots me a glance that I interpret as *Don't spook her.* But I want to hear. I want this woman to bear witness to her life and have someone believe every word. She deserves that.

'I was gardening,' says Blossom. She nods at the telly. 'That's the closest I get these days, but it was my job. I loved it. I studied it at college, learned everything about plants that I could. I had a list of clients, mostly older folks who needed help keeping up with things. One of them was his aunt. He was visiting her one day when I was laying a path and he brought me a cup of tea because he said I was working so hard. I thought he was kind. We got to talking and I thought he was nice.' She shakes her head. 'I was an idiot.'

'You were just being normal. Anyone would've done the same.'

'I thought he was lonely so I was friendly to him the next week. But I was always clear to him, I had a boyfriend and I wasn't interested in him. I did have a boyfriend, too. I wasn't lying. But when the phone calls started and the messages, Craig blamed me. Craig said that I must have done something, that I was leading him on, so he broke up with me. I thought maybe he was right, that maybe I'd done or said something that I didn't mean to.'

'It wasn't anything you did,' I say. 'It was all him, not you.'

I make a mental note to find out Craig's last name.

'I couldn't go to my gardens because he would find me there and try to talk with me. He found out where I lived and started sending flowers and letters. Letters every day, some in the post but some put through my door by hand. He was outside all the time. So I gave up my flat and I moved in with Mum, but then he found out and started here. I couldn't see my friends because if he found out who they were, he started on them, sending them messages about me, telling lies, asking them to get in touch with me for him. It got so I just didn't leave the house. It was better that way. Safer for Mum.'

'Did it affect your mum's health?' I ask.

'She had MS before, but it went downhill pretty rapidly during the trial. Especially since the press kept saying I was his ex-girlfriend. Which I was never! It was a lot of stress. I like to joke that it's a good thing I've developed agoraphobia, it means I can stay in and look after her all day and not feel like I'm missing out!'

I can't laugh at that, and neither can Jonathan. Blossom's brittle smile falters.

'It's OK,' she says. 'It's a good life, I'm glad I'm here to look after my mum. We have a good time together. I'd do it anyway, even if . . .' She spreads her hands in her lap and looks down at them. 'I do miss the gardening though. I tried some houseplants but they didn't get enough light. I've been thinking about terrariums, maybe.'

I want to grab a knife and cut a bloody swathe through mankind. I want to build a bomb and set it off under the patriarchy. I want to start a collection of violently removed testicles.

And the worst thing is that I'm so fucking angry, and yet Blossom is resigned. He's stalked her until she lost her job and her flat and her boyfriend and her independence and, worst of all, she's lost all of her fight.

This is why I do what I do. This woman, right here. And all of the thousands and millions like her. The ones whose only crime is being female and who don't have the specific skills and temperament to take things into their own hands.

This is why I can never, ever stop.

'Did he say he loved you?' I ask her.

'That's all he said over and over. He said it in court too.'

'It's not love.'

'Oh, I know. I can't trust most of my feelings these days but I do know that he doesn't love me and never did. I know what love is. I'm very lucky that way.' She glances at the baby monitor and then at the doorway leading to the bedrooms, where her mum must be resting.

'I'm so sorry that happened to you,' says Jonathan. 'You didn't deserve it.'

'Is he dead?' she says. 'I googled you and it says you write about murder.'

'I don't know. I've been talking with an inmate who claims to have some information. But as I said, it's not confirmed. You should still be cautious. The minute I know anything, I will tell you. I promise.'

'I hope he's dead.' Her eyes are glittering. 'I never wanted anyone dead. Mum would be shocked to hear me say this. She didn't raise me that way. But he took my life away from me and I can't get it back until I know he's in prison, or dead.'

* * *

We're quiet as we walk back to the car. After we get in, we sit in silence for a minute.

'She never said his name,' I say at last. 'Not once.'

'She didn't need to.'

'No, she didn't. Because what Tony Jones did to her was right in the room with us. It was practically drinking its own cup of tea. But he *is* dead, isn't he? You just didn't want to get her hopes up until you were certain.'

'I'm pretty sure he's dead.'

'I try not to think about it too much. How the things that men do to women can keep hurting them, even after the men are gone and the women are free.'

All those men I've killed. I can't kill the harm that they'd already done.

Blossom has a house full of flowers, and none of them can grow. God, that's depressing.

Jonathan asks me, 'What were you saying to her in the kitchen, when you were washing up?'

(Yes, I helped her wash up those floral mugs and dry them on a floral tea towel. No, I did not care if it ruined my manicure.)

'I told her that the charity had a discretionary fund to help with respite care and home nursing and that I could put her name forward if she wanted me to.'

'Will you?'

'To hell with the discretionary fund! I'm going to pay for a full-time nurse for that woman's mother and also an online therapist for Blossom.' I grip the steering wheel tight enough to wring its neck. 'She needs a lot more help than she's got now, and more than any charity can give her.'

Jonathan kisses my cheek. 'You're a good person, Saffy. You can't do that for every victim, though.'

'I can do it for her, and that's a start.'

I can do something else for her, too. I intend to do it as soon as possible.

Chapter Thirty-Four

BODY OF STALKER DISCOVERED

Oxfordshire Police have confirmed that the remains discovered yesterday by a fisherman on the bank of the River Isis belong to Antony 'Tony' Jones, a 36-year-old Tring resident who had recently been paroled from prison after serving half a four-year sentence for aggravated stalking.

'We have definitively identified the remains as those of Tony Jones,' said DI Miles Bashir at a press conference. 'Jones had gone missing after attending a first parole officer meeting and had not reported for subsequent meetings. Following a sighting by the public, we had been coordinating with detectives in the north of the country to locate him. We are treating this death as a homicide, but we have not yet determined Jones's movements before he was killed.'

Jones's remains were discovered by Benjamin Curzon, 72, a member of the Isis Angling Club, during a club tournament. 'They were in a green duffel bag sitting beside the angling platform,' said Curzon. 'They had some weeds chucked over them but I don't think they'd been there for long. I fished in this spot last weekend and I didn't see anything at all then.'

Forensic teams are still conducting a search at the site. Police would not confirm whether an entire body had been recovered or when the murder took place.

Jones's are the second remains to be discovered in the area in the same week. The body of missing MP Sir Rupert Huntington-Hogg was found in dramatic circumstances on Sunday at his estate in Berkshire, less than fifteen miles away. Oxfordshire and Thames Valley Police say that they are currently treating the homicides as separate and unrelated cases. DC Kira Bell of Thames Valley Police commented: 'While the timing is similar and tragic, and both bodies were discovered unexpectedly, we believe that the murder of a highly respected public servant and landowner is unrelated to the homicide of a convicted felon.'

DC Bell added that the current popularity of true crime documentaries and podcasts, particularly the keen interest in serial killers, has fuelled baseless speculation, especially online, where videos taken by witnesses of Huntington-Hogg's naked and mutilated body have gone viral.

'We respectfully ask the public to refrain from sharing sensitive content that will unduly upset a grieving family,' DC Bell said.

DI Bashir of Oxfordshire Police stated, 'We discourage individuals from visiting a crime scene or inserting themselves into homicide investigations in the name of amateur detective work or prurient curiosity. Murder investigations are best handled by trained professionals. If you have any information about Tony Jones's movements after being released from prison, please contact Oxfordshire Police or Crimestoppers.'

Tony Jones was convicted two years ago for aggravating stalking of his ex-girlfriend, Blossom Yan. Yan was not available for comment.

Chapter Thirty-Five

I KNOW I LIKE TO GIVE the impression that I am Superwoman: that I can gleefully murder and dismember a man without breaking a single nail, that I can keep smiling during endless fundraising events and still have time and energy to perform a gruelling beauty routine while simultaneously planning a perfect crime, that I can effortlessly flirt at parties and then go on to deadlift corpses while hardly breaking a sweat.

And it is true that I have more energy than most people, and I don't need as much sleep. I think it's because I don't have a conscience, so I don't have to spend all my mental resources beating myself up; and when I do sleep, it's the rejuvenating sleep of the untroubled angels.

But let me get real. I take a lot of vitamins, I have a personal trainer, I am extremely organised, and I outsource most of my non-homicidal labour to paid employees. I would never be able to achieve what I do, if I were a single mum working three jobs to put food on the table, or a sex worker with untreated addictions. Look at poor Aileen Wuornos, brutalised and penniless: the woman was fighting a good fight, but she never had a chance of getting away with it.

My hobby requires tremendous resources, both financial and personal. I don't need to check my privilege – I've literally built my life of crime upon it.

However. Even *this* superpowered one-percenter blonde firecracker gets tired sometimes. In the past week, I have literally hauled two bodies over multiple county lines (even though one of them was merely a head – Rupert was heavy enough to make up for it), while finding time to nurture my relationship and my mental health. Plus, I've discovered the worrying fact that someone has anonymously sent a photograph of my handiwork to my boyfriend.

Who was that? How'd they get the photo of Jones's head? I thought I'd kept it secretly stowed away.

And why did they send the photo to Jonathan, instead of showing it to the police? Not that I'm ungrateful ... I quite like sharing my hobby with my boyfriend. But why?

Those questions have given me a few sleepless hours.

And then there was that note on the roof (I'll go into that in a bit).

I'm tired.

In late morning I carry my duvet downstairs and install myself under it on the sofa. Jonathan, who's in the kitchen, calls, 'Coffee?'

'Please. Preferably in a bucket.'

Girl comes to the entrance of the room, sees that it's me, and backs out while not once breaking eye contact. Now that I notice, there are definitely dog hairs on this white sofa.

I'm going to have to do something about this. When I have more fuel in the tank. Right now I can't handle anything more energetic than a *Sex and the City* marathon. Or possibly another hate-watch of *American Psycho*. That man thinks he's so hot, but he's really just a bundle of fragile masculinity with good pecs. The film itself, though, is a pretty cool dissection of how the capitalist patriarchy consumes women and other vulnerable people. Official Serial Killer Rating: three and a half stars, not many useable tips other than plastic suits and skincare.

Jonathan brings me a triple espresso and sets it down on the glass side table. 'Are you feeling unwell?'

'I'm fine. Every now and then I figure that I need a pyjama day.'

(The pyjamas in question are Olivia Von Halle silk crêpe de chine because even when lounging on a sofa under a duvet, one should have standards.)

'That's a great idea.'

'You should join me.'

'Tempted. Yesterday was exhausting.'

Yesterday he spent the afternoon with his old friend DI Atherton, talking further about the photo of the severed head that he found in his inbox, which happens to be the same severed head that I dumped near a popular angling spot two nights before. He'd left his laptop with the police and they'd found no trace of the vanishing email and clearly thought Jonathan was making the whole thing up. The conversation was so frustrating for him that when I got home, quite late, he was stretching and pulling a lump of dough as if it were Atherton's face.

'Go ahead, take the day off,' I say. 'What's the point in being an unemployed wastrel if you don't enjoy it?'

He goes to put on his pyjamas and fetch his own duvet, while I lean back on the cushions, sip my coffee, and ponder yesterday evening's exertions.

On the way home from my hair appointment I had a sudden twinge of worry. Over the years I've honed my awareness of perverts to a sharp edge, until it's become almost a sixth sense; so when I get a twinge, I pay attention. I detoured via Sir Thomas's neighbourhood and lingered unobtrusively in the shadows until I ascertained that I couldn't see jack shit from this position.

So I ascended to my customary eyrie in the empty house. I kept my hand on the Taser in my handbag in case I ran into Mr/Ms/Mx Pot Noodle up there, enquiring into the whereabouts of their missing spoon.

But when I got to the roof, it was empty.

I sighed in relief (and a tiny bit of disappointment to be honest – it would have been fun to explain the spoon thing to someone between incapacitating and killing them). I turned my attention to my real goal: Sir Thomas.

I had to kill him soon, I knew. I had to find a way past his burglar alarms and bodyguard, and snuff out all of his future crimes as well as his insufferable smugness. What if he abused another child on my watch?

As I watched, Sir Thomas came to the window. He was wearing a casual sports coat and an open-collared shirt, and he had a sherry glass in his hand. He was talking to someone, though I couldn't see who it was. He laughed, flashing white teeth. So charming. So evil.

If he had a child in his house I could be downstairs, out of this house, over West's fence and breaking into his kitchen window within four and a half minutes. Even in a pencil skirt and these shoes. The alarm would go off, but I'd take that chance if it meant protecting a kid. I poised myself, ready to run.

Then he turned away from the window and I could see who he was talking to. It was a well-known newsreader.

I let out a deep breath and relaxed. Clearly nothing was going to happen tonight and if it did between these two, I really did not give a flying fuck. None of my business and I'd much rather not see it. My sixth sense had made a rare mistake.

It was only when I was about to climb back through the window into the house that I saw it. It was neon pink but only small, and stuck to the outside of the window frame, so not surprising I hadn't spotted it before, with my focus on checking whether the roof was empty and then what was going on with West.

It was a Post-it note with a message on it, printed in black marker:

HE'S MINE. LEAVE HIM ALONE.

* * *

So, I muse as I steadily ingest caffeine in silk pyjamas on my sofa, that's one riddle solved. This other person hasn't just chosen a handy rooftop for consuming Pot Noodle and leaving me cutlery/impromptu murder weapons. Someone else has their eyes on Sir Thomas.

This isn't good news. I want to kill Sir Thomas myself. Otherwise, how can I be sure it's been done properly?

And then there's the other bit of bad news: they also know about me. Unless they've taken a lucky guess, I have to assume that they've seen me watching Sir Thomas. I just have to hope that they haven't followed me long enough to witness any of my extracurricular activities.

This is two instances of someone meddling in my business. I need to watch my back.

Jonathan comes in wearing a pair of plaid flannel pyjama bottoms and a Pulp T-shirt, carrying a large mug and a plate of toast, his hair fluffing with static electricity on one side, and I can't help but giggle.

'What?' he says, sitting on the other side of the sofa under the duvet. His bare feet settle on top of mine.

'You look like such a dork,' I tell him. 'And I was remembering how, when I first met you, you were all brooding and dark and living in a hovel, and now you look like a nerd who's been dragged through a hedge backwards but likes it.'

'I thought I was a hot rodent.'

'Same thing.'

'Well,' he says, 'what can I say? I'm happier.' He tosses me the TV remote, which I catch with one hand.

What follows is a delicate negotiation between two people who are early enough in their relationship to want to please each other, but who have widely disparate senses of what is suitable to binge-watch on a day off. He agrees to watch *Grey's Anatomy*. I agree to watch *Bridge Over the River Kwai*. He agrees to watch *Rivals*. I agree to watch *Life on Earth*. I suggest *Mindhunter* to please him, but he thinks that has too many echoes of visiting Cyril in prison. He suggests *Friends* to please me, but I know I could never contain my deep-seated conviction that Ross should choke to death on a fistful of biscotti.

In the end, we settle for *Dexter*, which both of us admit we have watched three times apiece already. Comfort viewing.

It's nice. Sharing a sofa and a duvet, laughing at bloody shenanigans, feeding each other bits of toast. (I know – carbs – but

I have been doing a *lot* of exercise.) Girl stops hating me long enough to curl up on the floor next to us. We order in lunch. I have a little snooze and miss the end of season one. While Michael C. Hall measures blood spatter and drops chunks of people off his motorboat into Biscayne Bay, I absently scroll on my phone.

Susie has posted photos of herself and Finlay at a club night somewhere, which I vaguely remember her talking about the last time I saw her. They're in fancy dress. He's dressed as a surfer (duh) and she's dressed as a saucy schoolgirl: very short pleated skirt, knee socks, white shirt tied at the ribcage, loosened tie, hair in plaits.

There's something about her outfit that's familiar. I zoom in. She's wearing an Eton tie.

Casually, I text her:

```
Nice slutty schoolgirl look, babe. Saw
it on Insta.

Thanks! Years of practice ☺

I didn't know you went to Eton.

Aaaaa it's Finn's xx

He let you wear his old school tie?

Found it in his wardrobe, didn't ask per-
mission. You & J should come next week?
Couples clubbing xxx

Pigs might fly.
```

I zoom in further.

This Eton tie that looks very much like the Eton tie that I used to gag Rupert Huntington-Hogg, and which I planted in Finlay's wardrobe on the night of that dinner party on the off-chance that I needed someone to frame for his murder.

Shit.

'Shit,' says Jonathan, and I look up. He's also staring at his phone.

'What?'

'It's another photo sent from that same account. The one that sent the photo of Tony Jones's head. It's got the same subject line, too: *What do you think?* And the same message: *Dear Jonathan, I'd like your opinion on this photo.*'

'What photo?'

'There's only one this time. It's some sort of building.'

I scootch over next to him and he shows me.

'Looks like a warehouse,' he says. 'On an industrial estate somewhere. Why would someone send that to me?'

'Weird,' I say. Which is not technically a lie.

Because I know exactly what that building is, and why a picture of it was sent to Jonathan.

Chapter Thirty-Six

This message, like the last, disappeared from Jon's inbox within a few minutes of him opening it, but this time Saffy was able to snap a photo of its contents before it vanished. Some cropping and refining, and they were able to do a reverse image search which led them to an archived listing on an estate agent website, which led them to an approximate location on an industrial estate in West London.

They exchanged looks.

Jon said, 'It could be a trap.'

Saffy said, 'I'm up for it if you are.'

Ten minutes later they were both dressed and Jonathan was clipping a lead on Girl.

'We're taking her?' Saffy said. She had dressed all in black, with black trainers and a black baseball cap, like a sporty cat burglar. 'What if it's dangerous?'

'She's the nose of the operation.' He stooped and scratched Girl under her stubby, scruffy chin. 'And if we met any bad guys you'd bite them, wouldn't you? That's how we'd know they were the bad guys.'

Girl wagged her stumpy tail. Jon wondered how he'd ever thought he wasn't a dog person. What was wrong with unconditional love?

'I'm not sure I'd want to stake my life on the moral judgement of a mutt,' Saffy said, but she didn't object, and she laid down a blanket on the back seat of her sedan for the dog.

Travelling from the depths of moneyed Kensington to the depths of working-class Brentford took surprisingly little time. Several industrial estates lay in the approximate area indicated by the estate agent's website; they drove around them, peering at units occupied by car mechanics, refrigeration specialists, fabricators, importers, and pizza manufacturers. On the third estate they saw the building with the unit they'd been seeking. It was a small single-unit lock-up, unsigned and unnumbered, between a shuttered MOT garage and the premises of a heating engineer.

Saffy parked outside. 'What do we do now? Knock on the door?'

'Might as well.'

Jon looked around as they approached the unit. The heating engineer had a CLOSED sign on its door, and the unit directly across, a large fibreglass fabricator, seemed also to be closed. 'It's pretty isolated. Do you notice anything else unusual?'

'Um ... it's ugly?'

'I can't see any CCTV cameras. Can you?'

'Hmm. Now that you mention it ...'

'Maybe they're well hidden. But then they can't function as a deterrent, which is at least half the point.' Girl, who had been sniffing around some piled-up pallets, now pulled him along urgently towards the unit. Jon held her back a little to look at the cars that were parked in front of the garage. 'And these look like they've been written off, or they should be. Nobody's doing business here.'

'Recession?'

'Or something else.' He allowed Girl to pull him to the door, her nose to the ground, and tried it. 'Locked.'

'That's not surprising.' Saffy knocked hard on the door. There was a buzzer, too, which she pressed repeatedly. 'Do we have a story to explain our being here, by the way?'

'Looking to rent?'

'Do I look like someone who wants to rent a filthy industrial unit in the middle of nowhere?'

'Yoga studio?'

'Ugh. Artisan vegan dog biscuit factory. Possibly a front for organised crime.'

'Better.' Jon hit the buzzer a few more times. 'I don't think we need a story, however. No one is in.'

'Hmm.' Saffy considered. 'Why don't you and Girl go round the back and see if there's any way in there, and I'll see if I can pick the lock.'

'You can pick locks?'

She reached in her handbag and pulled out a metal nail file. 'Did I ever tell you about my misspent youth, sneaking out of my boarding school dormitories in the middle of the night?'

'I definitely need to hear more about that.'

Girl wanted to stay by the front door, but Jon dragged her around the side of the heating engineer's premises to the back of the building, which was cluttered with broken pallets and empty bins. There was a dusty window which clearly belonged to the heating engineer (he looked in it anyway, and saw a deserted storeroom with a calendar hanging on the wall, opened to March 2020), and a much smaller and higher window that might belong to the middle unit. He gazed up at it, wondering if it was big enough to allow a person through.

Girl barked and he looked down in time to see a large rat run directly in front of his feet. She lunged for it but it darted away under a pile of rubbish. Was he imagining things, or could he see the reflections of many pairs of beady eyes down there?

Shuddering, he tied Girl to a railing out of reach of the rubbish. 'I know you're not happy about this, but it will only be a few minutes,' he told her. 'Unless I fall through the window and break my leg.'

She barked again.

He checked inside a large plastic waste bin for creatures, and then pushed it up underneath the window, upended it, and climbed on top. From here, on his tiptoes, he could reach up and grab the windowsill. He pulled himself upwards, wishing he'd done more pull-ups for, like, his entire life, and managed to get high enough to look through the window.

It was boarded up. The whole thing was way too small for him to squeeze through anyway. Maybe Saffy could manage it, but this was several metres up – how would she get down once she was inside?

He gave up, dropped to the bin, jumped to the ground, collected Girl. She tugged him back towards the front of the building, her paws scrabbling on the asphalt in her haste.

When he reached Saffy, she was standing in front of the open door, bearing a look of great satisfaction.

'You picked the lock?'

'I told you, I have hidden depths.'

'Don't ever turn to a life of crime. You'd be frighteningly good at it.' He kissed her, and she returned it with enthusiasm.

They turned on the torches on their phones and walked through the door, Girl leading the way, with Jon following after, Saffy last, closing the door after them. It was only when they had set foot inside did he think that maybe it might have been a good idea to bring a weapon.

The unit was pitch-dark inside, but with his torch he could see it was one big room, open to the corrugated iron roof, with a concrete floor. All four walls were covered with soundproofing foam, like the inside of egg cartons.

Seeing that, Jon had to catch his breath, remembering with sharpness a similarly soundproofed room in a basement where he had thought he was going to die.

Saffy took his suddenly sweaty hand and squeezed it. 'There's no one here,' she said in a low voice. 'You don't have anything to worry about.'

He nodded and swallowed. 'Let's turn on the lights.'

She turned back and played her torch over the wall near the entrance until she found a light switch. Even though they hadn't been in the darkness for very long, the lights, when they came on, were bright enough to momentarily dazzle him. He blinked a few times before he could quite believe what he was seeing.

He'd expected one of two things: an empty dirty warehouse containing the rest of the remains of Tony Jones or some other victims; or a grisly killing floor out of a horror film, bloodstained and with implements of torture hanging from the walls, sputtering yellow-tinged lights, those inexplicable sheets of plastic that always seemed to be hung from the ceiling in these films, rats and spiders scurrying to their squalid hiding places.

This was neither. But it was possibly even worse.

The room was scrupulously clean. As in, ridiculously clean. The concrete floor was polished to gleaming. Not a single spider web dangled from a rafter; not a single speck of dust dared to soil a surface. The lighting was superb: bright and crystal clear, with not a flicker.

In the centre of the room was a large stainless steel table. It was empty and unmarked. Several stainless steel bowls were stacked underneath it. Against one wall was a stainless steel industrial sink. Next to it was a stainless steel chest freezer, humming. On the opposite wall was a stainless steel cabinet, about two metres high. All of this stainless steel shone with nary a smudge nor fingerprint.

'Maybe this, because of what we've been watching on TV,' Saffy said, 'but this looks like someone has been taking lessons off *Dexter*. Though . . . I guess it could be a dog biscuit manufacturer?'

'Let's hope so.' Jon inhaled properly for the first time since he'd entered. Bleach and Dettol. 'This place would pass a hygiene test, anyway. Maybe we should be wearing gloves.'

He realised he was still holding Girl's lead, and dropped it. Although she'd been so keen to sniff around the outside of the building, now that she was inside she seemed almost bored. She sniffed around in a desultory fashion, and then sat down and scratched her ear.

Saffy pulled her jumper sleeves down to cover her hands, then opened the cabinet and stepped back so that Jon could see inside too. Inside it was so orderly that he wasn't quite sure of what he was seeing and the significance of it until he'd looked at everything and began taking a mental catalogue.

On the bottom shelf, the widest one, were power tools. Drill, circular saw, jigsaw, chainsaw, Henry hoover, a couple of other things Jon couldn't identify because he had never really been very good at DIY.

The shelf above had hand tools, each of them laid out. Hacksaw. Axe. Hammer. Mallet. Chisel. Forceps. Scissors. Scalpels. Stanley knives. Incongruously: a comb. This also held stainless steel kidney dishes, and again incongruously, a turkey baster. Several tarps were folded neatly on one end.

The top shelf was the consumables. Bulk boxes of bin liners, clingfilm, latex gloves, face masks, paper towels, surgical gowns. And box after box after box of gaffer tape. Next to these were bottles of bleach and Dettol, packets of sponges, a glass bottle labelled CAUSTIC SODA, and a very large plastic bottle labelled LYE.

'Holy shit,' Jonathan breathed.

'I don't think this is a dog biscuit factory,' said Saffy.

'We need to call the police.'

'Because someone has a very neat and well-organised tool collection? We broke in here, remember?'

'If there's clear evidence of a crime, we need to report it.'

'Well, let's look for evidence of a crime, then.'

Both of them gazed at the chest freezer, humming against the opposite wall.

'That's more than big enough for a body,' said Jon.

'Maybe a few, if you stacked them up or chopped them apart.'

Jon shook his head. 'I've never had a pyjama day like this.' He started for the freezer, but Saffy stopped him with a hand on his arm.

'Why do you think you were sent a photo of this place?' she asked. 'Why you? If someone knew this was ... oh, a murder boutique, a dismemberment studio, whatever it is, why send it to you and not to the police? What do they expect you to do? And who sent it in the first place? Is it the guy who uses this place?'

'I don't know,' said Jon. 'They want me to investigate, that's clear.'

'So, a fan of yours? Like Simon Simons? Do you think they're watching us?'

'If it were a trap, it seems as if we'd've already had the jump scare.'

'Is it one of Cyril's little hideaways?'

'No, Cyril did all of his victims in his bathtub at home, after giving them a bubble bath. He says it helped the bodies relax and made them easier to cut up.'

'You have weird friends.'

'He's not my friend. Anyway, Cyril didn't kill Tony Jones. He says that and I believe him.'

'Sounds like he's a friend to me,' Saffy muttered, and then turned at the sound of a snort.

Girl had suddenly developed an interest in a small patch of floor and was sniffing at it, blowing air out of her nose in loud blasts between sniffs. She was so intent that she revolved around the patch with her nose as a pivot.

When they went to look, though, the spot looked like all the rest of the floor. No obvious bloodstains or evidence.

'Whoever cleaned this place missed a bit with the mop, I guess,' said Saffy, straightening. 'They're probably kicking themselves right now.'

'A sniffer dog and a forensics team might be able to find something,' said Jonathan. 'Have you got a pen to mark the floor?'

She rummaged through her handbag. 'I've got a Chanel lip liner.' She squatted and carefully drew a red circle on the floor around the spot. Girl looked disgusted. She sat down and started licking her arse.

'I guess we're planning on calling the police, then,' said Saffy, standing and examining the tip of her lip liner.

'I think we have to. We don't have the resources that they do.'

'I'm not sure how I feel about that, seeing as I just smeared my DNA all over the floor.' She bit her lip. 'Ugh, and I thought I was being clever.'

'We'll have to report it ourselves instead of calling in an anonymous tip. They'll be able to eliminate our DNA.'

'But we're going to look in the freezer first, right?'

'We are definitely going to look in the freezer.'

They approached it slowly.

'Do you think it has the rest of Tony Jones?' Saffy asked in a low voice.

'I guess we'll find out.'

She cringed. 'If so, I hope he has his clothes on. I've seen enough naked dead guys for a while.'

Jon pulled his sleeves over his hands, as Saffy had done, and gripped the lid of the chest freezer. He steeled himself before opening it wide. Better to find out all at once, than trying to peek inside.

It was clean, white, and empty.

Saffy peered in. 'Not even a pack of frozen peas?'

'Not even a fish finger.' Jon closed the freezer, trying not to think too much about the fact that he felt distinctly disappointed. He, too, had seen enough naked dead guys for a lifetime.

So why did some small part of him want to see more?

Chapter Thirty-Seven

THE NEXT MORNING, WHILE JONATHAN'S telling the police about our little adventure, I've a facial booked first thing, and then a blow-dry, and then I'm in the middle of a mani-pedi when Jonathan rings to say that Detective Inspector Atherton wants to see me at my soonest convenience.

'I'm sorry,' he says. 'I tried to keep you out of it.'

'That's fine,' I say breezily. 'Even Dr Watson had to speak with Inspector Lestrade sometimes, didn't he? I'll pop round after I've got my nails done.'

I keep my nails on the short and sensible side. I'd been planning on classic red, but since I'm going to the cop shop, I change to a pale, innocent pink on both fingers and toes. As I exchange a few words with Mandy, the nail technician, I absent-mindedly slip a small pot of wax into the pocket of my coat.

On the cab ride, while carefully dipping each of my fingertips in the wax, I experience a growing sense of curiosity. I've never actually been in a police station before.

Of course, I've been interviewed by the police. The first time was after Harold's death, and I've deftly avoided their questions after several other deaths, too. And I was debriefed after the whole encounter in that terrible basement. But all those times I was a potential witness, so all I had to do was feign ignorance, and also they were in the comfort of my own home or school.

I always sort of assumed that if I ever crossed the threshold of a law enforcement facility, I would be in handcuffs.

But here I am, tipping the driver, sashaying into reception, wearing head-to-toe Stella McCartney and looking better than anything the gormless spotty copper at the desk has ever seen in his life of dealing with lawbreakers and the general public.

'Good morning, I have an appointment with DI Atherton?' I say sweetly to him.

He goggles.

'I know,' I say in a lowered voice, smiling in a way calculated for maximum dazzle. 'I don't look like your typical criminal, do I?'

'Um,' he says, and clicks wildly at his computer. 'Name?'

Fortunately for him, another copper appears behind him at that moment and says, 'Ms Huntley-Oliver? We're ready for you. Please come through, door on your left.'

I tip the first copper a wink, go through the door, and follow the second copper down a corridor. She's got a poker face and either she's immune to my charms or she's straight.

I know you're dying for the details, but honestly I try not to notice as much of the interior of a police station as possible. I don't want it to haunt my memory. Suffice it to say, it's not The Ritz. It's not even a Travelodge. If the décor and (I'm sorry to mention it) the aroma are any indication of police funding in this country, it's no wonder that it takes a vigilante to tackle sex crime.

I meet DI Atherton in what I assume is a conference room. He's wearing his usual rumpled cheap suit. He rises when I enter.

'Hello again!' I greet him. 'It's so lovely to see you!' To his evident consternation, I kiss him on either cheek, as if I'm at a cocktail party. He smells of stale coffee and, interestingly, of dry shampoo.

'Ms Huntley-Oliver. Yes. Thank you for coming in.'

'You're looking well! When was the last time we met – in Jonathan's hospital room after he lost his toe? You've had your hair cut since then, I think?'

'Er. Yes. Thank you.'

He doesn't quite pull out a chair for me, but I can see he's wondering if he should.

I sink gracefully into one of the seats, graciously refuse an offer of coffee or tea, and position myself into a posture of courteous curiosity. He also sits. I notice that for a large man, he's quite a compact sitter. Not a manspreader.

'So,' I gush, 'I'm dying to know what you think of that place that Jonathan and I discovered! What do you think it is? Is it, like, a place where someone was murdered?' I let my voice sink to a thrilled whisper. 'What do you think the power tools were used for?'

'I can't comment on that, Ms Huntley-Oliver. However, I'd like to take your statement about how you came across it.'

'Oh, but Jonathan told you all about that already, didn't he? Really I was just along for the ride. Well, I mean, I drove my car, so that's a manner of speaking.' I giggle. It's so fun to play Dumb Blonde.

The uniformed officer, who's standing by the door, can't hide her expression of contempt. So much for female solidarity.

'If you can talk me through it,' says Atherton, patiently.

So I do, though (as agreed with Jonathan) I don't mention anything about picking the lock, and obviously, I also don't say anything about how I *actually* opened the warehouse door, which was with my own key. I go through the whole visit, including opening the cupboards and the freezer, and circling the spot that Girl was interested in with my own limited-edition lip liner.

'Then we left,' I finish. 'And Jonathan rang you.'

Atherton reads me back what I said. I had to leave out my own emotional thrills, so it's quite a boring account.

'That's right,' I say.

Atherton sits back and frowns. The familiar routine has given him some of his gravitas and grumpiness back.

'Did it occur to you at any point that you were committing a crime?' he asks.

My eyes widen like those of a fluffy bunny in a set of headlights. 'A *crime*?'

'Breaking and entering. Trespassing on private property.'

I wrinkle my nose. More fluffy bunny stuff. I can do this in my sleep. 'Well, we were sort of invited?'

'How do you figure that?'

'The photo that someone sent to Jonathan? Speaking of which, who do you think sent that photo? Was it a killer?'

This is the only part of this statement that really interests me. Who's been watching me? Why have they been sending stuff to Jonathan instead of confronting me themselves? It's rude.

'I can't comment,' says Atherton, by which I assume he means he hasn't a clue.

'Were we in danger?' I simper.

'Did you feel as if you were in danger?'

'Well. No. We had the dog with us, and she's quite good protection. Have you met Girl?'

'I have, yes.'

'So you know what I mean.'

Atherton frowns some more. Does he ever actually solve crimes, I wonder? Or does he get paid to be a grouch and leap to obvious conclusions?

'Since you met Mr Desrosiers,' he says, 'you seem to have been involved in several crimes.'

I think back. 'Well, one or two, I suppose. There was that whole thing with Simons, which was quite unpleasant.'

'Does that worry you?'

'It's Jonathan's job, isn't it?'

'Is it?'

I return his piercing stare with my best blank rabbit look. Not a thought in my head except grass and flowers, that's me.

'Ms Huntley-Oliver,' he says, 'it's not my place to give you relationship advice. But if you were my daughter—'

I have to bite the inside of my lip to keep from bursting out into incredulous laughter at this point.

'—I would ask you to consider if it's in your best interests to be involved with a man who keeps putting himself, and you, in dangerous situations.'

'Oh, I agree entirely,' I say.

'I'm glad to hear it.'

'It's *not* your place to give me relationship advice.'

He puts down his pen. 'But it is my place to advise you to stay away from amateur sleuthing, and allow the police to do our job.'

'You're not going to charge us with trespassing, are you?'

'Do you understand what I'm saying, Ms Huntley-Oliver?'

'I do understand. Yes.'

'Then no, I'm not going to charge you in this instance.'

I sigh in relief. My record remains spotless.

'Thank you,' I say.

He stands, and I stand too. This has been mildly entertaining, but only slightly more so than watching paint dry.

'Are we finished?'

'Almost,' he says. 'We don't have fingerprints on file for you, so PC Chowdery will take them.'

'Ooh, you want to fingerprint me? That's so exciting!' But then I frown. 'Hold on, you said you weren't going to charge me.'

'For elimination purposes,' he tells me.

I pout. 'I have another appointment in, like, five minutes. It would be much more convenient to do it later.'

'I'm all ready for you,' says PC Chowdery. 'It will only take a few minutes.'

'But I just had a manicure. Won't it get all inky?'

'We use a digital scanner,' says PC Chowdery. 'But I might have some of the old ink pads around here somewhere, if you'd rather.'

She's enjoying this.

'Do you need my DNA too?' I think about all of the crimes that could, conceivably, have my DNA all over them, stretching back years. I was as careful as possible, but what if I slipped up? I committed some of those crimes before my brain was fully developed. And at least one of them while drunk.

Though the less said about that instance, the better. Ugh, the hangover.

'That won't be necessary,' says Atherton.

'I suppose not. You can literally look up my ancestry in Debrett's.'

'No, I mean that we don't routinely take DNA samples for elimination.'

'So just fingerprints?'

'Just fingerprints.'

I consider. I'm a great fan of latex gloves, but sometimes I'm spontaneous. Fingerprints could possibly also be quite inconvenient.

'Do I have to? Like, is it illegal if I don't?'

'No. You don't have to. But it would be of great help to us if you do.'

'The thing is,' I say, 'I might want to have a career as an international spy at some point. Jane Bond? You know? It's one of the few professions open to people in my social class. But if I've got my fingerprints on file, where will I be then? I'll have to have my fingertips sanded off.'

'We'll give you a release form,' says Atherton. 'You can request that they are destroyed.'

'Or,' says PC Chowdery, 'you can tell MI6 to get in touch with us.'

That's it. They have me beaten. I could be the best actress and liar in the world, but I can't get out of this without looking suspicious.

'Fine,' I say. 'But please try not to ruin my nails.'

'I wouldn't dream of it,' says PC Chowdery, and I know I'm going to have to make an emergency stop at the manicurist right after this, before my appointment with Liza.

Fair enough. I can replace the pot of wax that I used to make my prints unreadable.

Chapter Thirty-Eight

I PRACTICALLY FLOAT INTO LIZA'S OFFICE and fling myself on the vulva couch. 'Oh my God,' I say to the Cabbage White ceiling, 'you are a miracle worker, you are amazing!'

Liza's hair is wrapped in an electric-blue silk turban today. She sits on her chair in the lotus position and says, 'You sound happy.'

'I really am.'

'That's wonderful. You were a little upset at the end of our last session. Can you tell me what has changed?'

'Well, I decided to follow your advice online about building intimacy, instead of focusing just on sex.'

'That's a wise idea. Intimacy in all areas is so important. How did it go?'

'Great! We've been spending time together, having fun. Exploring shared interests.'

'You've been letting him in?'

'I've been showing him things that I've never shared with anyone before.'

It's a shame that one of my favourite corpse disposal facilities has been compromised, but I have other ones scattered around

London and the world. And it was totally worth it, just for the expression on Jonathan's face when he saw inside the cabinet and all my lovely rows of tools.

Sure, someone is on to me, and this is worrying ... but Jonathan was *there*! It still gives me shivers of excitement!

'And how did that feel?'

'Fabulous. Really fabulous. I felt *seen*, you know?'

Liza grins. 'There's no better feeling than to be seen. It means we've been vulnerable, and our payoff for that is being accepted. Not just for our appearance or the act we're putting on for other people, but for who we really are deep down inside.'

'I mean, there are layers, obviously. And it's a process. I can't show Jonathan everything.'

'That's OK. It's early days. You're learning how to open up.'

'And one day ... maybe he'll be ready to see everything about me.'

'How does that possibility feel?'

'Good.' Although Jonathan has a worrying amount of faith in the police. Would he still have blabbed to Atherton if he knew that he was looking at *my* secret life?

'Well,' I amend, '... good in theory. In reality, I think there's a large possibility that things could go horribly wrong.'

'You're worried that if you reveal too much, he'll react badly?'

'That's an understatement.' Several consecutive life sentences is much worse than 'bad'.

'So ... how does that tie in with what we were talking about in our last session, about your fears?'

I should have known that she wouldn't just be happy for me, that she would want to keep digging. But I'm paying for this, and it has helped, so I think about it.

'I guess I am afraid that if someone sees all of me, the real me, that they won't like me.'

Liza nods wisely. 'So many of us have poor self-esteem, deep down inside. And we reinforce it with negative self-talk.'

'What do you mean by that?'

'You know, hyper-criticism. We look at ourselves in the mirror and we think, "Gosh, I'm fat." Or we make a mistake and we tell ourselves that we're bad at everything, and we'll never succeed.'

'That's all part of the patriarchy,' I tell her. 'If women can be brainwashed to doubt and judge themselves constantly, they don't have the energy or the confidence to challenge the prevailing order. Women are told we need to be perfect even to deserve the smallest reward, while all these mediocre men are just gobbling up all the power and benefits.'

'Well, yes,' says Liza. 'The personal is very much political when it comes to gender equality. Though I don't think low self-esteem is limited to one gender. Before I transitioned, I certainly suffered my share of it. But I was talking more specifically about you. Your own self-esteem.'

'Oh, I don't have that problem. I literally think I am the best.'

Liza blinks.

'Yes,' I say, 'I know, women aren't supposed to say that. I am probably a narcissist, but also I am beautiful and clever and fun and rich, so it's objective standards too. That's not a problem in my relationship, though. Jonathan also agrees that I'm beautiful and clever and fun and rich. We really think a lot of each other. He is also beautiful and clever and fun. He's not so rich, but he's extra beautiful and clever to make up for it, and also I'm rich enough for both of us.'

'So ... what are you afraid of him discovering about you?'
That I am a monster.
I don't say this. The silence stretches out between us.
But ... what else is there to say?
I don't believe I'm a monster. I believe I am a necessary force for the overall good of society. But Jonathan might think I'm a monster. And that would end everything.
I can't talk about that, though, obviously.
'I don't know,' I say at last.
Liza doesn't reply to this. She seems to be quite comfortable with silence. Usually, so am I, but only when I'm using it for my own benefit. In this case, I feel a bit like a butterfly at the end of a pin.
I squirm on the vulva seat.
'Can we talk about something else maybe?' I ask. 'I don't think this angle of questioning is leading anywhere productive.'
'OK,' says Liza, kindly. 'Let's take a different tack. You're a feminist, which I *love*! But last session, you mentioned that you wished you weren't attracted to men. Can we unpick that a little?'
'Sure,' I say, though it seems self-evident.
'Tell me about the men in your life. Let's start with the good ones. Who have been your great male role models?'
'Good men?'
'Yes.'
'I mean ... like Nelson Mandela. He was a good guy, right? Martin Luther King Jr. David Attenborough, he's a national treasure.'
'How about men in your life that you know personally?'
'I am offended that you think I don't know David Attenborough personally.'

She doesn't crack a smile. This woman is hard as nails.

'Jonathan's a good man,' I say.

'I mean earlier, in your formative years. What about your dad? Was he a positive force in your life?'

'I didn't know my biological father. I was five years old when he died. And by all accounts, he wasn't much of a hands-on parent. Nor was my mother.'

'Do you have any memories of him at all?'

I think. 'He wore glasses. I remember the scent of his aftershave. I think it was Chanel Homme. I suppose if I remember that, he must have held me.'

'But nothing else? Good or bad?'

I shake my head. 'As far as I know, he could have been a sociopath. In fact, that's likely. Lots of successful people are.'

'Do you have good childhood memories of any other men?'

'My stepfather had a gardener called Mo. He was a nice man. He carried photos of his grandkids with him in his wallet. He was very tall and once he gave me a ride on his shoulders around the lawn. I loved it. It felt like I could see the whole world from up there.'

'You felt safe?'

'Yes.'

'What happened to him?'

'One day he wasn't there any more. I assume he got fired. My stepfather went through a lot of staff.'

'So, the men in your childhood were impermanent and inconsistent?'

'I suppose so.'

'That must have made it difficult to trust.'

'*That* wasn't what made it difficult to trust men,' I blurt out.

She waits. And it's not like this should be a difficult thing to say. I know the answer.

It's just that I've never said it out loud before, to a person in the same room.

'It was my stepfather,' I say at last. 'It was Harold.'

Chapter Thirty-Nine

'You know what you look like to me, with your good bag and your cheap shoes?'

'A rube.' Jon sat down across from Cyril and squinted at him. Something was different about him, something subtle and sleek. His hair was still close-shaven, his face the same, he hadn't gained or lost weight, but he did look ...

'Have you had your prison clothes tailored?' Jon asked.

Cyril grinned. 'Of course not. Who in their right mind would give me needles and scissors? I could take out half the people in here.'

Jon couldn't help but flash back to the instruments in the industrial lock-up yesterday afternoon. The scissors: some of them small and delicate, some of them heavy-bladed and strong. All of them sharp.

'Just kidding you,' said Cyril. 'There are some lads over in low-security who are learning tailoring. They need guinea pigs. I sent them my measurements. No rules broken at all.'

Cyril glanced at the nearby guard, and winked at Jon.

'You like to fuck with my head, don't you, Cyril?'

'Whatever it takes, mate. Whatever it takes.' He leaned back in his chair and folded his manacled hands on his lap. 'I wasn't expecting to see you so soon, but then I read the news.'

'Tony Jones.'

'Was I right, or was I right?'

'You were right.'

'Did you tell your Scotland Yard friend that I was the one to tip you off? Like I said, I'm eager to build goodwill.'

'Atherton is keen for any information you have about your own victims.'

'In good time. When was the last time you saw him?'

'This morning.'

Cyril looked Jon up and down slowly. Jon couldn't pretend that it was entirely pleasant.

'*You* look different, mate,' Cyril said.

'How do I look different?'

'It's not your clothes, you've never exactly been a fashion icon. It's your carriage. The way you're sitting. There's a light in your eyes that hasn't been there for a while. What's up, Jonny? You in love with Atherton? Or is it that blonde?'

'I'm not talking about my love life with you.'

'Ah! That's it, then. Well, congratulations. I'm sorry I won't be able to come to the wedding.' He narrowed his eyes. 'That's not the only thing, though. You don't look horny and lovestruck. You look happy, yeah. But you also look like yourself. The way you looked when I first met you, years ago. When you were spending all your time hunting down the scumbag who killed Lianne Murray.'

He'd stopped being surprised when Cyril was insightful. After all, they had been friends for a while before Jon found out that he was a crazed killer.

In a way, although Jon kept on denying it, he and Cyril were still friends. Cyril might be his *only* male friend. Many of the people he'd considered friends had sided with Amy in the divorce and didn't speak with him any more. The rest he'd alienated when he disappeared off to Scotland for months.

He was close with his agent, Edie, and he was growing closer to Saffy. But he didn't have any men he could talk about this stuff with.

'You're right,' Jon said. 'After— all of that happened, with me finding the bodies and with you stabbing me in the kitchen—'

'I've said I'm sorry about that, mate. I really am.'

'I didn't know who I was. We discussed it last time I visited you. I'd defined myself by my job for so long, and then Amy left me because of it, and then I nearly died because of it. I wanted to distance myself. But I didn't know who I was, if I wasn't investigating a story.'

'Right. It's like what we talked about before. It used to be a job for life, bring home the bacon, drink on the weekend, a bit of football, a man could take some pride in his work. I mean, not for the homosexuals like me, but for the straights like you. No more. Now it's all absent fathers, mothers at work all hours, no youth programmes, no social clubs, impossible standards in porn, there's nothing for young men except for anger. It's the modern crisis in masculinity, Jonny. I can guarantee you that at least ninety-nine per cent of the men in this building have suffered from it. Including the screws.'

'I don't think that a lack of social clubs was your problem, Cyril.'

'Well, like I said, I'm different. Anyway, we're not here to talk about me. You said you've been lost. Are you found now?'

Jon leaned on his elbows on the table. 'My dad was a terrible father. He was a violent alcoholic. He beat my mother. She had permanent scars from it. But one thing he was good at was being a detective. He was very good at it. I chose journalism to be different from him, and to be honest, also to piss him off; but it turns out that I inherited his passion for investigating and solving problems. Over the past few days, on the trail of Tony Jones, I've felt more alive than I have in months and months. And not just because I'm solving a case – it's because I'm helping to right the wrongs he caused.'

'Inspirational.'

'So I have a choice: I can try not to be like my father at all, and deny the one good thing that he gave me. Or I can try to use that one good part to the best of my ability, to make this world a better place.'

Cyril clapped his hands. 'Bravo! Oh, good for you! I knew you'd come round.'

'Please don't ruin this by saying you told me so.'

He shut his mouth tight and shook his head. 'Mmm-mmh.'

'So yes,' said Jon, 'I will write that book about your crimes.'

At that, Cyril's slender thread of self-control was gone. He punched the air, rattling his chains. The guard stepped forward.

'Result!' Cyril cheered. 'Oh, you won't regret it, mate.'

'My agent is also going to be very happy.'

'I love that woman. Send her some flowers from me, will you?'

'I will not. That would be very creepy. However, Cyril, when I write this book, I am going to write it on my own terms. That means that it is not going to glorify what you did.'

'Of course not. I'm a terrible human being.'

'I'm going to tell the story from the point of view of your victims. I'm going to learn everything possible about them. They were men who had slipped through the cracks, who were vulnerable and frightened. I'm going to find out what led them into your web, and I'm going to write about what we can do, as a society, to make sure that other young men like them are safe.'

'See?' Cyril was beaming. 'This is why I knew you'd be the perfect person for this.'

'I mean it. I'm not going to make you a hero. Not even an anti-hero. This isn't going to be an ego trip for you. I'm going to show you for the inadequate misfit that you are.'

'Absolutely! Jonny, I keep on telling you: I loved those men that I killed. I truly loved them. That's why I kept their heads on ice, so they would last forever. I want nothing more than for you to immortalise them.'

'And while we're working on it, you might think about immortalising those victims that the police don't know about yet, by talking about them.'

'I'll think about it.'

'Time,' said the guard, and Cyril stood up.

'I guess you didn't remember the foot cream, huh?' he said, holding out his hands for the guard to detach him.

'I was in hospital for two weeks with the stab wound you gave me. I think you can suffer from athlete's foot for a little while.'

'Fair.'

Jon stood up, and before the guard could lead Cyril away, he said, 'One more thing. If you loved them so much, why did you kill them? Why couldn't you love them when they were alive?'

'Love and death are two sides of the same coin, mate.' The guard started walking, and Cyril peered back over his shoulder. 'You're falling in love, so maybe soon you'll know what I mean.'

Chapter Forty

Quite a bit of my self-image rests upon my belief that generally I am cool, calm, and collected. I am on top of most situations. Not someone who kills in the throes of passion, or makes stupid mistakes because of emotion: I am calculated and correct, poised and graceful, raised with a stiff upper lip and a disarmingly sincere-sounding charm. Look at the way I handled myself in the police station earlier.

But after my session with Liza I am none of this.

I'm unbecomingly sweaty, and my blow-dry has gone limp and is clinging to the sides of my face and neck. My clothes are wrinkled in places that clothes should not wrinkle. My mouth is dry; my palms are wet; my heart is pounding and my stomach feels as if I have eaten an entire live baby kangaroo who has very sharp teeth and claws.

I'm not accustomed to emotions that are beyond my control, so it's only when I leave Liza's inspiration-plastered office that I realise what I am feeling.

It's fear.

I stop dead in Harley Street, narrowly avoiding being run over by a woman pushing a pram with a Chihuahua in it.

I'm not afraid of Harold, am I? I used to be, when I was a child. But I haven't been afraid of him since I was twelve years old, when I killed him. When I transformed him from a large, strong, powerful man into a corpse floating in a pool. Then there was nothing to be afraid of any more. He couldn't hurt me, and he couldn't hurt Susie.

But now: heart racing, stomach roiling, pores leaking. I'm afraid, all right. Just from the thought of him. Just from saying his name.

He's powerless. Why does he still have so much power over me?

In moments of fear, real fear, when circumstances are totally out of our control, our primitive brains take over, and like animals of prey, we have only four choices of response: fight, flight, freeze, or fawn. Fawning is the least commonly understood of the four, but when you're vulnerable – especially when you're a child, or a woman, with nowhere to run and no chance of succeeding in a fight – sometimes it's the only choice for survival. Go soft, smile, play along with whatever he wants. Pretend you like it.

Forget that later on, when it's over and you try to get help, people will say, 'You must have wanted it. You must have liked the attention. You didn't fight or run away.'

Forget that people will blame you for what he did. And that maybe you'll believe them.

Just stay alive. And smile.

Fawning is what I did for six years, when I was a very little girl, while I kept Harold's secret. While I tried to figure out how to please him so he would stop hurting me. When I offered myself to him as a bribe, so that he would leave Susie alone.

It was only when I learned how to fight that I stopped being afraid. Fighting is how you take back your power. Fighting is how you make everything right again.

But right now, I don't feel as if anything is right at all. I feel as if all the fight has been punched out of me. A big, sickening sucker punch to the stomach.

I lean against a wall, my legs suddenly weak as a horrific realisation strikes me.

Harold is my origin story.

Everything that I am is because of him. It's because of what he did to me. That's why I kill bad men. But that's not the problem – I *like* killing bad men.

The problem is the fear that he instilled in me. The fear I thought I'd killed along with him. And for the first time, I see the connection between my love life and my murder life.

I've been stalking Sir Thomas, but I haven't been able to kill him yet – not because of the enormous hairy bodyguard or the home security or because I'm afraid of being caught. All of those are bullshit excuses. The real reason is because everything about Sir Thomas reminds me of Harold, and killing him would bring me too close to that terrible moment in my past.

I can't allow myself to be vulnerable with Jonathan, a man I'm falling in love with, because the last time I was vulnerable, it was with Harold.

I killed my stepfather.

But he's still the most powerful person in my life.

It's in that moment that something horrible happens. Something that I have spent my entire life avoiding. Something worse than showing my homicidal urges in public. Something worse than being stabbed in the course of duty.

Even something worse than being caught and thrown into prison and having to wear shoes with Velcro fastenings for the rest of my life.

I feel tears welling up in my eyes.

Chapter Forty-One

IN MY WORLD, THERE ARE only two cures for tears, and I don't feel up to homicide right now. So I hail a cab to take me to my sister's house.

As I arrive, I see a familiar figure emerging from Susie's door. After bursting into tears on Harley Street, the last person I want to see is my sister's feckless and sandal-wearing boyfriend Finlay. My reflexes aren't as sharp as usual, so before I can duck behind a post box, he spots me and comes striding over.

'Saffy!' he says cheerfully. Much too cheerfully. 'How's it hanging?'

'Fine.'

'You look clapped out, mate! Rough night?'

I'll show you what a rough night looks like. We'll start with an electric drill on your kneecaps. 'I'm fine. Everything's fine.'

He puffs out his chest. 'You should try what I'm doing. Installed a rail in my bedroom and I spend twenty minutes every morning hanging upside down to increase blood flow to my brain. I feel great! Biohacking is the new thing, you know what I mean?'

'Have you tried microdosing with arsenic?'

He laughs and claps me on the back. 'You're in a terrible mood, eh? You're not getting enough sleep! Too much night prowling, am I right?'

I wish. 'I'm just going to visit my sister.'

'Her place is a mess! She's been dogsitting your dog this afternoon!'

'It's Jonathan's dog.'

'Speaking of which, how's Jonathan getting on with my biography?'

'He's almost done.' I try to pull away from him, but he's got hold of my arm.

'You know, big sis, when we first met, I thought you were a psycho bitch, but the more I get to know you, the more I think we have a lot in common!' He winks at me, and lets me go. 'Don't do anything I wouldn't do!'

'Don't count on it,' I mutter, and stalk away. He saunters off, whistling in a key known only to douchebags.

No one responds to my knock on Susie's door, so I let myself in. Finlay was right: her place is a mess, littered with bottles, glasses, bowls of crisps, mugs, the remains of a sushi platter and, oddly, at least three Monopoly boards. Susie is nowhere to be seen, but I can hear the shower running so I go into her bedroom, where the bed is unmade and Girl is sprawled in the middle of it, with her own pink satin heart-shaped pillow. The dog greets me with a snarl. At least the dog, unlike Finlay, is honest.

'Nice to see you too,' I say, and keeping one ear trained on the sound of my sister in the shower, I open her wardrobe. In a rare stroke of luck, her saucy schoolgirl costume is lying in a heap on the floor. I deftly pluck out the Eton tie. The last thing I want to do is inadvertently frame my sister for murder. I've wadded it into my pocket before the water turns off and Susie emerges, wrapped in towels and looking fresh-faced and rosy.

'Saffy!' she says, delighted, and hugs me. For a blissful moment I hold her tight and I remember how when she was a little girl, whenever she would skin her knee or get a cold, whenever she fell off her pony or she got a splinter in her finger, she would come to me to soothe her small hurts and hold her until she felt better.

'How are you?' she asks.

'How are *you*? It looks like you had a party.'

'Oh my God! It was the best. Some of the other volunteers at the helpline came over and we had a board game evening. They are all so nice! And all different sorts of people, from all over. Have you ever met anyone from Wolverhampton?'

'Possibly?'

'I had to look it up! I feel like I have a whole new group of friends but for once they are people who really care about other people, you know? Like, their focus isn't on partying or shopping – there's nothing wrong with partying and shopping obviously, but they are deeper. And I feel like they really like me, for *me*.'

'You're a very likeable person.'

'I think maybe I've finally found my niche, the place where I belong. I can't wait for you to meet them!'

'I can't wait either. I'm really proud of you.'

Susie starts rummaging through her clothes. 'What were you doing in my wardrobe, by the way?'

'I was looking for my Alexander McQueen jacket.'

'The cropped one? It's in there somewhere.' She pulls on one of her many pink tracksuits and wanders off, leaving me to find my own jacket. Eventually I locate it near the back, half-off a hanger. 'I think it looks better on you anyway,' she calls.

While I'm in her wardrobe, I also locate faux-leather trousers, a vintage Agnès B chiffon blouse and a Hanae Mori pencil skirt, all of which belong to me. There is also a bra that looks vaguely familiar. Somehow I can't interest myself in collecting them all together, so I wander out and sit on the edge of her bed, watching my sister apply serum to her hair.

'What's up?' she asks me, catching my eye in the mirror. 'You're not yourself today. You're not even having a go at me for not using wooden hangers and alphabetising my shoes. And . . . have you been crying?'

'No.'

She sits next to me. Girl immediately gets up from her heart-shaped pillow and lies with her head in Susie's lap. My sister grabs my chin so she can look into my face.

'You have been crying! You look like a raccoon! What's the matter?'

'It's not important.'

'Saffy. *Tell me.*'

My little sister has become quite forceful lately.

'You never cry,' she says more softly. 'Please, tell me what's wrong.'

I swallow. This is much more difficult than discussing Susie's disregard for clothes care, even when those clothes happen to be mine.

'You know how we were talking about Harold the other day?' I ask.

'Yes, when we were talking about whether not having parents has prevented either of us from having functional relationships?

I'm not so worried about that any more, by the way. Finlay and I are getting on fine.'

'Does that mean he's stopped going dark for hours at a time?' This is a change of topic, but it's much easier to talk about my sister's terrible boyfriend and his bad choices than the central defining fact of my life.

Susie considers. 'I haven't noticed it so much? But then again I have been doing evening shifts at the helpline, and I turn off my own phone then anyway. I trust him, though. Why shouldn't he have some time to himself?'

'He's probably hanging upside down from a pole in his room like a man-size bat.'

'Yeah, that is bizarre. But his skin is amazing.' She scratches behind Girl's ears. 'Is that what you wanted to talk with me about? Do you know something about Finlay? He hasn't told you anything, has he? It's not cancer?' She suddenly grips my arm. 'Is that why he's doing all the weird health stuff?'

'As far as I know, he's doing the weird health stuff because he happens to be weird.'

'So why were you crying?'

'Because ... because of Harold. Because my session with Liza made me think about what Harold did to me, when we were children.'

'What did Harold do to you?'

I move my arm so that we are holding hands. I hold her tight, as tight as I can.

'You have to tell me, Saffy. Please. I can't stand you being upset.'

So I tell her.

* * *

Susie's face is wet. She's never had any shame about crying. She's holding both my hands, now, and sobbing as she asks me questions.

'The whole time?' she asks. 'Our entire childhood?'

'Whenever he was home, until he died.'

'Did Mummy know?'

This, I'm not sure of. But I know what Susie needs to hear, so I tell one of my rare barefaced lies.

'She knew nothing about it.'

'Did the staff know?'

'I think that was why he kept on firing people and hiring new ones.'

'And nobody helped you?'

I shake my head. 'I didn't tell anyone. He said it was our secret.'

'But why didn't you tell me?'

'You were a child.'

'No – I mean, why have you never told me before?'

I wipe tears from her cheeks.

'I've always wanted to protect you, Susie. That's my job.'

'But I'm grown up now.'

'That doesn't mean I have to protect you any less. I'm your big sister. And you . . . you think the best of people. You always have. It's your superpower. I never wanted to destroy that.'

'But I was going on about how Harold was my dad! How I missed him. That must have been awful for you. I'm so sorry.'

'You didn't know. Anyway, he was the only father figure you ever had. And he never did anything bad to you.'

Because I stopped him by knocking his head against concrete and holding him underneath the water until he died. But I'm not going to tell her about that part, either.

It's crazy how when I'm revealing myself, I have to conceal even more than usual.

'It's a good thing he's dead,' she says. 'Because if he weren't, I would *kill* him.'

'No you wouldn't. You believe in the sanctity of human life. But I appreciate the sentiment.'

Susie pulls me into a tight, tight hug.

'You don't have to protect me any more,' she says. 'We can protect each other now.'

I just hug her back, because of course I have to protect her. I'll always have to protect her. My love for Susie, and my need to protect innocent women like her, is as deep-seated and ingrained as my hatred for the men who commit these crimes.

If Harold's the dark side of my origin story, Susie is the bright side.

Chapter Forty-Two

I walk home from Susie's house, slowly and lost in thought, making a serious detour to explore every single spot in Kensington Gardens where it is possible for a dog to piss. Normally this canine meandering drives me sort of crazy, but today I need the time and space alone to think. I've thought before that maybe this is why people get dogs: you can talk to yourself while you're walking around outside without looking crazy. Girl doesn't like me, but at least she's a good listener.

Sometimes it feels like I've hardly had any time to rest for my entire life. I've been keeping secrets: first, Harold's secrets, and then my own. I've been working hard not to let anyone see who I really am, and keeping up a pretence of being a real person. I've been curating my wardrobe, maintaining frankly impossible beauty standards, and raising hundreds of thousands of pounds for charities. I've been finding bad men, and stalking them, and killing them, and disposing of their bodies in unobtrusive or very obtrusive ways.

And then there's the worry about getting caught. Someone knows what I've been doing. If they found my murder lock-up, they know that I killed Tony Jones, at least. And instead of going to the police, they've emailed my boyfriend about it, which means they probably have some sort of agenda. I've got to be specially on my guard, and that is exhausting.

Even my relationship with Jonathan has involved a lot of effort: plotting and planning behind the scenes, to lead him into the honey trap of my arms. Trying to seduce him, and failing to do the deed, tempting him with murders, and launching myself into therapy to try to improve our relationship.

'I'm tired,' I tell Girl. 'Is this, like, eldest daughter syndrome? I never give myself the chance to rest, I have to keep on achieving and achieving and achieving? Do you think a man would have treated himself to a little vacation by now?'

Girl, as usual, doesn't answer. She shits on a bed of marigolds.

She was probably the youngest in her litter. She'll never understand.

* * *

When I arrive at my bijou mews house in Kensington, Jonathan is ensconced on the sofa surrounded by papers. He jumps up and although Girl is greeting him as if they've been separated for ten thousand years, he hugs me and kisses me on the forehead before he notices the dog. At least that's a small win.

'Here,' he says, 'sit down, I'll clear all this out of the way.'

I take his place on the sofa, which is nicely warm, and he collects the scattered papers into a pile. 'What are you reading?'

'I started reading Finlay's autobiographical notes.'

'You *didn't*.'

'Just the first few pages.'

'Oh my God, you can't. Imagine the smirk on his face.'

'It's much more interesting than I expected.'

'No!'

He laughs. 'Seriously. Did you know he was a child actor?'

'No. Actually that explains quite a lot.' I wrinkle my nose. 'What else?'

'I don't know. Like I said, I only read a few pages.' He shoves the papers into the manila envelope. 'Are you OK? You look a little pale.'

'It's been a bit of an intense day. I'll be all right.'

But will I?

Right now, I'm not entirely certain. And that's so unusual for me that I'm shaken.

Normally, if I feel a little unbalanced, I'll go right out and kill a bad guy in a satisfyingly gory and schadenfreude-inducing way. I am Justice, I am Karma, I am Woman. But today's revelation that my entire body count, from the very beginning, was all due to Harold ... well, that takes the savour out of it.

Like, at what point does it stop being vengeance and start being a tribute?

'Do you want to talk about it?' asks Jonathan.

'No. Tell me about your day. Where have you been while Susie's been looking after the dog?'

'I've been at the prison visiting Cyril. But there's something much more exciting to tell you. Hold on.'

He goes into the kitchen and appears a moment later with two flutes and a bottle of champagne in an ice bucket. It's a decent château and vintage, but it's not from my cellar; I recognise it as a favourite at the bijou and pricey wine shop down the road. I watch as he pops the cork, a little clumsily but endearingly, and pours it. 'To you,' he says, holding up his glass in a toast.

'Why are you toasting me?'

'Because you've helped me more than you can possibly know.'

'Well, you're welcome.' I sip my champagne. Not bad. 'What have I specifically helped you with?'

'After I went to visit Cyril, I spoke with my agent. I've decided that I'm going to start writing again, and I've accepted a very generous contract.'

'Writing true crime?'

'It's the only thing I'm good at.'

I clap my hands. 'Jonathan! This is wonderful! I love your books!' I throw my arms around him and kiss him. 'I mean of course I'm supportive of whatever you choose to do, but I think you were meant to work in the true crime field and solve murders. You've got a gift. I'm so excited that you're going to use it! Oh and also you are good at lots of things, including cooking and kissing.'

'Thank you.' He grins at me and I can see that he's genuinely happy. Maybe for the first time since I've met him, he looks like a man who's completely in control of his life.

Unlike me. I am not in control of my life.

I can, however, put on an act.

'Who are you going to write about? Cyril? I hope it's Cyril.'

'Cyril.'

I clap my hands again. I'm the one who helped Jonathan solve that case, so I feel I can take some of the credit for this success. Of course Jonathan doesn't know that, but I can use all the success I can get right now.

'He's eager to cooperate with me, but I had to explain the parameters to him.'

'What parameters are those?'

'I want the focus of my work to be about the victims of murder, not the killers. I always tried to do that as much as I could, but I want to push it further with Cyril's story and use it to examine systematic inequality, male loneliness, and how young men slip through the cracks. I'm not interested in what Cyril did, so much as why it happened to these particular young men, and how we can stop it from happening again.'

'Because not all men are bad,' I say, before I know I'm going to say it. And then I catch up with myself. 'Listen to me, not-all-men-ing. There *are* a lot of bad men out there, Jonathan Desrosiers. And even more men who aren't good enough. But you are not one of them.'

'So I'll have less time to bake sourdough.'

'That's OK, though my personal trainer will be disappointed to lose the extra sessions. What made you change your mind?'

'I think it was talking with Blossom.'

'Yeah, it was tough to see her.'

'It was, but I was also inspired by afterwards, when you decided to help her by offering her nursing care and therapy, but in a way that preserved her dignity. That really touched me, Saffy. It made me realise I had to do whatever I could do, to help, and this is really the only thing I'm good at.'

'Wow.'

Well. This makes me feel a little bit better.

'Yeah.' He toasts his glass with mine again. 'Thank you.'

'Oh, you're welcome. Is it a *very* generous contract?'

'Very.' He grins and kisses me. 'Very very.'

'Oooh, goody. I've always wanted to date a rich guy who actually *earned* all his money.'

'Seriously, though, Saffy. You're a very generous person, and I know it doesn't matter to you, but it's been tough for me, dating someone who's wealthy. I know it sounds like a ridiculous problem to have, but a large part of my self-image has always come through my independence. And I grew up in a household where the man was the main provider. Those are deep foundations, and they're hard to ignore. The financial inequality has been making me feel a little shaky in myself. It shouldn't, and it's not your problem or your fault – but I'm relieved that I'll be on a better footing.'

'Wow. That's a lot to unpack. Have you been seeing a therapist on the side?'

He smiles a crooked smile. 'Sort of. I might have talked with Cyril. Not about our relationship, but about masculinity in general.'

'Romance advice from a serial killer. Now *that's* a book or four.'

He settles back on the sofa and snuggles me up against him.

'It's my turn to romance you,' he says. 'And I might not be very good at it, because frankly, I've never done it before. And I know we've had some ups and downs in the past few weeks.'

If only he knew.

'I think we both need some time off,' he continues. 'Proper time off, so we can spend some time together. Once I start working on this book, I'm likely to disappear for quite a while, into my own head. And that's what killed off my marriage. I don't want to do it again.'

'That's really sweet,' I say, 'though I am nothing like Amy.'

'No, you're not. But *I* want to be a different kind of man this time round. I want to give this, whatever we've got between us, the best chance. I think you're something special, Saffy.'

I squeeze his hand. 'How did I manage to find the only decent man in the world?'

'Well. Not the only, obviously, but thank you. So, I hope it's OK, but I've arranged a little surprise for you.'

Even in my depleted state, I manage an enthusiastic squeal. 'What? What surprise?'

He reaches for his phone. 'Full disclosure – I can't take the credit for this. Susie rang me when you were on your way home and said that you needed some pampering and extra care. And I'm not the world's greatest expert on pampering, so she suggested this.'

On his phone is a photograph of Il Piacere di Artemisia, in Florence.

'This,' I say, 'is one of my favourite hotels, in one of my favourite cities.'

'What do you like about this hotel?'

'The beds are to die for. The views are stunning. The service is sublime. The food is gorgeous. The spa treatments are decadent.'

There is no CCTV anywhere in the entire hotel.

'We're going there tomorrow.'

My squeal this time is completely genuine.

'Really?'

'Really. Four nights, five days.'

'You booked it?'

'I did. Well ... my credit card did.'

'Can you afford it?'

He shrugs. 'Future me will be able to afford it, yes. And after everything you've done for me, I want to do something for you.'

I fling my arms around him and kiss him all over his face and hair. 'Omigod, I love Florence! The art! The wine! The architecture! The food! The music! The light! The completely touristy carousel in Piazza della Repubblica! This is amazing!'

He accepts my kisses, but he's blushing. 'This can't be a big deal for you. You could go any time you wanted.'

'Yes, but you arranged it just for me.' I kiss his adorable pink cheek. 'You are the best boyfriend, ever.'

'And no murder, no corpses. Nothing related to my weird line of work, whatsoever. I promise.'

'Me too,' I say.

And in that moment, I mean it. I need a break from killing, while I reassess what it means to me, and whether I can ever separate it from my past. Plus, there's whoever has found my murder lair and has been sending Jonathan emails. It's a good idea to lie low.

Maybe it will be nice to be a normal, non-lethal person for a while.

Chapter Forty-Three

I FIRST VISITED FLORENCE WHEN I was a university student as part of my course in Art History. I spent an entire summer term there with hundreds of other Art History students, ostensibly to study the art and architecture, attend lectures and seminars, and (unofficially) to shag as many Italians as possible.

The university housed us in dinky student digs, piled up on top of each other like sardines in little cells with tiny windows and no natural daylight or ventilation, and shared bathrooms furnished with cracked porcelain. After the first miserable night, I procured for myself an airy and frescoed appartamento in San Niccolò, with a beautiful view of the Ponte Vecchio.

Heaven. I love New York and I adore London and Paris, Milan and Barcelona and Tokyo and Bangkok and Mumbai, but Florence will always have my heart, for that appartamento and for the espresso and the way the light reflects off the stone. I spent only as much time as necessary with the other students, chattering in English like crowds of starlings in the cafés and flirting with waiters and hopeful young men, and instead discovered the back streets, the small galleries, the ancient alleys, the places where artists sipped the cheapest wine and the places where bodies could be concealed. I perfected my Italian and I soaked in all the art I could manage.

I spent hours in the Uffizi in front of Artemisia Gentileschi's painting of Judith beheading Holofernes. The light. The strength in those arms. The blood on pale skin.

Sometimes I went hunting, but I was yet fresh in the ways of murder. The previous summer, I'd killed for the third time – my former New York neighbour, the cocaine-snorting, wife-beating, sidewalk-splattering Chad Brett – but I'd been in quiet Durham since, and a suitable candidate hadn't presented himself. Here in Italy, entitled masculinity was rampant. It was impossible to walk anywhere without being wolf-whistled or to buy a coffee at a bar without having your arse pinched. Even the priests looked at your legs. But repulsive as it was, it was a cultural norm. If I killed everyone who did it, only half the population would be left.

Anyway, I was busy glutting myself on art and culture. Homicide, I figured, could wait.

I had already done a little modelling in New York and I signed up to do life modelling for an all-woman artist collective called Le Costolette Extra, who liked to sketch by candlelight.

That's where I met Annunciata. She did life modelling in every artist's studio and art school and boasted (in strongly Tuscan-accented Italian) that she 'had the most famous living tits in the city'. This was plausible, as she earned the bulk of her money doing sex work and even when she was fully dressed, most of her bosom was on display.

They were very gorgeous tits, but Annunciata herself was the real prize. Once she discovered that my hair wasn't a wig and that I was a natural blonde – rare in her experience – she took to me immediately, and in a ramshackle bar, drinking Chianti from smeared glasses, smoking cigarette after cigarette, she told me about her life. She'd grown up devout and destitute in a village in the mountains and started sex work in the city when she was a teenager. She had no shame about fucking men for a living, and she went to confession every week so none of her supposed sins would be on her soul.

But she preferred to talk about what she called her 'eternal work', and she could list every single gallery and show in Italy that had ever held a drawing or a painting that she had posed for. There were a lot.

'I am a muse,' she would say, in between correcting my Italian and lighting another cigarette.

She thought it was hilarious that I was rich and while she had no compunctions about accepting money or gifts of food or clothing or books from me, she also insisted on paying her share of the wine we drank.

'I can only afford the cheapest,' she said, pouring out glasses from the bottle, 'but there is no bad wine in Florence.' This wasn't strictly true, but it was true that Annunciata knew how to find good cheap wine.

For me, she epitomised Florence more than the image of David that adorned every tourist shop in the city. David was perfect and beautiful, timeless and pure and innocent, God's vision of Man, with a great arse and a tiny dick. Annunciata was tough and generous, modern and vibrant, the vision of Capitalism and Art, with an equally great arse and huge breasts. David was divine; Annunciata was divinely human. I thought she was wonderful.

I happened upon her in the darkness of one very early morning, when I was returning from a party thrown by an ambassador's son, and she was finishing her night shift. She linked her arm in mine and brought me to the Mercato di Sant'Ambrogio. The market was just waking up, greengrocers and fishmongers and butchers unloading vans and trolley in the darkness. Annunciata and I joined a group of what I assumed were other working girls who were breakfasting on lampredotto sold from a sleepy street vendor. I declined the breakfast (cow's stomach lining boiled in broth, doused in spicy sauce, and slapped in a bun) but accepted a plastic glass of Chianti from the bottle attached to the cart and we stood around comparing our evenings. They thought it was hilarious that I had started my night drinking champagne with an ambassador. They quizzed me about the clothes, the canapés, the men, they taught me how to say 'rich wankers' in Italian, and then they began talking among themselves.

The other girls used so much slang that I could barely follow them, but I gathered they were discussing politics rather than their nights on the street. Annunciata had a passion for economics.

Even though I couldn't make out most of what they were saying, I understood it immediately and totally when they all stopped talking at once.

A man walked by. He was wearing a dark suit, white shirt open at the neck, gold bracelet at his wrist. He was smoking a cigarette. He wore tennis shoes without socks. He seemed completely unremarkable to me, but the eyes of all of the women never left him as he passed them without a glance, and continued down the street, past the market and around a corner out of sight.

Then Annunciata spat on the ground. Her friends all did the same.

* * *

'His name is Giacomo Francese, and he is a policeman,' she told me a few days later, in our usual café, drinking our usual wine. 'He fucks the girls for free, in trade for not arresting them on false charges.'

'Bastard,' I said.

'Oh no, that is not why we hate him. Giacomo is HIV positive, he will not take treatment, and he will only use his own condoms. But he puts holes in them. He does it on purpose, because he hates us. My friend Luciana tested positive after he did it, and my friend Maria-Agnes too.' She screwed up her beautiful face as if she wanted to spit. 'We can't report him. He is police. We can't refuse him either. He wants to make us sick.'

And that was it. I'd found my art; I'd found my friend; and now I'd found my victim.

What more could you want from a perfect city?

* * *

Jonathan has never been to Florence before, so of course I have to show him the essential tourist things on the first day. We visit the Duomo; we queue for *David*; we share fiori di zucca and a gelato in Santa Croce and we savour a spritz in the Piazza del Duomo. It's late in the afternoon when we venture off the tourist trail to a gallery I remember in Oltrarno.

It's tiny, on a back cobbled street, in an ancient building. There is a small handwritten sign outside: MOSTRA D'ARTE SPECIALE. We climb two flights of stairs to a bright white-washed garret. We've got the place to ourselves. The man behind the desk, dressed in a black polo neck and black trousers and glasses with thick black frames, says 'Ciao' and returns to his book.

I see her right away: Annunciata.

The real Annunciata is no longer in Florence. She retired years ago to the Dolomites, married a well-to-do widower who could hardly believe his luck, and had twin girls. We exchange letters every Christmas, in which she still manages to teach me at least one new swear word every year.

This is an oil painting by an artist called Zoë Zello. I was hoping we'd see it when I'd found this exhibition online. The painting is slightly smaller than life-size, framed in gold, rendered in bold strokes of orange and green and pink. Annunciata is sitting on a backless stool with her hands clasped behind her head, one foot caught behind the rail of the stool, one leg swinging free. She seems about to grab her satin robe from the back of the nearby chair, light a cigarette, and start complaining about elected officials.

I grip Jonathan's hand, intending to lead him over to it, maybe talk about how great her knockers are, reminisce a little bit about my friend, but he's stopped.

'Is that . . .'

He trails off, but I follow his gaze to another framed artwork on the opposite wall. This one is only a pencil drawing, not a painting, but it's been framed and mounted.

'Is that you?' he asks.

It is. A drawing, beautifully detailed, of me.

I'm lying on a chaise, one leg drawn up, my arms spread to either side like wings. My hair is piled on top of my head and I'm regarding the viewer with a small smile on my face. Although the drawing's in black and white, Zello has managed to capture the blush of my cheek, the small moisture of my licked lips.

And, of course, I'm naked.

'It is!' I cry, delighted. 'It's me! I remember the day that was drawn!'

I very particularly remember the night *before* the day it was drawn. It had been an extremely fruitful and enjoyable night, and the proof of that was in my miniscule Porto clutch bag, sitting with the rest of my clothes out of sight behind a silk and paper screen. Giacomo Francese's penis, sealed in a sterile plastic sandwich bag.

The rest of him was out in the Tuscan countryside somewhere attracting insects, but I couldn't resist holding onto the frankly undersized part of him that had caused so much pain and devastation. That was the reason for my small smile, my flushed cheeks, my lush lips.

So much joy. So much passion. So much purpose. I was in my youth, and the world dangled in front of me like a ripe peach for the taking. I thought I had everything under control. That I was invincible.

I was so innocent. I thought I had conquered my past; not been defined and shaped by it.

'I had no idea this was here,' I say. 'Do you think I should buy it?'

Jonathan doesn't reply, so I turn to him. He is staring, rapt, at the nude. His mouth is slightly open. He might even be drooling a little.

I can't blame him, really. I am smoking hot and a natural blonde and though my tits can't compare with the bounty, gravitational defiance, and sheer nipple architecture of Annunciata's, they are classically and perfectly formed. You would not find better ones on any of the Venuses or Dianas in the Uffizi.

I leave Jonathan to ponder his monumental good fortune at having snagged such a total babe, and speak with the man in black to purchase the drawing and have it shipped to London once the exhibition is over. I hand over my platinum card, and he goes to put a small sticker on the frame to indicate that it's been sold.

'Così bella,' he says to me, with a smile that says he recognises the subject. He winks at Jonathan, a little show of chauvinism which I'm inclined to forgive because it's sweet to be reminded of happy memories. The world at my feet and a cock in my bag.

But all of that past cockiness – forgive the pun – was based on denial. I had a large gaping emptiness in the centre of me, a hole that Harold hollowed out. He took some vital part of me and filled it with trauma and pain. I could only function by ignoring it. By killing bad men like Harold again and again. But the hole never went away, no matter how many men I killed. It was waiting, all that trauma and pain, and growing, filling the hole and spilling out, until it got too big for me to ignore.

That's why I strangled my boyfriend Manuel – not because he was a bad man, or because he triggered some killer instinct in me, or because I enjoyed killing him, but because in that instant that he touched me without my expecting it, I was a little girl again. Except this time, I had the strength and skills of an accomplished murderess.

The young woman in this drawing has this fear inside her, but she doesn't know it. She thinks she doesn't care. She believes she can make the world a better place.

Will I ever feel that carefree again?

Chapter Forty-Four

In Jon's opinion, Florence was even more beautiful by moonlight. The shadows were more velvety than in London. And somehow Saffy seemed to fit right in. She spoke fluent Italian and knew her way around the maze of streets; knew a story behind every artwork and the quirks of every building.

He shouldn't have been surprised to see a drawing of her in that gallery, he reflected. She was always beautiful, but here, the elegance of the city reflected her beauty and seemed to enhance it. She could be a Renaissance lady, a medieval maiden. She could be carved out of white marble and painted on frescos.

These weren't thoughts he was accustomed to having. Maybe it was the city affecting him. Maybe it was the wine. Quite possibly it was the picture of Saffy totally nude.

They had dinner by the light of a dripping candle at an intimate restaurant tucked away on a side street. He let her order, and he wasn't exactly certain of what they'd eaten, but he knew it was vegetarian and delicious. Saffy charmed the waiter, and the sommelier, and the owner of the restaurant, and after their meal they were brought altar wine and biscuits.

Afterwards, holding hands and walking back towards the hotel, they stopped at a wine window – a peaked aperture on the side of a bar, just large enough to fit a single glass of wine – to share a final glass of red. And there, with the moonlight reflecting off the cobbles and gleaming in Saffy's eyes, he got up the courage to say what had been on his mind since seeing that picture. But before that too.

'I want to talk about sex,' he said. 'And about why we haven't had it yet.'

The wine glass halted on the way to Saffy's mouth. A part of him, the cowardly part – let's face it, the typical British male part – wanted her to jump in and reassure him that it was fine, that they didn't need to talk about this, that it would all happen naturally without any discussion whatsoever.

But she didn't, so he had to carry on.

'I've been afraid,' he admitted.

'Afraid of me?'

'Afraid of sex. But yes, a little afraid of you. You're so amazing, Saffy. And I've been struggling with my idea of who I am. I've been worried I won't measure up.'

'Oh, Jonathan, it's not the size that matters, it's—'

'It's not the size. I'm not worried about that. I mean – I think I'm normal.'

'I think you're better than normal,' she said kindly.

'I've been afraid that I won't be sophisticated enough, or romantic enough, or energetic enough. I've been worried that you'll be disappointed in me. That I'll fuck it up, like I felt that I fucked up the rest of my life before I met you. So I've … allowed myself to be distracted, or to pick a fight with you, or to turn to work instead. It's been easier.'

'I understand.'

'But it's not you. You are sexy and desirable. I desire you. I would love nothing better than to rip your clothes off and make love with you all night long.'

'Or, fuck me up against a wall.'

He was momentarily distracted by her frankness and that image.

'Or ... that. Yes. That would be nice, too. I've just got in my own way. But I wanted to say to you, before we go back to the hotel—'

'—Where we are sharing a bed—'

'—Where we are sharing a bed, yes. I wanted to say that I'm over that, now. I feel more secure in myself. And whenever you're ready, I am ready too.'

Saffy took a long drink of their shared glass.

'Thank you for your honesty,' she said. 'And your vulnerability. That's ... a rare trait in a man.'

'It's how I feel.'

'So I owe you the same in return. I also want to sleep with you, Jonathan, in the worst way. Bed, wall, shower, chair, back seat of a car, every which way. But I haven't been ready either. I've got some things that I've had to work through.'

'I thought so.'

'Have you? Ugh, I hate that I'm so obviously weak.'

He touched her shoulder. 'Don't. Please don't. It actually makes me feel a little better, that we've both been having some struggles. And – well, you're a little scary sometimes, Saffy. This makes you less so.'

'Does it?' She sighed.

'You've been muted for the past few days. Not quite yourself. I can tell that something's been on your mind.'

'It has.'

'If you want to talk about it . . .?'

She shook her head. 'No, I don't. Not yet, anyway.'

'Do you have someone else you can talk to about it?'

'Yes. I've been talking with Susie. That's probably why she suggested to you that we come here.'

'OK. Well, I just want you to know that when you're ready, I'm ready too. But not before then. I can sleep on the floor tonight. For the whole time we're here. I can get another room, if that makes you more comfortable.'

'No. I trust you, Jonathan. And I don't say that to many people. Almost no one.'

'And if you're never ready, then that's OK too.'

'Oh, I'll be ready,' she said, and a bit of her usual spark came into her eye. 'Sooner or later. I'm not dying before I see you naked.'

'Hmm. Well, I've seen that picture of you naked already so I guess I can die any time.'

She punched his shoulder lightly, and they grinned at each other.

'Thank you,' she said.

* * *

They entered the marble and gilt hotel lobby with their arms around each other. Jonathan felt lighter for having had that conversation. It was the sort of honest and vulnerable conversation he'd never had with Amy; the sort of conversation that his parents would never have dreamed of having with each other.

It made him hopeful. And just because he was more than a little drunk, and every time he closed his eyes, he could picture that drawing of Saffy naked, or think of what she said about fucking against a wall, or in the back seat of a car . . . well, that was OK. He could wait.

Piano music was coming from the bar, and he was about to suggest they drop in for a nightcap, when:

'Boo!'

He and Saffy whirled around. Behind them stood Susie and Finlay.

'Susie-sue!' Saffy took her hand out of her pocket and embraced her sister. 'What are you doing here?'

'We were coming anyway,' said Finlay. 'Ouch,' he added, as Susie elbowed him.

'We *also* made a spontaneous decision to have a little Florence fun,' Susie said. 'But our room isn't on the same floor as yours, I checked, so we won't cramp your style.'

'Oh my God, you should see the drawing I bought,' said Saffy, pushing a lock of Susie's hair back behind her ear. 'You will scream.'

'You really will,' agreed Jonathan. Maybe he should be annoyed that Saffy's sister and her boyfriend had crashed their romantic getaway, but he was OK with it. Saffy had said she'd been talking with her sister. It might make her feel more secure to have her here. Anyway, it was a big city – they were bound to find their own space.

'You read those notes I sent you yet, bro?' asked Finlay, as the four of them walked together into the gold and mirrored hotel bar.

'As a matter of fact, I did make a start. I tucked them in my rucksack in case I have some free time when I'm here.'

'Epic!' Finlay slapped him on the back. 'You won't regret it. It's going to be explosive.'

'But I have just agreed a new contract for some new books, so I won't be able to commit to anything else for the foreseeable future.'

'Oooh, something to celebrate!' said Susie.

They slid into a leather-upholstered booth and Finlay gestured towards a waiter. 'Bottle of fizz, my man.'

'Per favore, potremmo avere una bottiglia di Franciacorta?' said Susie.

'You speak Italian too,' said Jonathan.

'Swiss finishing school.' She made a face. 'Full of girls obsessed with cocaine. So boring. What did you two get up to today?'

Saffy gave her a rundown of their day as the waiter returned with a bottle and an ice bucket. There was a respectful pause as he popped the cork and poured out four glasses, and then Susie raised hers.

'To family,' she said. '*Real* family. The people we can trust, and who take care of us.'

Jonathan saw her and Saffy exchange a significant glance. Yes, maybe it was better that Susie was here.

They drank, and then Susie bounced up and down in her seat, and she said, 'Guys guys guys! This is so exciting and I'm so glad that I ran into you! There is a party tomorrow night that you absolutely have to come to! Everyone will be there! I scored us all invitations!'

'What do you mean by "everyone"?' Saffy asked.

'Isabella Q Amato! God, I love her.'

'Who's Isabella Q Amato?'

'She is, like, *the* Italian street fashion influencer. Oh my God, you should see her stuff!' Susie pulled out her phone and started scrolling madly.

'Let's go to the party,' said Jonathan.

Saffy raised an eyebrow. 'Are you sure? We'd have to shop for outfits beforehand, and that's not your thing.'

'It's your thing, though.'

'And you don't like parties.'

'But *everyone* will be there,' said Jonathan.

She covered his hand with hers. 'We don't have to stay long.'

'Just long enough to make you happy,' he said, and squeezed her hand.

'You two are adorable,' said Susie happily. 'It makes me sick.'

Chapter Forty-Five

Susie loves meeting new people and having adventures with them, and taking selfies in glamorous places, and becoming besties with celebrities she admires. In short, she loves a party. I see parties as more of a practical matter: it's a way to scope people out, learn gossip and secrets, choose targets, cultivate an image. Susie parties joyfully, and I party transactionally. Maybe this is the way we approach life as a whole, the product of our different upbringings. Or, possibly, I happen to be a psychopath and she is not.

However, I do love to shop, and so does my sister. In that way, we are peas in a pod.

After a leisurely breakfast in bed, we assemble in the hotel lobby. Well, we were meant to assemble – but when Susie tumbles out of the lift, all messy ponytail and bare midriff, she's alone.

'Where's the F-bomb?' I ask her, attempting to hide my relief.

'He's working out. He says he already has an outfit and to have fun without him.'

She's acting cheerful, but I know I have to follow up on this. So I show mercy on Jonathan by choosing a suit for him at the very first shop we go to (to be fair, quality Italian tailoring is so gorgeous that men can afford to play it simple) and then ensconcing him in a café with espresso, pastries, and a good book about the Pazzi conspiracy to assassinate the Medicis. And then, while we are browsing in Gucci, I confront Susie.

'What's wrong with Finlay?' I demand.

'What? Nothing.' She holds up a strappy wisp of a top. 'Do I suit a pussy bow?'

'He passed up an opportunity to corner Jonathan and bully him about writing his biography. That's not like him.'

'He likes working out, that's all.'

'And he did not insult me once last night, or try to feed me mortadella.'

'I told him to be nice to you.'

'Did you tell him why?'

'Of course not!' She decides against the wispy top and puts it back. 'He was a little annoyed that you were coming to Florence,' she admits. 'But he's come round.'

'How long have you had this planned?'

'A week or two. It's no big deal. I want you here.'

I have already decided that I don't fancy anything in this collection, but I stall, because Susie can't hide her worry from me. 'Is he treating you properly, Susie?'

'Yes!'

'Is he?' I give her a hard look. 'Because it's one thing to have independent lives, and it's another thing to avoid your girlfriend when you're on a romantic break together.'

'He's preoccupied,' she admits. 'Spends a lot of time on his own.'

'And do you still trust him?'

'Yes! I mean—'

'You mean what?' I've given up all pretence of shopping.

'I look at you and Jonathan. And you're so lovely together. So connected and strong. He's kind to you, and supportive. He looks at you like you're a goddess. And that is totally what you deserve, but ... well, that's just not the way Finlay looks at me. Or at least, not lately.'

Never, as far as I'm concerned. I have never seen what my sister sees in that man. However, because I am not stupid, I keep my mouth shut.

'But I love him, Saffy. I love him so much. If I lost him ... if he left me ... I don't know what I would do. I don't know if I could carry on.'

'Of course you could.' I take both her hands in mine. 'You're strong. You work at a suicide hotline, for goodness sake.'

'But I've lost way too many people. And when I think about what you've gone through ... all by yourself ...'

'Stop it,' I say firmly. 'You're not going to lose me. And you're not going to lose Finlay, either. Not if he knows what's good for him.'

I mean this. I don't like Finlay, and I think Susie would be better off without him. But she wants him, and I will torture him to within an inch of his life if it means he promises never to leave her.

* * *

Jonathan looks so good in his Italian tailoring that before we even leave our hotel room, I utterly ruin my lipstick before a public appearance by snogging the breath out of him.

'Whoa,' he says afterwards, looking dazed. 'What was that for?'

'That was for rocking an ankle-length trouser and a slim-cut shirt.' I wipe the lipstick from his mouth, but I purposely leave a bit of red on his neck, just above his collar.

I don't compete with other women as a rule, but this one is delicious, and he is mine.

I've always been a big fan of mutual consent when it comes to sex. But I never truly knew how sexy it was for a man to tell you he'll wait until you're ready. Maybe that sounds old-fashioned, but if it is, screw it. I need to have at least one traditional moral value.

We share a cab to the party, which is being held in a crumbling yet beautiful palazzo by the banks of the river. It's raining and the streets are misty. Men in suits meet our car with umbrellas to shield us. The golden lights from the building reflect off the wet stone and glitter on the Arno below. Through the door, I can hear a string quartet playing music from *Turandot*. A cliché, but a beautiful one.

'Do we have to follow your rules about no canapés tonight?' Jonathan murmurs as we enter.

'I'm not on the clock so eat whatever your heart desires.'

It will be interesting to be at a party where I don't have an alternative agenda. It will be almost normal.

It will probably be very boring.

* * *

We have no sooner arrived in the vast, frescoed hall and been given drinks than Susie spots her influencer crush on the other side of the room, near a towering arrangement of red and white roses. In her usual winning way, she hustles us all over to the flowers and immediately manages to charm her way into Isabella

Q Amato's circle and to introduce us all to each other. Isabella Q and several of her friends are interestingly dressed, so I prepare myself for an evening of talking designers; there are worse things to do, especially when you are sipping a well-made amaretto sour.

Then one of the friends says in English, 'Wait, are you Jonathan Desrosiers?'

Suddenly everyone's attention is laser-focused on my date.

'I've read all your books!'

'I listen to your podcast!'

'I saw you in London!'

And just like that, my boyfriend is the most famous person in the room.

Jonathan, in his newfound peace with his job, good-naturedly handles a barrage of questions while I gaze around me. Susie is visibly pleased to have brought someone so popular to the party. While she's busy and distracted talking with Isabella Q, Finlay touches her waist and murmurs something in her ear. Then he breaks away from our group and slips into the crowd.

Where's he going? What's he doing? Am I going to have to torture him after all? Would that be so bad?

I whisper to Jonathan, 'I'm just popping to the ladies'.' He's answering so many questions that he doesn't have a chance to respond, but even in that short time, Finlay has disappeared.

I put my mostly full glass on the tray of a passing waiter and wander the floor. The interior of the palazzo is gorgeous: there are soaring ceilings and arches, there are gods painted on the walls, all of it lit by candlelight and tasteful fixtures. But I can't really take any of it in, because I'm searching for my sister's errant boyfriend.

He's cheated on her before, and all the signs are there again now. I don't even need much proof; finding out that he's got Snapchat installed on his phone would be enough evidence for me. But ideally, I'll catch him in a clinch and get a picture of it. Normally I prefer out-and-out violence to blackmail, but at this point I'll use whatever I can, to make sure that my sister doesn't have her heart broken.

However, as I pass the string quartet, I spot someone else. Someone who makes me stop dead in my stiletto heels.

Sir Thomas West.

It's a sign of my distraction that I didn't have an inkling that he was in Italy. He's wearing a black suit and a white shirt, with a silver cravat that matches his hair. His pinkie ring glints on his hand as he sips from his drink and speaks with another man. As I watch, he accepts a small sweet pastry from a waitress and gives her a fatherly wink.

The string quartet swells with the climax of 'Nessun Dorma'.

And all at once, I'm hit with a revelation. A bolt from the blue. A message from God, if there were a God, and he was kind to women and serial killers.

This is a sign. Like the drawing of me as a younger woman, naked and unashamed, smiling demurely while a pervert's penis sits in my handbag.

I can't sit around worrying about Harold and what trauma he inflicted upon me. He is dead. I killed him. And in the years since, I have made my life the way I want it. I've taken all that trauma and inflicted it upon other people who deserve it.

I don't have to carry it any more.

Which is good, because normally I am quite cheerful and it's been a real drag being in touch with these terrible feelings.

Tonight, I will kill Sir Thomas. No more messing around or procrastinating or planning or fantasising or chickening out. I will make my opportunity, and I will seize it. I will lay Harold's ghost to rest for good, and I will do it with my own hands.

Even Finlay can wait.

First, Sir Thomas West must, at last, die.

Chapter Forty-Six

THE SUBTLE APPROACH LEAVES TOO much room for me to back out, so I walk right up to Sir Thomas as bold as brass. His devotion to maintaining the outward appearance of being a gentleman is such that he ends his conversation with the other man and greets me.

'Well, hello! We met recently ... at that charity gala, wasn't it? We met in the lift?'

'Yes, we did. Saffy Huntley-Oliver.' I hold out my hand to shake his. Needless to say I'm wearing my most charming smile, but only years of practice make it possible for me to keep it on my face when, for the first time, his skin touches mine.

I'd pictured this moment happening when I had my hands around his neck.

'Tommy West,' he says. His hand is dry and cool. I try not to think about the things it has done.

'Oh, I know who you are, Sir Thomas!' I laugh modestly. 'What brings you to Florence? Business or pleasure?'

'At my age, Ms Huntley-Oliver, it's all pleasure. Didn't I meet your partner, as well?'

'Yes, Jonathan is over there.' I nod to where he is still being grilled by his fans.

'I must say hello. He was so kind.'

'He'd be thrilled. Actually, I hope you don't mind, but may I intrude on your pleasure a tiny bit with some business?'

'When such a beautiful woman asks it, I don't mind at all. Shoot.'

If I had a gun, I so would. My gaze flickers to beyond Sir Thomas's shoulder, where Mullethead is lurking in the shadows of a marble pillar. Tonight, not even a beefed-up eighties throwback can stop me.

'We met at the Save Our Asses gala,' I say, 'and I'm on the board of that charity, but I'm also on the board of several other charities that are also very worthy causes, helping women and children specifically. I think you would be a great fit for some of our fundraising projects. If you have the time, of course. I know you already do a great deal for charity.'

'I'm always keen to do more for children.'

Ugh.

'I knew you would say that. I'm so grateful. I don't want to bother you with any of the details now, but would it be all right for me to take your number?'

He laughs that famous genial laugh. 'Oh, love, you don't have to give me any excuse to have my number! I'll give it to you willingly.'

His flirtation is easy and convincing, even though I'm at least twenty years too old for his tastes.

Harold was like this in public. He gave such a masterful performance of being a kind, decent man of the world. Raising his deceased wife's two daughters. I used to hear people talk about what a wonderful father he was.

I take Sir Thomas's number and thank him, and force myself to engage in five more minutes of chit-chat before I excuse myself and hurry to the powder room to wash my hands over and over.

*　*　*

But I rise, I rise from the ashes and my memories, and emerge to the theatre of battle even more beautiful than before.

As much as I've prepared over the past months to slay Sir Thomas, I'm not prepared tonight. The most lethal thing in my bag is an emergency tampon. I don't even have gloves. I'd been planning to give the old murder game a rest. But I've got a now-or-never feeling about this, so I need to find a place far from the madding crowd.

I wander, feigning slight tipsiness, along a red-carpeted corridor until I reach a stone stairway under an arch. Cooler air wafts in through it, and the scent of rain. There's a red velvet rope draped across the entrance to stop less curious guests. I duck under it and follow the stairs in a tight spiral up and up and up, until I emerge in a wide gallery, lined on one side by a series of unglazed gothic arches which offer a view over the Arno. This would make a spectacular roof garden, and there are some spindly olive trees in large terracotta pots eking out a living, but it hasn't been finished or used for some time. Many floor tiles are missing or loose underfoot. Above, the roof is also missing tiles. I can hear the coos of nesting pigeons and, as I watch, I see a bat flit from a rafter and out through an arch.

I peep over the ledge of an arch and know immediately that I've found my spot. This is a health and safety nightmare. You could push an unsuspecting children's television star through one of these arches and he would plummet several storeys to the cobblestones below. With nothing to break his fall, he'd have a broken neck and a smashed skull.

It's as close to perfect as I'm going to get. And there's no time like the present.

I pull out my phone to text Sir Thomas, planning a message that will lure him up here without making him suspicious, that will appeal to his fake chivalry and self-image. I can't use the normal sexual come-on, so it's a little difficult. I tilt my head, considering. Maybe blackmail is the best path. I start typing:

```
I need to talk to you about something
secret.
```

But before I can add anything else, or press send, someone grabs me by the throat from behind.

Chapter Forty-Seven

An arm around my neck drags me back from the ledge; a hand grabs my arm and pinions it behind my back. I jab back with my free elbow, hitting solid muscle and not eliciting even a grunt. I stomp hard with my stiletto heels, trying to find a foot.

My attacker lifts me in the air by my neck and I kick backwards, making a plan. Hit him in the shin, hard enough to make him drop me so I can tear off my shoe and stick the heel through his eye.

But he's strong, this guy. And big. And he's taken me by surprise while I'm unarmed. What is he? A common opportunistic rapist? A thug from an Italian kidnapping ring?

I've got my phone in my free hand and I strike back with it at the same time I kick, trying to get the guy in the face. This time, I land two hits at once.

'Fuck!' he says. In English.

In a voice I recognise.

'I already told you, West is mine!' he says.

And that's how I realise that my sister's boyfriend Finlay is not only a douchebag, but is also the other person who has been stalking Sir Thomas West.

He's the watcher on the roof. The consumer of Pot Noodle. I *knew* I should have killed him ages ago.

On the bright side: it's his DNA on the lobotomised upskirter. I stop struggling.

'Let me go, Finlay,' I say in a choked but calm voice.

'That depends. What'll you do?'

'Besides discussing with you how you plan on explaining to my sister that you assaulted me?'

'You have a few things to explain to her first.'

'Let me go, or I will jab my shoe into your leg so hard that you will have to retrieve your knee from the Boboli Gardens.'

He lets me go and quickly backs away. We face off next to an olive tree in a large terracotta pot.

'My sister thinks you're having an affair.'

'Clearly I'm not.'

'What are you doing up here?' I ask him.

'What are *you* doing up here?'

'Getting some fresh air.'

'Bullshit,' says Finlay. 'You were about to lure Thomas West up here and push him through a window.'

'What makes you think I'd do something like that?'

He smirks. 'You've been obsessed with West for months.'

'Well, he's an interesting person. Maybe I want him for my charity campaign.'

'You usually recruit spokesmen by stalking them? Looking into their houses with binoculars?'

'That *was* you on the roof.' I keep my fists raised, ready to throat-punch him if I need to. 'I thought you were biohacking. Protein junkie. What are you doing eating Pot Noodle?'

'Everybody needs a cheat day.'

'Right. So you've been watching Sir Thomas too. What happened, did you see me going into his neighbour's house?'

'That's right.'

'So you stole my surveillance spot.'

'I had it first. You stole it from me.'

We're circling each other now, slowly. Eyes on each other's face.

'And you left me the Post-it note,' I say.

'Bravo, Einstein.'

'So why were you watching him?'

'Why were *you* watching him?' he retorts.

'Let's just say that Sir Thomas isn't as squeaky clean as he appears to be. I've been making sure he behaves himself.'

'Like the police? Or a nanny?'

'Just like that. A police nanny, that's me.'

'I know his secrets,' says Finlay. 'Just like I know yours.'

That stops me for a split fraction of a second. Not enough for him to notice. I hope.

'What secrets do you think I have?' I ask.

'Susie doesn't know,' Finlay says. 'She has absolutely no fucking idea. Not the foggiest. Do you think she'd still idolise you, if she did?'

'Care to enlighten me with what you're talking about?'

The self-satisfaction on his face could power a jet. Reason 2,682 why I hate this dude. Also, I notice for the first time that he is wearing leather flip-flops.

'Do you ever wear proper shoes?' I ask him. 'Is there a reason why you want everyone in the world to see your toe cleavage?'

'Remember that time weeks ago when you asked me to help track down who had sent Jonny-boy an email? Right before you went after him and got involved in that enormous bloodbath where he lost a toe in a serial killer's basement.'

'Yes.'

'Well, you might also remember that Susie went to bed before I found out who'd been sending the emails.'

'Yes.'

'So I was curious about what you were doing. So I followed you.'

'You followed me . . . to Simon Simons' house?'

'No. I followed you to the place where you went first.'

That warehouse. My murder lounge. I stop circling and he stops too.

'You were in and out of there fast, and I realised I could either follow you, or check out the warehouse. And frankly, I didn't care what happened to you.'

'Rude.'

'So I looked in the warehouse. Imagine my surprise when I found a bunch of power tools and a severed head in the freezer.'

Ah. Mystery number two solved.

'You took pictures of the head and the warehouse. You're the one who emailed them to Jonathan.'

I should have known. Disappearing untraceable emails. Tech bros will be tech bros.

'You're on fire tonight, babe,' says Finlay. 'What did you pick up from the warehouse that night, by the way? Was it Fanducci's head?'

Yeah, like I'm going to tell him that.

'Where did you get the other photos that you sent Jonathan, of the heads in Cyril's and Simons' houses?' I ask.

'Dark web. There's some sick shit on there. Probably posted by a police officer who wanted to make some extra Bitcoin. I just wanted to show your boyfriend that I was legit.'

'If you think you know so much about me, why haven't you told the police?'

'Because I love Susie. And Susie loves you. Can you imagine how she would feel about me if I told her that her big sister was a serial killer? If I was the one who put her away forever?'

He's not wrong. It's a similar reason for why I haven't killed him.

At least I'm grateful that his love for my sister is greater than his moral compass or concern about other people dying. I might even like him a little bit better now.

'Why did you send clues to Jonathan?' I ask.

'It's his actual job, right? To track down killers? I don't care if *he* hates you. Or if Susie hates him. Also, it's gross that he doesn't know that he's fucking a serial killer.' Finlay frowns. 'Or wait, have you guys fucked yet?'

'Shut up, Finlay.'

He smirks again, eroding what little respect I'd gained for him in the past few moments.

'Anyway,' he says, 'you might have killed a bunch of people, including the one whose head I found, and that guy who Jonathan found on his doorstep and, I'm guessing, also Rupert Huntington-Hogg and those two kids in the park that Jonathan stumbled across.'

Damn him. I knew his clueless demeanour was an act.

'Probably some others,' he continues. 'That guy I read about in the news who was hog-tied in the alleyway – that has your name all over it. But you're not going to kill West.'

'Why not?'

'Like I said, he's mine.' He looks at his fancy health-tracking watch. 'And he's on his way up here any minute now, so bugger off.'

I narrow my eyes at him. 'You're not a killer though.'

'What makes you say that?'

'I'd know. I'd be able to see it. I've met a lot of violent men. You're a narcissistic dickhead, but you're not a murderer.'

'And I'm trying to change that? So get out of here.'

I don't budge. 'But why do you want to kill him?'

He rolls his eyes. 'Your celibate boyfriend didn't tell you?'

'Tell me what? Why would he know?'

'He read the notes for my autobiography, duh. It's all in there. Explosive stuff, like I said.'

'He only read the first few pages,' I say. But something else is slotting into place in my head. Something Jonathan did mention.

Finlay was a child actor.

He said his biography would blow everything wide open.

'You worked with Sir Thomas when you were a kid?' I ask. Quietly.

He nods.

'He did it to you?'

And Finlay doesn't even have to answer for me to see the truth.

As much as we hate each other, he and I have this terrible, monstrous, fearful thing in common.

Chapter Forty-Eight

THIS CHANGES EVERYTHING. THE ONLY person who deserves to kill Sir Thomas more than I do is one of his victims.

'OK,' I say. 'You have priority. But what makes you think you can kill him? Have you done it before?'

'No, I've never killed anyone, are you for real?'

'Are you certain you can do it?'

Finlay looks me dead in the eyes. 'I haven't been able to think of anything else for months now. I keep on thinking about him. When I try to sleep ... I see him. What he did to me, I dream about it. Nothing I do helps. It's like he's imprinted on me, like he's poisoned me.'

If I hadn't killed Harold, I would have felt the same way.

But Finlay isn't me.

'Did you come to Florence especially to kill him at this party?'

'I *threw* this party so I could kill him here.' He shakes his head. 'Nobody knows, I've done it through a shell company and a planning firm. I've been working on it for months.'

'You really want justice, don't you?'

'Wouldn't you?'

Well. Exactly.

'It's not too late to go to the police,' I say. 'There have been other children. Lots of them, over the years. If you stand up and say something, they will too.'

'*You're* telling *me* to go to the police?'

'Normally, I would say go for it. Kill him and dance on his corpse. And then I'd have something on you, and you'd have something on me, and we'd both be safe. But there are other ways to justice, Finlay. Think about it. So many people must know what Sir Thomas is. He's been abusing children for years. At best, they've ignored it. At worst, they've enabled it. If you speak up, you could bring it all down.'

'I thought you liked murder.'

'I'm thinking about my sister. I'm thinking about what will happen to her if you get caught. She loves you, more fool her.'

'I can't,' says Finlay. Actual tears glitter in his eyes. 'I can't say it aloud. What he did. I can't say it in front of her.'

'She'd understand. Maybe better than you think. She *wants* you to be vulnerable with her.'

'No. She wants me to be strong.' He dashes the tears away. 'I need to kill West. That's the only way I'm going to get rid of this feeling.'

So much for my career as a couples therapist.

'OK, well,' I say. 'You do you, I guess. Though I'd have worn shoes with better grip.'

He glances at his watch again. 'He's on his way up here *right now*.'

'Is Mullethead with him?'

'No, I told him to come alone, and I think he will. You need to leave.'

'How?' Beside the staircase, the only way out is through the windows. 'There's no time. I'll hide.' I scuttle behind the big terracotta pot.

'Don't come out,' Finlay says.

'Fine. Just make sure you do it properly, OK? I don't want to get implicated for a murder I didn't even commit.'

'Just stay quiet.'

'And also, no monologuing.'

I crouch down. It's dark behind here. I can barely even see the pot.

I can, however, hear everything. I can hear Finlay breathing. He's agitated — exactly the wrong state of mind for getting away with murder. If I were smart, I would have taken him out and done this job myself.

But fair is fair. He deserves to do this.

If he can.

I hate to see a bungled killing, though, so I promise myself that if I hear him getting into any difficulties, or even if I hear him talking for the sake of hearing his own voice like some sort of Dr Evil, I'm jumping out and pushing Sir Thomas over the ledge myself. I owe it to Susie to keep her boyfriend safe.

'Is that you, Finlay?'

The douchebag wasn't kidding. That's Sir Thomas's voice. He's here, on the terrace. My skin crawls, the way some people's does when they see a spider or a snake.

'Little Finn. It's been a long time, hasn't it?' says Sir Thomas. 'How have you been doing for yourself?'

'I'm not here to chit-chat,' says Finlay. From here, he sounds shaky. Maybe he won't go through with it.

Sir Thomas, on the other hand, sounds smooth as silk. 'Then why did you invite me up here?'

'To talk about what you did to me when I was a child.'

A pause.

'I'm afraid I don't know what you're referring to.'

'In your dressing room. You said it was our secret. I was nine years old. I bled afterwards.'

Behind the pot, I wince.

Finlay should just get on with it. But I'm curious to know what Sir Thomas will say. Whether he'll deny it in a fit of righteous rage. Or admit it, and paint himself as sorry victim of his own uncontrollable urges. Whether he'll blame a child – all those children – for seducing him. Or say he was misunderstood.

Or a combination of all of those things, because one thing that successful, narcissistic, powerful predators never, ever do is take full responsibility for the damage they have done.

'How much?' says Sir Thomas.

Finlay must be as surprised as I am, because he takes a beat to respond.

'How much what?'

'How much do you want to keep quiet?' Sir Thomas is, of all things, weary. 'Name your price. It's got to be a one-off, though. I can't have you turning up at all junctures demanding more for your silence.'

'This isn't about money.'

'Of course it is. You think you can ruin me. You threaten to ruin me. But you haven't done it in all these years, you haven't said a blessed word. Ergo, you must want something.'

Sir Thomas isn't frightened or angry at all. He isn't even mildly worried. He's *annoyed*.

He's done this many times. These exact same accusations; these exact same words. So often that it's an inconvenience to him.

All those children.

'So tell me, little Finn: how much?'

This has gone far enough. I suck in a deep breath and start to stand, to come out into the open and take things into my own hands. But before I can, I hear a scuffle and a shout.

I crouch back down. He's finally making his move.

Good work, Finlay.

It's difficult to tell exactly what's happening from here, but there are grunts and sounds of a struggle. Heart issues aside, Sir Thomas is a well-kept elderly man, but Finlay is so much younger and more built than him that there shouldn't be much in it.

I listen as they move inch by inch closer to the ledge. A gasp and heavy breathing. Feet scrabbling on loose tiles.

They're close to my pot now – I could reach around and brush their trousers with my fingertips – but I don't. Finlay is an infuriating mansplaining gasbag, and he's a terrible boyfriend for my sister, but he deserves this victory all for himself.

There's a low moan of pain, or horror. More heavy breathing, more exertion, more scrabbling. And then a final shout, trailing downward.

A distant thud.

Then nothing.

Good work, Finlay. Now it's time for you and me to sort out how we're going to keep our mutual secrets.

But as I'm rising, I hear the sound of footsteps running away. Rapidly across the tiles, and down the stone stairs.

'Finlay, you rat,' I say, standing and brushing off my dress. My legs have stiffened. I wobble around the side of the pot when something occurs to me.

Footsteps. Running.

Not flip-flopping.

'Shit,' I say, and hurry to the nearest window ledge. I don't want to be seen, but a glance is all I need.

Finlay lies face-up on the cobbles below. His legs are twisted at unnatural angles. Blood is pooling out underneath his head. There's quite a bit of it, which maybe proves that all that hanging upside down has made some difference.

One of his flip-flops has landed a metre away. I *knew* those were the wrong shoes for murder.

I duck behind the ledge.

And at that moment, I hear the worst sound in the world.

My sister screams in horror and pain.

Chapter Forty-Nine

I HAVE NEVER RUN SO FAST in my life, not even that time five years ago in Aberdeen when I was fleeing from the cops after cutting it close with the murder of that terrible wee gynaecologist, Dr Date. I fly down the stairs, hardly touching them with my feet, push my way through the partygoers, through the crowd clogging the door, along the pavement and through the clump of people surrounding Finlay's body on the ground.

Susie is on her knees beside him. She is cradling his head in her lap. It's too floppy on its neck but she doesn't care. She's sobbing and kissing his mouth, his cheeks.

Jonathan is crouching beside her, holding Finlay's wrist as if taking his pulse. Typical optimism on his part. He reaches out for me when I appear but I drop to my own knees next to my sister.

'Susie,' I say, wrapping my arms around her. 'I'm here. Sweetheart, I'm here.'

She doesn't respond. I hear sirens approaching.

'What happened?' I ask Jonathan.

'We were— she wanted to look for Finlay, so we stepped outside. And then, we saw him falling.'

'Where did he fall from?'

He jerks his chin upwards, to the row of high-arched windows.

'Where have you been?' he asks.

'I got caught in a conversation I couldn't leave,' I say. 'Then I heard— Susie, darling. Sweetheart. Look at me, honey. Look at me.'

She can't look away from Finlay's dead face.

As the crowd parts for the paramedics, I stand and look around. I should have gone after Sir Thomas as soon as I realised that he'd killed Finlay. I should have slaughtered him then and there.

But I don't see him or his bodyguard anywhere. And my sister needs me.

* * *

Finlay is clearly dead, but Susie and I ride in the front of the ambulance anyway. Finlay is in the back with a sheet pulled up over his head. She's shivering hard, her teeth chattering. I wrap Jonathan's jacket tight around her and hold her as close as I can. There's no need for the ambulance to speed or for them to sound their sirens. It's a quiet ride.

At the hospital, they take Finlay's body away and guide us into a small waiting room. Within minutes, two poliziotte arrive and sit down with us to take down the vital information. Susie has subsided from screaming to sobbing to silent crying, clutching my hand. I answer all the questions that I can, but she has to supply the details about Finlay. His full name, his address, his next of kin. Why he was up on the roof terrace.

'I don't know,' she says. Even though she's in shock, her Italian is perfect. 'He said he was going to look for a friend of his.'

'Which friend?'

'He didn't say. A school friend, I think. Someone he knew as a child.'

Cold touches my spine at that.

'Do you know why he was up there?' the policewoman asks me. 'It was a forbidden area.'

This is when I could tell the truth. I could tell them that he threw the party, that he'd arranged to meet with Sir Thomas, and that Finlay had beef with him. I wouldn't even have to place myself at the scene; I could say that he'd confided in me. I could give them the lead, and they could follow it, and arrest the man who killed Finlay. There's even evidence against him in Finlay's own handwritten pages.

But that would prevent me from taking my own revenge.

'He didn't tell me anything,' I say.

'Forgive us, we have to ask this, although it is painful – do you know of any reason that he may have wanted to harm himself?'

'No,' says Susie, vehemently.

'He had been keeping secrets,' I say.

Susie glares at me. 'He would not want to hurt himself.'

They ask more questions, and tell us that they will check in with us tomorrow, and notify Finlay's next of kin if we would prefer, and ask us if we are able to make our own way back to our hotel. They say, however, that we should not be in any hurry, and should take all the time we need. They give us their condolences, and a leaflet, and leave.

And then it's Susie and me, sitting in this green-painted waiting room with plastic chairs. Both of us have dirty knees. She has blood on her frock. Her teeth are still chattering.

I think about how Finlay planned this entire party so that he could kill his nemesis, but he still took the time to invite Susie's idol, Isabella Q. It was probably to distract her, but he knew it would also make her happy.

'I'll get you a glass of water,' I say, standing. 'Or a can of Coke.'

'*Sit down.*'

I sit.

'You are not going anywhere until you tell me what really happened,' she says.

'What makes you think I know?'

She merely looks at me.

'I will tell you later,' I say. 'When you've recovered a little bit from the shock.'

'You will tell me *now*.'

I'm going to have to do this very carefully. I double-check the waiting room for cameras.

'I didn't tell the police this,' I say, 'because Finlay did not want anyone to know. I was trying to persuade him to tell you.'

'Tell me what?'

'When he was a child, Finlay was abused by a man who was famous in children's television. His name is Sir Thomas West.'

'What?'

Her face goes impossibly paler. I'd think she was about to faint, but she has my thigh in a death grip.

'He's kept it secret all these years. It wasn't his fault, but he was ashamed of it.'

'He told you this?'

'Yes.'

'Oh, Finlay.' Her eyes start leaking tears again.

'Thinking about it, it can be especially difficult for a man to speak up. They don't only have to deal with the trauma from the abuse, but the stigma of the loss of masculinity.'

'Saffy, stop traumasplaining to me, my boyfriend was just killed.'

'Right. Sorry. This was just to say why he didn't want to go to the police, or why he didn't tell you.'

'Why did he tell *you*?'

'I think ... he knew that we had something in common. If that makes sense?'

'He could have told me. It wouldn't have made me love him any less.'

'That's what I said to him. I said you'd understand. But he wasn't ready.'

She sits with this for a moment.

Then she asks, 'But what does this have to do with him being up on that roof?'

I dislike lying to my sister. Which might sound ironic, given that I am essentially lying to her all the time, and also that lying is so far down the scale of moral severity from murder that it shouldn't even register with my conscience. But there it is. I don't like doing it.

Here, I have to tell a bit of a lie to protect both me and Finlay, and therefore Susie.

'Sir Thomas was at the party. It was triggering for Finlay. So the two of us went up to the roof terrace to talk.'

She swallows hard.

'Did he jump?'

'No.'

'How did he fall?'

'He was pushed.'

'*What?*'

She jumps out of her chair.

'Sir Thomas came upstairs,' I tell her. 'I think Finlay had arranged a meeting somehow. I don't know, he didn't tell me. But he did tell me to hide and not to say anything. He wanted to confront Sir Thomas. So I hid behind a plant pot. And I heard them talking. Sir Thomas was offering Finlay money to keep quiet, and Finlay was refusing, and then I heard a scuffle. And then … oh, sweetheart, I heard a cry, and I thought Finlay had pushed Sir Thomas over, and then I looked, and it was Finlay.'

'You were there?'

'I was hiding.'

What little colour is left in her face drains away. I have never seen her like this.

'You let him fall?' she says.

'I wasn't— Susie, I wasn't close enough to do anything.'

'You could have talked him down! You could have refused to hide! You could have called the police! You could have made him come downstairs and talk to *me* about it!'

I can't reply to any of this. Because it is true.

I could have done any of those things. And Finlay would not be dead.

'I didn't think—' I begin.

'You never liked him! You never wanted us to be together! You wanted him gone.'

This is also true.

'Susie—'

'Well, now he is! Does that make you happy?'

'Susie, I never—'

I get up and reach for her. She backs quickly away.

'Don't touch me,' she says. 'Don't come near me. I don't want to talk to you.'

'But, darling—'

'No! You promised to protect me! And then you let this happen.' She backs to the door. 'You kept secrets from me. You say it was to respect Finlay, but you didn't respect him! You hated him. And you just stood by while he died. I don't want anything to do with you. Just leave—leave me alone.'

My sister, the only person in the world I truly love, turns away from me. She flees down the corridor.

Chapter Fifty

By the time I reach the door, Susie's out of sight. I try following her, but the hospital is a maze and when I finally exit the building, there's no sign of her.

I stand near the entrance, next to a dozen chain-smoking Italians, and try to work out what to do.

The obvious answer is to find Sir Thomas West and kill him. But to do that, I need to feel powerful and murderous. And though historically I have not been that good at parsing my emotions, I've learned enough to know what I'm feeling now is the opposite of powerful.

I'm hurt, sorry, and bereft. I'm afraid that my sister will never forgive me. And the truth is, being present when Finlay died and not stepping in to prevent it are only the teeniest fraction of the terrible things that I've done.

Imagine how much Susie would hate me if she knew?

* * *

So I don't look for Sir Thomas. I walk to the hotel, keeping my eyes out for Susie. The lobby is empty and there is a card on the reception desk saying Per favore suona il campanello. I knock at the door to Susie and Finlay's room but there's no answer, so I go to mine on the next floor up.

Jonathan's there. He's had a shower and has re-dressed in jeans and a shirt, but his hair is still wet. He rushes to the door when I step in and holds me in his arms.

'Are you OK?'

'No,' I say to his chest, clinging to him.

'How is Susie?'

'She's awful. She's devastated. I've never seen her in this much pain.'

'Poor Susie. It's horrible.'

'I can't help her. There's nothing I can do to make it better. And she blames me.'

'What? Why?'

'Because I never liked him.'

'But that's not your fault.'

'And because I talked with him right before he died.'

'You did? What about?'

I look up at his face, full of concern.

'We were both abused as children,' I say. 'Finlay and I. Sexually. We ... were discussing it. And it upset him. And then ...'

'Oh, Saffy. Oh, sweetheart. I'm so sorry.'

'I could have done something. I could have prevented him dying. It is my fault.'

'Saffy—'

'And what if she hates me forever? What if she never speaks to me again?'

At this moment, speaking it out loud, it feels like a real possibility.

Tears erupt from me. And this time, I can't stop them or pretend them away. I sob helplessly in Jonathan's arms.

He holds me and lets me cry. He strokes my hair and my back. He murmurs soothing words. He lets me wipe my nose on his shirt. He holds me and holds me, while I sob. He doesn't try to tell me I'm wrong or stop me from being upset. He doesn't argue with my feelings. He doesn't insist that I explain myself. He doesn't make me need to pretend that I'm all right, that I'm strong.

He just holds me.

I don't remember ever crying like this before. It feels as if it will never end. It scrapes out the inside of you and stops you seeing or hearing anything except for your pain.

It goes on forever. Until suddenly, it's over.

I can't stand any more. My legs are weak, my body wrung out. Jonathan gently picks me up cradled against his chest and carries me to the bed, where he sits me down. He kneels and takes off my shoes. Then he helps me get under the covers. He disappears for a moment, a moment that instils unfamiliar panic in me – *don't leave me alone* – but then he returns with a damp flannel, a box of tissues, and a glass of water. He helps me sit up a little. He wipes my face with infinite care. He gives me a tissue to blow my nose. He gives me the glass of water and when my hands are shaky, he puts his hand over mine to help keep the glass steady so I can drink.

'Thank you,' I say to him. 'I've never had anyone look after me like this.'

He kisses my forehead. 'Try to sleep,' he says.

He goes to stand up but I grip his hand.

'Stay with me. Please?'

Jonathan climbs into bed beside me. I crawl into his arms and he holds me tight, so tight I can feel his heart beating against mine.

'What if she never forgives me?' I whisper.

'She will always forgive you. You're her sister.'

'But what if she thinks I'm a monster?'

'Shh. You're not a monster. She's angry, but she knows you love her. You just need to give her some space.'

He feels so much better than anything else right now. I start to unbutton his shirt so I can get closer to him. The skin on his chest is warm, and so comforting. I've never looked to anyone else for safety before.

I kiss him on the lips. They're soft, like medicine. I kiss him again and again. I wrap my legs around his hips and draw him closer. I want to meld with him, I want to borrow some of his strength and kindness. He kisses me back and I reach behind me to unzip my dress, so I can pull it over my head and get even closer. And then we're skin to skin and it feels better than I could have possibly imagined.

'Make it stop hurting,' I murmur in between kisses. 'Just for now. Please.'

His hand on my bare back. I push off his shirt. I reach for the button of his jeans.

Jonathan stops me. He gazes into my eyes. His breath is on my lips. I don't think I've been this intimate with anyone who has lived.

'Are you sure?' he asks.

'Yes,' I say.

And this is how we finally make love. Slowly, and gently, with whispers and touches, with comfort and consent. With so much pleasure and giving, and nothing taken at all.

Chapter Fifty-One

AFTERWARDS, I LIE WITH MY head on Jonathan's chest, feeling it rise and fall, listening to his breathing. 'I didn't know it could be like this,' I murmur. He trails his hand languorously through my hair. I'm warm and floaty, tingling and heavy, washed clean by tears and orgasms.

He kisses the top of my head. 'Everything is going to be OK,' he says. His voice is sleepy. It rumbles through his chest and into my ear.

It's the thing that people say, I know. But in this moment here with him, it seems possible that everything might work out.

Susie will forgive me. The police will decide Finlay's death was suicide. I'll kill Sir Thomas West. Jonathan and I will have a great sex life. I will continue to grow into an emotionally literate psychopath. Susie will find a boyfriend who treats her better. Everyone who deserves to live, will live happily ever after.

As I lie there, wrapped around him, his breathing slows and deepens. His hand lies still on my hair.

'Jonathan?' I whisper. But he's fast asleep.

I gently disengage from him and slip out of bed. In the bathroom mirror, my makeup is ruined and my eyes are red from crying, but my skin is glowing and I've got bed hair. I wash my face, splash cold water on my eyes, and brush my hair before quietly and quickly getting dressed in soft, casual clothes and a pair of trainers. I wrap a cashmere pashmina around my shoulders and, after dropping a kiss on Jonathan's cheek as he sleeps, I creep out of our room, closing the door silently behind me, and head downstairs to Susie's room to check if she's back yet.

There's no answer at her door. That could be because she's ignoring me. But my head is clearer now, and I know which path to take to solve everyone's problems.

So I do what I've often done at this hotel before, late at night when I wanted to be discreet: I take the service lift down to the basement, flit through the dark and empty corridors, ancient and only wide enough for a housekeeping trolley. I stop by the kitchen to slip a small razor-sharp paring knife into my waistband.

I exit the building by the tiny door, which is set next to the loading entrance, like an afterthought. I prop it ajar with a loose cobble, and emerge in the alleyway behind the hotel, unseen and unsuspected.

I love this hotel.

The streets are empty. It's stopped raining and the moon has appeared from behind clouds. I'm not sure what time it is, but it's that hour when only the transgressive are alert: sex workers, murderers, insomniacs, lovers on secret trysts.

Incredibly, a simple Google search on my phone for 'Sir Thomas West Florence' brings up a recent article in an Italian interiors magazine with photographs of the outside of his house, and an equally simple reverse image search gives me his address in Santo Spirito. Sir Thomas may be an elderly nonce with a dickey heart and at least one murder on his conscience but he really is out here acting like a man with nothing to hide.

I slip between shadows, moving like a predator through the night, taking back alleys, swiftly crossing the Ponte Santa Trìnita. I feel like a ghost of my younger self: full of spirit, lust, and beautiful righteous rage. I remember how good it felt to sink my knife into Giacomo Francese, all those years ago.

This is going to feel even better. I'm doing it for Susie.

Sir Thomas's house is at the end of a little cobbled cul-de-sac, silvered in light from the moon. Typically for Florence, it's built right onto the street, with large varnished, double-arched wooden doors. I wrap my pashmina around my hand and try the doorknobs, but they're locked and probably bolted, too.

I've been stymied by Sir Thomas for too long, so something minor like a couple of fortified doors aren't going to stop me now. But it takes a little bit of thought. I prowl around to ascertain that there isn't a back entrance, but if there is one, it's via a courtyard enclosed by other buildings. I could ring the buzzer and see what happens. I could light a fire and try to smoke him out. I could phone him and try to talk my way inside.

I look up. One of the first-floor windows overlooking the street is slightly open. And there's a convenient wisteria winding its way up the front of the house.

Bingo.

I tie my pashmina securely around my waist and hoist myself up the vine. It's not the sturdiest of bushes, but I'm a size zero. The sandstone walls give some traction, with ledges in between the stones that are wide enough for the toe of my trainer. There are still a few late blossoms left, which smell divine. All in all it's not an unpleasant experience, but by the time I reach the level of the window I realise that the plant doesn't quite reach it. There's a gap of about a metre.

No problem. I'll reach over, grab the windowsill, and pull myself—

My pashmina won't come with me. It's stuck on a branch.

I'm gripping the windowsill with both hands, so I attempt to free myself by wiggling my backside back and forth and up and down. The wisteria rustles. I'm basically twerking in mid-air halfway up a sixteenth-century Florentine building, which is not the way I expected my night to go.

A particularly vigorous shake of my booty dislodges the pashmina but at the same instant, I feel my stolen paring knife slip from my waistband. I cling helplessly to the wall as it tumbles away. I see the glint of its blade, falling, and then I hear it clatter on the cobbles below.

An echo. The hoot of a distant urban owl. Otherwise, all is quiet.

No more knife. I'm going to have to improvise.

I'm about to make the jump from vine to window when suddenly beneath me there is a creak and a shaft of light. I freeze, holding my breath.

One of the big double doors opens and a large figure steps out. It's Mullethead. From this vantage point, I can basically see the breadth of his shoulders and the gelled-up curls on the top of his head. He's starting to go slightly bald at the crown. Bad luck for him.

He stands just outside the door. I wait for him to spot the knife lying on the cobbles nearby, or to look up for the cause of the rustling. But he does neither. The flare of a lighter illuminates his face for a moment as he lights a cigarette.

And this is my chance.

I let go of the windowsill, push myself off from the vine, and leap onto Mullethead's shoulders. Fortunately they are a very large target. He staggers, but doesn't fall as I clamp onto his back with my legs and clench my left elbow around his throat.

My knife is out of reach. I am not strong enough to strangle him manually.

I grab the long back hank of his mullet and, while I still have the element of surprise, I wrap it around his thick throat and pull back with all my weight.

He makes choking sounds and claws at his neck. But his hair is in beautiful condition, strong as a silk garrotte and securely attached to the back of his head.

Is he a bad man? I don't know, frankly. I may be making a moral mistake here. But if there is a hell, I'm going to it anyway and Sir Thomas is *so* bad that a little collateral damage has to be worth it. I pull back harder and the bodyguard launches against the house wall, bashing me against it. He does it again and again to try to get me off him. My breath is knocked from my body, I can barely hold on and gosh, I am going to be sore tomorrow but I don't let go. I twist his hair in my hands and hold on for dear life. Mine, not his.

Finally, Mullethead falls to his knees. I brace myself against his broad back and keep strangling. His hair is making furrows in my hands but it is strong and surprisingly efficient. His hands drop from his throat and he goes limp. I have to scramble out of the way to stop from being crushed under his man-mountain bulk.

Is he dead, or merely unconscious? His eyes have rolled back into his head and even in the darkness I can tell that his face has swollen and turned purple. His frantic efforts to scrape me off him have brought us right to the end of the cul-de-sac, several metres from Sir Thomas's open front door.

I unwind myself from his hair and grab a limp ham hock of a wrist to check for a pulse. It seems a pity to waste such impressive muscles, but he's dead.

Incredibly, no lights have gone on inside any of the other houses in the cul-de-sac. Maybe they're empty holiday lets, or maybe they're inhabited by people who don't hear all that well, or perhaps nobody cares in the city of the Borgias. In any case, it's my lucky day, because there's no way I'll be able to drag this guy out of sight without using some sort of heavy machinery.

With my foot, I snuff out Mullethead's still-lit cigarette on the ground, then scoop up my knife. Noiselessly I slip through the doors into Sir Thomas's house, shutting them behind me.

I hurry through a tiled hallway decorated with scrolled mirrors and potted palms, towards the open doors of what looks like a salon, where lights are blazing and there's the faint sound of classical music. Soon I get close enough to see Sir Thomas.

He's standing in the centre of the room, in profile to me. He's changed out of his suit and into a purple silk smoking jacket and black silk pyjamas, slippers with fancy gold tassels on them. His snow-white hair is perfectly swept back. In one hand he holds a bottle of wine; in the other he holds a glass.

This is my moment of triumph. This is where I should have been ages ago: in private, with this monster, with a knife in my hand. I'm going to end his terrible life. I always had to be the one who ended it. Finlay wanted revenge for himself, but I want revenge for every single child whose innocence was stolen.

Every. Single. One.

I raise my knife, ready to run into the room and strike. To see his blood, to feel it. To smell it. Watch the life draining from his terrible eyes.

Then I realise that something is strange.

He isn't looking at me at all. He's staring at something else, something I can't see because the wall is blocking my view. Not speaking. Not drinking. Just staring, his mouth slightly open.

It doesn't matter. Whatever he's looking at so intently, it means I have the element of surprise. I creep closer to the doorway, my rubber-soled trainers making no sound on the marble floor. A step closer, and another. Now I can smell his cologne, and the sweet scent of the open bottle of dessert wine in his hand.

He shows no sign of noticing me. Not a flicker of an eyelid. But as I reach the threshold, he says, in his practised charming television voice, 'Now, dear. Are you sure you want to do this?'

I open my mouth to answer, because who else is he talking to but me and my knife? But before I can, someone else answers for me.

'Yes,' says a voice.

A voice I know as well as my own.

My mouth falls open and, throwing caution and surprise to the wind, I rush inside the room to see who is standing there, the person that Sir Thomas is talking to.

It's my sister Susie.

Chapter Fifty-Two

SUSIE LOOKS LIKE SOMETHING OUT of a horror movie. Her hair's come loose and hangs damp and limp around her face. Black mascara smudges her eyes. Her bare knees are bloody, and Finlay's blood has dried on the sequinned skirt of her Emilio Pucci dress. She still wears Jonathan's jacket across her shoulders, but it's about to fall off. Her lipstick has smeared across her cheek. Her tiny clutch bag dangles from one hand, almost dragging on the ground.

In the other hand, she is holding a gun. She is pointing it at Sir Thomas.

Her face is pale and lifeless, her eyes glittery and blank.

'Susie!' I cry, at the same time that she pulls the trigger.

The explosion shatters the room. Her arm jumps up with the recoil from the gun, and she staggers back a step or two as if drunk. But then she takes aim again, and fires.

Sir Thomas falls silently backwards. His chest has been blown open. His eyes stare sightlessly at the elaborately plastered ceiling.

Finally, he is dead.

I didn't expect it to happen this way.

Susie drops the gun on the floor. It lands on the thick carpet and hardly makes a sound.

Instantly, I dart forward, pick it up, and wrap it in my pashmina. Then I grab Susie's wrist.

'We've got to get out of here, now,' I say.

'No,' she says. But she lets me tug her out of the salon and through the hallway. I hip-check the door open and hustle her through it, past Mullethead lying on the ground outside, out of the cul-de-sac, and drag her as quickly as I can along the back streets, sticking to the shadows.

I can't hear any sirens. Not yet.

But they'll start soon. Strangling a man with his own hair is one thing, but two bloody loud gunshots in a residential neighbourhood is something completely different.

As we run, I rub the gun down with my pashmina. Once at the bridge, I chuck it as hard as I can into the Arno. We can travel a bit more quickly now, though Susie seems to have no sense of urgency or will; she's just coming along with me like a puppet or a doll. Her skin is cold and her eyes are glassy.

Finally, we reach the alley behind the hotel and the back door that I've propped open. The hotel is still dark and quiet; her room isn't far from the service lift and we encounter no one. Once inside, she stands near the door, staring straight ahead at nothing and shivering.

She and Finlay have a suite. Her clothes, and Finlay's, are strewn all over the place. The bed is unmade and there are empty water bottles, coffee cups, makeup, and open toiletries on most surfaces. I go straight to the bathroom and start running a hot bath, then guide Susie to an armchair, where she obediently sits down.

Susie is *never* obedient.

'You're in shock,' I tell her.

She doesn't respond.

I make a mocha, and add three lumps of sugar and a cognac from the mini bar. She accepts it and takes a sip. Then another one. Some faint colour appears in her cheeks.

'Are you OK?' I ask her, crouching down before her and rubbing her cold legs. 'Are you hurt?'

She blinks, and seems to focus on me for the first time.

'Saffy,' she says.

'Yes, it's me, darling. I'm running you a bath, so you can warm up and get clean.'

'I killed him,' she says.

'Yes. Yes, you did. Did he hurt you? Is that why you shot him? Was it in self-defence?'

'I shot him through his heart,' she says. 'He killed my heart. So I killed his. Fair's fair.'

Chapter Fifty-Three

Now.

I have to put in a word here in my own defence. A lot has happened in the past few hours. Even for someone who's used to a fast-paced, jet-setting, high-crime lethal lifestyle, it's been intense. And part of my therapeutic journey is to feel and honour my emotions, rather than repressing them into homicidal urges. (While still feeling and honouring the homicidal urges, of course.)

To say I am experiencing some emotions is an understatement.

Astonishment. Dismay. Alarm. Protectiveness. And, I will admit it, a certain amount of pride.

I never expected Susie to kill a man.

Is this ... a family trait?

'You've never killed anyone before, right?' I ask, because tonight has been so strange that I have to check.

'What? No. What do you think I am?' She holds up her empty cup. 'Can I have another one of those?'

In a daze, I stand and make her another spiked mocha. I also turn off the bath taps before the bathroom floods. You would think this would give me a little space to process what has just happened, but not really.

I sit beside her in the second armchair. 'Where did you get a gun?'

She rolls her eyes. 'Saffy, I was at finishing school with the daughters of half the Italian Mafia. I made a phone call.'

'And you just . . .' Actually, this is quite sensible and probably relatively safe, from an evading law enforcement point of view. 'Wow.'

She gets up and raids the mini-bar for a bag of chocolate truffles.

'How did you get into the house?' I ask.

'I googled the address. The door was open.' She returns to the armchair and rips open the bag. 'So I walked in.'

This must have been while I was strangling the bodyguard. 'Why do you think the door was open?' I ask, trying to play it safe, trying to work out if she saw me doing anything.

She shrugs, uncaring and uncurious. 'Maybe he was expecting someone? It doesn't matter. I found him sitting in an armchair and drinking a glass of wine. Like it was a normal evening, like he hadn't just killed the love of my life. And he offered me a glass of wine, and I took the gun out and shot him.'

'Twice.'

'Was it twice? I don't really remember.' She bites into a truffle.

'It was twice. I was there. I saw it.'

For the first time, she seems to see me. 'Why *were* you there?'

'I followed you. I was worried about you.'

The last bit is true.

'Why didn't you tell the police that Tommy West pushed Finlay?'

'I didn't think they'd believe me.'

This is a lie. A large lie. And it doesn't even make any sense. I'd make at least a credible eyewitness.

Susie doesn't seem to notice, though. She considers the half-eaten truffle. 'These are good. You know, I don't feel as bad as I thought I would after murdering a human being. I'm probably still in shock. Do you think I'm going to be racked with guilt in a bit?'

'I really don't know.'

'The thing is, he deserved it.' She pops the rest of the truffle in her mouth. 'Anyway, I'll take that bath and change what I'm wearing and then we can go to the police.'

'Hang on. You want to go to the police?'

'Yeah, of course! I need to turn myself in.'

'You are not turning yourself in.'

Susie looks at me like I'm an idiot. 'I just murdered someone. I'm a criminal.'

'I am not allowing you to spend the rest of your life in prison.'

'What life have I got left anyway? Finlay is dead.'

I get up and I take hold of Susie by the shoulders. 'I know that Finlay is dead. And I know that losing him hurts you, a lot. But if you go to jail, *I* will lose *you*. And also, Susie, you will not like it in prison. There is no Deliveroo. There are no linen sheets. You have to wear the same clothes and watch the same television programmes as everyone else.'

'But I killed a man.'

'Who, as you said, deserved it.'

Susie squints at me. 'Saffy, I don't think this is right.'

'None of this is right! Thomas West molested Finlay and then he killed him. Now West is dead. But he brought it on himself, by choosing to molest children in the first place. You going down for life isn't going to change the past, or bring Finlay back.'

And if Susie goes to prison, it will be my fault.

My fault, for getting cold feet and not killing West all those times when I had the chance. My fault, for letting Finlay die. My fault, for prioritising my own revenge and not telling the police that West pushed Finlay off the building.

I've killed quite a lot of people, and I feel zero guilt for most of them. But if Susie loses her freedom because of me...

I'm not sure I can live with that.

'You are not telling the police,' I say. 'Mummy would not want you to. Finlay would not want you to. And I'm your older sister, and I don't want you to. So it's final. Give me your phone.'

She takes it out of her handbag and gives it to me. I put it in my pocket. Then I unplug the hotel landline phone from the wall, wrap it up in the cord, put it on the room's balcony, and lock the windows, putting the key in my other pocket.

'What are you doing?' asks Susie, through another truffle.

'I'm making sure you don't call the police.' Briefly, I consider stealing all of Susie's shoes and putting them out on the balcony with the landline, so she won't leave the room, but I dismiss that idea immediately. She has way too many shoes.

'Take a bath,' I order her. 'A long one. And scrub your hands. Do you hear me?'

'Yes,' she grumbles. She gets up and trudges to the bathroom. The whole thing reminds me of when she used to try to get out of doing homework when she was in primary school.

Meanwhile, I've got to dispose of Susie's bloodied dress, make sure my pashmina doesn't have any twigs in it, retrace the whole evening in my head, worry about witnesses, convince Susie not to tell the truth, and invent an alibi for her.

I've never been so glad that my sister isn't a serial killer.

Chapter Fifty-Four

s I'm fortifying myself with a coffee and room service sfogliatelle, I get a text from Jonathan:

```
Are you OK?

Yes, I'm with Susie.

How is she?

Still in shock. I'll come find you when
she's settled.

You are incredible x
```

Yes, I am, rather. Strangled a man with his own mullet. Gun safely disposed of in a body of water. Smuggled my sister into the hotel without anyone seeing me. *And* I didn't even break a nail.

Susie has fallen asleep in the bath. I top up the hot water for her and sit beside her, holding her hand where it dangles over the side of the tub.

I remember bathing her when she was a baby. I'd check the water temperature on my wrist before lowering her into the baby bath. I'd hold her head up with one hand while I washed her with the other, making funny bubbles on her tummy.

I remember playing in the bath with her when she was a toddler, then a pre-schooler, floating rubber ducks around and making the flannels into puppets with funny voices.

I remember sitting on the toilet seat while she took a bath during school holidays, listening about her stories about the boys she fancied and the girls she admired.

'Everything I've ever done has been for you,' I whisper to her. 'It's been to protect you, or to protect women like you. I couldn't bear it if you left me. I couldn't bear it if you didn't love me any more. I'll do anything I can to make sure I can keep you.'

* * *

Some time later in the morning, after I've tucked Susie up in bed and tidied the suite, there's a soft knock on the hotel room door. I'm expecting Jonathan, but it's the two female police officers from the hospital yesterday.

'I'm sorry, she's asleep,' I say in hushed Italian. 'Thank you for checking in, though.'

'We have to take a short statement.'

'Didn't we tell you everything yesterday?'

'There are new circumstances. It's a matter of urgency.'

I let them through to the sitting area and offer them coffee, which they decline. 'Do you need to speak with both of us? My sister is still in a state of shock.'

'Sì, signora.'

Well, at least here I'll be able to control the conditions a little bit more than at the police station. I bring Susie an espresso, set it on her bedside table, and shake her shoulder gently. 'Susie-sue, you need to get up and speak with the police again.'

'Hnnghmn?' She sits up blearily, her hair half-covering her face.

'It will only take a few minutes. You remember what we talked about last night, don't you?'

'Hnnghmn.'

'Just follow my lead, OK, dear heart?'

'Finlay is dead,' she says, and starts to cry.

I hug her. Much as I hate to see my sister in pain, I can't help thinking that her grief will be a point in her favour with the police.

If she can refrain from sacrificing herself, that is.

I help her pull on a robe and slippers, and we join the police officers. We sit close together on the sofa, knees touching.

'Many apologies for disturbing you so early, signora,' says the elder officer. 'We require an update on the statement you made yesterday.'

'My boyfriend is dead,' says Susie.

'We're very sorry indeed.'

'Do you know when I'll be able to take him home for a funeral? He wanted to be composted.'

'I'm sorry, I can't answer that question. Someone will be in touch in due course.'

The younger prepares her notebook. 'Can you please tell us about your movements after we spoke to you yesterday, at approximately 21.50 hours?'

'We came back here,' I say quickly, before Susie can answer and mess it up.

'Both of you?'

'Yes.' I press my knee against hers.

'Can this be verified? Did someone see you? Hotel staff, for example?'

'The receptionist wasn't at the desk,' I say. This fact is such an incredible stroke of luck that it's practically divine proof that we're doing the right thing by lying. 'She must have been on a break, or dealing with another guest.'

'Did you take a taxi?'

'We walked together,' I say.

'Actually—' begins Susie, but I interrupt her.

'We had a little disagreement in the hospital and Susie left before I did. But then I caught up with her just outside and we walked together.'

'And then what happened?'

'Since then, we've been here in the suite. I've been looking after my sister.'

'Why are you asking this?' Susie says.

'There was another incident last night,' says the elder. 'We are trying to determine if it is connected to the death of your partner.'

'What was the incident?' I ask, gently increasing my pressure on Susie's knee. I use whatever tiny vestiges of ESP our shared genes might give us to send her a message: *Don't be an idiot.*

'Two men were killed. We have reason to believe they attended the same party as you and Finlay Smythe. Do you know Sir Thomas West?'

'Yes,' says Susie, with some venom.

'Yes,' I say quickly. 'He's a television presenter. I've met him several times. I spoke to him at the party last night, in fact. We're on the board of the same charity.'

'Were there witnesses to your meeting?'

'Several. Though I don't know their names. I asked for Sir Thomas's personal phone number so that I could speak with him about another charity I represent. He was killed? That's horrible.'

'Yes,' says the elder, 'and his employee, too.' She turns to Susie. 'You sound as if you also know him personally, signora.'

Don't be an idiot, don't be an idiot, don't be an idiot.

'I don't like children's television,' says Susie.

'Did you also see Sir Thomas at the party?'

'No.'

'Can you tell us who you did speak to? To assist us in putting together a timeline of the event.'

Susie reels off her list of celebrities and pals. Bless her.

'And can you please tell us where you were this morning, between the hours of midnight and two?'

'We were here,' I say. 'In the suite. Susie took a very long bath; her fingers are probably still like prunes. Then she went to sleep. I've been looking after her.'

'You were together the entire time?'

'Yes.'

'Do you agree?' the elder asks Susie.

I hold my breath.

'Yes,' Susie says. 'My sister likes to be in control of every situation.' She turns to me. 'Why did you tidy the room? His things are all I have left of him.'

'I just want to make things easier for you.'

'I'm a grown-up, Saffy. And I've just lost someone I love. I should be allowed to make my own decisions.'

I stand and turn to the officers, eager to get rid of them before Susie makes the decision to spill her guts. 'Is that all you need? We have a lot of things to discuss.'

'That's sufficient for now. We'll be back in touch if we need anything else.'

I do my best not to appear to hustle them out the door. But when I've closed it behind them, I draw a sigh of relief.

'I think that went well,' I say, following Susie back to the bedroom. 'It was a good idea to bicker with me to make them want to leave.'

Susie opens one of the wardrobes and takes out a large and very wrinkled hoody. She clutches it to her.

'I wasn't bickering with you to make them leave. I was bickering with you because I'm furious at you.'

'Pardon me?' I say. 'I literally just saved your life.'

'You literally just made me lie to the police about doing something which I believe I had every right to do. You literally try to control my life. You literally could have prevented all of this from happening and my boyfriend from dying. And the way you lie so easily is literally terrifying. So.'

She holds the hoody up to her face and inhales deeply. Then she pulls it on over her pyjamas. It comes down to her knees.

'So?' I repeat, my heart hammering.

'So, I meant what I said last night. I want you to leave me alone. I don't want anything to do with you.'

'Susie . . .'

'Go away. Literally. Get out of here.'

And that is when I can literally feel my heart breaking.

Chapter Fifty-Five

I stumble out of Susie's suite and blindly press the button for the lift. Both buttons, up, down, I don't care. I want to see Jonathan, I want him to hold me, but it's more important to get away from Susie right now, to give her the space she needs while I figure out how I can get her to love me again.

But what if I can't manipulate her, like I'm able to manipulate everyone else in the world? We share so many traits, after all. One of them is stubbornness.

The lift dings and the doors slide open. Preoccupied with my thoughts, I start to step in, and then I realise there's someone in it already.

It's Jonathan. Adorably messy-haired, unshaven, his shirt untucked. The man who held me and comforted me and respected me as no man has ever done before.

'Oh,' I say, 'am I glad to see—'

Then I see who else is in there.

Two burly male police officers standing either side of him, armed to the teeth and looking stern.

Jonathan's hands are behind him.

Has he been cuffed?

'Saffy,' he says. 'They wouldn't let me send you a message.'

'What's going on?' I wedge my foot in the doors so they stay open.

'Signora, per favore.'

'Is Susie all right?' Jonathan asks.

'Yes, she's fine. What's happening?'

'Tommy West has been shot,' he tells me quickly. 'They found one of my credit cards at the scene. I've been arrested for his murder.'

'You've been arrested?'

'It's all right,' he says. 'It's all a mistake. I have an alibi. I was here with you.'

'. . . With me.'

Oh, shit.

I've given my sister an alibi. And denied Jonathan his.

'Signora, please remove your foot. We must go.'

'They're taking you to jail?' I ask stupidly. 'You? They think *you* shot Sir Thomas?'

The pages in Finlay's handwriting testifying to Sir Thomas's abuse. Giving a motive for his murder. They're in Jonathan's backpack.

Which is, I see, currently in a plastic bag dangling from one of the officers' hands.

I have three choices right at this moment, as far as I can see.

One: I can hand my sister over to the police.

Two: I can let Jonathan go down for a murder that my sister committed.

Three: I can take on two heavily armed men in an enclosed space, somehow kill them both without killing Jonathan as collateral damage, and go on the run with my boyfriend through Europe.

Right at this moment, none of these options seem remotely plausible.

'We'll fix this,' I say to him. 'I promise you.'

I don't know how.

Keeping my foot in the door, I lean forward and kiss Jonathan on the lips. The policemen tense.

'It will be OK, don't worry,' he says to me. His eyes gaze into mine. 'I love you.'

My heart, previously in pieces, gives a little flip of pure joy. I didn't even know I wanted to hear him say this. But I do.

I want a good man – *this* man – to love me. Apparently I always have.

And now . . . it's quite possibly too late. I might have to give him up forever.

'I know,' I say.

I step back. The doors slide shut between us.

Chapter Fifty-Six

Jonathan's and my hotel room is now a crime scene – yellow tape across the door and everything – so I spend some time at the front desk arranging another room. Then I pop out to buy toiletries and a new outfit so I can take a long hot shower and work out how to solve this problem.

Even shopping doesn't give me a needed lift. I trudge to the hotel and, despite what Susie said about never wanting to see me again, I knock on her door. There's no answer, so I go back down to the front desk.

'Would it be possible to have a key for my sister's room?' I ask with all the sweetness I can muster. 'I've picked up a few things for her and I think she's asleep.'

'Oh, Ms Huntley-Oliver,' says the charming receptionist, 'Ms Susan Huntley-Oliver checked out half an hour ago.'

'Did she say where she was going?'

'I'm sorry, no.'

'Did you call her a cab?' Maybe I can ring the company.

The charming receptionist shakes his head.

I check my phone for messages. Nothing. I call her, and her phone rings in my handbag. I've forgotten that I confiscated it from her so she couldn't confess.

I go up to my new room to fret and pace the floor.

It's been nearly thirty hours since I last slept. Right now Susie is God knows where, and Jonathan is in a Florentine jail, most likely being strip searched by someone other than me.

If I retract my statement about being with Susie the whole night and tell the truth by saying I was with Jonathan, my sister might be implicated in killing Sir Thomas. She might even choose to confess, once she hears that an innocent man has been arrested. If she doesn't, the police are going to wonder why I've been lying. It might not do any good to Jonathan anyway. The suspicion could fall on any one of the three of us.

The truth is, I have to choose between my boyfriend, my sister, or myself. And even if I do choose, the wrong person might end up getting the blame anyway.

In this situation, I can't do anything. So I take a long, hot shower as I intended. I realise, halfway through, that I am washing Jonathan's scent off my body – all evidence of the first, and possibly the last, time we made love.

But by then it's already gone down the drain.

I crawl between the fresh sheets. It's a long time before I fall asleep.

* * *

I'm awakened by my phone going crazy beside me. When I pick it up I see that it's nearly six o'clock in the evening, and that my housekeeper Tilly is calling me. I also see that she has called me several times already and I haven't picked up.

'Tilly,' I answer. 'Is everything OK? Is the dog OK?'

Tilly has been staying in my Kensington house with Girl while we've been away. I hope against hope that the animal hasn't been hit by a car or developed a deadly illness. Jonathan doesn't need to be kicked while he's down, and the last thing I need is to have to make life or death decisions about a dog who doesn't even like me.

'Saffy,' wails Tilly in a tone of voice I've never heard from her before, not even when I confessed to drinking the single malt I'd brought back for her from Scotland. 'You've got to come back to London right away!'

'I'm sort of tangled up in something here,' I say, sitting up in bed. 'Can't it wait?'

'They've kicked me and the dog out of the house! They won't even let me fetch my vape!'

'Who's kicked you out?'

'The police!'

Blasted fucking wanker shitbags.

It's all over.

I immediately begin planning Saffy Huntley-Oliver's exit from the known universe. My closest stash of fake documents and cash is in Paris. How can I get there without being seen? Not for the first time, I mentally curse the UK for withdrawing from the EU. No more free movement across borders for serial killers.

Then Tilly says something that changes all my plans.

* * *

Even flying privately (yes, I know, it's destroying the planet, but this is an emergency), it takes me hours and hours to arrange a flight, land in London and get to Kensington. Every single minute is nail-bitingly agonising.

I needn't have worried, though; when I jump out of the cab on the other side, my manicure worn down to stubs, the search of my house is still going strong. They've blocked the entrance to the mews with a police van and a wooden barrier.

My neighbours Gaye (one house over) and Suella (across the mews) are standing by the van, sharing tea from a flask and peering over the barrier. Gaye spots me and waves frantically, chunky silver rings flashing.

'What's this then, Saffy?' she says with some urgency. 'They're not doing all the houses, are they?'

'I think your upstairs herb garden is safe,' I tell her. 'They've got bigger fish to fry.'

She sighs with relief and offers me a sip of her tea, which I decline. Knowing her, it's laced with her home-grown marijuana. 'I hope they'll be done soon,' she says. 'I've got a fertilising schedule.'

'Were you hiding immigrants in there?' asks Suella.

'Um. No. Pardon me, will you?'

I push aside the barrier and am stopped by a uniformed officer. 'You can't go through there, ma'am.'

'It's my house you're searching,' I say, pointing. From here I can see that lights and tape barriers have been set up around my little house, and that my door is open and all the lights are on inside. There are two more police cars and a van parked nearby, and people in white coveralls milling around. The whole thing looks like an episode of *CSI*. 'I believe that I'm entitled to see a warrant.'

'Wait here.' The PC goes to find someone with a higher pay grade. I'm not waiting to approach my own property, so I walk right up to the front door.

Surprise, surprise. The next person to emerge is Pound-Shop Columbo, DI Atherton himself.

'Ms Huntley-Oliver,' he says. 'We meet again. I heard that your sister has suffered a loss. Please pass on my condolences.'

'Decent of you. Why are you searching my house?'

'Would you like to sit comfortably in one of the cars while we chat?'

'No. Please tell me why you are searching my house.'

The last time I saw a man this self-satisfied, he was about to bleed to death in my bathtub, in the very house they are searching. Right now, I'm hoping really hard that my cleaning skills are as good as I think they are.

'Your boyfriend Jonathan Desrosiers was arrested in Italy for murder, wasn't he?'

'He's innocent.'

'It's touching that you're so loyal. However, law enforcement in Florence have been in touch. They discovered evidence pertaining to two other murders on Desrosiers' phone, and thought we would be interested.'

'What murders?'

'The park stabbings.'

'The two bodies he discovered and reported to you? Did he take some photos? He's a journalist, DI Atherton.'

'A journalist who always seems to fortuitously stumble upon homicides, don't you think?'

'You've been trying for ages to frame him for crimes he hasn't committed.'

'It was enough for a probable cause search of his last-known residence, Ms Huntley-Oliver. And a good thing it was. We've found some very intriguing things indeed.'

'For example?'

Please, please, please, no bloodstains.

'An old school tie,' says Atherton. 'From Eton. Did you attend Eton?'

'Of course not, it's a boys' school.'

'Interesting. I know for a fact that Desrosiers didn't. And yet The Right Honourable Rupert Huntington-Hogg's family did, for nine generations. Oh, and Desrosiers also happened to be on the scene when his body was discovered. What a coincidence!'

'Lots of people have Eton ties.'

Lots of people do not have Eton ties covered with Rupert Huntington-Hogg's saliva.

'Well,' says Atherton, 'the DNA evidence will tell us the truth, I trust. Just like it told us that the bodies of both Tony Jones and Francesco Fanducci were held in the freezer of that lock-up that Desrosiers led us to.'

'Why on earth would Jonathan lead you to a place that implicated him?'

Atherton clicks his tongue. I have never wanted to stab a man more.

'Desrosiers always did think he was smarter than the police,' he says. 'I suppose he's finding out now. I wonder what Italian prisons are like?'

'He's going to be exonerated in Italy.'

'Fair enough. By then I'll have enough to extradite him here to the UK. By the way, I'll need you to give us a full statement as to your whereabouts when all of these murders occurred.'

'Fine.'

Not that this will supply Jonathan with any alibis, as I happened to be out committing the murders at the time.

All the murders that Atherton wants to pin on him.

Damn, damn, and treble damn. Why couldn't this have happened before I fell in love with Jonathan? He would have been the perfect fall guy. If I didn't care about him.

I dismiss Atherton with a wave of my hand and head for my front door.

'You can't go in there!' he says.

'Am I under arrest?' I ask.

'No.'

'Is this house my property?'

'Yes.'

'Then I'm going in. My housekeeper needs her vape.'

I march inside.

The place is chaos. My white carpets! My white walls! How do the forensics team expect to find anything of value when they're so busy making a mess? I straighten a painting, and shudder. Whatever happens after this, I'm going to have to move. The memories will be too awful.

'You're not to remove anything,' says Atherton, who is following close behind me.

'Except this,' I say, scooping up Tilly's purple Voopoo pen from a side table. 'Unless any of the victims have been vaped to death?'

He sighs. 'Fine. Now can you ...'

I go to Jonathan's bedroom. The bedroom where, once upon a time, I had hoped to fuck Jonathan's brains out. Now, it's full of white-suited forensics bods putting his clothes in plastic bags.

I'm going to have to clear his name, somehow. I've only just found a decent man. I've only just found my own mojo. And if my sister now hates me, Jonathan is the only person I have left.

But how can I prove he's innocent?

I gaze around the room, looking for something, anything, that will be able to help Jonathan without also incriminating me. The wardrobe door is open. And just visible inside it is …

Wait.

Is that a Jimmy Choo sandal?

Is that *my* Jimmy Choo sandal, left of a pair, with teeth marks in the heel?

I give out a cry and stride to the wardrobe. Inside it is another one of my shoes. A Louboutin, chewed in half. And another. And another.

A whole slew of designer footwear, piled up on top of each other like tiny corpses.

Jonathan Desrosiers is not such an innocent man after all.

Chapter Fifty-Seven

'NOW THAT HE'S DEAD, I CAN SPEAK OUT'

The murder in Italy of Sir Thomas West, OBE, shocked the world this week. But even more shocking are the allegations that have emerged in its wake, as victims of an alleged and monstrous campaign of paedophilia stretching back decades have bravely spoken out about their experiences at the hands of the children's television star.

Italian police have arrested British citizen Jonathan Desrosiers, a well-known true crime author and podcaster, on suspicion of the shooting. In a statement released yesterday, they alleged that the motive for the murder was vigilante justice. Police found handwritten testimony, written by Desrosiers' friend Finlay Smythe, a former child actor, accusing West of abusing Smythe when he was nine years old.

Smythe, 27, died in Florence just hours before West, falling from a building under circumstances that are still under investigation.

Since the statement from Italian police several other alleged victims of West have come forward, speaking on social media and to various news outlets, including this paper.

One such alleged victim, who has waived her right to anonymity, is radio DJ Shehla Razavi, known professionally as She-Rah. Razavi posted yesterday evening on her Bluesky account: 'Tommy West abused me when I appeared on his show twenty-five years ago. I was ten years old. He told me it was our secret. When I was a child, I was too scared to say anything. As I grew, Tommy told me that my success in the industry was all down to him and his special interest in me. He told me that if I said anything, he would make sure I never worked again.

'It only happened once, but it has haunted me for my entire life. I believed I wasn't worthy of my own success. And I believed I was the only one he had hurt.

'Now I know I'm not alone. My heart breaks for the other children. And I would never wish death on anyone, but in my soul, I believe that Jonathan Desrosiers is a hero.'

Chapter Fifty-Eight

I'M HOLED UP IN THE Rosewood in Holborn, which is the only five-star hotel in London that had an available suite and which will permit dogs. Yes, I've got Girl with me. No, I'm not particularly happy about it, and neither is she; but she's my main tie to Jonathan and I wasn't going to leave her in a kennel.

As soon as the press got hold of the story about Jonathan Desrosiers, true crime podcaster, bestselling author and amateur sleuth, being arrested for shooting a beloved children's television presenter in Italy, I could no longer go out in public. And it's even more intense now that the news has come out about what Sir Thomas did. Everybody wants a picture of Jonathan's beautiful, wealthy, tragic girlfriend. Everybody wants to ask me if I ever suspected anything? If I ever feared that my life was in danger? If I knew my boyfriend was a vigilante?

I have to stay in the hotel to stop myself from committing wholesale slaughter.

The news hasn't broken yet about the other murders that Jonathan has been framed for. I presume that Scotland Yard is waiting until he is extradited. Or maybe for people to stop saying that basically he's Batman.

In any case, it's only a matter of time.

Meanwhile, my shoes – the ones that are left – are locked in the room safe. Girl is walked four times a day by a designated hotel employee. As far as I know, they pick up her shit with a solid gold spade.

Personally, I have been doing very little for the past several days but pacing the one hundred square metres of this suite, fingering the wrinkle that has definitely dug in between my eyebrows. The news has played non-stop on the telly. Every hour or so, another one of West's victims speaks up. My rehab actress friend has given an exclusive first interview to Sky News.

I know that Susie did the right thing. I wish I could have done it myself. I don't really mind Jonathan taking the credit for it, but I don't want him to take the fall.

They say that psychopaths don't have any empathy, but that doesn't apply to me. I can easily put myself into Susie's shoes. On a wider scale, I have a lot of empathy for the half of the population who identify as female. I pay my taxes, *all* my taxes, on the dot, and I give enormous amounts to charity, because I have empathy for others who are less fortunate than I am. And I've spent so many odd moments, through the years, imagining what it would be like to be shut up in a prison, that I have enormous empathy for Jonathan right now.

I miss him so much. His presence in our shared space. The scent of his skin. The soft bristle of his chin. The hollow of his neck. The way he pushes up his glasses when he's thinking. His laughter. His encyclopaedic knowledge of serial killers. His moral compass. His gentle breathing as he sleeps. Even his naïve trust in law enforcement.

I've tried ringing the Florentine police to contact him. They refuse. I don't even know where he's being kept.

I'm beginning to seriously wonder if I am even a psychopath at all, because they also say that psychopaths can't feel guilt, and I feel guilty as hell.

The news plays in the background while I prowl from sumptuous bedroom to well-appointed living area to spacious dressing room to marble-clad bathroom. Susie turning into a killer, Jonathan being framed, every single bit of it is my fault. I could have avoided it all if I had just kept killing quietly. Put the poison in West's coffee. Not got so showy with the heads. Refrained from displaying Huntington-Hogg like a slaughtered prize pig at a county fair.

But do I want to admit what I've done and go to prison for it myself?

No way.

That means I have to, somehow, get us out of this situation.

'But how?' I ask Girl, who's been furnished with her own dog bed courtesy of the hotel, but who prefers the velvet sofa.

She growls at me slightly and then startles herself by farting. Serves me right for asking intellectual questions of a dog.

My phone buzzes, which is nothing new. I'm checking it obsessively, in case there's any news of Jonathan or Susie, but it's only been calls and messages either from people I know, supposedly to ask if I'm OK but in fact wanting to know the tea, or from journalists asking for my side of the story. Am I standing by my man? Or am I ready to throw him under the bus for the sake of a headline and a photoshoot, or possibly a Channel 4 documentary?

I snatch it up anyway. It's a text from an unknown number:

Meet me at The Ivy for brunch.

Odds are, it's a journalist. Or an amateur true crime sleuth. Or a social acquaintance, wanting some hot gossip.

Or. It could be something else. I hardly dare hope.

I text back: `Which Ivy and when?`

I get no answer. Which could mean nothing, or it could mean everything.

In any case, I can't stay in this hotel for much longer or I'll start licking the wallpaper. So after I call down to the front desk to arrange for a dogsitter, I put together a disguise. Big sunglasses, hair tucked up in a baseball hat, black polo neck and trousers, trainers, voluminous jacket. Surgical face mask (what with the masks and the gloves, the pandemic did a *huge* favour to serial killers).

And then I head for The Ivy in Covent Garden – the original one – to arrive at exactly quarter past one o'clock.

As soon as I step in, I see her. She's also wearing black. She's sitting at our usual table with two Bloody Marys in front of her.

A smile blossoms under my mask. I glide across the room, slip into my seat, and reach out my hands to her.

'You look stupid,' Susie says.

I take off the hat and the sunglasses and the mask. 'I'm so happy to see you!'

She briefly squeezes my hands. 'Drink your drink,' she says. 'I've already ordered us another round.'

Obligingly, I suck on my paper straw. At this point I would jump off The Shard if Susie asked me to.

'Where have you been?' I ask her.

She shrugs. 'Rome. Milan. A few other places. Doesn't matter.'

'Why did you come back?'

'I have to arrange a funeral.'

'Is that the only reason?'

'It's easier to follow the news about West here.'

'Is there a third reason?'

The waiter arrives with two more drinks. I'm on tenterhooks until he leaves.

'OK,' she says. 'I've been doing a lot of thinking.'

I wait.

'I was angry,' Susie continues. 'And a lot of what I said is true. You are *very* bossy. But I love you, and I know you do everything because you want the best for me, even when you're wrong. And I know you didn't mean to let Finlay die.'

'It wasn't my intention, no.'

'Also, Finlay's gone and Jonathan's in jail. You and I literally have no one but each other now.'

'Gosh, you know how to make someone feel loved and appreciated, don't you?'

'You know what I mean.' She pushes away her empty Bloody Mary glass and starts on her second. 'We have to stick together. You were right, it's what Mummy would have wanted for us.'

'I love you so much, Susie-sue. When I thought I'd lost you, I wanted to die.'

'I love you too, Saffy-san. Let's not fight any more, OK?'

'Yes, please.'

We lean over the table and embrace each other. I have to brush a tear away from my eye.

See? Not a psychopath. Emotional growth.

When we've sat back down, Susie says, 'I'm sorry about Jonathan.'

'Yes. Me too.'

'They'll free him, won't they? I mean, they can't have any real evidence. I could kick myself for dropping his credit card out of his jacket by mistake.'

'You're not going to tell anyone the truth, are you?'

'I will if I need to. But I know why you don't want me to.'

She doesn't know half the reasons.

'I can see now why you didn't tell the police about West pushing Finlay off the roof.'

'Why?' I ask, trying to hide my alarm.

'Because you wanted to protect him. You didn't want everyone to know he was a victim of abuse. I get it. You know how it feels. And you hid it from everyone for a very long time.'

'It was difficult to say it out loud. I didn't – I *don't* want to be pitied.'

She nods. She squeezes my hand.

'Anyway,' she says, 'I'm glad it's come out. And I think if Finlay knew, he'd be fine with it. The truth is important. It helps the survivors. I think he'd be proud of everyone who's speaking up now.'

Would he? Did Finlay ever think a day in his life about other people, aside from Susie?

I don't know. I would have guessed not. But my sister believes in him, and maybe that changes my mind a little.

'I have to tell you something about what's going on with Jonathan,' I say, and I quickly outline the search of my house, the murders that Atherton has accused him of.

She twirls her paper straw in her blood-red drink, considering.

'He didn't do it, did he?' she says. 'All of those murders here in London?'

'No. He can't have.'

'I didn't think so. He doesn't seem like the type. He's too nice.'

'So you're an expert on murderers all of a sudden?' I ask.

'I'm starting to have a certain insight, yes.'

My eggs Florentine arrive, and Susie's buttermilk pancakes with extra maple syrup and crispy bacon. When we're together, we no more have to order brunch than we have to ask which Ivy to go to.

'It's a three-er today,' Susie says to the waiter, who goes off to fetch us more drinks.

'I miss him,' I say to Susie.

'I miss Finlay, too.' She takes a big bite of pancakes, and speaks through it. 'Maybe everyone will think Jonathan is such a hero that he'll be let free.'

'I'm not sure it's that easy.' I pick at my eggs.

'Babe,' says Susie, shovelling bacon into her mouth, 'we'll sort it. We're together now. You and I can do anything.'

Acknowledgements

My everlasting thanks to my agent, Teresa Chris, my partner in crime.

Thank you to Ben Willis, Georgia Marshall, Rianna Houghton, Holly Milnes, Eleanor Stammeijer, Stella Giatrakou, and all of the team at Bonnier for encouraging this madness. Thanks too to my fabulous publishers around the world who have made Saffy the international jet-setting serial killer that she truly is.

Enormous, homicidal, and bloodstained, thanks to all the readers, bloggers, fellow authors, booksellers, and reviewers all over the world who have asked for another Saffy book, and especially to those of you who said, 'In the next book, we need more men to die,' and *especially* to those of you who offered me examples of bad men who should die in truly horrific ways.

This one is for you. You know who you are. You're all sick and I love you.

Thanks, too, to everyone who was worried about Girl. She's going to be fine.